The Craving

Scott Wojtowich

"The Craving," by Scott Wojtowich ISBN 978-1-951985-97-4 (softcover); 978-1-951985-98-1 (ebook).

Published 2021 by Virtualbookworm.com Publishing Inc., P.O. Box 9949, College Station, TX 77842, US.

Alsace, Europe

1317, third year into The Great Famine

Chapter 1

GUARIN LAY IN HIS BED, wondering if today might be his last. Pain and nausea swept over him in great cramping waves, like a blacksmith pounding on his back and abdomen simultaneously with his fists, and then with hammers, becoming stronger and harder every minute, beating him to the heights of agony before mercifully subsiding—until the next wave struck. He couldn't stop the shaking chills that chattered his teeth uncontrollably like the sound of a woodpecker.

But deep underneath all this misery lurked a feeling of such utter despair that it almost made him relish the pain, tearing at his soul as though he deserved it, like some impending and inconceivable dilemma he had been avoiding was finally at hand. Straining to remember what he could have said or done to feel so empty and loathsome inside, he thought of his starving young children, Han and Greta. *I'm so sorry, I tried to get us through this but I'm afraid I am failing you, my sweet children.*

Sinking deeper into his thoughts, searching for the true source of his despair, the answer finally struck him like a blow to his heart. "Oh God, what have I done!" he groaned, rolling his head side to side as he recollected Lutrud's pleading words from the night before: "So, you see? There is simply not enough food to sustain all of us. If we perish, then they will be left alone, soon to follow us to our graves."

With his strength withering away and his body racked by pain and fever, he felt too weak and listless to respond about their dire situation. Trying to tune out her droning and annoying

I

voice, he no longer wanted to worry about how he was supposed to feed his family anymore. Overwhelmed with exhaustion, he really just wanted everything to end.

"Yes, perhaps you're right dear," he finally succumbed before drifting off.

Those fateful words now echoed in his aching head. With trembling hands, he wiped the sweat from his fevered brow.

Just then he realized how silent his cabin was. *How long have I been asleep?*

"Lutrud?" He tried to call out but choked as her name escaped his dry throat. He reached over to his nightstand, lifted his head, and brought a cup of water to his mouth, drinking it down in large audible gulps.

"Han, Greta? Anyone there?" he rasped, struggling to raise his voice. He tried to sit up in his bed, but his shaking arms gave way beneath him as another wave of pain struck. *How could it have come to this?*

Suddenly, he heard a loud and urgent rapping at the door, startling him from his thoughts.

Three hard knocks, like someone pounding with the bottom of his fist—BOOM-BOOM-BOOM—each as loud as the other. He jerked himself up to a sitting position, shaking his head like a dog as a wave of nausea struck him from the sudden movement.

As he stood and dressed himself, he heard a man talking with an unfamiliar voice. "What have you done, Lutrud?" he muttered. He instinctively reached for his great axe hanging on the wall but quickly realized that he no longer had the strength to wield it. Instead, he tossed his tunic over his head, tucked his hunting knife into the inside pocket, and threw open the bedroom door.

The silhouette of a hooded figure stood just outside at the doorway, his black cloak snapping and whipping with the wind. The mysterious visitor turned his gaze toward Guarin and stepped inside, uninvited. Everyone held their breath as he entered; the only sound was the clunking of his heavy boots on the wooden floor.

The man flipped off his hood, unleashing long dark hair that spilled around his neck and shoulders. He looked to be around thirty years old, solidly built with a square jaw, cleft chin, and confident smile. His large wide-spread eyes seemed to take in everything at once with a quick sweep of their home.

Greta gasped when she saw his face. "It's you!"

He turned to her and smiled as if to offer reassurance. "Don't be frightened little girl. I'm not here to hurt you. I'm here to take you to your new home."

Guarin, barely able to stand, somehow mustered up enough strength to confront the intruder. He clenched his jaw and growled through his teeth. "The hell you will!" He advanced in a slow prowl and continued in a steady, gravelly voice. "You think I would let you walk into my home and take my children away from me? Lutrud, who is this man?"

"My dear, we talked about this. You agreed that we cannot feed them. We must let them go!" She looked earnestly up into his eyes, took hold of his hand, and pressed on. "What happens to the children if you don't make it through this illness? You expect me to feed and raise your children on my own? Then what happens if I go next? Without enough food to sustain all of us, I'm afraid we won't make it to see the summer. Don't you see? By giving them away to someone more fortunate than us, we are offering them the best chance to survive."

"The lady speaks with reason," the stranger interjected. "Some families have become desperate enough to abandon their own children in the forest, even little babies. I've discovered them myself." The corners of his mouth curled into a smirk as he continued. "One poor wretch decided to make a meal of her half-dead child before—"

"Enough!" Guarin tried to shout but was stifled by a dry cough. Without taking his eyes off of the intruder, he jerked his arm free and continued to close the distance, sliding the knife from his pocket. "Han, take your sister and run! Now!"

He leveled his weapon at the man's chest. Without hesitation, Han snatched his bag with one hand and tugged Greta by the other as he dashed out the door.

Even though Guarin stood a full head taller, the man just smiled up at him with a smug look of pretentious pity.

"Stop this nonsense and listen to me!" Lutrud cried out. "This man knows of a healing lady who—"

He held his trembling arm outstretched, clutching his blade that now seemed much heavier than he remembered. He pressed on with a measured but gravelly voice. "Now you will leave my home and never—"

Before he could react, the man gripped his wrist, tightening like a vice and twisting until the blade dropped from his hand. He glared up at him with wild green eyes, his mouth stretched into a sneer, his hand still gripping and twisting his right arm, daring him to make another move.

"Yes, I will leave your home now, and I *will* take your children with me."

Guarin tried to knee him in the groin, but he quickly pivoted away, his knee glancing off the man's hip instead. He swung his left fist around and struck him in the jaw, but without being able to wrest his other arm free he had no leverage; the intruder didn't even flinch. Suddenly, his assailant crouched and then lurched back up and forward in one quick motion, shoving both hands against Guarin's chest with all of his momentum. He felt an amazingly powerful thrust that sent him flying backwards off his feet, his body crashing against the wall behind him, the back of his head resounding with a sickening thunk. He tried to suck air into his lungs but instead had to settle for short spasmodic gasps. Somehow, he still managed to clamber back to his feet, but as soon as he did, he saw his fist coming. He didn't see anything after that.

Chapter 2

JUST TWO DAYS EARLIER, Guarin awoke feeling optimistic about heading into the town of Riquewihr, hopeful to obtain some desperately needed food or grain to sustain his family for another couple weeks. They simply couldn't last much longer on sparse berries, bugs, and bark.

A brisk but refreshing draft blew in through the open door, filling the cabin with the fresh scent of pine. He pulled on his gray woolen tunic, tightened his belt, and stepped outside. He shivered from the blustery wind that whipped up, spitting cold drizzle into his face.

He looked over to Han, only twelve years of age but as tall as most fifteen-year-olds with the attitude to match. He watched him throw his ball as high as he could, then catch and sling it back up with one fluid swing of his arm. His dirty blond hair, straight as straw and pointing in every direction at once, flopped around as he jumped. He always thought it looked like someone just picked up a patch of hay and stuck it on top of his head.

He heard him call out the name of his old friend as he tossed the ball back into the air and pretended to talk to him like he used to. He felt his throat tighten up. *My poor dear son, lost his mother and his best friend this past year.* He used to watch them play games and pass the ball to each other in the yard, but now he just passes it to himself. *I should really spend more time with him. Why haven't I?*

Shaking his head of these sorrowful thoughts, he trotted out toward Han and shouted, "I got this one!" He reached up and snatched the ball on its descent, then threw it high in the air for Han to catch. Unfortunately, the ball got lost in the canopy of trees, until finally dropping onto the roof of their house and rolling off the back.

"Nice throw, Papa," Han teased as he ran around the house to retrieve it.

He turned to see Greta walking across the yard, carrying an armful of orchids and wildflowers, hugging them against her chest. He smiled as she reverently laid the flowers over her mother's modest gravestone. Lutrud stood behind her with hands pressed together, her head bowed in prayer. He lost his smile. *How did my life become ensnared by this toad of a woman?* Lutrud looked up at him and waved as the wind blew her white hair into her face. He raised his hand and smiled back at her.

He reminded himself why he took her into his family. *What kind of a man would I be if I didn't honor my wife's dying wish?* "Please," Kaetherlin had said before she died. "It will make my sister very happy to have a family and you could use her help. She has been so lonely and has never known love." *Well, it's easy to see why. I would rather she had asked me to carry her ashes to the holy city, or even to the highest mountain peak in the land for that matter; at least I could move on with my life. Living with her is like languishing in purgatory.*

He walked over and knelt beside Greta, a slight wisp of a girl just a few years younger than her brother with bright green eyes that shined like her mother's. He offered her an approving smile and placed his arm over her bony shoulders.

"I can still remember when Mum looked pretty, before she got sick and stopped eating,"

Greta said softly.

"Me too, Sunshine, me too," he replied, running his fingers through her soft blonde hair, so light and fine that it was almost imperceptible to touch. He loved the way it perpetually floated above her head, taking whatever form the breeze decided to style it that day.

She looked up at him as if she needed to confess a hidden shame. "Sometimes I think I forget how pretty she was, but today I remember."

6

His eyes glazed with tears, and he felt a warmth in his heart that only she provided anymore. He picked her up and kissed her on the cheek. "Oh sunshine, that's alright. I'm very glad you remember her now, as I do. When you get a little older, if you can't remember how she looked, you will be able to just look at your own reflection."

She beamed her biggest smile at him. "Thank you, Papa!" She giggled, giving him one last embrace before darting away to play with Han. He loved it when she rewarded him with a smile like that.

They ate what little unripened berries and edible roots they could find and filled up some traveling vessels with rainwater they collected from an oaken bucket.

"Go put on something warmer and then let's head to town," he said. "We'll need to get there early to have a chance at any offerings. Even if it's just some grain, we can be thankful."

He began walking toward the forest path and cast a despairing look at his wood-cutting equipment, rusting and rotting away into useless artifacts. "I was really looking forward to teaching Han all I know about carpentry before these incessant rains began. Will they ever stop, Lutrud?"

"Lord, if I know," she replied, looking back at Han as he came back out carrying some warmer clothes. The deep crease between her brow suggested she hadn't gotten over their quarrel from last night. He turned and watched as Han handed Greta her torn woolen coat and scarf, then tightened her leather wraps onto her feet while she playfully mussed his hair.

"He's a good boy, Lutrud. I wish you would consider what he's been through before letting your anger out on him."

She jerked her face into his so fast that her wet hair whipped him across his cheek, her blood-shot eyes casting daggers at him. He winced and stepped back from her wrathful glare. Her sudden outbursts of anger never ceased to surprise him. "So, this is all my fault then, is it? You allow him to raise his voice to me, even question God's intentions like a little devil, and I'm supposed to just remain silent?"

"The fault lies with me, not him. Let me handle the discipline from now on, alright?"

7

"Pah! If only you would," she scoffed and turned away from him.

Swallowing his anger, he looked toward the muddy path to town and sighed. He always looked forward to the short hike through the forest of the Vosges mountains, eastward to the town of Riquewihr. Lately, with his stamina sapped by the famine, he thought it more like a daunting uphill trek over the sodden ground and encroaching shrubs.

Han didn't seem to be nearly as affected as he zipped past him toward the trail. "Papa, let's race to that big old tree just before the turn down there. I bet I'm faster than you now!"

"Hold up, Han," he called out before turning back to Greta who remained at the doorstep.

"Coming, Sunshine?"

"I think I have to go really quick," she said, reaching for her tummy, raising her eyes like she needed his permission.

He smiled. "Of course, take your time."

"You two go on ahead. I'll wait for her," Lutrud offered.

He mustered up what energy he could and ran after Han. His son was right, he couldn't keep up but at least gave himself credit for at least making it to the tree without falling or tripping over a tree root. Han raised his arms and shouted as though he just won the town race, his shouts echoing off the canyon walls towering above them like the cheer of a crowd.

He felt suddenly invigorated by the run and by the beauty of the trees sprouting fresh growth in every shade of green imaginable. Large beech, oak, pine, and maple trees surrounded him. The lush and verdant forest was alive with birds chirping their morning song and the occasional woodpecker tapping out its rhythmic beat. He realized with wonder how the vitality of the forest seemed so paradoxical to the ongoing famine.

As they continued along, he heard the rush of the waterfall ahead, its refreshing cascade beginning to drown out the other sounds of the forest. Though he had seen it countless times, he always found himself enchanted by its beauty, its appearance ever-changing with the seasons. Lately, the heavy rains amplified the waterfall, gushing with more than twice its usual intensity, the once gentle stream now overflowing its banks with a rushing current. He gazed up at the falls, long serpentine streams intertwining and plunging down the lush but rocky slope. Each of the multitude of streams locked in a dance with the others as they merged into small pools and then separated again around massive boulders blanketed by a soft, green moss.

"Come on Papa, whatcha waiting for?" Han said as he swept passed him. They left the path and made their way toward the falls by hopping over boulders and fallen tree trunks alongside the stream. A bearded, brawny man of impressive stature washed himself under the cold spray, boldly singing aloud. His white stallion grazed nearby, its flanks laden with baggage.

"Ho there!" greeted Guarin from a distance as they approached.

The man quickly jerked his attention toward them, but then waved and began to dress himself. His steely gray hair and beard, weathered skin, and heavily chiseled features showed his age, but he managed to maintain a remarkable physique despite the ravages of famine.

"Even his horse is better fed than we are. He must be a man of some importance," he said to Han. The big man donned a bright crimson woolen cloak, fastened his belt, and then brushed back his long, thick, wavy mane of hair. *If only I had half the hair he does,* he thought, feeling clearly inadequate.

"Sorry to interrupt your bath, I didn't want to sneak up on you. My name is Guarin, this is my son, Han."

The man offered him a firm handshake, introducing himself with a southern French accent and the deepest voice he ever heard. "My name is Barous. A pleasure to make your acquaintance." He then smiled at Han and tousled his hair. "You have a very fine-looking young son. Once he puts on some weight, he is sure to be a big strong lad, as I'm sure you were before the famine."

Han's eyes widened as he noticed a long sword strapped to his mount in its fine leather scabbard. "Are you a knight?"

Barous beamed with pride toward his young admirer. Despite his weathered face, Guarin thought he looked quite handsome. The lines that stretched from the corners of his eyes to his graying temples only added to his charm. "Yes, I am, or at least I used to be. I fought as a young man in the Crusade of 1291 for the city of Acre."

Han fumbled for words. "Wait, you fought for…you were a…"

The knight looked around and finished his question in a lowered voice, "A Templar?" Then he nodded with a wink and a half smile as he pulled on his heavy leather boots. "Unfortunately, knights have had a bad reputation since the fall of the Templars."

Guarin stared at him in stunned silence before he could speak. "But I don't understand, the Templars were executed to the last man a decade ago. How is it that you are still alive?"

"Believe it or not, many of us survived the purge, all living abroad in secrecy. Some of my brothers are rumored to have been captured since they escaped, but from what I can gather, about a dozen of us live to tell our side of the story. Of course, certain angry zealots would like nothing more than to see me burn."

He became intrigued. This was a major topic of discussion and one of great controversy over the last few years. "I'll be damned," he said, scratching his beard. "If you wouldn't mind, we would love to hear your side of the story. The word passed to down to us is that the Templars became corrupted by greed and heresy."

Barous took a swig of ale from his leather skin and offered it to Guarin. "Baseless lies to be sure. King Philip simply grew hungry for our treasury and would do anything to tarnish the reputation of our order, even involving The Pope himself in his schemes." He furrowed his brow and leaned in toward Guarin. "Sure, there were admissions of guilt by some of the Templars, but most were forced under such unimaginable torture that they were left with little choice: either confess to something they didn't do or endure unending agony. Some of the noble knights still refused to admit to such treachery, until their bodies could take no more and perished during the persecution. Those that confessed fared no better, as King Philip publicly burned a hundred thirty-eight of my brave brothers in a great conflagration of unholy horror, claiming to purge their sins with the everlasting flames of hell. Even while their wretched souls screamed and shrieked in torment, they protested their innocence to their dying breath.

"As for the Grand Master, despite imprisonment and torture over the course of seven long years, he still refused to capitulate. Philip Le Bel ordered his public immolation before the great cathedral of Notre Dame. I mingled in with the crowd, disguised as a dirty peasant, so that I could witness this unhallowed, heinous spectacle and pay my respects to this brave and honorable man who I had admired since my childhood. I watched as the flames licked and consumed his mortal flesh, and I listened to his rising shouts as he passionately invoked a curse upon the King as well as the Pope. Long live the Grand Master, Jaques de Molay!" With that, he flipped a coin to Han along with an assuring wink, before warily shifting his gaze behind them.

Han stared down at the copper coin, stamped with the seal of the Templar Cross, then slowly looked back up at him incredulously. "He cursed the King and the Pope before he died?"

Barous nodded gravely, then shifted his gaze behind them. "We have some more visitors it seems."

They turned to see Lutrud and Greta approaching along the trail, still too far away to have heard anything over the rushing falls. He waved to them and then turned back to Barous, "That is Lutrud and my daughter. Speak none of this to her, she does not grasp the complexities in life, if you know what I mean." Barous acknowledged with a firm nod of his head. He turned to Han, "Do you understand me, Han? Not a word and put that coin away quickly."

Han nodded but rolled his eyes. "Why did she have to come along?" he asked, sneaking another glance at the coin before shoving it into his pocket. Guarin let it pass.

"Well, good journey to you and your family. May God bring a bountiful harvest this year and put an end to this despicable famine." He swung himself onto his saddle and paused, staring out ahead of him with a solemn expression. "I believe the destruction of the Order has unleashed a darkness unto this land, and the worst may be yet to come. Some have named Philip Le Bel the anti-Christ for destroying The Knights Templar, the first of the Four Horsemen, mounted upon his

White Steed. Now it appears The Black Horseman has unleashed this famine upon us.

Perhaps next shall come the pestilence, endless wars, …Apocalypse."

With those ominous parting words, he wheeled his mount around and cantered off toward town, his crimson cloak billowing behind him.

Chapter 3

HAN LOOKED ON WITH FASCINATION as the knight's steed galloped up the hill ahead of them, wishing that he had a strong, beautiful stallion to carry him to town, or anywhere else he might desire to venture off to. Then he looked over to his stepmother and his spirits dropped.

"Who was that man?" Lutrud asked as her lingering gaze followed the stranger away.

"Just a wealthy traveler passing through, a merchant so he says," replied his father.

He then quickly changed the subject and went on about reminding him and Greta how to behave in the town and not to go wandering off, but Han didn't really listen. He thought about his shiny new coin and wanted nothing more than to take it out and get a better look at its engravings. He put his hand in his pocket so that at least he could feel its shape and weight and smooth surface. Then he noticed Lutrud eyeing him suspiciously. *Why does she always have to spoil everything?* he thought to himself.

"He tossed you something before he left. What was it?" she asked, her eyes probing into his.

"It's nothing, just an old coin, that's all."

Her eyes lit up. "Well, that might be enough to buy us some food when we get to town.

May I see it?" she said, holding out her hand.

He exchanged uneasy glances with his father. Lutrud pressed her hand forward, a bluish-purple vein beginning to bulge in her left temple. When he stepped back, she took hold of his shoulder.

"Let go of me!" he shouted, grabbing onto her arm. She raised her other hand, threatening to strike but he didn't flinch. "Are you going to hit me again!"

Her grasp on his shoulder felt like a pincer. He tried to pull away, but her grip held firm.

In an instant, she smashed him across his face, then across his other cheek with her back hand, swinging her whole body from the waist with her arm fully outstretched. Greta screamed for her to stop, but instead she went for a third cross—mercifully arrested by his father in mid-swing.

"Lutrud!" he shouted. "Enough of this, I've already asked you earlier to stop hitting him. He is old enough to think for himself." He drew a deep breath before continuing. "Listen, I made him promise not to say anything." Han barely heard him under the ringing in his ears and throbbing in his head. "It's ok, Han, let her see it."

Her eyes widened as she inspected it. "This has the seal of the Templar Order. Why would you hide this from me?"

"We weren't hiding the coin, simply trying to protect the man's identity," his father explained.

She stared up at him for a long moment, her expression one of shock and betrayal. "You? Why would you want to protect a criminal?" Another pause while she stepped closer. "How could you hide secrets from me, Guarin?"

"I didn't want you stirring up trouble when we get into town with rumors of an escaped Templar knight, that's all. He was very kind to us, so I would appreciate it if you wouldn't say anything about this to anybody. Now hand that coin to me. I'm afraid it would arouse suspicion. Besides, you won't be able to purchase anything with it unless I can find somebody willing to melt it down into a nugget."

She stared him down with silent scorn before dutifully handing the coin to his father and then strutted indignantly back toward the trail. Han glared at the back of her stringy, long white hair as she walked ahead, his father tailing quickly behind her, continuing to plead his case like a boy to his obstinate mother. After she walloped him across the face last night and now this,

his seething hatred for her surged into a boiling rage, his mind swirling with animosity like a tempest, yet he said not a word—not to his stepmother, and not to his father, who seemed more concerned about upsetting Lutrud than his own son whom she just whacked.

Greta walked to his side and took his hand, looking up at him sympathetically. "Are you ok, Han?"

He accepted her hand but didn't reply or look at her. He didn't want her to see his eyes all red and teary.

"She hit you really hard! You should see how red your face is. If she hit me that hard, I would be crying my head off, unless my head didn't already go flying off when she hit me."

Han grinned. He liked the way she always tried to cheer him up when he became upset.

Greta smiled back at him.

"I really don't know how much longer I can stand her. It's like she's not right in the head. Why the hell did Papa let her live with us anyhow?"

"Don't you remember? Mum said he needed her help to raise us until we're big enough to live on our own."

They continued on in silence as they hiked up a steeper grade. He noticed a look of consternation on her brow. "Do you want to rest, Greta?"

"No, I'm ok," she replied. Then she looked up to him with sadness in her eyes. "I wish

Mum didn't have to die. I really miss her a lot."

A pang of guilt shot through him. "Yeah, me too."

He felt her gaze linger upon him.

"How come you never talk about her?"

Her question took him off-guard. "Don't I?" He paused to think of how to reply. "Maybe I just wish I'd spent a little more time by her side when she was sick like you did, that's all." It relieved some of his burden to say it that way, but he couldn't bear to say the real reason. He didn't like thinking about the last few days before she died. "Anyhow, I don't need anybody taking care of me anymore. As soon as this famine is finally over, I'll get a job somewhere and live my own life."

Greta laughed at him. "Come on, you? What could you do on your own? You're not even thirteen years old yet!"

"I can do a lot of things," he replied. "I can build my strength up by chopping wood for a while, then maybe I'll go to Strasbourg and apply as a squire or something."

She blew through her lips and laughed again, "Yeah, right! You!"

"Sure, why not me? You'll see."

"I'm just teasing, I could maybe see you doing that when you get older."

"Greta, before we get into town, I need to warn you about what I heard stepmother say, but I don't want you to freak out or anything."

She pinched her eyebrows together and wrinkled her forehead. "I promise. What is it?"

He lowered his voice. "She wants to be rid of us, and she is trying to convince Papa too."

"Come on, she wouldn't say that." Her worried expression softened but then her eyes suddenly widened. "I can see if she wants to get rid of you but not me," she teased.

He didn't smile. "I'm serious, Greta. I overheard them talking last night after you fell asleep. She wants to put us in an orphanage."

Her pale face and sunken cheeks looked up at him warily and asked, "Isn't that where children are sent if their parents die, or they don't want to take care of them anymore?" Han nodded his head and gripped her hand a little tighter. "Papa wouldn't allow her to do that, he still loves us," she added, almost pleadingly.

He shot her a quick glance and bumped his eyebrows up. "I hope so Greta, because I won't go to no orphanage."

Chapter 4.

THEY EMERGED FROM THE FOREST at the crest of a vast rounded hill overlooking the town of Riquewihr. Guarin stopped to catch his breath and take in the view. The verdant slope of the hill fell gently below them, down to the small farms, vineyards, and homes that spread out from the fortified stone walls and towers surrounding the town. Broad swaths of yellow daffodils brushed the vast green fields of the valley and surrounding foothills. Low clouds spilled a heavenly white mist over the distant mountains that drifted down into the valley and toward the town. From this vantage point, it seemed to offer security, order, and hope—especially in this time of desperation.

The forest path joined with others to form the main road leading to the western entrance gate at Dolder Tower. Standing guard over the town at a height of over five stories, this lofty tower climbed higher than any other building in town, including the church. As a young child, he watched his father help build this tower from the timber, brick, and sandstone cut from the nearby forest. He remembered feeling awestruck when they installed the giant new clock near the top, just under the steepled belfry. Looking back now, he can see how it truly ushered in a new time in history. Before the arrival of the clocktower, all of the merchants, town administrators, and other businesses organized their day according to the bells of the church; now they organized their day to the chimes of the clock.

As they made their way down the slope, he noted how the cold rains reduced the grape vines to useless stalks and stumps drowning in the sodden earth.

Greta pulled one of them out of the mud. "What are these ugly things in the ground, Papa?"

"They're grape vines, Sunshine. It's what we use for making wine. This area is famous for its vineyards—our biggest crop—but with all of this cold weather and heavy rain over the past couple years, we haven't been able to bring them to harvest, just like everything else we try to grow."

The last time he passed through town just before winter set in, Guarin noticed how guards at the gate had grown more suspicious and asked more questions, merchants had overcharged for their goods and food, and thievery had become rampant and unenforced. The noblemen stayed clear of the peasants for fear of contracting disease or suspicion of looting, and the poor regarded the wealthy with downcast expressions, filled with self-pity or envy. Lost was the sense of optimism and good will that had pervaded the town. He expected worse after suffering yet another brutal winter.

Indeed, they hadn't even descended the hill when Greta called out, "Papa, what are they doing? Are they pretending to be cows?"

Lutrud gasped and crossed herself. He had to refocus his eyes to believe what he was seeing. What he initially assumed to be grazing livestock from a distance were actually starving humans, crouching onto their hands and knees, gnawing at the grass in a desperate attempt to fill their bellies.

"God help us," he lamented. "How dreadful have things become that humanity has been reduced to grazing like animals?"

As they approached Dolder Tower looming high above them, the town guards forced them to wait and stand back at a distance while a large wooden cart was wheeled out. As it exited the gate, he could see why they were being kept away. Laden with emaciated and decaying human corpses heaped on top of one another, they were being carried out to be buried in a mass grave. A giant ox pulled the cart forward, which was steadied by two men wearing scarves over their faces, while two others walked beside to keep people away and to pick up any body parts that fell out along the way.

The cart lurched as it rolled over a bump, causing the pile of bodies to flop as one giant bunch, knocking one of them loose. Its massively swollen belly jiggled wildly as it struck the ground. He was surprised it didn't burst open and spill its guts when it landed. Two of the men promptly picked the body up by the limbs and tossed it back in with the others as if it were nothing more than a sack of grain.

Next, a second cart followed as big as the first, this one loaded with a potpourri of dead animal carcasses. Whereas the appearance of the animal carcasses was not nearly so disturbing as the human bodies, the reek of the animals was unlike anything he could possibly fathom. Diseased and rotting from the inside out, many of the bellies had ruptured, emitting their pestilential miasma as a thick choking cloud of noxious vapors. Any remaining bystanders quickly scattered even further away. He couldn't imagine how the men pushing the cart could even breathe, scarf or no scarf.

At last, they were permitted entry through the gate into town. As they walked past the dilapidated buildings and homes along main street, they had to stay clear of the peasants and animals that lie dead or dying of disease and starvation, ignored by all except for the rats feasting voraciously on the rotting flesh. It seemed the death carts couldn't keep up with the body count.

The shouting and the laughter that he remembered so fondly were replaced by the lugubrious groans and cries of the suffering. He almost cried himself when he passed by a wretched-looking mother, weeping and singing for her dead baby cradled in her arms.

Even those healthy enough to walk and carry on with their daily lives looked pale and malnourished with their red eyes, bleeding gums, rotting teeth, and swollen bellies, giving him the impression that they were creatures back from the dead. He darted his eyes toward his family to reassure himself that they were not beginning to look like these walking corpses.

They passed a boy whose face was so disfigured by disease that he appeared freakishly inhuman, almost monstrous. His skin was thickened in areas and eaten away in others such as his upper lip and part of his nose, baring his upper teeth and gums and contorting his mouth into a frightening rictus sneer. Although he had never seen a leper before, he'd heard of them, about how awful they looked, but they always remained separated from the community until now.

As they passed through the market area, he scoffed at the ridiculous prices which had inflated to at least ten times what they charged just last fall, prices only noblemen could barely afford and even they looked incensed. The only thing he could afford was some cheap ale, a small piece of molded cheese that he bought at a discount, and bread tough enough to break his teeth on, but nothing to sustain them for the weeks ahead as he had hoped. He asked around and heard that the town was offering free handfuls of grain from their emergency reserve.

As they neared the town square, a crazed man dressed in rags ran through the streets, waving his arms and screaming that he was on fire. Guarin could see no flames, only that his feet and hands were mostly black from gangrene and missing a few fingers. The next moment, he began spinning and waving his arms madly around in circles before spewing vomit and then finally collapsing in a spastic fit of convulsions. His limbs stiffened and locked up in an outstretched position, while his back and neck arched back uncontrollably. After about a full minute of this, his body unclenched and began to writhe as though possessed by a demon.

Lutrud began tugging at their arms, "Leave this man now, the devil is in him!"

Guarin walked backward completely mystified and continued to stare at the poor wretch, wondering if he truly was a soul being possessed. He bumped into a man standing behind him who steadied him and delivered a stern warning, "Don't eat the grain." The voice sounded familiar.

"Barous, my good man!" Guarin smiled and clapped him on the shoulder, then gave him a confused look. "I'm sorry, did you say don't eat the grain?"

"Indeed. I believe he may be poisoned from the tainted rye grain that they are giving away—St. Anthony's Fire, as they call it in Paris. He is the second victim I've seen today like this."

Lutrud tightened her mouth and rebutted him. "It's the devil, I say! Eating grain doesn't make anyone act like this. You're a fool if you believe that!"

"Please, Lutrud, try to be more respectful," he implored, feeling embarrassed for her outburst. "Let me talk to the man and hear what he has to say." He apologized before continuing, "I thank you for your advice and trust what you say is true, but how do you know of this? You've seen others like him?"

"Indeed. I used to visit a friend in one of the Templar hospitals in Paris. The disease seems to go around when the weather is cool and wet like this. The physicians suspected tainted rye grain was to blame. Black limbs, lunacy, muscle spasms, and seizures just like him. For some reason they often complain or cry out that they feel part of their body is on fire, hence the name

St Anthony's Fire. You may have heard of The Feast of the Burning Ones?"

He shook his head with revulsion. "Why should I have heard of this? It sounds like a devil worship ceremony!"

Barous chuckled, "Yes, indeed it does, but quite the contrary. It is a day celebrated by the church to commemorate the miraculous healing of these victims by the holy relics of St.

Genevieve almost two centuries ago."

"Thank the Lord that you are familiar with this disease. You must alert someone to have them stop the handouts. The town will be wiped out by this lunacy!"

"I've already spoken to the town physician who assured me they would dispose of the rest. Don't worry, it seems not everyone who consumes the grain becomes ill, in fact probably only a small number. Needless to say, don't take your chances," he reassured. "Now follow me, there is a public persecution about to begin that I think you will want to see."

He took one last look at the poor man who continued to scream and writhe on the ground in agony before moving on. Barous led them to the town square which was filled with onlookers. A group of four men and a woman walked through the crowd and up the steps to a broad, raised, wooden platform. Two guards pushed forward a young red-haired woman who looked exhausted and disheveled with her head bowed low. Her hands were tied behind her back and she wore shackles on her feet. Closely behind them followed a cleric in a black hooded cloak, and a well-dressed man in a fancy green hat and breeches who sported a wide mustache that curled up at the ends.

After taking their places on the stage and silencing the crowd, the man in the fancy hat began to speak. "Behold, gentlemen and ladies of Riquewihr!" He boomed as he circled his arm around and gestured toward the woman with an open hand as if he were introducing a circus act. "Before you stands a witch!" He paused as he cast a stern look upon the crowd.

Guarin had heard of witches, of course, but he had never heard of one being prosecuted for it. The crowd murmured, looking upon one another in confusion and ignorance, except for Barous, he noted, who listened intently, and Han who stared with fascination at the woman on the stage. He felt Greta clutch onto his leg, so he scooped her up in his arms.

The cleric stood motionless and expressionless with his hands clasped in front of him, in contrast to the other man's gesticulations as he continued to prosecute his case. "Once this heresy became known, I realized that I had to involve the church." He gestured toward the cleric. "Father Linhart graciously obliged us in this difficult case and began his own line of questioning. Utilizing interrogation skills that he learned in Paris, he was able to confirm that she was indeed using dark magic and cavorting with demons. Moreover, and most concerning to all God-fearing people, she even admitted to cavorting with and signing a pact with the Devil himself!" With this proclamation, he stomped his foot and opened his arms wide to the crowd, who erupted with hysterical shouts of terror and outrage.

He slowly turned back to the woman and gave her one last chance to defend herself. "Tell us, do you deny these charges?" He paused, then spit out his last word with vehement contempt: "Witch!" The accused remained still and continued to stare at her feet, her face partially covered by her straggly red hair. Her disposition suggested that she was resigned to her fate.

"Burn her!! Burn the witch to Hell!" the crowd roared around him, throwing their fists in
the air.

A smile crept across the prosecutor's face. He looked to the cleric who had remained motionless as a statue, but now gave him a brief nod of his head. "The church and the town of Riquewihr pronounce the sentence of death by burning at the stake, to be carried out this very evening!" His voice rose to a shout over the growing ebullience and fervor of the crowd as he triumphantly raised his fist to the heavens.

Greta buried her face into his chest and hugged him tightly.

"It's alright, my dear," said Lutrud, pulling her from his arms. "We don't need to stay and watch this farce of a spectacle. I'm taking Greta to the church. Service will begin soon, and we all need to pray to the Lord for better weather—and for this poor woman's soul. Please meet us there and don't be late. Come along now, Greta," Lutrud said, taking her hand and leading her away.

"Thank you, Lutrud. We'll see you in a few minutes. Ok, sunshine?" He kissed her on the cheek and turned back to the stage.

The guards escorted the woman off the stage, fighting off the raucous mob as best they could, but they still managed to pelt her with fists and sticks. More guards came to assist and gradually made their way through the mass of pressing bodies, back toward the town prison in

Thieves' Tower.

As the crowd dispersed, he noted that Han's attention lingered on the witch. He knelt down in front of him to get his attention, "You alright, son? Ready to head over to church?"

He watched Han's eyes continue to follow the woman as they forced their way through the streets, before finally looking up at him. "What makes someone become evil like that witch anyhow, Papa?"

He leaned in closer. "Are you convinced that she is guilty then?"

Han tossed his arms up. "I guess. She admitted it, didn't she?"

"Yes, he said that she did, didn't he? But do you remember what our friend Barous here told us about how they made the Templars confess, under torture?" Han nodded and looked up at Barous, towering above them. "So, if someone blamed you for something that you didn't do, and then tortured you for days or for weeks, don't you think you would eventually confess even though you didn't even do it, just to stop the pain and suffering being inflicted upon you?"

Han thought for a moment and replied with a puzzled expression. "That makes sense, but then why would they torture people, even if they're not sure whether they committed the crime or not?"

Guarin gave it some thought, but then just shook his head without a good answer before Barous interjected. "I may be able to shed some light on that, if I may? Being a soldier all my life, I can say without a doubt that this is probably the best way to get information from the enemy. We don't really have any choice, because the information that they can provide could mean life or death for our entire army, victory or defeat. So, we would torture prisoners for information quite often. This method has unfortunately carried over to civilian life and became an accepted method of obtaining information for the courts as well. From what I understand, once the accused confesses under torture, they must ask them again the next day when they have rested and can think straight again. We did not see her deny the charges against her today, did we?"

"No, she did not deny them." Han paused and thought for a moment before continuing. "What would make someone become evil like her?"

Barous scratched his beard. "Well, I'm still not so sure I would agree that she is truly guilty of being a witch as they claim, even if she did admit to it. But to answer your question more generally, I believe that people may turn to a life of sin and corrupt their souls for any number of reasons; but I also believe that they can be redeemed as long as they recognize and mend their malevolent ways. So, in that sense, I'm not sure I would consider all of these people evil."

Barous hesitated before continuing as his expression assumed a more solemn appearance, as though he was struggling with whether he should continue. "However, I'm afraid this may not be true for everyone, unfortunately. I wish I could tell you otherwise--that the power of redemption could heal us all. I wish I did not believe that what I'm about to say were true, but I have seen it first-hand." He took a deep breath, crossed his arms, and leaned back against the stage.

"I will tell you that there was indeed some corruption within the Templar Order, but most were womanizers and petty thieves, and some let's just say were less holy than one would expect of a Templar." Then he furrowed his brow, taking on a most disturbed look of deep contemplation and dread. "There was one knight, however, who was unlike anyone else I had ever known. When I first met him, I thought he was a little odd, that was all. But later I discovered what a truly despicable man he really was-- a murderer, a rapist, and a sadist. He didn't just commit these crimes to get what he wanted or to take revenge; he killed and tortured women and even children simply because he took *pleasure* in it, and he never showed any remorse. Not even on the day of his execution, as he walked to the block with that sinister smirk. I would swear that smirk remained on his face, even as it rolled in the dirt. This man was evil in its purest form. I can't say whether I know if he was born that way or something turned him that way. Alas, I'm afraid some people are truly and irredeemably evil."

His ominous words seemed to hang heavily in the air, provoking a cold, tingling sensation to creep up the back of Guarin's neck.

"I'm sorry, I should have left you with more encouraging words than that, my boy."

"It's alright, sir. I enjoy talking to you and I appreciate your honesty." Han replied with an almost reverential smile.

Guarin noticed a gleam of admiration in his eyes that he had not seen in quite a while, which made him realize how long it had been since his son regarded him with as much esteem.

Chapter 5

AS HAN FOLLOWED HIS FATHER back to the church, he fantasized about charging into battle on a war horse, brandishing his sword, his armor gleaming in the sunlight, his red cloak billowing behind him, as he led his valiant companions into the fray. Why should he have to remain a stupid woodcutter all of his life like his father when he could become a gallant knight like Sir Barous, traveling to the great cities of Paris, London, and Florence?

He looked up at his father and sighed. This was not the man he had grown up admiring. The father he remembered was strong and confident, not this lanky stick with ripples of worry written across his balding head. He used to watch him swing his axe with those once-powerful arms and broad shoulders capable of splitting logs twice as fast as the other men, impressing the hell out of everyone including the blacksmiths with his imposing stature.

He wanted to look up to him with pride like he used to before the famine, before his mother died—he really did—but how could he when he sees him giving up on his family like he has? He figured it was only a matter of time before Lutrud convinced him to send Greta and him away somewhere.

Lost in his thoughts, he would have tripped right over an old lady's corpse if his father hadn't stopped him. She seemed to be staring right up at him, her mouth gaped widely to reveal the sickening cavity within, her dry lips sucked in over her gums, and her black tongue protruding like a leather stump. He jumped back in revulsion and nearly tripped over a dog scampering by, a dog so emaciated that he figured it would also be dead by the end of the week. As he stepped around the dead lady, he wondered why nobody had moved her body, and why nobody seemed to care.

He thought about the witch lady too as he looked up at Thieves' Tower, looming above them on the northwest corner of town, where she awaited her execution. He wondered how she must feel knowing that she will be burned alive tonight, knowing that she will never live to see another day, knowing that she could do nothing about it, even if she wasn't guilty of what they claimed. Convincing himself that she really was an evil witch made him feel a little better about it, so that is what he did.

He felt his father's hand rest on his shoulder. "Is something still on your mind, son?"

"What? No, not really."

"You sure? It looks like there is something you'd like to get off your chest. Are you still upset about what happened this morning?"

He thought hard about how best to express his thoughts before continuing. "I heard stepmother talking to you last night. I know she doesn't want me around anymore. To be honest, I'm not sure I blame her. I just want you to know that I think I'm old enough now to take care of myself. I mean, the way things are…if we can't stay with you…"

"Listen, I'm going to talk to her some more about hitting you, but believe me, if I had to choose between her or my children, who do you think I would choose?"

He became distracted by the sound of children singing from the churchyard just ahead. Rounding the corner, he saw about twenty-five filthy children of all ages holding hands to form a circle, their emaciated bodies barely covered by rags, swaying and singing to a rhythmic rhyme. At the final chorus line, they all threw their arms up, screaming and laughing as they chased one another around the yard. He noticed that they were kept behind a fence in a dirt clearing—*not much different than livestock*. To Han they appeared to be child skeletons prancing about, while others resembled little gnomes sitting all by themselves, lonely and dejected. He couldn't imagine a more deplorable existence.

Then he noticed Lutrud and Greta standing along the fence, watching the children. Lutrud turned her head back toward Han as he warily approached. She wore an eerie, crooked smile, waving her hand for them to come closer. "Han, come over and see the lost children! Look how happily they play together."

He saw the word "ORPHANAGE" written on the building. He didn't read very well, but he had seen the word before and knew what it meant. He glanced back to Greta, clearly distraught, tears streaming down her cheeks. While panicked thoughts raced through his mind, an awful sense of dread sunk into his chest.

"What have you told her, Stepmother?" he demanded.

But she just maintained that weird smile, beckoning them to come closer. "Why don't you come and talk to some of the children? Get to know them a little bit."

So, this is why they brought us here.

"What's the matter, son?" his father asked, eyeing him curiously.

"She finally got to you didn't she, Papa? You lied to me."

At first, he felt helpless, unable to move as he looked from his father to Lutrud to the orphans and back to his father—then he fled. He turned and ran down the narrow, cobbled streets as fast as his legs would carry him. He didn't even know where he was running, as long as it was away from the orphanage, and away from Lutrud. He heard his father's desperate calls, but he didn't care—he just kept running, shoving people aside, hurdling over carts and corpses and stray animals and piles of crap that stood in his way. He turned down an even narrower deserted alleyway, rounded another corner, and then smacked into the heavy chain mail armor of a town guard.

"Ho there, son! What be your hurry?" The burly guard asked, grabbing hold of his arm.

He gasped and panted for breath, his mind still racing. He had to say something, anything, to get away from Lutrud and that orphanage. "Please help me, my stepmother is a witch! You must arrest her!" The accusation spilled out of his mouth before he even thought it through.

The guard grinned, shaking his head in disbelief but holding firmly to his arm. "Why do I keep hearing that word lately? One lady gets blamed and now it seems they're everywhere. You realize this is a very serious accusation? If you get caught lying…"

Han nodded.

The guard studied him a moment, then exhaled audibly. "Tell me why you are running. Is she chasing you?"

"She is over by the church. She wants to put me in that orphanage!"

He shook his head again, "Lots of that happening too, lately, I'm afraid." He scratched his black beard and thought a moment. "Is your father somewhere around here too?"

Han nodded, still trying to catch his breath.

"Come along then, bring me to your father and your stepmother. We shall have to settle this properly."

As they turned to walk back, his father rounded the corner in a huff, a look of relief washing over him. "Oh, thank you sir. I'm so sorry for the trouble, I am his father." He bent down on his knee and rested a hand on Han's shoulder. "What is it son? Why did you run?"

Han cringed and pulled himself away from him, feeling like he could no longer even trust his own father. "She convinced you after all, didn't she? You brought us here to put us into that orphanage! Admit it, you can't take care of us anymore and would rather just be rid of us!"

His father stared down at him in disbelief. "No…no…no, I wouldn't do that to you, believe me, Han. I agreed to no such thing!"

Although he appeared earnest, Han remained unconvinced. He glared back up at him and pressed his argument. "Stepmother has you under her spell and you don't even know it," he sputtered, tears welling up in his reddening eyes.

"Han!" he barked, abruptly rising back to his feet. "I told you not to speak like this in public. What has come over you?"

The guard eyed him suspiciously. "So, you have had conversations like this before, eh?

You are aware that he believes your wife is a witch?"

"You told him she is a witch?" His father looked incredulous as he shifted his attention to him, before turning back to the guard again. Han could see that he was getting nervous as a small crowd began to gather around them. "She is not exactly my wife, but no sir, he…he never told me that. I swear to you."

Seemingly out of nowhere, his father cried out and doubled over in pain, his right hand reaching for his lower back, the other on his knee to support himself.

The guard quickly turned to see what had happened, his hand instinctively gripping his sword hilt. "Did somebody strike you, sir?" he asked, clearly alarmed. He surveyed the area, but nothing appeared amiss.

"It certainly….*felt* like I was….thumped in my back," he groaned again, "but I can assure you…. I was not." His voice was strained, barely able to grunt out the words, his mouth locked in a grimace. "It feels like a stone again, I'm afraid."

"I'm sorry, sir. I've heard those can be quite painful," said the guard, lending his shoulder for support. "Let's go find your wife—sorry, his stepmother. I'll have to bring you all to the tower. Don't worry, they'll just want to ask you some questions, and then I suspect you'll be on your way."

Chapter 6

GRETA SAT QUIETLY IN A DARK DUNGEON of a room within Thieves' Tower while the two men she saw on the stage talked to her family. The cold stone chamber was mostly empty except for a large wooden table lit by candles at which they sat, along with some chairs and a heavy wooden chest beside the table. On the wall hung a large yellow shield emblazoned with a star at the top and what looked like three antlers underneath. A small window crossed by iron bars shed some extra light into this otherwise cavernous gloom.

In the corner lurked another man, leaning casually against the stone wall and watching silently from the shadows. She took him to be a guard but then noticed that he wasn't wearing any armor. He wore long hair too. She had never seen a guard with long hair before.

The man with the funny-looking green hat and curly mustache did most of the talking, while the hooded cleric nodded and listened intently. She did her best to listen but didn't understand half of what they were saying and didn't like any of this talk about witches. She knew her brother was just being a brat—he only said this to get stepmother in trouble for threatening to put them in an orphanage; she hoped the men would see it that way too. She didn't want to go to that orphanage either, but she didn't hate her stepmother like Han did and certainly wouldn't want anyone to light her on fire.

Muffled screams and cries coming from somewhere below them distracted her attention. *Could one of them be the witch lady?* She shivered and rubbed the goose pimples down that spread across her arms, trying to convince herself it was just from the damp chill inside the room. Once in a while she caught the man in the corner stealing glances at her which made the hairs on the back of her neck prickle, but other than that, nobody seemed to pay any attention to her at all.

She noticed that her father didn't seem to be listening very well either. He looked too sick to pay attention as beads of sweat trickled down his rippled forehead, and he shivered even more than herself. She knew this was because of the pain in his back, and maybe the cold too, but certainly not because he was scared. *Adults never seem to get scared, even that witch lady didn't look scared when they told her that she was going to be lit on fire tonight.* She couldn't imagine ever being that brave.

She wanted to go sit on his lap to make him feel better. He could brush her hair with his hand like he always does, but she knew this wasn't the time or the place. So, she just sat, and shivered, but did her best to listen.

Finally, the cleric began to ask some questions, his deeply lined face half-concealed and buried deep within his cowl, his penetrating eyes flashing an intensity that belied his aged face.

He didn't use as many words as the other man, but rather spoke slowly and deliberately.

"Tell me, boy, what exactly did she tell you that made you think she is…evil?" His deep voice reverberated off the walls, imparting an extra depth of gravity and importance to his words.

Han swallowed deeply and avoided looking at his stepmother. "It isn't so much as what she said to me….as much as the way I see her look at me sometimes. Like when she is about to punish me or hit me, she….she gets this weird smile on her face….and I….I just know that most people don't smile that way when they want to hurt someone…..especially someone they're supposed to care about."

Her stepmother scoffed.

"I see," said the cleric, nodding his head. "Does she hit you often?"

"Lately she has. Just last night actually and again this morning. It still hurts," he added with a frown, reaching for his ear.

Father Linhart studied her brother's face for a few long moments, his lips pursed, and his eyes focused in concentration, before continuing. He tended to open his lips with a slight smacking sound just before he spoke. "So, you are telling me that she is mean to you, but many parents strike their children when they do something wrong. What makes you think she is a witch? Have you seen her perform any spells or talk to the devil?"

Before answering, Han pinched his brows together like he does when thinking hard about something. "No Father, but I used to see her talking to our animals. Like her cat....and our old goat." Greta noticed the old cleric's eyes suddenly perk up with great interest.

"Liar!" shouted Lutrud, rising to her feet and shaking with rage, no longer able to hold her composure. She pointed her finger at Han, her mouth tightening into a lipless pucker, "You lying little devil!" Then she snapped at her father. "I warned you he would get us all into trouble, didn't I? Why don't you tell them what he said last night?" She looked over to the two men who stared back at her, their eyes wide with dismay. When Guarin didn't reply she answered for him.

"He said he didn't even believe in God, didn't he?"

Her father just put his hands over his face and shook his head as though he didn't seem to know whom to defend at this point. He didn't even seem to have the strength to say anything.

The cleric stared intently at her in silence until she took her seat once again. "We shall return to this new accusation in a moment," he said before turning to address her father again.

"Tell me Mr. Guarin, have you ever seen or heard her speak to animals, as your son claims?"

He removed his hands from his face and shook his head, "No, of course not. No more than a mother might talk to her baby," he replied softly, wiping the sweat from his brow.

Greta could see her brother's face turning red. He usually held his anger inside when around adults, but this time he looked like he was about to blow. "Tell them what *you* said last night, Stepmother! You threatened to *eat* us like some parents do in other villages!" Greta had seen him angry many times but had never seen him talk back to anybody like that.

33

Her father finally decided to speak out. "Come now, Han, she wasn't threatening you; she was just trying to get your attention and put our situation into perspective—that we're not nearly as desperate as some families—that is all she meant. You know she would never do anything like
that."

By the livid expression on Han's red face as he glared at her father, she worried that he was about to start yelling at him too.

A long silence pervaded the room, and then the two men conferred in quiet whispers. Her eyes glossing over with tears, she crossed her arms over her chest as she continued to shiver and rubbed the goosebumps on her arms. Still, nobody seemed to notice her—nobody that is, except for the silent man in the corner.

Finally, the man in the green hat stood and loudly pronounced, "We thank you all for your time. You three are free to go for now, but we have some more that we would like to discuss with the lady alone. It shouldn't take long, but if you wouldn't mind waiting outside." He gestured toward the door.

The old cleric rose more slowly and spoke to her father before he left the table. "I do hope you get over whatever it is that ails you. A stone, you say? I have had a few of those buggers in my day. Be sure to drink plenty of beer or clean water, and it should pass soon enough. At least water is one thing that we are not in short supply." He smiled and escorted him to the door, gently placing a hand on his shoulder.

As they waited outside, she could see that her father grew restless as he paced the courtyard, clutching his right flank.

Han shot him a look with a mix of disappointment and frustration. "You wouldn't even defend me against her in there. You just sat there like you always do, doing nothing."

"You know I would defend you, but these are all lies! You know what you said in there was not true. How could you lie to a cleric? How could you expect *me* to lie to a cleric, Han?" he rebuked, his voice growing louder until he suddenly clutched at his back again with a loud grunt.

Greta finally decided to interject. "But Papa, don't you remember how she used to talk to her kitty all the time, and even the other animals? Han wasn't lying about that."

He softened. "Well yes, of course, Sunshine. I'm sure we've all talked to our animals, but that doesn't mean.....Oh Christ, I have to take a piss." He closed his eyes with a grimace and took a long slow deep breath before continuing. "You're correct, Greta, he didn't actually lie about that, but they're going to think...." He doubled over again. "Excuse me kids, I'll be back in a moment," he groaned and then shuffled stiffly to the side of the building.

After a minute or two, Greta and Han peaked around the corner to see if he was ok. Greta screamed as she saw bright red blood pouring out of his penis, splattering against the stone wall and puddling towards his feet. "Are you ok, Papa?" The burly guard looked over and quickly covered his mouth, gagging in disgust.

He waved his hand in the air without looking up, "It's ok everyone, I just have a stone. I'll be alright....eventually." With that, he promptly vomited up what little he had in his stomach, mostly just green bile and berries, which mixed with the bright crimson swirls of his urine into a grotesque but kaleidoscopic blend of a painter's pallet.

Chapter 7

HAN SAT QUIETLY ON THE FLOOR OF HIS CABIN, trying to carve a small block of wood into some semblance of a horse. He glanced up again at his stepmother who seemed rather tense this morning—about what, he wasn't quite sure, but he had a suspicion, one that he kept pushing out of his mind. He turned to look out of the window. He couldn't really see anything through the blurry, translucent glass other than indistinct shapes and shadows and raindrops trickling down, but it was enough to create illusions in his imagination to pass the time.

He used to gaze into their fire pit before going to sleep each night, embracing its warmth, watching the flames as they danced above the crackling logs and glowing embers, following the smoke as it spiraled upwards. Now, with no dry wood to burn, it just sat there in the middle of the cabin, an empty ring of cold stones, rendered as useless as his father had become. Even the holes in the ceiling, which once served to release the smoke from the cabin, now served no other purpose than to let the cold air seep through and the rain to leak down upon their heads.

While his father slept late into the morning, Greta played with her hand-made doll on her bed of straw. The only thing talking to him at the moment was his stomach which gurgled and burned with hunger like usual.

He started bouncing his ball against the wall to pass the time. He remembered the day that his father made it for him many years ago. He'd watched as he carved out a ball of wood from a special tree, covered it with a thick layer of moss to make it softer, then wrapped it in a thin pliable leather that he stretched tightly around the ball and sewed it shut. His mother taught him how to stitch it back together when the seam came loose. He loved how it made the other kids jealous because his was the only ball that actually bounced. A knot tightened in his throat as he thought about his friend Amis, recalling the many hours they spent tossing it to each other. *I hope you're having more fun than I am, wherever you are.*

His stepmother set down her knitting and cracked her knuckles. He hated when she did that. She kept darting her eyes to the door and around the room. *What is she so nervous about?* She stood up and said she would check on his father when an unexpected loud thumping on the door made everyone jump.

His stomach turned. *Who the hell would pound on our door like that?* But he knew exactly who it must be. He quickly tossed his ball and carving knife into a small sack containing his wooden figurines, as his stepmother lurched to open the door without hesitation.

He held his breath when the stranger entered. *This can't really be happening!* He hadn't even noticed his father step out of his room, looking frail and haggard and barely able to stand.

But when he told him to run, he bolted without a second thought.

He ran as fast as Greta was able to keep up, tugging her by the arm and trudging through the thick, cold, wet muck that squished between his bare toes.

"I told you it would come to this! I won't go to no crappy orphanage, I won't!" Han whispered harshly as he urged her along.

"Where are we going?" Greta asked breathlessly, trying her best to keep up.

"Just trust me and keep your voice down. I know of an old mine up ahead where we can hide," he huffed.

They heard Lutrud scream from inside the house. Realizing they would be caught if he kept to the path, he made a sharp turn and kept running through the brush. As they got further from the path, the vegetation became so thick that running became impossible, at some points forcing them to crawl through the mud to get underneath the brush. "Let's stop and rest here for a little. If we keep low, he won't be able to find us."

He heard the man curse in the distance as he came out to hunt for them.

"That's the man that stood in the back of the room when those men were questioning you. What do you think he did to Papa?" Greta whispered.

"I'm not sure. We can go back and check later but right now we have to hide."

He thought about what his stepmother said just before he told him to run. *Did he really agree to let this man take us away?*

He stopped to listen and catch his breath while they cowered low in the brush. Greta shivered uncontrollably next to him, so he hugged his arms around her, holding her close. "Do you hear anything?" whispered Han.

Greta shook her head.

What if he just follows our footsteps in the mud? He glanced up at the gloomy sky, becoming heavier with deep blueish-gray clouds, gathering and growing darker by the minute. "A storm is building," he said, just as a low rumbling thunder began. The wind whipped up with great force, angrily throttling the trees. "We have to keep moving toward the mine, or we'll get caught in this storm. Follow me, but stay low and don't say a word," he whispered. "He'll quit chasing us once it starts."

Just as they started to move on, they heard him call out again, this time he was closer— much closer. "I know you are out there, and I know you can hear me, children. There is no need to keep running. It is not hard for me to find you. Your footsteps have led me this far. Soon I will see your breath. I really don't want to have to keep searching for you in the rain. You have my word that I will not hurt you if you come out on your own. I don't want to have to get rough with you."

They continued to crawl through the mud, trying to keep quiet, as spiders and worms and those long critters with a hundred legs scurried around them. Lutrud called out their names, pleading for them to return.

He popped his head up above the brush and spotted the mine. "Let's move, we're almost there. I can see it!"

The rain turned to a deluge with frantic intensity, heavy and drenching and all at once. A splintering crack echoed from a nearby tree as one of its heavy branches snapped off, crashing to the muddy ground right beside them.

"Keep running, just a little further!" Han shouted, darting aside from the falling tree limb that nearly took his head off.

They arrived at the edge of a clearing, about thirty steps away from the opening to the mine with nothing to conceal them the rest of the way. A deafening blast of thunder from directly over their heads shook the earth under their feet, rattling them to their core. Greta let out a scream which she quickly stifled, drowned out by the booming thunderclap.

He peered out in all directions and could neither see nor hear any trace of their pursuer. "I need you to run as fast as you possibly can to that mine, do you see it?" She nodded, her eyes wide with alarm yet intently focused. "Good, now don't make any sound and don't stop until you are through. Once we are inside, it will be very dark, but I'll lead us to a hiding spot so don't be scared. Are you ready?" Her eyes grew wide and determined as she nodded her head vigorously.

"Ok, Let's go!"

They took off through the clearing at a full-on sprint, not even bothering to look around, his vision focused ahead, intent on reaching the opening in the rock wall. He had never felt so exhilarated and alive! Bounding through into the darkness, he turned to grab onto Greta just a few steps behind him.

"Congratulations, you made it!" came a startling shout from the darkness behind him as a powerful arm wrapped around his neck. He heard Greta scream while he choked in his grasp. The man reached out to grab her and then threw them both violently to the ground. "I told you I would find you. Now you made me get rough!" He kept his hand on the back of his neck, smashing his face into the muck. Han heaved and sputtered to catch his breath, but his mouth was now full of mud. He felt the pressure from his hand lift off his neck, but quickly replaced by the hard sole of his boot, then forced his wrists behind his back and bound him like a hog. As soon as he felt the pressure lift from his body, Han flipped over, spitting mud in his captor's face. The man just smiled, kicked him in the face, gagged him, and then went to work tying up Greta in the same fashion.

He then snatched the sack that Han was carrying, brought out his carving knife, and slipped it in his pocket. He continued to shuffle through his remaining items without much consideration. "You can keep those," he said, tossing the bag back on the floor next to Han.

"There, see how nice I can be?"

He sat back against the wall, tossed his hair back with a sweep of his hand, and smirked at them as they lie helpless and bound on the cold cave floor. *Does he ever stop smiling?* He looked as though he had just finished a round of playful wrestling and now sat back for a break. "Did you silly things really think you could escape from me? It was really quite easy to follow your tracks in the mud, the rustling of the leaves, your breath in the cold air…it wasn't difficult to see where you were heading. Well, you made me get rough with you, but that's ok. It doesn't bother me. It didn't bother me when I got rough with your father either," he chuckled. "Your stepmother assured me he wouldn't put up much of a fight, which is true I suppose."

He paused to wiped off the mud from his face, then turned toward Han again, his voice calm and steady. "I'm not sure why you were running from me, boy. You don't really want to go back and live with that nasty stepmother of yours, do you? What did you call her yesterday, a witch?" He tossed his head back and let out a chuckle. "You really think she is a witch or were you just trying to get rid of her?" Han could only stare back at him from the ground. "You best be careful when you accuse somebody of a crime just to get back at them. Do you know what happens if the court finds you guilty of a false accusation?" His captor smiled and leaned forward, "They give you the same punishment that the accused would have gotten. In this case, they would burn you alive," he said, his smile widening, clearly enjoying the anxiety this provoked in Han. Then he pinched his eyebrows together and tilted his head a bit, mocking a show of pity. "Should I take you back to town again and see whose side they believe? No? Then maybe you should just cooperate with me, and I'll take you to your new home. I think you'll like it. The Lady is very kind. I think you'll like her too."

Chapter 8

GRETA SHIVERED ON THE COLD, WET GROUND in the shelter of the cavern, watching the tempest wreak havoc in the forest. The wind roared and the trees flailed as they struggled to keep upright. Rain poured down with a wild ferocity, the chaotic wind whipping it angrily in every direction, even slashing through the entrance and spraying onto her face. She witnessed another tree become completely uprooted, creaking and groaning as it careened onto its side like a dying animal.

Still in shock, she struggled to process everything that had just happened. She had so many questions and tried to work up the courage to ask the man holding them captive. She almost felt grateful that he at least unbound her wrists so that she could hug her thighs to her chest against the cold. He refused to extend the same privilege to her brother though. She looked with pity down at Han, lying on his side, bound and gagged, and staring out into the storm.

She turned to her captor who sat with his back up against the wall, studying a map in the dim light. Then she looked past him into the dark depths of the cave and shuddered, wondering what might be lurking in that black void. A spectacular display of lightening briefly illuminated the empty darkness within, followed by another ear-splitting crackle of thunder directly overhead. When a second bolt struck, she noticed the man's eyes flash a brilliant green just as he caught her gaze, inducing a sudden fresh chill to run up her back.

"What is your name?" she asked, breaking the silence between them. Her whispery, squeaky voice hissed off the cavern walls, lending it a ghoulish quality.

"My name is Roland, my dear Greta. It's my pleasure to make your acquaintance," he replied eloquently with his usual smile before returning to his map.

"You smile a lot; but only with your mouth, not with your eyes," she said, putting on her best pouty expression.

"Is that right?" he chuckled. "Well then, I shall have to work on that."

"Did you kill my Papa?" she asked after a few more moments of silence.

Roland lowered the map just below his eyes and peered over at her. "Noooo, I did not need to kill him," he answered like a teacher correcting his student. "Nevertheless, I wouldn't get your hopes up that he will be coming after you anytime soon. He is not in any condition for that. Given how sick he looks, I doubt he will last another week anyway," he said in a casual, dismissive tone. "But don't worry, my dear, once we get you to your new home, you'll forget all about your Papa. A lot of children are losing their parents these days, so don't feel sorry for yourself. It would be best for you both if you start looking ahead to the future and not the past."

She continued on. "Where are you taking us?"

He didn't respond so she tried a different question. "Does my stepmother know?" Silence.

She sighed with exasperation. "Can't you at least tell us how far we have to walk?"

"So many questions from such a little mouse," he replied as he finally dropped the map and put it away. "If this continues, I shall have to cover your mouth like your pesky brother there. But I'll answer you this last time. We have quite a long walk and may take a couple of days to arrive at The Lady's home. There are not many who know where The Lady's home is, but I know, so you better not wander away from me and get lost in the forest. There are lots of bandits out there looking for little boys and girls like you to take home with them, and believe me, you wouldn't want to go home with one of them."

Another chill went up her spine after his warning, so she decided not to ask any more questions. A cold silence hung in the cavern between them for a long while. She sat and gazed up at the turbulent sky as it put on a dazzling show with brilliant flashes that illuminated the storm clouds. As she watched, a lurid bolt of lightning arced across the sky in successive bursts before striking down to earth like a jagged spear from the heavens. She listened to the sound of the heavy rain, interrupted by crashes of thunder, cracking branches, and the eerie whistling wind.

She scooted back further away from the opening to escape the cold breeze and spattering rain. A mysterious sound coming from somewhere within the cave caught her attention again.

Turning towards the darkness, she tried to peer as far back as she could while her eyes adjusted. She heard another curious sound, like a faint squeaking or chirping. *Probably just dirty rats*, she thought. *But then what is that? Is that breathing?*

"Roland, do you think a bear could be——" but then she slapped her hands over her mouth as she remembered his threat about asking any more questions.

Roland stood up and walked several feet in front of her into the darkness and stood there in silence, looking and listening. She could barely see the outline of his motionless body, standing like a sentinel at the threshold of the cavernous black void. Lightning flashed in quick succession, casting his flickering shadow back and forth across the walls, followed by a tremendous blast of thunder that made them all jump. A moment later the squeaking and chirping grew suddenly louder, and then another sound caught her attention—a flapping sound.

"Bats!" he yelled, his cloak flaring out behind him as he turned to run. "Get down!"

She watched as his silhouette suddenly became engulfed by countless tiny black flapping shadows all around him, squealing like flying rats. He dove forward onto the ground at her feet, covering his head with his cloak. She screamed as they flew rapidly toward her, throwing herself onto the ground, covering her head with her hands. The sound became a screeching storm as the cloud of bats fluttered over them.

She couldn't stop screaming, even after the swarm had past as one of the bats became entangled in her hair, clawing into her scalp. She thrashed wildly on the ground trying to pull it out. Finally, she felt a ripping sensation throughout her entire scalp—and then it was gone. She looked up to see that Roland had torn the bat free, a wad of her hair dangling from its claws, as he rushed to throw it outside.

Blood dripped down her face, into her eyes and mouth, her scalp searing with pain. She couldn't stop screaming and crying; never before had she been struck with terror such as this. Then someone took hold of her. She looked up—it was Roland. Afraid he was going to beat her or suffocate her, she panicked and fought wildly against his grasp, but he held her firmly, reassuring her with his soothing voice until she calmed down. Greta knew she hated the man, but his strong and warm embrace was enough to make her feel a sense of security for the first time all day. He reached in his pocket and carefully wiped the tears and blood from her face with a rag, telling her that she was going to be ok. He held her as she sobbed and panted for a couple more minutes, and then he let her be.

He turned to look outside, studying the weather for a while. "We have wasted enough daylight this morning, and it looks like the worst has passed over."

He stepped out to soak his rag in the rain, then returned and knelt down beside Greta, pouring water over her scalp while gently rubbing the rest of the blood away to inspect the wound. "It looks like it should heal just fine but may take some time, that's all," he said with a conciliatory smile.

He turned to Han and shot him a stern look. "I'm going to take off your bondage, and I expect you to cooperate with me. If we run into anyone on the road, then you must keep silent and let me do the talking. Is that understood?" They both quickly nodded their heads. "I don't want to have to get rough with you again, but I will if you make me." They shook their heads without hesitation. He then resumed his unfriendly smile again as he untied them.

Reaching into his backpack, he pulled out their rain cloaks. "Your stepmother wanted me to give these to you to keep you a bit warmer and dryer for the journey."

"Thank you," they mumbled under their breath.

"What was that?" he chided them, cupping his hand behind his ear. "Did you just thank me?"

"Thank you, Roland." they said, louder this time.

"Well, what do you know? Bad guys *can* do good things for people sometimes, can't they?"

Chapter 9

GUARIN OPENED HIS EYES TO SEE LUTRUD standing stiffly over him, her expression grave, almost menacing. He realized that his wrists and ankles were bound.

"You are about as useless to me now as the balls of a priest," she said, glaring at him. "How could I have ever hoped for any love to grow between us? I've been lonely my entire life. When you asked me to stay with you after Kaetherlin died, I…. How stupid and silly I was, giving into my naive emotions like a little girl. I opened up an empty space in my heart like a deep well of vulnerability, but instead of nourishing and filling it with love, you crapped in it like a latrine. You and your lying filthy son."

He tried to speak but his mouth was so dry he could barely open his mouth.

She knelt down and wiped the blood from his face. "Am I so irrelevant in your life?" she said softly as tears welled up in her eyes. But then her expression hardened again. As though frustrated and disgusted by these emotions that she no longer wanted to feel, she began to beat on his chest, slapped his face, and screamed out loud, "Why did it have to come to this? Why couldn't you show me just a little love, just a little companionship?"

Outside, he heard a storm begin to rage. He worried for his children. He tried to ask where they were, but no words came out as she continued to beat and slap him. Howling with despair, she dropped her face and arms across his chest and sobbed, spilling out her pent-up resentment and emotions until they were all dried up. All he could do was just lie there and wonder with trepidation what she might do next.

Slowly, she lifted her body from his and sat back on her heels with one last heavy sigh. Then, as though reasserting her sense of dignity, she wiped the tears from her face, straightened her white hair back behind her shoulders, and looked down upon him once again, but this time with a face of stone.

"Goodbye, Guarin," she said, rising back to her feet like a changed woman. Without looking back, she opened the door to the fury of the wind and rain and thunder. With weariness pressing down upon his senses, he watched as she stood at the threshold, gazing out at the churning sky, letting the storm rush through her, violently whipping her hair around like a white flame. As though impervious to the ravages of the storm, she stepped outside and strode steadily back to Riquewihr.

Chapter 10

PULLING HIS WOOLEN CLOAK OVER HIS HEAD, Han followed Roland, along with Greta, out from the shelter of the cave and into the driving rain, noting the devastation wrought by the storm. He saw massive trees uprooted and blown to the ground or caught between the branches of its neighbor, another with its thick trunk split in half by a lightning strike, exposing its splintered edges like so many sharp jagged teeth within its gaping maw. The storm clouds remained a grayish-purple hue, but the strong winds and lightening had subsided.

As they arrived back on the main path, Han turned to look back toward his cabin in the distance.

"Something on your mind, boy?" snapped Roland.

Han jerked his attention back to Roland and shook his head. "No, sir." He glanced down at his feet, then back up at him quizzically. "I was just wondering how my father is doing, that's all. Did you hurt him pretty bad?" he asked, eyes glistening on the brink of tears.

Roland considered his question for a moment before replying. "Let's just say if he doesn't recover, it won't be from anything I did to him. It looks like that kidney stone has him in a death grip, but I'm sure your stepmother will do the best she can to get him some help." He paused and heaved a heavy sigh. "Like I said before, you need to start looking past your family now. They can't take care of you any longer, just like many other families, believe me. Your stepmother has seen fit to make arrangements for you at least. You should be thankful that they didn't just abandon—"

"Abandon us in the forest to die, we know," they interrupted almost in unison.

Roland almost chuckled. "Alright then, I see you get the picture. Let's be on our way then."

They set off more or less in a westward direction, away from the town of Riquewihr. Han and Greta both gave one last lingering look at their home as he led them away. They passed by some of the sporadic forest dwellings situated just off the path. He knew some of the families that lived in them, especially if they had children. At least he used to know them, back when their chimneys still smoked. Many of the homes looked abandoned now and in dire need of repair, some collapsed in ruin. He thought about the days when he used to see neighbors out talking with each other or diligently working in their gardens or tending their livestock; those days now seemed like nothing more than a lost memory. Gone was the daily steady beat of axes chopping in the distance, the myriad sounds of free-roaming chickens and pigs and dogs mixed with the laughter of children. These days, he only heard the sound of rain.

From one of the homes further along the way, an old man with weathered face and long white beard leaned languidly against his doorway. He silently watched them go by, perhaps with a hint of suspicion, he couldn't tell. Han had seen him before talking to his father. He made ropes from tree bark or some such thing if he remembered correctly, and he enjoyed birds—trapped and sold them—but that was about all he knew about him. He wasn't very friendly, kept to himself mostly.

They walked on in silence for hours along a fairly arduous uphill path, the rain and wind remaining mostly steady but whipping up at times. They trekked further that day than Han had ever been with his father before. When they reached a fork in the path, he made sure Roland wasn't looking, then tossed one of his miniature wooden carvings to the ground. Once he escaped from Roland, or from the lady's house, he wanted to be sure he knew the way back home. Greta looked up to him as if to tell him he dropped it, but Han put a finger to his lips before she uttered a sound. He just hoped there wouldn't be too many more forks in the trail going forward, since he only carried five carvings.

By mid-afternoon, the rain slowed to a drizzle. They stopped to rest near a patch of bilberries, still too hard and tasteless to enjoy this early in the season. Roland removed his backpack and set it down, then unbuckled his sword belt and hung it from a tree branch, letting out a little moan of relief as he stretched back and forth. He pulled out the carving knife that he took from Han and used it to scrape some bark off a birch tree, chewing it as if it were a tender fruit.

"Want some?" he offered when he noticed them staring at him.

Greta wrinkled her nose and shook her head, but Han decided to give it a try. He had tasted it mixed up in a paste before but never straight from a tree. He bit off a chunk and chewed it with disgust but had trouble swallowing. It sucked his mouth dry and tasted like dirt and wood, so he spit it out.

Roland laughed, "You're supposed to eat the inside of the bark, not the whole thing. Try it again."

He used his front teeth to scrape off the inner layer which was indeed softer and less bitter. He still gagged on it a couple times but was able to finally get it down on the third try.

"More?" Roland offered again with a broad smile.

"No, thank you. I'm sure I couldn't swallow it again if I tried," he replied with a grimace.

He then looked over to Greta again who appeared weary and exhausted. "You need to try to eat something, young lady. We've a long way to go yet, and you're going to need the energy to keep up."

"I guess I'll just stick to the berries then," she sighed.

They rested on a fallen tree trunk for a while longer while Roland ate his tree. He then searched around the area and came up with some edible greens that he used to spice up his bark meal and gave the rest to Han and Greta. "Try this, it's the best I can do."

For the first time since they left, Han heard faint sounds of distant conversation and laughter. As they came around a bend in the path, Han could make out four people walking towards them; three of the men were armed with swords at their hips and seemed to be guarding a woman.

He could see Roland studying the party but maintained a casual posture, leaning against the tree. Without taking his eyes off of them, he whispered a warning to Greta and Han. "You don't speak unless spoken to. And keep your hoods on. I don't want any extra questions or suspicion. Understood?"

They both nodded their heads, but Han wondered if this might be his only chance for escape. He could see them much more clearly now as they approached. Their laughter ceased. He noted they were wearing leather armor as well. Three trained, armed men against one unarmed man wearing nothing more than clothes and a heavy cloak. *This will be too easy*, he thought as they came near enough to make out their faces. *But then why am I so nervous?* He wanted to call out for help, but instead he felt paralyzed, unable to utter a sound. *What if they decided to mind their own business despite my plea for help and continued on, leaving me to Roland's wrath?*

They nodded their heads curtly to Roland, who returned the gesture. "Good day to you, sir. Nice weather for a hunt," one of the men quipped. He looked to be the older of the three men, probably the captain.

Roland chuckled, "Looks like you boys had a successful hunt, at least. Good day to you gentlemen."

Two of the men laughed, but the third cast him a look of disdain. His face bore a sullen, stern appearance and sported a short patch of black hair on his chin. It looked as though a perpetually scornful expression had chiseled deep creases into his cheeks and between his brow. He motioned with his head towards Han and Greta. "Yeah, but it looks like you were twice as successful as us," he said, his voice thick and deep.

"Mind yourself, Eudo," Roland shot back at him, holding onto his casual smile. "Their parents have asked me to escort them to stay at their aunt's while their father is sick. I get paid just as you do."

"Bah! I know the type that fills your dirty pockets," growled Eudo as he spit towards Roland's feet.

They know each other, thought Han, a bit discouraged, *but at least they don't seem to like each other much.* The third man in the group drew his attention, younger and taller than the others. He didn't recognize him at first with his beard but noticed his tic when he kept blinking and then he remembered him clearly—his best friend Amis's older brother! He used to help cutting trees with his father sometimes. A few years ago, he moved into town to become one of the guards. Han had only seen him once more at Amis's burial but remembered that he was kind to him. *What's his name? It sounded like... friendly...friend... Ferrand! That's it! Surely this is providence! God must have heard my doubts and placed this savior in my path.* He could only blame himself if he let this opportunity go by. *I must act now!*

Han flipped off his hood, stood up, and shouted: "Ferrand! It's me, Han. I was a good friend of your brother, Amis. Remember me? And my sister, Greta?" He jerked Greta's hood back and heard them gasp in alarm at her condition. He pointed to Roland. "This man is lying! He barged into our house this morning and beat up our father. We don't even know where he is taking us. Please help!"

Swords flashed. The Captain stepped back from the others to the far side of the path with the woman, making way for the ensuing fight, holding her close with a dagger at her throat. "Don't you try to run, little lady."

"Do you know these children, Ferrand? Does he speak the truth?" asked Eudo without taking his glowering eyes off of Roland.

"Han?" Ferrand studied him, his expression slowly turning to one of recognition. "Step away from him and we'll protect you. Come across the path to our friend, Bertran." He pointed to the Captain with his longsword. Han noticed that his sword shook ever so slightly despite gripping it with both hands. "We'll take you back to your father. Come along now."

Han didn't hesitate to walk over but was surprised by the sudden assertive command of Roland: "Sit down, boy. You're not going with them."

Han stopped short and glanced back to find him in the same relaxed position, leaning against the tree. He shaved off another piece of bark with his carving knife and chewed some more, waving the little knife at the guards with short flicks of his wrist as if shoeing away flies. "My business with these children does not concern any of you. I can assure you gentlemen that their stepmother made arrangements for my escort, and I have the papers to prove it. I will keep them safe until they arrive at their destination. He is just scared, that's all, but he will be fine. Won't you, Han?"

Han didn't reply. He didn't move either.

"Eudo, bring the young girl to me first, and then the boy," commanded the Captain.

Ferrand shifted his eyes to Greta and then back to Roland. "It doesn't look like you're keeping her safe so far. What did you do to the poor girl?"

"We sheltered in a cave during the storm. A bat became entangled in her hair, I pulled it off." He replied simply. "Now put away your weapons before someone gets hurt."

"Now, Eudo!" shouted the Captain.

The events unfolded rapidly at this point. Eudo quickly lurched toward Greta to pull her away, but almost instantaneously Han saw his own carving knife zip across his vision and enter into his neck. Eudo screamed and tore the blade free, opening up a gash that unleashed streams of blood spurting through the air, some of it striking Han in his face and mouth. The warm, metallic taste of blood on his tongue made him want to retch, even as he watched him thrash around in a pathetic panic. He didn't expect such a haughty man would ever make such a sound, such a pitiful shriek, which quickly changed to a gurgling wheeze as his neck swelled and blood poured from his mouth.

Greta screamed and darted behind a tree, cowering with her eyes shut tight and hands covering her ears, as though trying in vain to shut out the appalling violence going on around her. His adrenaline surging, Han turned his attention back to the furor of the battle.

Ferrand raised his sword to attack Roland, roaring out a battle cry as he advanced, but before he could deliver his strike, Roland spun away from the tree in a blur of motion. Leaping and twisting his body through the air, he kicked the outside of Ferrand's knee like a whip, collapsing his leg inward, snapping it into a gruesome angle that knees were not meant to bend. He went down hard, angulating his knee even further beneath his weight. Han heard it crack a second time and watched in horror as his jagged and bloody bone pierced through his skin and breeches. His face lost all color and his eyes rolled back in unimaginable pain as he released an agonizing groan.

Almost in the same fluid motion, Roland turned his spinning momentum into a forward roll toward the unsuspecting Captain's feet. Bertran shoved the woman away and leveled his dagger to defend himself from the impending assault. Roland came out of his roll onto one knee, letting out his breath with a hiss and delivering an awesome, open-handed upward thrust to the bottom of his sternum. The power of his blow lifted the man completely off his feet and sent him flying backwards before landing spread eagle in the mud, jarring the dagger from his grip.

Han watched in amazement as though he were enjoying a circus act, mystified by Roland's graceful dance of death. *An acrobatic assassin*, he mused. Bertran lifted himself back to his feet and looked warily at Roland. He stood hunched forward with his mouth open, one hand on his chest and the other held out as if to ward off a second blow. He could tell that the man struggled to draw in a breath. Roland just stood completely still and silent, even smiling as he watched the Captain's face turn blue and his eyes bulge from their sockets. Then he began to drool, his legs shaking uncontrollably before collapsing onto his knees. At last, he inhaled a giant sucking breath but then puked bile instead of exhaling.

What have I done? It was only then that Han realized his predicament. Becoming desperate, he looked down at Eudo, choking to death on his own blood, staring blankly and gasping in his final slobbering breaths. He turned to Ferrand, still agonizing on the ground, his lower leg twisted grotesquely up toward his hip, his blood draining into a puddle beneath him.

Han knelt down in the dirt beside him. "Please, Ferrand, forgive me! I'm so sorry to bring you into this," he pleaded, tears streaming down his cheeks.

He heard guttural, choking sounds coming from the Captain. Jerking his head up toward the sickening sound, he saw Roland straddled over the chest of his dying victim, hands clasped around his neck. "Please, Ferrand, you must do something. He's going to kill us next!" he begged, knowing full well that he was crippled and helpless.

"Don't worry about me. Just take your sister and run!"

Han almost took him up on it. He considered it and began to rise but then shook his head vigorously. "I can't just leave you here. I'm the one who got you into this."

Ferrand propped himself up on his elbow. "Can you hold my sword, Han? Take it, stand over me. Even if you can't wield it, just distract him. Bring him closer. I may be able to surprise him with my dagger," he whispered in staggered breaths.

Han shook his head at first, but then realizing this was their only chance, he grasped the hilt and rose to his feet. He raised the sword above his midline before the weight forced it down again. He wiped his tears on his shoulders and lifted the blade again with sheer determination, his arms shaking with strain. "Roland!"

Slowly, he turned his head around with a sinister grin. It was different from his usual absent smile, more intense. *He really seemed to be enjoying this,* Han observed with revulsion. Roland looked back down at the Captain's purple face, giving his neck one last violent shake; then he rose to his feet and strode swiftly over to Han.

"Han! Look at you trying to wield that sword like a man! Is that what you've become today, Han? A man?" he mocked. "Where is your sister? Did she run away into the forest all by herself?"

Han stared him down with fury in his eyes and didn't back away. Ferrand remained motionless, feigning unconsciousness. Roland quickly closed in on him with brisk strides, easily evading his feeble swing, and reached out to grab the sword from his hands. Just as he did, Ferrand thrust his dagger up toward his groin, gashing his upper thigh. Roland shifted his weight at the last instant to avoid a deadly blow to his artery, then kicked the dagger from his hand with a flick of his other foot. Han swung down again with all his might, aiming for his neck, but he was much too slow. Roland barreled his shoulder into his chest, knocking him backward and jarring the sword loose, dropping uselessly into the mud. Han staggered backward from shock and fear.

Roland clutched at his bleeding thigh. His perpetual smile was gone. He looked wild now, snarling like a feral beast, his radiant green eyes ablaze with fury. In a fit of rage, he bunched his fists and let out a blood-thirsty roar. As he wiped off the spit from his lips, his bloody hand streaked a crimson smear across his mouth, leaving the appearance of a freakishly wicked sneer. He crossed over to Ferrand and stomped on the thigh of his maimed leg, pinning it to the ground. As if oblivious to the desperate man's agonizing screams, he grabbed hold of his ankle with both hands and jerked it violently, separating the only remaining fragments of bone and ligaments that held it together, ripping the severed limb completely away from his body. Ferrand screamed with an ululating pitch that sounded even more pathetic than Eudo did with the blade in his throat. He shrieked and wailed like a mortally wounded animal in his death throes, blood spurting out of the open stump in giant arcs as he thrashed on the ground.

Roland hoisted his leg into the air like a trophy, straggly bits of tendons and blood vessels dangling from around the protruding broken bone. "Don't worry, you won't be needing this anymore!" Roland yelled, and then hurled the limb far into the forest, as though it were nothing more than a walking stick. Roland watched him agonize with maniacal fascination, his eyes feasting on the gruesome spectacle he had created. Jerking his attention back to Han, he mocked him with his blood-stained grin. "You see what you made me do? None of this had to happen. I asked you to keep your mouth shut, but you couldn't do it. I told you I would have to get rough. I was going to let this man live, but then you had to get clever. Now you're going to watch me kill him, and that will be your punishment for what you've done. Do you understand? If you look away, I'm going to get rough with you too." He walked over and heaved Ferrand up from the ground, propping him up onto his one leg, facing Han.

"No, please don't kill him! He was only trying to help me!" Han cried out. "His brother just died; his parents won't have any children left."

Ferrand thrashed his arms about trying to break free of his grasp, but he became weaker and more sluggish as blood continued to drain out of his stump.

"There now, that's better. Why don't you calm down now, I think your friend has something he wants to say to you. What do you want to say, Han? Is there something you want to tell your hero before I kill him? Do you want to tell him thanks for trying?"

"I'm sorry!" Han cried out in utter despair, fresh tears flowing down his cheeks. "I'm so sorry," he repeated and buried his face in his hands.

"Ah-ah-ah! Remember to watch, Han! There you go, that's good," Roland said as he grasped Ferrand's head with both hands like a melon and jerked. He heard a loud, sickening snap that rendered his neck as twisted and crooked as his leg had been. Roland let go of his head which flopped backward and to the side, as his lifeless body crumpled back down to the ground.

Han howled in despair as he wilted down to his knees, weeping and shaking his head with disbelief. "It's my fault, this is all my fault. I'm so sorry."

Chapter 11

GRETA REMAINED HIDDEN BEHIND THE TREE, hunched over and trying to shut herself off from the screams and shouts and sounds of death. But now, everything suddenly became silent except for her brother's sobbing and muttering. *Why did he have to try to be a hero? Roland is going to kill him now. He might be breaking his neck right this second! Then he will come for me.* Paralyzed with fear, she didn't move; she didn't even open her eyes.

She heard voices now—Roland talking to the woman—but too distant to hear clearly. The squishing sound of footsteps approached her, trudging through the muck. They stopped short. His voice suddenly louder and very close. "You help me find your sister now, boy. We don't have time to search. Call out to her."

He didn't call out, he just kept sobbing.

Roland raised his voice, "If she does not return, if you do not find her, then I abandon this mission and throw your dead body in the river with your hero friends, understand?"

With that threat, Greta promptly rose to her feet and stepped away from behind the tree, wiping her eyes. "I'm here. I was just scared. I'm not going to run."

"There's a good girl," he said as the phony smile returned to his face. "Come over and sit next to your brother while I search these men. Sendy, come over and sit with the children, if you please."

Greta looked her over as she walked toward her. She was a young woman with long curly raven black hair, dark eyes, and a kind face—pretty, she supposed. Her skin appeared darkly tanned, but not burned like most people's skin would become if out in the sun too long. She smiled at them both as she sat down and gently tousled their hair. "Hello lovely children. My name is Melisende, but most people just call me Sendy. Can you tell me your names?" she asked.

"Greta," she replied like a mouse. She hated the way her voice squeaked when she felt shy or nervous.

She then turned to Han and rubbed her hand gently on his back. "And how about this brave boy? Can you tell me your name?"

His eyes were still glazed with tears, his face covered with dirt and blood as he sat looking at the ground. "Han," he choked out in a raspy voice.

"Well, that's an unusual name. I've heard of Hansel and Hans before, but not Han." She winked at Greta to let her know she was lightly teasing him.

When he didn't respond, Greta answered for him. "Our Papa said he didn't like the name Hansel as much as our Mum did, so they agreed to call him Hans. But after a while he didn't see the point since there was only one of him," she said, smiling. "He always likes telling people that. I guess he thought it was kind of funny."

"That actually makes sense!" Sendy giggled. "Anyhow, I like the name Han better as well." She brought her face closer to his so he would look at her. "I've never seen a boy your age act so bravely! That kind of action can really impress a lady like me. Tell me, do you want to be a knight when you grow up?"

Han glanced back at Roland as he rummaged through the guards' pockets and bags. She could see his eyes begin to well up with tears again and his lip quivered. "Ferrand told me that he wanted to be a knight someday."

Sendy lightly touched her finger on his cheek and turned his face toward hers.

"Let's try not to look upon the dead as their souls leave their bodies. It isn't proper, don't you agree? Let's instead turn and look into the beauty of the forest. It is much nicer to look at what is alive than what is dead. If you listen closely, you can hear the trees speak to one another. They whisper with the breeze." They listened in silence for a while to the rustling of the leaves. "Can you hear the birds now that the rain has stopped? I see a pretty one with a red breast looking down at us. Just there, can you see him?"

They nodded as she pointed it out. Greta could feel the tension leaving her already as the sparrow chirped happily down from its perch. She stole a glance back to Sendy, who smiled warmly at her. Greta shyly returned it. She noticed that Han was starting to get some color back into his face and his eyes dried up. Sendy kept them distracted by pointing out and explaining other interesting things in the forest that they otherwise would not have noticed or understood.

"Where were they taking you? Were you in trouble for something?" Greta asked.

A subtle change came over her expression as she gazed into the forest, as if deciding how to answer. "They were taking me to stand trial in Riquewihr."

"Did you steal something?" Greta asked.

She shook her head slowly and then looked back to Greta, her dark eyes penetrating into her own. "They say I'm a witch."

Greta rocked her head back and gasped. "But you're not though, right? I mean, you're much too nice and pretty to be a witch."

She laughed and brushed Greta's cheek. "It seems nobody really knows what a witch is. Pray tell me, how did you come to hear of this?"

"I saw a witch on trial in Riquewihr just a couple of days ago. They said that she spoke to the Devil and that they were going to burn her alive!" Greta exclaimed, her eyes growing wider with each word.

"My Papa said that she probably didn't even do those things that they claimed. He said they tortured her until she admitted it so they wouldn't hurt her anymore," Han interjected.

"Well, I think your Papa is a very smart man. And do you know they would have tortured me too if Roland hadn't rescued me from those men?"

Greta noticed Han's face perk up when she said that, as if she had just relieved him of some great burden. He then looked up at her with the same quizzical look he gets when he questions somebody: lifting one eyebrow and scrunching up the other side of his face. "Did you and Roland know each other, before today, I mean?"

"Would you believe me if I told you that he brought me to the same lady to whom he is bringing you? In fact, I think I was just about your age?" she said grinning, pointing her finger and touching the tip of Greta's nose.

"Really?" They gasped as their eyes and mouths gaped open.

She cast them a reassuring smile as she nodded her head. "My father had been killed in some kind of a skirmish when I was quite young. My mother was not able to provide for me, and we didn't have any other family around. One day I woke up to my mother sobbing, and then I heard a knock at the door. It was Roland." She glanced over to him and then whispered to Greta with her hand next to her mouth, "I found him quite handsome, don't you agree?"

Greta giggled and tried to hide her reddening cheeks with her hands.

"I must admit that I was shocked and scared at first, but he made me feel safe and protected. Once I met her and found how nice she was to me, I felt much better. Some of the children call her "The Fairy Lady," but others just call her "The Lady." She is a very wise woman who opened my eyes to new ways of thinking. She taught me to heal the sick, and to respect nature, and so many other things that I could never have imagined on my own. I shudder to think how different my life would have been without her. I think you will come to love her and respect her as much as I do," she said as she caressed a finger under Greta's chin, lifting it slightly as though she were a kitten.

"Will you come with us, Sendy? Please?" Greta asked.

"I will come along with you the rest of the way, but don't be afraid of Roland. He only sounds mean and gruff when you don't listen to him. If you do what he says, you will see that he is very kind, and he will do everything he can to protect you. I'm sure you can see by now that he is quite capable of that."

"I'm going to need some help with these bodies," Roland called out. "We need to drag them away from the path, hide them in some brush or something."

They walked over to where he gathered their items into a pile. There wasn't much, just their weapons and ale and a few pieces of hard bread which they shared between them. She also noticed some other items that were more peculiar: a couple of pouches and jars containing powders, ointments, feathers, some dead toads, the paw of some small animal like a cat, and a wad of hair sprinkled with bits of nails and small teeth.

"We'll drink the ale and leave the rest," Roland said, then looked toward Sendy with a look of mild disgust. "Is this your junk?"

"Yes, we should bring them along. They can be useful to us."

"Isn't this what they were planning to use against you in trial?" asked Roland.

"Yes, but like I said, they can be most useful"—she gestured toward his wound—"for healing."

He shrugged his shoulders and tossed the items back in the sack. "If you say so," he said, handing it over to her.

Roland pulled the Captain's body by the ankles, while Han and Sendy each grabbed one of Eudo's legs and slowly dragged the corpses away from the path. Greta walked ahead of them, knowing better than to look back, having no desire to witness the horror of them pulling dead bodies through the muck. After disposing the body in a shallow ditch, they went back for Ferrand's corpse. They left the remainder of his leg wherever Roland threw it for the animals to devour. After covering the bodies with wet dirt and leaves, he told Han and Greta to kick some mud over the blood stains, while Sendy tended to his wound.

Greta peered over to watch with interest. First, she poured some ale over his thigh and cleaned away most of the blood using a patch of grass that was growing nearby. Then she mixed some powder from one of the jars with an ointment from another, rubbing it over his wound. He grimaced as she rubbed it deeper into the opening. She covered his thigh with a patch of mud, and then wrapped it with some of the fabric that they had torn from one of the men's pants. As she went about her craft, she sang a pretty song that Greta hadn't heard before. Its calming melody made her feel better just by listening to it.

After she finished, she walked over to Greta with a warm smile and tenderly applied the remainder of the ointment to her scalp. She asked Greta to hum along with her as she sang her song, which had an even greater calming effect upon her.

"What is this?" Greta asked, lifting a heavy metal medallion that hung over Sendy's chest. To Greta, it looked like a circular head with two giant crescent-shaped ears.

"This is the symbol for the three phases of the moon—waxing, full, and waning. We can also think of it as the three phases of a woman's life—maiden, mother, and crone."

"What is a crone?" Greta asked with a funny smile. "Is that what we become when we get old and wrinkly?"

Sendy stooped over and tried to transform herself into her best impression of an old woman. "Yeah, when we're so old that we can't even stand up straight, and our teeth fall out, and our hair turns white, and we talk like this…" she trailed off forcing a gravelly strain in her voice as Greta laughed along with her.

"Kind of like this?" Greta asked with her own strained voice as she pulled her lips over her teeth and stooped over. "A crone sounds a lot like stepmother. Doesn't it, Han?"

He chuckled, "That's *exactly* what I was thinking."

As Roland searched through the weapons, he only took one of the swords and a dagger, then threw the others into the forest. "Let's head out," he called to the others. Just before leaving the site of carnage, however, Roland stopped in his tracks and shook his head as a half-smile crept across his face. He turned to Han and held out his hand. "Let's have it, boy."

Han looked at him blankly, as if to play off like he didn't know what he meant. Roland took a step toward him, again extending his hand out to him, along with a sharp look as if to suggest that he knew damn well what he meant. Han gave up the ruse. He reached into his pocket and handed back his carving knife.

They continued throughout the afternoon and into the evening. Sendy would occasionally stop to pick some plants and dig up some roots that she found useful. The rest of the day was uneventful except for stopping to assist a merchant that had his heavy wagon stuck in the mud. He said he would have offered them a reward, but that he had just been robbed and his guard was killed by bandits the day before. They only left him with his life and this empty wagon.

As the daylight waned to dusk, the sky gradually cleared from the ever-present gloomy cloud cover. Through the canopy of the trees, a bright full moon emerged in time to shed some light on the darkening forest. As the night settled in, the temperature steadily dropped. Greta rubbed her arms and wrapped her cloak about her tighter. Her nose began to run, and she could see puffs of smoke from her mouth when she breathed.

She usually went inside and buried herself in warm blankets when the cold nipped at her like this, but instead she now found herself surrounded by ominous-looking oak trees. She always loved looking at their long graceful, curving branches and dark green foliage, but now many were reduced to stark corpses of the once beautiful trees, killed off by foul weather and disease. At this time of the night, she thought they looked creepy and mysterious—like hulking, gnarled black giants with long twisted arms that could stretch out and drag her into its dark shadows.

As they continued on at a relentless pace, exhaustion and hunger increasingly took their toll on her. Her legs felt weak and shaky, while her empty, burning stomach made her lightheaded and nauseated. She found it hard to keep up and kept lagging behind the others until finally tripping over a tree root and collapsing onto the cold, wet ground. Her body trembled and refused to go on any further.

"Poor girl needs to eat something," Sendy said as she knelt beside her, offering the last of the berries she had collected along the way. She put three plump ones in her mouth and chewed slowly, savoring the juice on her tongue for as long as could.

"How come they have never tasted that good before?" she asked.

Sendy smiled. "They say we can never fully appreciate the value of anything until such times that we crave it most."

Greta thought about that, not just the taste of a fruit, but realizing how much more she would appreciate her mother if she came back to her now.

Sendy asked Roland if he could carry Greta on his shoulders, which he grudgingly obliged. *Sendy was right; he did have a way of making me feel safe,* she thought, sitting atop his sturdy shoulders. The steady rhythm of his stride lulled her closer and closer toward sleep, so she folded her arms over his head, nestling her face in the crook of her elbow.

Just as she fell asleep, she suddenly lurched backwards, nearly falling off his shoulders from a screech that pierced her ears.

"What was that?" gasped Han, looking almost as startled as she felt.

"It's just an owl, that's all. A very noisy owl, that's for sure. He even startled me!" Sendy reassured them. "You're going to be hearing a lot of those noises tonight, but this one was really close!"

Another hoot from the owl made her jerk her head back around. Roland tried futilely to track it for food.

"Let's not waste any more time. There is a clearing up ahead where we can rest for the night. I know you are all exhausted," said Roland.

They continued to walk along in silence as the temperature dropped even further. A cold wind began to stir and whistle hauntingly through the trees. The branches of the trees creaked and groaned like dying old men. *Or ghouls rising from the graves*, she imagined.

She could hear Roland whisper to Sendy, "There is something about this cold tonight. It doesn't feel...natural. Do you feel it?"

"Indeed," she said, "Let's hurry along."

Her eyes became heavy again, but she tried her best to stay awake. She looked ahead through the trees, searching for any more owls that might try to scare the wits out of her again. But what she saw next was so unexpected and disturbing that it paralyzed her with fear. Perched on one of the twisted branches, a child stared down directly at her, as if boring its eyes into her soul. Sudden terror slammed into her chest and sank deep into the pit of her stomach. Through the twilight and shadows, she could clearly see the child's wild hair— and menacing eyes that appeared to be swallowed in blackness.

She pointed and tried to scream but her throat constricted with the fear that consumed her. Roland looked up but the child vanished in an instant.

"What is it, dear? What do you see?" asked Sendy.

Greta blinked and rubbed her eyes and looked again, but the child was nowhere to be seen. Roland continued to study the tree and the area around it.

"Sweetheart, you look like you just saw a ghost! Pray tell us what has frightened you."

At last, she found her voice. "There was…" she swallowed hard, "there was a small child sitting up in that tree! He…or she…or whatever it was," she swallowed again and took a breath, "stared at me with those big black eyes. He had long wild hair and dressed only in tattered rags. You saw him, didn't you Roland?"

"I saw something moving on the tree, but I couldn't make out what it was," he said as he continued to survey the area.

They all continued to peer ahead into the trees as they walked silently along, listening closely for any footsteps or other unusual noises.

After a couple minutes, Sendy looked back up at Greta with a look of concern. "My dear, you must be so exhausted and hungry and scared. The waning light in the forest this time of the evening can make it difficult to see things as they truly are. Do you really think a child would be alone this far out in the forest, especially in this time of night?"

"I suppose not," Greta surmised, "but I swear I saw someone staring at me. It didn't look like a regular child though; it looked wild…it looked evil."

"She always thinks she sees something that frightens her at night," said Han.

"Shut up Han! I was right about the bats in the cave, wasn't I?" she countered.

"It's alright children, there is no need to argue. She saw what she saw, so let's just leave it at that," said Sendy.

As they continued on their way, they didn't see any more sightings of this strange child. Perhaps her mind was playing tricks on her after all, she tried to tell herself, but the haunting image of that sinister face staring down at her convinced her otherwise. And she couldn't shake the strong feeling that someone—or something—was watching them, following them.

She heard more scurrying and scratching sounds all around her now that the darkness deepened and the nighttime creatures had arisen. The queer call of a bird, sounding more like a very loud cat, repeatedly cried out, and then a more distant cry from another returning its call. Next, a cacophony of shrill, wicked laughter erupted in the distance as a pack of coyotes moved in on its prey.

At last, they reached the clearing that Roland was looking for. He set Greta back down and stretched his arms and neck out. They all shared the extra ale that they had taken from the guards.

"It is best to huddle together for warmth. You two can share your blankets and lie close to each other. My lady, with your permission, we should do the same," he suggested with a charming smile.

"Yes, of course," she said, returning the smile. "We will be right over here children, so do not be afraid," she said. Then she drew in her breath sharply like he pinched her behind, then expressed a playful giggle as they walked to the other end of the clearing.

Greta hugged her brother's warm body tightly to hers, listening to the crickets and frogs and owls all around her. Every time she closed her eyes, she kept seeing that face with those black eyes staring down at her. Something was watching her right now; she was certain of it. She peered around in the trees but became so frightened of seeing that face again that she decided to keep her eyes shut, not daring to open them again.

Before long she heard soft, soothing sounds of pleasure coming from Sendy. It reminded her of the sounds her mother used to make with her father in their bedroom at night—back when everything was normal, she thought as she drifted into a deep sleep.

Chapter 12

GUARIN AWOKE TO THE SOUND OF FOOTSTEPS around him. He opened his eyes to see four men staring down at him, his vision so blurred that he couldn't make out their faces. He had no idea how long he had been laying on the floor. His tongue felt like leather, his head pounded, and his right lower back still throbbed with pain.

He heard the men murmuring to each other about what they should do with him. He felt a splitting pain when he peeled his dry lips apart, and his tongue stuck to his mouth when he tried to talk. He tried to stand but could hardly even bend his legs or push himself up with his arms.

The men lifted his limp body under his shoulders and dragged him outside to a wooden chair, stripping him of his soiled tunic and letting the rain wash the filth from his body. One of the men put the pale of water to his cracked lips which he drank down aggressively with large gulps, letting the excess spill down his face and neck. When finished with his long drink, he took a deep gurgling breath and coughed for a bit.

Feeling more aroused now from the cold rain and quenched thirst, he surveyed the men standing around him and their horse-drawn cart. "Lutrud sent you to help me?" he croaked.

They smirked and exchanged glances with one another before one of them replied. "Yes, of course. She said you were very sick and in need of assistance. We feared you might be dead when we arrived. Are you feeling any better?"

He shrugged his shoulders, his unshaven face grimacing up at them. He recognized him as the burly guard that brought them to the tower: rugged face with thick, black eyebrows and a long mustache that dangled below his jaw. "Not really, but the cool air feels good. And I thank you for the water."

"Here, maybe this will make you feel a bit more satisfied," another man said, thrusting his waterskin towards him. "Drink, it's good ale."

He upended it and sucked down the delicious, cool ale with vigor. This was some of the best he had tasted in a long while. "Thank you," he said, then belched loudly before handing it back to the guard.

"We met in town yesterday, but I haven't properly introduced myself. My name is Captain Erec. I wanted to ask you some questions if you don't mind," asked the tower guard.

He looked them over again as a scowl crept across his face. "I have some questions of my own if you don't mind my asking. Can I ask where my children have been taken? Why they were taken without my consent? Why I was assaulted in my own home and left to die?"

They exchanged awkward glances with each other again before the captain replied. "I'm sorry. We do not know where your children have been taken; that man does not officially work with the guard. We were only told that your wife is the one who made these...arrangements."

"My wife?" he let out a brief chuckle and then spat on the ground. He looked back up at the guard with dour expression. "My wife died last year. Lutrud is just staying with us for a while, but I guess that sounds about right." he replied, dropping his eyes. "Where is she now? Did she not come back here with you?"

"She is providing some information to Father Linhart regarding a different matter," Captain Erec said matter-of-factly. "We want you to tell us about a man who goes by the name of Barous. He passed through this area on his way to Riquewihr a couple of days ago on horseback. Have you seen him?"

That fucking bitch. He stared up at them, trying to hide his dismay. "Yes, I met him. Very nice fellow."

"What can you tell us about him?" pressed the Captain.

He shrugged his shoulders again. "Not much. I didn't talk to him for long. He was a merchant just traveling through on his way east from France. There is nothing further I can say about him. As I said, very nice fellow."

"I see." He knelt down to make eye-level contact. "The thing of it is, Mr. Guarin, we have reason to believe that he was not a merchant, as you say he is. You know something about him, something that he did not want the town to know about."

Guarin felt him studying his face as he spoke. The scrutiny was palpable. He had to focus to maintain his composure. "I'm sorry, sir. I don't know anything else. I don't have any more information that I can offer you about him." He paused, showing an expression of concern. "Why, is he in some kind of trouble?"

He noticed the Captain clench his jaw but remain calm as he continued his interrogation. "Well, in a way you could say that he is. He may not be this *'very nice fellow'* as you call him. We believe he may be part of an illegal organization, one of the remaining Templars, in fact. He is a wanted man, Mr. Guarin. He is wanted by the Pope and the King of France himself. If we find that you are withholding information from us that might lead to his arrest, then you could be in *'some kind of trouble'* yourself." He flashed a smirk as he mocked these last words. "I can offer you some more of this delicious ale if you can tell me what I think you know about him; otherwise, you will make this more difficult on yourself. What will it be? Your choice."

He stared him down. His threats meant nothing to him now. "I've told you all I know about him. I'm sorry I can't help you gentlemen." He winced, reaching his hand around to his back.

"Something the matter?"

"It's my stone. The pain flares up like this every couple of hours. I've just never felt so miserable like this before." He felt like he was about to pass out. "Please, I have to go lie down. I'm not feeling right."

"Of course. Tell us what you really know about this man. Tell us this secret of yours and we'll let you lie down in your bed. You can drink as much ale as you like. There is no need to…" The words drifted off as their faces blurred into darkness.

Chapter 13

ROLAND SAT BOLT UPRIGHT FROM THE GROUND, drenched in sweat and panting, looking around with alarm. Sendy lie next to him, just beginning to arouse, while the children remained asleep. The unexpected transformation of the forest since last night nearly made him forget what he thought he heard. *Am I still dreaming?* A sheen of glittering white frost blanketed the forest. Scattered snowflakes sparkled as they drifted gently downward, coating the surface of bushes and trees with a thin powder, bestowing upon the forest a magical, supernatural quality in the early dawn of the new day.

Sendy sat up beside him and gasped with delight, a look of wonderment in her eyes. She rested her hand on his knee. "It is so beautiful!" she whispered.

"Yes, it is. But listen closely, do you hear anything?" he asked, placing his hand over hers.

"Are you alright? You're sweating. You look like you just awoke from a nightmare," she said, wiping the sweat from his brow.

"I did, I grant you that, but I'm sure I heard something."

"It looks so peaceful out here," she said, resting her head on his shoulder. "Tell me about your dream; what was it about?"

"Wolves."

His word hung in the chill, silent air. Then they heard it—a distant howl calling out from deep within the forest. Then a second returned the call, distinct from the first. The howls seemed to be coming from somewhere north of them.

71

He rose to his feet. "We should be on our way. Gather your things and rouse the children."

"Don't be alarmed by wolves. They are misunderstood, natural creatures. We used to see a wolf come by our yard often enough, a curious but harmless beast, and magnificent to look upon," she tried to reassure him.

"I wouldn't be so certain anymore, not in these times. They're hungry and their food source is scarce. Besides, we still have a long way to go, and I'd just as soon have these children out of my charge." He winced as he bent over to pick up his supplies on the ground.

"Let me have a look at your wound at least before we leave here," she said, reaching for his belt.

"I'm fine, really. You've done a nice job with the packing so let's not disturb it so soon. We really need to go," he replied with urgency in his voice.

"Wow, look at this! I didn't think it snowed anymore this time of year." Han exclaimed, marveling at the white wonderland around him.

Greta yawned and stretched and rubbed her eyes, while Han jumped to his feet. Scooping up a large handful of snow, he rolled it into a ball and whipped it at Greta.

"Ouch! Stop that you brat!"

"Come on Greta, get up! Check out this snow, it's fun!" Han said as he jumped and swiped at a tree branch, scattering more snow on top of her.

Greta jumped up about to yell at him as Han laughed out loud. Roland quickly clapped a hand over his mouth and cast a sharp look at Greta with his finger to his lips, stifling her outrage. "Keep your voices down. There may be predators about," he cautioned, his tone low but harsh.

"They didn't know, Roland. Please don't be hard on him, he was just having some fun," pleaded Sendy.

Roland withdrew his hand from Han's mouth. His head and shoulders dropped as he walked away, looking withdrawn again. He noticed Sendy looking upon the boy with pity in her eyes. *It seems I crushed his only moment of lighthearted fun amidst all of this gloom that had been thrust upon them.*

"Hey, sorry, Han. We just need to keep it down for now, alright?" He offered his apology but could see that his body language didn't change.

"Sure," was all he said, looking deflated at the ground, wiping his wet hands on his tunic.

He was a stubborn, insolent boy that really had a way of getting under Roland's skin. *If only he would just listen to what I say and obey me!* He had almost ripped his head off yesterday in his rage, but thinking back on Han's actions now, he rather admired him for his courage. *He reminds me of myself sometimes.* Looking over at his moping face and stooping posture, Roland felt almost ashamed of himself. *I suppose I'm being too hard on him, blaming him for the deaths of those men and all.* He shook his head and then noticed Sendy looking up at him with her lip in a pout. *Damn, she looks cute when she does that.*

"Didn't know what?" asked Greta, interrupting his thoughts.

Roland looked at her with confusion.

She turned to Sendy. "You said we didn't know. Didn't know what?"

"Nothing, sweetie. We just heard some wolves making noise before you awoke, but they seem far away and shouldn't bother us," reassured Sendy. "We just need to keep our voices down a bit, that's all he meant."

Another distant howl erupted from the north.

Greta's face blanched and her raised eyebrows expressed worry, but she didn't say anything in return. Roland went back to packing up his supplies. Sendy came over to assist and whispered to him, keeping her eyes fixed empathetically on Greta, "Did you really see something in the tree last night that frightened Greta so terribly?" she asked.

He paused momentarily and cast her a grave look of concern. "Aye, I know what she saw, I just can't believe it," he admitted, then resumed packing. "I've heard stories of the black-eyed child lurking in this part of the forest. Surely you must have as well. I think I may have caught glimpses now and then, but it disappears so fast that I can't be sure. Ghost stories—they fuck with your mind is what they do, that's all." He finished tying his pack, paused on one knee, and fixed her eyes with intense solemnity. "But it seems she has never heard the story, and yet she described the ghastly face exactly as the others."

A look of curiosity transformed her face just then. "That is strange indeed."

"We're heading out," he commanded. "We have more than half a day's journey yet ahead of us, then you can eat and rest once we arrive."

Roland passed the last few swallows of ale around to share between them before they set off again. The snow was a welcome change from the rain and seemed to go a long way toward brightening the children's spirits from the horrors of the day before.

They walked for over an hour before they heard the wolves again. It started with a single low howl that rang out from deep in the frost-covered woods. He thought the lonely sound would never end as it sent chills up his spine, evoking feelings of despair and desolation. Soon, one by one, other wolves joined in its mournful song. They each sang with a different pitch that resonated and harmonized together, rising into a crescendo until it reached a shrill cry. Some sounded more like a growl that rose to a roar, and still others yapped and shrieked with shifting pitch like coyotes. The forest became alive with the wild cries of the famished wolf pack.

He turned to the others, Sendy's usual calm and reassuring expression now turned to alarm. Han and Greta trembled as the cries grew in number. He felt uneasy himself. This wasn't the first time he heard wolves in the forest, but something seemed very different and troubling now. Maybe he was spooked by his dream, but they sounded more desperate, more urgent, more persistent.

"Most of them seem to be coming from our right. They might be tracking us, gathering in numbers. We have to keep moving, faster now," he urged them on as the beastly chorus continued to harass them relentlessly.

They continued along the path through the crisp, morning hours, maintaining a brisk pace. So far everyone was keeping up, even Greta who held tightly to Sendy's hand. Soon another howl pierced the air from behind them—much closer this time.

They jerked to a halt and turned with sudden terror, knowing full well that this one was meant for them. They gazed helplessly at one other, their frosty breath hanging visibly in the air between them.

"Come on, we can't stop here!" he warned as they broke into a run. He turned to Sendy, trying to maintain his sense of control. "We may have to separate. Try to stay with the children, climb the trees if you must. I will try to hold them off, take them out one by one. But take this just in case," he said, handing her a long serrated dagger that he had pilfered from one of the guards.

Despite their pursuit, they tired quickly and slowed to a staggering walk, punctuated by short bursts of running once they caught their breath. Another howl burst forth from ahead of them this time, shrill and menacing and dangerously close. Roland searched the forest but saw no sign of a wolf. Every couple of minutes, they would hear an ear-splitting howl—one from the northwest, another from behind, then another, this time directly ahead of them.

Sendy grabbed his wrist tightly. "They are surrounding us! I'm scared. We must protect the children."

Roland had faced near certain death many times, but always with courage. The thought of dying wasn't something that ever occurred to him in the heat of a battle or a fight. So why did he feel such dread now? Death felt imminent; he could feel it closing in on him, choking his breath. *Not me, not now!*

He felt the crushing weight of others depending on him, encumbering his thoughts, tensing his body; a sense of duty and responsibility like never before tugged at him. He had taken these children from their father, this woman from her guards. He must see them to safety. As this revelation poured into his awareness, his senses suddenly aroused, his vision sharpened, his alertness heightened, and a scowl of anger twisted his face.

Sendy began to chant in a strange language behind him. Greta whimpered and Han's lip trembled but made not a sound. He kept them moving forward, but now at a slow, cautious pace. Instead of the howls, they now heard yelping and barking, the threat coming from all different directions and closing in on them. He heard scuffling sounds, rustling of bushes, and panting in the woods close by.

Then he saw its breath, rising above a bush to his right about twenty paces away. A surprisingly large wolf stepped out and stared him down with calm, icy blue eyes. He expected it to rush him but instead trotted forward in the direction they were walking, keeping its distance. He slowly slid his sword from its sheath, keeping his eyes fixed on the wolf.

Suddenly he heard brisk movement immediately to his left. Before he could even turn to face it, the beast was upon him, diving at his chest and knocking him to the ground, its mouth tightening around the bracers of his forearm, snarling and drooling into his face as he wrestled with the feral creature. He heard Han and Greta screaming nearby and only assumed the worst. He kicked it off his chest, but its teeth remained firmly clenched on his arm and quickly pounced on top of him again. Then it yelped as though wounded, the weight of its body suddenly going limp on his chest.

Throwing the dead wolf aside, he sprang to his feet to see that Sendy had stabbed it in the neck. Decrepit and emaciated, it somehow possessed incredible strength and quickness in its desperation. He surveyed the area, spotting at least three more wolves nearby, but hearing many more. As they resumed their flight down the path, their pursuers trotted forward along with them, yelping incessantly while gradually closing the distance.

Ahead of him, one of the wolves darted straight toward Han. "Han, to your right! Catch!" he shouted, tossing him his carving knife.

Just as he grasped the knife from the air, Han was struck by the charging wolf, knocking it out of his hand as they crashed to the ground. The wolf landed hard on its side next to him but immediately got back to its feet to finish the kill. Roland could see the knife handle sticking straight up out of the mud, as Han desperately looked from side to side. Roland lunged toward the wolf with sword upraised but knew he wouldn't reach him in time. Han finally snatched the knife as the wolf pounced on top of him, its snarling maw moving ferociously for his neck. Han swiftly jabbed it straight up into the soft underside of its muzzle, its mangy head rearing back with a yelp but poised for another strike. Roland finally closed in, piercing his sword through its ribs all the way to the hilt.

He kicked it off of Han and slid the sword back out, raising it just in time to deliver an arcing blow to another wolf, slicing it in half as it dove towards him in midair. They charged at them now from all different directions. Roland pointed to the only opening he could see, yelling at them to run. "Remember to climb the trees if you must!"

He needed room to wield his sword without striking too close to the others. Fortunately, he didn't have to say it twice. The fear and tension he felt earlier had vanished. His mind was now clear and determined, his movements as fluid and effortless as water, and his body pulsed with the infinite energy of the present moment. His body and sword became one as he spun through the air and across the ground, felling one beast after another. He could see and sense everything around him, hear the crackling of frost beneath his dancing feet and the whirring of his sword through the crisp air, and smell the blood of the wolves growing stronger with each death stroke.

But despite his savage slaughter, they kept attacking him relentlessly. He kept his blade spinning as though it was a torch to ward them off. For a moment it seemed to be working as they kept their distance, but then he realized they were encircling him. They glared and snarled with feral ferocity, their black lips curling over sharp fangs, their blood-red tongues flashing aggressively like fiends. Still more approached, bristling their fur as they growled and barked, wildly snapping their jaws in the air, biding their time.

As he stared them down and whirled his sword, he realized he couldn't hold them off for much longer. All it took was one wolf to begin the charge and his flesh would be devoured in an instant. Then he heard the most peculiar sound, a loud chant calling out from the direction in which the others ran. *Sendy?* He could hear desperation in her voice, but the power sounded immense, like nothing he had ever heard or felt before. The magical rhythm boomed and echoed through the forest like a chorus of monks, seeming to transcend beyond the limits of the forest and out to the heavens. He wondered if they were surrounded just as he was. *This must be her death song or a*

*prayer to her God. Surely, she wouldn't be trying to draw the
wolves toward her and the children.*

The wolves heard it too, dropping their savage expressions,
perking their ears, and searching for the sound. A brief but
welcome respite, it allowed him to catch his breath and rest his
shoulders, but eventually they began to flash their threatening
fangs and lashing tongues back upon him. Some lurched and
snapped at the air between them before backing away from his
spinning steel. He tried to keep his focus directed toward the
largest of the wolves, assuming the alpha would initiate the final
charge.

Indeed, he watched as it began the assault in a crouch as a
low steady growl escaped its mouth. Then its face turned from
threatening to ravenous as the alpha leaped towards him,
immediately followed by the others. He could feel his blade slice
through several bodies of flesh as he spun in a pirouette. He tried
to leap over the circle of snapping teeth surrounding him, but
they pounced too quickly, ripping and tearing at his flesh. He
reached for the dagger in his boot and slashed blindly.
Screaming with rage, he kicked and thrashed and bit and
somehow managed to push himself to his feet.

He spotted something unexpected moving rapidly from his
periphery. It looked like a great horned beast from the darkest
pits of hell charging straight at him. It didn't matter though, he
was already a dead man, he thought, as the wolves brought him
down again. While fangs pierced and ripped through his flesh, a
loud shriek split the air, and a moment later he felt the impact of
the beast colliding into the pack. He heard more shrieking and
squealing and yelping and barking as the wolves left him and
focused their attention on the new threat.

Lying motionless on his back and panting for breath, he
watched the savage battle ensue before him. More wolves died
and some scattered before they finally brought down the great
beast that he now recognized as a wild boar.

He began to lose consciousness as his vision faded, then felt
himself rising into the air. He turned to look down upon the
carnage below in a dream-like state. He saw his body lying at
the center of a circle of death with over a dozen carcasses and
their bright red blood splattered all over the pure white snow.

His own blood oozed out from the countless wounds inflicted upon him as well. Like the vivid contrast of crimson paint over a vast white canvas, it was a sight both gruesome and beautiful to behold.

Suddenly, he dropped back into his ravaged body, racked with excruciating pain. Too weak and exhausted to move, he simply lay there listening to the guttural sounds of the wolves enjoying their hard-fought feast. He heard them tearing the flesh, slopping it around in their mouths as they chewed, and growling to ward off other wolves that returned to share in the meal. The tasty pig flesh kept them busy for now, but he knew that he would be their dessert. He just hoped he was dead by then.

As he waited for his life to mercifully slip away, he watched the snowflakes drift down over him, opening his mouth to feel them tingle as they dissolved on his tongue. Before long, he heard footsteps crunching toward him over the frozen ground.

"Sendy! You must go, leave me please," he croaked as blood trickled from his mouth. "I cannot walk, and the wolves will smell my blood. Save yourselves! I'm a dead man," he pleaded with her to no avail.

She retrieved his pack lying on the ground nearby and tossed it onto her back, then grabbed his ankles and dragged him over the slick snow-covered surface. He felt like one of the corpses they dragged through the forest yesterday. The remaining wolves ignored them, busily devouring or awaiting their turn on the fresh kill.

"Where are the children?" he asked.

She met his question with silence as she pulled him along through the forest, far enough away from the carnage. Eventually, they stopped in a small clearing where Han and Greta dropped down from their perch in a tree. He felt his spirits lift.

She sent the children to kick some snow and dirt over the bloody track they made from pulling his body across the ground. Kneeling down beside him, she surveyed his wounds, quickly tending to the worst of them as best she could with snow and mud and some of the herbs she had gathered along the way, then covered him with a wool blanket from his pack. After that, she placed stones in a circle around him and carved lines and symbols in the ground with a heavy stick.

"Sendy, I heard you chanting while I fought off the wolves?" He paused as his expression turned to one of wonder. "It sounded ... magical...powerful!"

She stopped and turned her face back toward him, tossing him a half smile. "I called to the forest for help."

"I'll be damned, I think it worked! But don't you have one that would just calm the wolves instead of summoning that raging beast from hell?" he asked with a wink.

Her half smile turned to a smirk. "I did, you may have noticed, but wolves have very short attentions, and I can't keep chanting all day, now can I?"

"Thanks for coming back for me," he rasped, then gestured to the stones and markings on the ground. "but is this to be my shallow grave?"

She crumbled some dry leaves from her pack between her hands and blew the dust into the circle that she carved around him. "I'm going to have to leave you here for now until I can return with help. I placed a protective ward around you which should keep you safe." Finally, she cut the top of her hand with the knife and squeezed some blood into the ward as she spoke a brief incantation. "That should do it. Come along children, we don't have a lot of time."

He looked around at his precarious position, lying helpless in the forest. Ward or no ward, he didn't feel safe. "Hey, wait!" he called out. "Can't you at least throw some tree branches over me to conceal me a little better?"

"It might disrupt the ward that I've cast," she called back.

He didn't place much faith in magic and wards but didn't want to tell her that. He propped himself up on his elbows so she could see the exasperation on his face. "I'll take my chances!"

Feeling a little safer after they covered him as he suggested, he watched them walk away until they could no longer be seen. He then turned to look back at the direction from which they dragged him, noticing the feeble attempt to cover his long track of blood. "Great," he muttered "just great."

Chapter 14

GUARIN AWOKE FROM A SUDDEN, FIERCE POUNDING on his right flank. He cried out from the pain which escalated with each successive paroxysm. His fever raged as well, his skin emanating heat and beading with sweat. He opened his eyes and found himself in a dark, dank prison cell of some kind. A single narrow window in the stone wall that he took to be an arrow slit offered what little light and ventilation it could. Still too weak to move, he just lay there, looking forward to the next time sleep overtook him. Other than the occasional groan or snoring from one of the nearby cells, the room was mostly silent.

After a while he heard footsteps, the clang and scrape of metal, and the grating sound of rusty hinges as his cell gate opened. He pushed himself up to sit on the edge of his cot as an armed guard issued in a white robed figure. He recognized him as the cleric that questioned his family the other day. It could have been a week ago, he really had no idea.

Father Linhart studied him closely before making that moist smacking sound that he did with his lips just before speaking. "Well, well, Mr. Guarin, we meet again. You look very sick, much worse than when I saw you last."

"Where the hell am I, a hospital or a prison?"

"You have been brought to Thieves' Tower for questioning, but I can see that you are not ready for that yet." He turned to the guard standing outside the cell. "Bring this man some food and drink, and a wet cloth from the kitchen, please." Returning his attention back to Guarin, he said, "You look feverish and dehydrated and in terrible pain. You need to drink and eat something if you can. A small meal will do you good. I will return once you feel better."

"My children, do you know where they were taken?" he asked hoarsely, then doubled over in a coughing fit.

"I'm sorry," he shook his head somberly. "Those arrangements were worked out between your wife and the city official whom you met. I did not involve myself in those affairs. I will inquire as to their whereabouts, but I'm afraid I'm not at all familiar with these remote lands."

He bowed his head, "Thank you, Father. I would greatly appreciate that."

The cleric returned the gesture and exited his cell. Moments later the guard returned, presenting him with a jug of weak ale from which he drank deeply and a bowl of rice and beans, more food than he had eaten in years. Despite the nausea, he managed to keep it down. Feeling better than he had in days, he lied back down on his cot, rubbed the cool, wet cloth over his face, and then fell into a more restful sleep.

He awoke sometime later with a tremendous urge to empty his bladder. He struggled to rise to his feet and nearly blacked out when he finally did, so he flopped back down onto his cot. He closed his eyes and pressed his palms into his forehead until his head cleared. More slowly this time, he used the edges of the stones in the wall to help pull himself back to his feet and steady himself, then made his way to the chamber pot. It was only steps away across his cell but may as well have been a mile. The liquid fire that shot out of his penis made him grimace and groan. He felt something spasm and shift from his back to his abdomen, causing excruciating agony.

Carefully, he made his way back to the cot and took another swig of ale, swishing it around in his mouth to let it soak into his parched mouth and leather tongue. His fever subsided for now and his head stopped aching, so all things considered, he felt pretty good.

After a couple more days of eating gruel and hydrating with watered-down ale, he began to feel better and get some strength back. As his physical ailments abated, however, the yearning for his children and the guilt that he felt for losing them only grew. *Did I really agree with Lutrud to send them away?* His words continued to echo in his head like a curse that he couldn't escape. *"Yes, perhaps you're right, dear."* It felt as though the words had opened up an abyss in his soul, and the more he thought about it, the deeper he sank into this abyss. *What depths of desperation must it take for a father to abandon his own children?*

Around mid-morning of the third day in his captivity, he heard the heavy door to the prison room open, followed by shuffling footsteps making their way to his cell. The guard unlocked his cell gate, set a wooden chair inside, then resumed his position just outside. Father Linhart entered and sat down across from him. His sparse grey hair, deeply lined face, and piercing blue eyes imparted the visage of a wise sage.

"Your color looks better at least," he said, nodding his head with an approving smile. "It looks like you might even live to see another day."

"I thank you for the nourishment, Father. You are very kind. I understand that you must want some information from me in return."

Father Linhart nodded deeply. "We believe in treating our guests of The Tower humanely. We also expect that you regard us with your utmost respect and cooperation. Is that a reasonable request, Mr. Guarin?"

"You have my respect. You may ask me anything you like, Father."

Guarin felt his unwavering gaze upon him for several long moments as he studied his face. Then he began by audibly parting his pursed lips, the quiet but distinct sound amplified in the small hollow cell. "Is your wife a witch, Mr. Guarin?"

"You mean Lutrud?" *Why does everyone keep calling her my wife?* "She is my sister-in-law actually, supposed to be helping me with my children. But no, of course she isn't," he replied with a light smile.

"Of course. But how can you be so sure?"

"Look, I know what my son told you, but…" he almost said Han was just angry at her until he remembered the penalty that incurred. "I just don't believe in witches."

"Ah, but you would if you heard the confessions I have."

Yeah, tortured confessions, he thought, remembering his conversation with Barous. "Perhaps you are right, Father. But to answer your question, I have no reason to believe that Lutrud is a witch. She is a devout, practicing Christian and has been for as long as I've known her."

"Is your son a devil worshiper?" he asked with surprising bluntness, his expression fixed like stone, his gaze steady and intense.

Guarin almost laughed. "No, Father. I can assure you he is not."

"Lutrud says he is. She says he even questioned the very existence of God."

"Please understand. He recently lost his mother and his dear friend. He simply wondered why God would allow this famine to continue to claim the lives of those we love."

Father Linhart rubbed the scruff of his chin before countering, drawing his attention to the considerable loose fleshy folds spilling down his neck. Some people called it a turkey neck, but he thought it looked more like an old man's scrotum.

"But tell me: did he not accept a Templar coin from your devil worshiping friend?"

"Look, I don't know what Lutrud has told you—"

"It doesn't matter what she has told me. I expect YOU to tell me!" his voice suddenly loud and sharp, echoing off the walls. The jowls of his neck shook from his sudden furor as his bony finger extended dangerously close to Guarin's face.

I haven't seen that coin since placing it in my pocket after leaving the waterfall. I was so sick I forgot I even had it. It's probably still in my soiled tunic, lying in the mud in front of my home. Doing his best to maintain his composure, he found it difficult to look into those cold, piercing eyes for so long, and his trembling neck folds didn't make it any easier. *Surly there must be a pair of balls contained within that ample sac of loose flesh.*

"I don't know any Templars, and I don't know what coin you're talking about." He felt a subtle tug on his lower eyelid as he lied to the cleric, whose eyes astutely shifted their focus directly upon it.

"I see," he said, nodding for a few moments before continuing. "This man that you met by the waterfall riding horseback, who was he then?"

"He told me that he was a merchant, traveling from out of town."

"Did he now?" exclaimed the cleric, raising his eyebrows sarcastically. "A merchant? Did he mention his name, where he was from, where he was headed?"

"Yes, he told me his name is Barous. I believe he said he was from the south of France, but I'm afraid he didn't tell me where he was headed. He may still be in town for all I know. He is easy to spot—a big, bearded, well-dressed man on a horse, sporting a beautiful scarlet cloak."

"Yes, a man of that description was spotted in town days ago. We have since searched but alas…perhaps he has moved on by now. If not, we will find him." His eyes remained locked on Guarin's for another long silent minute. "So, you don't remember anything about this coin that he gave your son?"

"I think Lutrud must have imagined this coin of which you speak. There aren't many people just handing out coins these days. Believe me, if I had seen him receive a coin, I would certainly have spent it on food and drink by now, but as you can probably discern by my famished appearance…" he trailed off, gesturing to his face and emaciated body with his bony hand.

"So you say." Father Linhart reached into his pocket and produced the coin. "But I don't think many merchants would dare accept this as currency, do you?"

He stared incredulously at the coin, its surface gleaming with the heretical Templar Cross. "Lutrud gave you that coin?"

"I expect better from you, Mr. Guarin," he said, rising to his feet. "Our next round of questioning will not go as easy."

As he turned to leave, Guarin called out, "Father, if I may…" the cleric halted, snapping his head back around. "Why do you want this man so badly? I mean, even if he were a Templar, they are disbanded, powerless. What threat could he pose?"

Father Linhart squared his body around to address him directly, speaking with authority and making him feel like an insolent student talking out of turn in class. "What threat, you ask? The Pope has found the Templars guilty of heresy. I was personally involved in the trial of many of these men, and I have reason to believe that this particular man was a high-ranking officer in The Order. He goes by the name of Barous Vaillant, sentenced by Papal decree to be burned at the stake along with the other Templar officers. For now, he has escaped justice and remains one of the last living Templars to roam freely in this land. Bringing him to justice will yield great favors from our new pope. Furthermore, we do not need him spreading the seed of heresy among our people. Your testimony will strengthen our case, so I expect your full cooperation once we have him in custody." He then turned and strode out of the cell gate, clanging it shut behind him.

Chapter 15

AS THEY TRUDGED ALONG THE UPHILL PATH, Greta had trouble keeping up with Sendy's pace. Hunger and exhaustion weighed heavily upon her. Han seemed to be struggling as well.

"We must leave the path for the last part of our journey. The Lady's house is hidden deep within the woods." said Sendy. "Please stay close together. It is easy to become lost, and we don't want to become separated here."

She led them through a thick patch of trees and brush and into the densest part of the forest that she had seen. The heavy canopy darkened the daylight, and a queer silence pervaded the forest around them. Even their own voices reflected back to them as though they were in a cavern. She turned back to look from where they came, but already they were swallowed by the woods, as though they had entered into a new world, isolated from everything else. Her skin crawled as she remembered that child's sinister face staring back at her.

"Why does she live so far away from everything?" Asked Greta, her voice sounding louder than she intended.

"The Lady enjoys her seclusion and privacy," Sendy replied softly.

"How did the guards find you way out here anyhow?" Han asked.

"Oh, I don't live with her anymore. She raised me until I was old enough to live on my own, then I moved to a nearby village."

"Can't we stay in your village instead of way out here?" Greta asked.

"No, I can never go back," she said, making her way forward through the brush, being careful not to let the branches swing back into their faces. "I shall have to find another village to make my home, unfortunately."

She looked up at her hopefully, "Does that mean you will stay with us for a while at least?"

"Yes, my sweetling." She smiled at her. "I will stay for a little while, but not too long. As I said, The Lady does enjoy her privacy, so I don't want to overstay my welcome."

After a short distance longer, Sendy pointed ahead. "There, do you see the gate?"

Greta saw only green leaves and trees but nothing that resembled a gate. "I don't see anything," she said, squinting as she tried make it out.

"It is cloaked in the colors of the forest. Don't you see the ivy-covered wall just ahead? Look closer," she said smiling as she outlined it with her finger.

"Oh, there it is!" They both shouted almost in unison.

She thought it looked like an illusion from a distance but gradually took shape as they approached. She could now make out the decorative and elaborate gate between a brick wall covered with ivy. The gate was made of twisted metal rods fashioned to look like snakes that converged towards the center, spiraling into and out of a circle, thereby forming an intricate shape resembling a rounded triangle or clover. Thick tangles of vines coiled around the snakes, sprouting large yellow flowers that hung upside down like bells.

Peering through the gate, she saw the house set back in a large open field. *My new home,* she thought, realizing that she must remain in this secluded place for many years to come. An ominous sensation gripped hold of her just then, as though the house had been waiting for them to arrive. She swallowed hard and shuddered.

Her attention was shaken when Sendy suddenly snapped at Han, who began chewing on the large flowers hanging from the gate. "Don't eat that! Those flowers can make you sick."

Han shot her a look as though she were crazy. "These aren't flowers. They're candy. Try one," he said, picking another off the vine.

Sendy snatched the flower away from him, a look of concern crossing her face. "I'm very serious, you could die if you ate too many of these," she said, holding up the crumpled flower in her fist before throwing it to the ground. Then she paused and her expression softened. "You're just very hungry, Han. Everything is starting to look like food to you now. Trust me, she will have a lot of good food for you inside."

"If you say so. I suppose I can wait a little longer," Han conceded.

She patted him gently on his cheek. "Good, now open your mouth, let me see your tongue." She plucked a leaf off a nearby branch and scraped the remaining bits of the flower off his tongue. "Now don't start eating my finger!" she teased.

Greta giggled. "You're brave. I wouldn't put it past him right now."

"There, that should do it. Now let's see if we can get somebody to open this gate."

Sendy called out for someone to allow them entrance. After a while, a tall, black-skinned man appeared from behind the house and walked across the field toward them. Greta had never seen a man with black skin before. She didn't even know it was possible to have skin that dark. As he approached, he smiled warmly at Sendy—a great big friendly smile, unlike Roland's, she thought.

"Welcome back, my dear Sendy!" he boomed in a deep voice as he opened the gate. "It has been too long. What, two years? And you keep getting prettier every year," he added, embracing Sendy in a bear hug and spinning her off her feet. He spoke with an accent that she had not heard before either.

"Indeed, I miss seeing your happy face every day. It is very good to see you again, Jehan."

"I see you have brought some guests," he said, smiling down at them with large white teeth. "Han and Greta, this is Jehan. He is the groundskeeper for The Lady."

"How do you do?" Han greeted him, shaking his hand, followed by Greta.

His oversized meaty hand engulfed her own as he knelt down to her eye level. "You all look weary from your journey. Come with me and we will fill your bellies," he said, giving her belly a poke.

She wanted to tell him all about the wolves and Roland but Sendy spoke first.

"That is most kind of you, Jehan. But if I can ask of you a great favor, I will be deeply indebted to you," she asked as a solemn and urgent expression washed away her smile.

"Of course, my dear." He straightened himself back up and placed his hands firmly on her shoulders. "What is it? Are you in some kind of trouble?"

"I was, but my friend, Roland—you know him—he rescued me from some guards that were escorting me to stand trial in Riquewihr. I owe him my life but now his own is in grave danger. He is badly wounded and lost a good deal of blood." She could see the whites of his eyes grow bigger with alarm as she continued, but he did not interrupt. "He lies not far away—less than two hours walk without the children. I would be most grateful if you would help me bring him back to The Lady for healing."

"Of course. We must leave swiftly then. Bring the children into the yard while I gather supplies to carry him back," he said before hurrying off across the yard and around the side of the house.

Sendy held open the gate as they passed through. She felt an unnerving finality as she clanged it shut behind her. As they approached the house, however, her spirits lifted a bit. It looked very unusual, not the kind of dreary old house that she expected an old lady would live in at all. She actually thought it quite a grand and beautiful house, accented with the crossed timbers she had seen on the fancy homes is Riquewihr. But unlike the boring, monotone gray or brown homes in town, this was painted bright yellow and even the crossed timbers were painted blue, providing a unique contrast of colors that made her smile. An inviting arched wooden door with a circular window centered atop a modest brick porch. Flanking each side of the door, two large windows looked out to the yard between bright red shutters. Flowers draped down from the windowsills, and a red brick chimney that matched the porch smoked atop the fat red roof, adding a sense of comfort. She laughed out loud when she got close enough to see artistic decorations of little candies and cookies attached to the walls.

They walked towards the house through an open grassy field, lightly dusted with snow and sprinkled with a menagerie of daffodils, daisies, and lavender growing all around them. Apple trees bloomed pink and white, while forsythia sprayed yellow flowers like fountains up from the ground. Closer to the home, she noticed garden beds that actually grew tomatoes and chubby little berries.

She asked Sendy if it was ok to eat some of them. With her approval, they headed straight for the blueberries and sat down on a wooden bench next to the porch to enjoy them.

"How is it that she is able to grow all of this food when we haven't had a harvest in almost three years?" asked Han with that half-scrunched face of his.

Sendy shrugged her shoulders. "She seems to be able to grow crops much better here for some reason. Maybe because we are up on the slope of a hill, so the rain doesn't flood the soil. There is also a little-known secret about this area. It seems to get a little more sunlight than everywhere else around here." Then she looked up and beamed at Jehan as he returned. "Or maybe because Jehan is such a good groundskeeper!"

He carried a long pole and a blanket that he hurriedly stuffed into a bag. "You're too kind," he said, smiling back. Then he turned to the children, "The Lady will be with you shortly, I already informed her that you've arrived. Here are some dry clothes for you to change into."

Sendy offered one last word of advice before departing, "I trust you will be on your best behavior when she comes out. Please stand when you greet her and be respectful."

"Yes, we will. Thank you Sendy!" Greta shouted back, waving goodbye.

They immediately changed into their fresh set of clothes and began to warm up right away. She thought Han looked silly because his tunic was much too short, covering less than half of his skinny thighs. Hers draped all the way down to the ground.

She had to hold it together at her neck to keep it from falling off her narrow shoulders.

"Look at those big red berries, Han," she said, reaching for one of the shallow baskets on the window ledge. "They look like little hearts, don't they?" The juice gushed forth from their mouths as they slurped the strawberries. She sat down and closed her eyes, letting the flavor wash over her, filling her soul with nourishment.

At that moment she heard an unfamiliar voice from behind her. "It seems I have some new guests at my home."

Greta sprang back to her feet. She stood as straight as a pin and didn't know if she should smile or not—or say something or not.

"Well, aren't you two beautiful children? Come a little closer so I can get a better look at you," she tittered in an unnaturally high-pitched voice. "Won't you tell me your names?"

The first thing she noticed about her was her unusual hat, its brim overflowing with flowers. Colorful feathers from some exotic bird rose high above her head, giving her a most ostentatious appearance. The next thing she noticed was her height, taller than any woman she had seen before—about as tall as her own father and nearly as broad in shoulders. She covered herself with a long black shawl over a green chemise. Over her chest, hung the medallion of the three moons, or three phases of a woman's life, the same medallion that Sendy bore. *She is most certainly the crone.* Long black boots jutted out from beneath her shawl.

Greta stepped forward cautiously and squeaked her name as she introduced herself. The Lady stooped down and smiled at her. Then, seeing her face under the hat more closely now, she understood why she had trouble seeing them from where she stood. Her eyes appeared cloudy, as though partly glazed over by a film of some kind. She saw this before in very old people in the town, but this lady didn't look as old as they did.

"Oh, look at your pretty face, my child. Don't be shy, I won't bite you or anything," she said, followed by a burst of unexpectedly loud cackling and fetid breath. She had a very wide smile that stretched across her face, revealing her few remaining decrepit and decayed teeth. A blood red paste of some kind neatly colored her lips, and a smaller amount smudged over her cheeks, as though she were trying to make herself appear younger. Her chin jutted out much too far, creating an almost masculine appearance, and even sported a few long strands of hair that she didn't bother to pluck. Her nose, however, was her most impressive feature. Perhaps it provided some balance to her protruding chin, she thought, but still disproportionately large for her face. The nostrils flared out at the base, and while the bridge of her nose began with a prominent hump, it tapered down in the middle until finishing off with a fleshy bulbous tip, topped off with a lumpy red wart. A single strand of hair grew from the wart like the stem of a wilted cherry.

She raised her eyebrows as an expression of concern transformed her smiling and welcoming face. "What happened to your hair, my poor darling dear? It looks like it's been ripped apart."

"I was attacked by a bat!" she exclaimed with widening eyes. "We had to shelter in a cave from the rainstorm yesterday. A bunch of bats flew over me and one of them got stuck in my hair until Roland tore it loose. Sendy tried to clean it up for me as best she could. It doesn't hurt as much as it did yesterday."

"Ooooh my, that is quite a perilous story! You must have been scared to death, weren't you, my pumpkin? Not to worry, I have just the thing to fix you up and make it all better. You can also wear one of my hats to cover it up until it grows out if you like." She gave her a quick embrace and then turned her attention to Han. "And who do we have here? What is your name young man?" she asked, her mysterious glazed eyes peering out from under her wide brim.

Han stepped toward her; his apprehension seemed to have been wiped away. "My name is Han. It's nice to meet you. I really like your hat," he complimented with a broad smile.

Her face lit up. "Oh, thank you for saying so! I always wear my favorite hat when new guests arrive," she said, patting and brushing the feathers on top. "I have other hats too. I love to wear hats. I have a collection of them, one for each of my moods," she giggled, "but this is my favorite. Maybe you can make one for me as a surprise some day, would you do that for me?" she asked, pinching his cheek vigorously.

She couldn't tell if Han's expression was one of embarrassment or pain as he tried to back away.

"I like your hat too, it's really pretty," Greta said, opening up now. "And I really like your house! It's so colorful and almost looks like it's made of candy."

"Oh, thank you, my little darling!" The Lady replied, excitedly clapping her hands together. "The children do love to look at my house with wonder when they come to visit me. I like the children to be happy when they arrive."

"Yeah, it looks like it's made of gingerbread; makes me want to take a bite out of it," Han said, staring at the wall like it was a basted, succulent turkey dinner.

"Oh dear, you can eat my berries, but please don't eat my house!" she tittered, shaking her head with a teasing smile. "I must say, you children look very hungry. Dinner is almost ready. Since Jehan will not return until later, would you mind feeding my animals in the stable around the back? I would greatly appreciate it. I'll leave a bowl of soapy water on the porch for you to wash up and have dinner on the table by the time you're done."

They walked around to the yard in back of the house, which was even more expansive than the front yard. The brick wall extended back about two hundred paces, holding off the thick forest of trees beyond. Not far from the back porch sat a large empty black stone cauldron atop a circular, red brick fire pit. Against the side wall, a half-enclosed wooden stable or barn sheltered a few pigs, goats, sheep, an ox, and even two cows. Several chickens pecked at the ground nearby. In the center of the yard stood a giant oak tree.

"Wow, look how huge that tree is! It must be ancient! Let's see how high we can climb?" Han said excitedly, charging toward the tree.

Greta called out to stop him as he leaped up to grab onto the lowest branch. "Han, don't you dare! You have to ask permission first. Besides, she asked if we could feed the animals for her. Come on!" she demanded, stomping her foot.

"Oh yeah, you're probably right." He hung onto the branch for a moment, then dropped himself back down. He arched his back and craned his neck trying to see the top of the tree. "I bet I can climb way up there. We could probably see for miles if we climbed to the top."

She walked toward the stable and then turned back to call Han who was still eyeing the top of the tree, but something quite odd and unexpected caught her eye. Carved deeply into its massive trunk was a large five-pointed star within a circle. She stood transfixed in front of it for a while before bringing it to Han's attention.

"What do you think this means?" she asked.

Han stood next to her, staring wondrously at the mysterious symbol. "I don't know, but it's kind of creepy, isn't it?"

She felt a cold chill rush through her. "It's weird, but I wouldn't say creepy," she said, trying to deflect her growing fear.

They continued to look it over before Han broke the silence. "Well, I think it's creepy."

She felt that cold chill again and shook like when someone sneaks up behind her. She looked past the tree to the back of the house and saw a figure staring out through one of the windows. "Han, come away from the tree. I think she's watching us."

Chapter 16

AFTER FEEDING THE ANIMALS AND WASHING UP, they walked back to the house, eagerly anticipating the first good meal in over two years. Han could already smell the dinner by the time he stepped onto the porch. He looked at Greta who smiled back at him with delight, then closed her eyes and sniffed the air slowly.

The Lady greeted them at the door and ushered them inside. "Please take off your dirty shoes before you come inside. Ooohhh, I must say! You should probably wash those feet of yours while you're at it!"

He had never been asked to remove his shoes and clean his feet before, but as he stepped inside, he realized why. Dark wood planks covered the floor and unlike his own floor, looked immaculately clean. Three cushioned chairs and a wooden rocker surrounded a large rectangular rug decorated with intricate lacy patterns. All were situated in front of a prominent red brick hearth, its flaming logs and glowing embers shedding its warmth throughout the room. Unlike the central fire pit in his own home, and any other home he knew of for that matter, this hearth was built into the wall. He nudged Greta with a sly smile and pointed to a large tapestry hanging on the wall to his left, displaying naked women dancing around a tree. Beside the tapestry, on the far side of the room, stood an arched threshold to a dark hallway.

He looked up at the vaulted ceiling, rising high above him, much like the church in Riquewihr. The windows on each side of the door brightened the home considerably, even though the afternoon sky remained shrouded by heavy clouds. The smoky scent of the wood burning in the hearth gave him an immediate sense of comfort, while the savory aroma of her stew— something that he hadn't smelled in a very long time—made his mouth water.

A heavy slam of the door behind him forced him to jerk his head around as the Lady bolted the door. It suddenly dawned on him that he and his sister were now alone in this strange lady's house, a lady that they were going to have to depend on for the next several years. A suffocating sense of dread came over him at that moment. The room that just moments ago seemed to him so spacious and warm, suddenly felt small and cramped, the air heavy and thick, the sudden silence almost palpable.

"We can never be too safe, now can we my little dumplings? Lots of bandits out these days. We wouldn't want them to come in and GET US!" she teased, lurching toward them, her hands positioned like claws. They both startled and then giggled nervously while exchanging awkward glances. "Oooh, you're a couple of little scaredy cats, aren't you?" she tittered, evidently pleased with herself.

She led them through to the dining room where a large wooden table was set with their plates and eating utensils. On the center of the table rested a large black stone bowl, steaming with flavor, drawing him towards it and easing his anxiety. A shiny metal pitcher sat beside it, glistening and dripping with beads of cool condensation, along with a freshly baked loaf of bread.

"Have a seat, please. I'll pour some stew into your bowl so you can get started," she said, pinching his cheeks. "Oh dear, we shall have to fatten you up. Won't we my poor starving boy? No sir, that won't do at all…" she added, clicking her tongue and shaking her head.

He waited patiently as she filled Greta's bowl and then his own with a large dipping spoon. "Enjoy," she said, setting the bowl in front of him and patting him gently on his head.

Stirring around the contents in his bowl, he noticed carrots, mushrooms, celery, and large chunks of pork. When he tasted the first spoonful, his mouth became overwhelmed with flavor, forcing him to close his eyes, allowing his tongue to roll over each tasty morsel before swallowing.

"Wow, this is fantastic! Sendy didn't lie, you're a great cook. Thank you," he said, dipping his soft bread in the hot, savory stew.

She smiled down at him as she filled her own bowl. "Oh, you're too kind, aren't you, my sweetling? You're more than welcome to help yourself to more if you like."

He couldn't seem to take his eyes off her nose when she looked at him, even though he knew it might hurt her feelings or get him in trouble if he kept doing it. There were just so many things about it to take in: the hairy nostrils, the hump, and the fleshy wart at the bulbous tip. He felt like he could stare at it for hours and still be entertained.

"Oh, I see you like my nose. I must say, I get so many compliments about my nose. I don't mind if you look at it, just so long as you don't look in it!" she said, slapping her thigh and shaking her head as she laughed at her own quip.

He forced himself to join her with a nervous chuckle. Then through her laughing, she burst forth a tremendous blast of gas, so unexpected and loud that he and Greta both stopped and gawked at her. Her mouth and eyes momentarily opened wide with embarrassment, but then she erupted with that explosive, shrieking cackle that pierced his ears and reverberated off the walls of the house. At first, he was startled by her outburst(s), but then seeing how she laughed it off, he lost all self-control. What started with a tickle in his belly, it blossomed into ten thousand butterflies fluttering throughout his body, making him double over in ecstatic elation.

"Oh, my goodness, what was that? Who let the ducks in the house!?" she called out, looking behind her. Then, showing a look of disgust, she pinched her nose shut and waved her other hand in front of her face, "and the pigs too?" she screamed, raising the hysterics to a new level.

The three of them were all rolling with glee now, finding it hard to breathe. He looked back up at her beaming grin stretched over that long chin, her ridiculous nose, and that audacious hat! He had never seen an old lady acting so hilarious and cackling this hard at her own expense. This had to be the funniest thing he had ever witnessed!

"Laugh now little ones, but when you get to be my age let's see if you can hold it in. My, my, my…I can't believe I did that," she said, wiping tears away and waving her hand in front of her flushed face.

"I like you, you're funny," Greta said, looking up at her, wrinkling her nose as she smiled.

"Oh, you're too sweet, my duckling. Now let's eat up before we all die of laughter," she said with one last burst of cackling.

They enjoyed their meal while talking more about their journey, and their parents, and sharing some more amusement. Just as he thought he was becoming full for the first time in years, he began to smell the sweet scent of a freshly baked pie coming from her kitchen. Greta smiled next to him, closing her eyes and lifting her nose in the air.

The Lady finished off her wine, wiped her mouth with the cloth napkin, and rose from her chair. "Help me clean the dishes, and then we can enjoy the gooseberry pie for dessert."

They thanked her for the wonderful meal and carried their bowls into the kitchen with smiles, their stomachs satiated for the first time since they could remember. They placed their bowls in a large bucket filled with water and lye to let them soak.

The smell of the pie drew their attention to the brick oven. A charcoal fire crackled in the lower half, heating the stone surface over which the pie baked, along with another loaf of bread for the morning. She removed the pie and bread from the oven using a flat, square piece of metal with a long handle and placed it on the top shelf to let it cool, then placed the large cauldron of stew back into the oven to keep warm for the others when they returned later.

They sat back down at the table and she served them each a large piece. He licked his lips as the berries spilled onto his plate and the sweet scent wafted into his nose. When he took his first bite, everything seemed to slow down, letting each bite stay in his mouth as long as he could before swallowing so that his tongue could swim in ecstasy. The warm, gooey sweetness mixed with the tartness of the berries tasted better than anything he could have imagined. They all ate in silence and before he knew it only the crumbs remained.

He looked up at The Lady who smiled across the table at them. "I can see you enjoyed my pie. You haven't spoken a word since you started."

They broke their silence by speaking over each other, emphatically declaring how delicious it was and how they never knew anything could taste so good.

She laughed and clapped her hands and resumed her cheerful, shrill voice, "I thought you would enjoy it, everybody loves my gooseberry pie. If you behave like nice children, I'll make it again for you some day." She turned to Greta. "Maybe I could even teach you how to make it with me. Have you ever baked with an oven like mine before, my dear?"

Greta shook her head. "Our mother just used to hang a big pot or a spit of meat over the fire pit until it cooked. She said I was too young to help her back then, but I'm definitely old enough to learn now."

"Oh yes, I daresay you are, my sweetling. A year or two can make a big difference for a young girl," she said, before turning to Han. "I have a favor to ask of you Han, I have a load of firewood in the stable that I'd like for you to bring down to the cellar. Can you do that for me?"

He nodded.

"Very good. You will find the cart next to the pile of wood. Bring as much as you can carry, and I'll meet you on the side of the house. In the meantime, Greta can help me wash these dishes and clean the oven, won't you dear? After you've finished, I'll show you to your beds so you can get a good long night's rest." She brought her hands together in front of her chest and sighed, "Oh, it is so wonderful to have children back in my home again."

Chapter 17

IT DIDN'T TAKE ROLAND LONG TO REALIZE that he had been left to die. That wouldn't be a bad thing, he thought. Anything would be better than having to endure this agonizing pain that seared through every inch of his body. The wool blanket and bed of branches and leaves that she threw on top of him before she left only took away the chill of the breeze, but little else it seemed. The frozen earth beneath him gradually penetrated deep into his bones, making him shiver uncontrollably. Every sound he heard, made him jerk his head around in fear of a rabid wolf coming to finish him off.

Eventually though, his senses dulled and his eyelids grew heavy. The shivering settled down over time until he didn't even feel cold anymore. In fact, he felt quite warm. Soon the blanket on top of him felt suffocatingly hot. It took all the strength left in him just to toss it aside so that he could breathe again, but his throat became so dry that he choked for breath.

Then the strange visions began, too surreal for him to believe but there they appeared before him. A wolf sauntered up sniffing around but did not come within an arm's reach. Instead, it sat casually before him on its haunches with its tongue lolling out to the side, appearing as relaxed as though it were his own dog watching over him. Then a great deer with heavy, majestic antlers approached and stood beside the wolf. Above him in the tree, a half-naked child with long hair perched on a branch like a vulture, staring down at him through large black eyes, as though awaiting his death with intense interest.

Finally, he closed his eyes one last time and sunk into oblivion—a state of timeless nothingness. He possessed no thoughts, no feelings, no emotions, and no memories; only awareness. But who was he? He was no longer Roland, no longer even human, just pure consciousness existing in an eternal moment of transcendence.

Then a single point of light appeared before him. This tiny light became the only thing that existed, or had ever existed, in this realm of infinite darkness. It began to pulse with a rhythm that defined time, infusing a sound that he could both hear and feel. This light became a gash, as though sliced open by a cosmic sword, rending the blank fabric of the void. This gash grew into a fissure of light towards which everything, including himself, began to flow inexorably. It sucked him in closer, slowly at first but then pulling exponentially faster and stronger, the fissure expanding immensely in size until it overtook the blackness, the pulsing rhythm amplifying with intensity as he approached this strange, new universe.

As he plunged through the chasm, a single thought pervaded his awareness: aversion, a single emotion: fear, and a single sensation: pain. His full consciousness suddenly thrust itself back into his body in unimaginable agony. He tore his eyes open to perceive his world upside down. Several hooded figures shouted at him in Latin with the same rhythm that pulled him out of the void. His body was restrained, tied to something hard and rough. He smelled and tasted blood trickling down his face and into his mouth. Immediately, a frantic torrent of terror flooded through him, a terror like the ferocity of a thousand demons ravaging his soul, as he screamed his agony into the unholy night.

Chapter 18

WITH HIS MIND FINALLY FREE from an incessant preoccupation with hunger, Han took his time to enjoy the beauty of the yard on his way to the stables. *This place looks like a dreamland!* Yellow butterflies, little red hummingbirds, and dragonflies flitted all around him in the tall grass. The sun, only a couple hours from setting, shined its golden rays between the clouds, countless shards of light angling down to earth. He always imagined that must be what heaven looked like. Perhaps because it had been so long since he saw this much sunlight, it seemed unusually bright; every flower in the yard popped out at him with incredible vibrancy. The house appeared almost cartoonish with its contrasting bright colors and childish decorations attached to the walls. He stared spellbound as the wind blew wisps of snow on the roof into swirling tufts of glitter that sparkled in the sunlight.

Making his way to the old stable, he found the large pile of chopped wood sitting on a raised platform and loaded it into the two-handed cart. He slowly managed to wheel the cart around to the side of the house where The Lady stood waiting. He heaved a deep breath and rubbed his hands after setting it down. Next time he wouldn't load it so heavy, he decided.

She stepped toward him and stared intently into his eyes, her nose just inches from his own—any closer and she would be tickling him with her wart hair. Finally, she smiled and said, "Ah, I think you have been eating things that you shouldn't be eating, Han. Am I right? Did you try those pretty flowers on my gate, perhaps?"

Han nodded. "I was so hungry... I thought they were candy." He spoke slowly and had trouble finding his words.

She nodded her head slowly as he spoke. "That *candy* is called Devil's snare, or Hell's Bells as some like to call it. And how many flowers did you eat, my silly boy?"

"I only took one bite before Sendy slapped it out of my hand. I didn't really swallow much of it. She said they can make me sick."

"They certainly can; they can even make you see things that aren't really there."

"Yeah, I kind of noticed," he realized.

She poked his belly with her long, gnarled finger. "If you eat too much it can kill you too. I would hate to wake up tomorrow and find you dead in your bed! Tsk, tsk, tsk," she shook her head and clicked her tongue with a teasing smirk. "With only one bite though, I think you should be just fine by tomorrow. Let's finish these chores then so you can sleep it off."

He bent over a trap door situated on the ground and jerked the handle up, but it was much heavier than he realized and slammed back shut. With a second effort, he heaved it up and swung the door open over its large rusty hinges, then let it fall heavily onto the other side. As it croaked open, he thought it sounded like the groans of many tormented souls escaping from their prison in the blackness beneath his feet. He looked down to see a steep stairway plunging underground into darkness and under the house itself. A faint light flickered on the lower stairs. He looked up at The Lady as if to see that she really wanted him to carry the wood into the depths of that dark place.

She motioned with her hand to proceed. "Go ahead, my boy. You can see better once you're down there. It looks like the furnace is still lit from yesterday, but we need to add some more wood and charcoal, so it doesn't go out on us overnight. You can toss the wood inside the furnace door, but the charcoal goes underneath. Two shovelfuls ought to do it."

He grabbed an armful of chopped wood from the cart and hugged them against his chest, then carefully descended the steep, narrow steps into the cellar, keeping his eyes focused on the light flickering at the bottom. The air felt suffocatingly still, like he was entering into a crypt. The odors of damp earth, dry smoke, and coal dust stifled his breath. Trembling, he forced himself to continue down the creaky, old wooden staircase, its agonizing groans amplified in the still silence, threatening to give way with each step.

As he stepped off the final stair, his feet crunched onto the gravelly surface of the cellar floor. He entered into a large, cavernous room with several thick posts supporting the ceiling and weight of the house above. Against the far wall, a low red flame of coal embers provided the only light, casting flickering shadows all around. Above this lurid glow appeared to be some kind of giant black squatting beast. As he stepped closer, it materialized into an enormous brick furnace or kiln of some kind, covered in black soot. A pair of bellows used to stoke the flames sat beside it. The whole contraption looked similar to the blast furnace used by the blacksmith in Riquewihr, but much larger. A hinged metal grating on its front allowed access from the cellar while most of the smoke vented up through a broad pipe opening to ground level. Most of the excess smoke that escaped through the grating wafted up and out through a small open vent adjacent to where the pipe exited the cellar.

The noxious odor became heavier next to the furnace, drying his throat, but underneath he sensed something disturbing, as though he could taste the stale, rank stench of death and corruption. His pulse quickened as a mounting sense of dread threatened to burst his brain into a full-blown panic. Dropping the wood on the floor, he charged back up the stairs, tripping himself twice, scraping his shins and elbows along the way. As soon as his head emerged to the surface, he leaped up, throwing himself out the rest of the way onto the grass.

The Lady gawked down at him with surprise and laughed hysterically. "Oh my goodness, you are a little scaredy-cat, aren't you?"

Han lay there panting with fright, looking back up at her and hoping she would say that was enough for today. But she didn't.

"You better get used to it down there, this will be your job from now on. Now finish this load and then fill up one more cartload to bring down. Don't forget to feed the charcoal to the flames. We don't want that fire to go out."

It took five trips down the stairs with each cartload before he finally finished. Exhausted from the exertions of the day, he lifted and swung the heavy door shut and went back inside to tell The Lady that he had finished.

She led them quietly through the living room and down the dark hallway, lit only by her candle, to a pair of doors across from each other. He had never been in a house with so many rooms before.

"This will be your room, mine is just down the hall," her voice creaked along with the sound of the door as it slowly swung open. He looked in from the hallway as she stepped inside. The consuming darkness of the windowless room seemed to press against the glow from her candle, diminishing its brightness to just a small ineffectual droplet of light at the end of her candle stick. The Lady walked over to a wooden dresser and lit another candle, this one about as long and thick as his thigh and surrounded by a globular cascade of hardened wax from previous use. Two straw mattresses lay side by side, covered neatly with wool blankets and stuffed pillows for their heads.

"I've left some toys from my previous guests in that box over there," she said, gesturing with her candle to a small box tucked into the corner of the room. "You can play with them when you wake up in the morning if you like."

She reached into her pocket and produced a handful of little balls, each of a different color, glistening in the candlelight. Han reached for one and popped it directly into his mouth. He bit down hard and immediately reached for his jaw with a grimace of pain.

"Oh dear, I forgot to tell you that you're just supposed to suck on them. If you keep doing that you'll end up with as many teeth as me," she said with a broad smile, showing what remained of her teeth before pealing off another loud cackle.

He took it out of his mouth and held it up in front of his eyes to study it more closely, marveling at the bright red color. When he held it up to the candlelight, he noticed a darker shade of red swirling toward the center. He placed it back into his mouth and let the flavor of cherries melt over his tongue. *This is too good to be true*, he thought.

"Try one, my sweetling. They're made of hard sugar, don't be afraid," she said, extending the handful to Greta. She placed it on her tongue and closed her eyes to indulge in the sticky sweetness.

"The candy will help you sleep better in your new beds. When the others return, I would hate for us to awaken you. Just blow out the candle when you're ready to go to sleep," she said, closing the door behind her.

They walked over to the toy box and giggled quietly as they pulled out a rattle, a smelly stuffed cat, a couple of hats, several marbles, a set of clogs that were even too small for Greta, and an old wooden baby pacifier. Next to the box leaning against the wall stood a long stick with a crude representation of a horse's head at the top, complete with worn, ratty yarn for a mane.

"Here's one for you, Greta," Han said sarcastically as he pulled out a doll made of yarn and cloth.

She winced and backed up a step as he held it up to her. "No way, that thing gives me the creeps."

He studied it more closely in the dim candlelight. "You're right. Who would want to play with this ugly thing?"

With large black buttons for eyes and a mouth stitched to appear wide open, it looked as if it were screaming. Long course black yarn hung down for hair. Its rigid arms stretched out to the sides like the victim of a crucifixion.

"Can you put that back in the box now? I don't even want to look at it," Greta said, turning away toward her bed.

Han took one last look into its big black eyes and shuddered, tossing it back into the toy box. As he pulled off his tunic, he succumbed to a deep yawn, arching his back into a long satisfying stretch. He then blew out the candle before climbing under the warm blanket of his new bed, smiling as his head hit the pillow.

"This is way more comfortable than our bed," he sighed, hugging the soft pillow against his cheek. He fell asleep with the candy still in his mouth.

Han dreamed that his body lifted from his bed, levitating in motionless silence halfway to the ceiling. He felt completely paralyzed, but calm and at peace. After a while, he rose higher until he passed through the ceiling and found himself outside in the cool night air, still rising steadily above the trees and up toward the clouds. He could see for miles around in the moonlight, all the way east to the Rhine River. From this height, it seemed like he could travel there in just minutes, but instead he continued to rise up to the clouds. Before he knew it, he passed through the billowy white haze, tasted the cool moisture on his tongue. He felt no tension up here among the clouds, no feelings of hunger or guilt or worry, no shame or anger or fear— just pure serenity. Finally, pushing through the clouds, he gazed with fascination upon the countless stars cast across the eternal heavens like tiny sparkling jewels.

Then an unsettling wave of nausea rushed through him as he began to fall, plummeting endlessly through the sky, the stars fading away into the white mist. Passing through the clouds, he saw them overhead once again, appearing much heavier now, pelting his face with rain as he continued to fall. They began to churn and rumble like the coming of an epic storm, transforming into the ghastly visage of Ferrand, glaring down upon him with his glazed eyes and bloated face and swollen black tongue. The face bellowed down from the clouds like thunder, "You shall suffer unspeakable terror for bringing death upon me!"

Han flailed his arms, grasping for anything to hold onto but kept falling helplessly downward. He managed to flip himself over to see where he would land. At first, he saw only treetops and grassy hills, but then he could make out a single house with a red roof far beneath him, growing larger and closer until he plunged through it and then through his bed. At last, he stopped falling and found himself alone in the cellar.

But the soft glow of the coal embers was now a roaring conflagration. The great beast squatting above it was alive with flames licking out of the metal grating of its mouth and the two dampers above it like burning orange eyes, its black smoke choking his breath and stinging his eyes. Underneath it all, he heard blood-curdling screams of children that seemed to be coming from inside the monstrous furnace itself. Suddenly a blast of flames erupted through its mouth, shooting straight towards him, transforming into a giant fist that gripped his body and began pulling him inside the roaring beast.

He jolted awake with a sudden terror, panting for breath and drenched with sweat. In the pitch-black darkness of his room, he could still see the face of the giant glowing furnace, bursting with flames, as though seared into his mind. He reached up to pull off the candy ball stuck to his cheek and flicked it across the room.

He heard Greta asleep beside him with her slow quiet breathing. More faintly, he heard people chanting from somewhere outside and wondered if he might still be dreaming. He shook his head to clear it, but the distant sound of chanting continued. He rose out of bed but lost his balance, reaching blindly for the wall to keep from falling. After steadying himself, he slid his hand along the wall, finding his way to the door. He turned the handle, slowly creaked open the door, and stepped into the dark hallway. A single candle glowed dimly in the living room, guiding his way through to the dining room.

He cautiously peaked out the window to the back yard and saw several robed figures with deep hoods pulled over their heads, huddled together behind the large oak tree. Intrigued, he wanted to get a closer look to see what they were up to. To avoid notice, he decided to exit the front door and move around to the side of the house.

As he stepped outside, the cold breeze blew away any sleepiness that remained. As he crept around to the back yard, the rhythmic chant filled his ears with wicked clarity, sending a chill up his spine. It sounded like a litany of both men's and women's voices singing rhythmically in an unfamiliar language, each short verse starting slowly, growing faster and louder, punctuated by three quick shouts of the final word in the verse. They repeated the chant again and again, each time louder than the last. The mystical sound piqued his curiosity, compelling him to discover the reason behind it.

Peering around the corner, he saw them more clearly now. Seven robed figures intently focused toward the tree; one of them making strange gestures like a sorcerer, another restraining a goat by a leash, and the tallest wielding a great two-handed axe. *They must be praying to that symbol carved into the bark of the tree.* He thought about heading back inside, but instead decided to get a closer look at what else might be going on.

He crept along the shadows against the brick wall of the yard until he reached the concealment of a bush behind their gathering. He could now see the five-pointed star that they saw earlier, but something else caught his eye, something that seemed to be tied directly to the thick trunk of the tree. At first, he couldn't discern what it could be. The candlelight dimly illuminated the tree as he studied it, trying to make it out. As his eyes worked their way down, a sudden rush of horror and nausea flooded through him once he finally realized what he had been looking at. Underneath the symbol, was the body of a man tied upside down to the tree, his arms stretched out beside him, just like the doll in his room, in the manner of a crucifixion.

Every hair on his body pricked and tingled, and he felt his dinner starting to come back up. In utter revulsion, he pulled himself away from the grisly spectacle and threw his back against the stone wall, closing his eyes tightly. *Oh God, Oh God! What the hell are they doing to him?* His eyes teared up, and a sour, acrid taste hit the back of his throat, forcing him to wretch. He struggled to control his breathing by taking slow, deep breaths.

The chanting continued to grow louder and more passionate, now screaming their verses into the night. *I must be seeing things, this can't be real*, he thought as he wiped the cold sweat and tears from his face. He couldn't just retreat back to his room in fear; he needed to figure out what the hell they were doing. Shaking his head like a dog to rid himself of any hesitation, he returned to peer over the bush again. The candlelight flickered over the man's body, revealing innumerable bloody, gaping wounds. His long hair spilled downward, almost touching the ground. *Roland!*

A sudden movement of the tallest figure caught his eye as his large axe swept down over the neck of the goat. A gush of blood splashed and spurted over Roland's naked body, spilling downward over his face and hair before trickling down onto the grass. As their screaming voices rose to a fever pitch, he watched in amazement as Roland's limbs began to twitch and then quiver and jerk until his whole body shook violently. At last, his eyes ripped open in a rage of fury and his head thrashed from side to side as he spewed forth a most hideous shriek.

Han stared in shock and disbelief until he realized that he should not be out here witnessing this infernal resurrection. Just as he started to sneak away, he noticed one of the hooded figures had turned to look towards him, its face just an empty blackness looking out from beneath the deep cowl, before turning back to Roland. He didn't look back as he returned along the wall, then sprinted like mad to the front door of the house, closing and locking it behind him before hurrying back to his room, where he stood with his back against the door, panting and sweating in the pitch-black silence.

Chapter 19

GUARIN ROUSED TO THE MUFFLED CLAMOR of guards wrestling a man up the steps of the prison tower. Once they managed to open the door to the prison, loud shouting and cursing and the scuffling of heavy boots erupted through the room, echoing off the stone walls.

The new prisoner sounded drunk as he fought against his captors, "Get your fucking hands off me you little pricks! You have no idea who I am and no right to hold me against my will! I swear to God, I will break free of these chains and rip your ugly fucking heads off your skinny little necks!"

"You're not breaking free of anything, so just shut the hell up and calm the fuck down," hollered one of the guards.

Guarin rose to his feet and peered out of his cell gate. *They got him.* He looked on with regret as the unmistakable figure of Barous, cursing like a drunken sailor, hands chained behind his back, was wrenched toward the empty cell next to his by a pair of guards.

The older of the two guards, a cadaverous looking man bearing a deep scar on his left cheek, slammed his armored hand into the gate directly in front of Guarin's face. "The fuck you lookin' at? Back away and mind your damn business, prisoner!"

They shoved Barous violently into his cell and swung the gate shut with a loud echoing clang. "Get used to your new home, pig fucker."

The younger guard locked the cell gate, then turned to the other, "That bastard was a fuckin' handful. We should get a special reward for bringing in this big fish," he boasted.

The older guard smirked and clapped him firmly on his shoulder. "Don't count on it, but if we do, I know who I'm spending my reward on."

"You still hot on that skinny little number? How old is she anyhow, thirteen?"

"The fuck difference does it make? She wants my money; I want her pussy. 'Nuf said, am I right?"

The younger guard shook his head but smiled nonetheless, "You're a dirty old man, Joff. That's all I gotta say."

"Dirty old man?" Barous shouted from his cell. "That's all you can say to a man that likes to fuck little kids? Dirtier than my unwiped asshole; that's what you are, you piece of shit! I'm going to rip your dick off and shove it down your throat, balls first! I'll leave your snake hanging out of your mouth so everyone can see how stupid you look after I twist your head off and mount it on a pike!"

Joff looked to the other, feigning a look of shock, shaking his head and pointing his thumb toward Barous. "Can you believe the mouth on this guy?"

"Never in my life..." the younger guard played along as they turned to leave.

Barous continued his verbal assault on the two guards as they made their way out of the prison room and even long after they had shut the door, inciting the other prisoners in the cells to shout back at him to shut his damn mouth. Once the commotion settled down, Guarin quietly called out his name but his only response was loud snoring. *What a mess you've caused, Lutrud. What will tomorrow bring?*

The muffled sound of tortured screams and mocking laughter ripped Guarin away from his dreams. It seemed to be coming from the other side of the wall from the prison cells but disturbing, nonetheless. He'd been awoken to screams before, but today he knew who was screaming, and it made his stomach flop. If Barous didn't give up his identity, Guarin knew he would be next. It seemed to go on for hours, the whipping sound of lashes against his skin and blood-curdling shrieks, followed by the defiant insults hurled from Barous. Eventually, the screaming became less intense until it finally stopped altogether. A few minutes later, he heard the prison door slam open, the rattle of chains, the grunts and chit chat of the guards as they dragged his limp body across the floor.

"I've never seen anyone suffer through that much of a beating before going under, and he didn't stop runnin' his mouth none, neither."

"I'd say so, I hope we didn't kill him. Is he dead?"

"He's breathin', ain't he?"

"I guess so."

"Then he ain't dead, genius. Open the door to his cell. I've got him."

Guarin winced when he heard the heavy thud of Barous's head hitting the stone floor of his cell. He sat quietly as he listened to the loud clang of his cell gate closing shut, the scraping of the key in the metal lock, the scuffling of their boots across the floor, the slamming of the prison door followed by the usual series of locking mechanisms, then silence—until he heard himself weeping.

Some hours later, Guarin heard the sounds of Barous rousing, his breathing becoming more labored and audible, gradually turning to groans. He moved toward his cell gate and sat down on the floor, resting his back against the wall adjoining their cells and folding his arms over his knees.

"Barous, can you hear me?"

"Who's that?" he croaked.

"It's me, Guarin. I met you at the waterfall the other day with my son."

"I'll be damned, what the hell are you doing here?"

"I'm afraid it was Lutrud... she...she found the coin you gave my son," he whispered.

"Well shit, you did warn me about her." He coughed and let out a stifled groan. "It's all starting to make sense now, why they brought me here. Except, why you? What the hell did you do to her, beat her up, kill her?"

"I didn't do anything to her. They want me to admit that you were..." he lowered his voice to a whisper again, "...a

Templar. Don't worry, I told them you were a merchant, not much more than that."

Guarin heard coarse laughter coming from Barous, "They actually threw you in here just for that?" He coughed again until he groaned from pain. "Ah shit, I think they broke my ribs."

"Well, look on the bright side, unless you have something on your person that marks you as a Templar, like more coins or one of those Templar crosses tattooed on your ass, they really don't have anything else except for what Lutrud may have told them."

"Fortunately, I didn't have my sword or other belongings on me when they arrested me last night. I left them at the house I am renting, and I paid the man handsomely to keep it discrete. As long as they don't go searching all of the houses in town, they should remain safe."

"He said you were pretty damn important in the Templar ranks, worth a lot of reward money. He said you are one of the last of them."

Barous took a while to answer as he struggled to slow his breathing. "He's right about that. Listen Guarin, I'm sorry I laughed at you earlier. I shouldn't take what you did for me lightly. That is very admirable, and I owe you a great debt of gratitude. If only there were more men like you around, men who still value their integrity above their own self-interests. In times like these more than ever, it seems everyone is just looking out for themselves."

"Thank you, Barous. I can see you are a good man. You certainly don't deserve to be here either. My son also holds you in high regard; I could tell by the way he looked upon you as we talked by the town square. It even made me feel jealous. It has been too long since he rewarded me with such a gleam of admiration. I think if I ever get the chance to see him regard me again in the same way, it will wash away all of my regrets. So, to assist them with your capture or, God forbid, execution, based on trumped up charges from many years past..." he paused, shaking his head, "I would never even feel deserving of such admiration from my son again."

"How is your son doing? I like him, a very smart and inquisitive boy. Han is it? I think you should give them the information they want and get back home to him and your darling daughter. Integrity is one thing but responsibility to your family reigns supreme, don't you agree?"

"I'm afraid I have nothing to go back home to. Both of my children were taken from me soon after we met."

"Taken? By whom?"

"Believe it or not, Lutrud had a hand in that as well."

"Why does that not surprise me?"

"I became gravely ill with a kidney stone shortly after we parted ways. We both thought I was going to die. We've had so very little food for so long…she said it was best that we send them away…that she had made arrangements." He hunched forward over his knees as his breathing turned to short spasms, his face distorted into a grimace, and tears rolled down his cheeks. He took a deep, shuddering breath and then continued his lament. "I protested against it, but she wouldn't let up. I was so sick and so tired…I guess you could say that I just finally gave in."

"I am so sorry, my good friend. It tears me up inside to hear such sorrow. Only God can know the depths of despair that you have endured. Let no one judge your actions in such a state, let alone yourself. You seem a loving and caring father, and I know you would only put your children's safety first."

"A loving and caring father? What kind of a father allows his children to be taken from him? You tell me that! What kind of a father can't even provide for his children? What use is a man if he can't defend his own home? What kind of a husband would eat his wife's food while she lies dying right next to him?" He let out a series of sobs and pressed his palms to his weeping eyes. "I keep telling myself that we had no choice, but I remember how I felt in that moment. I felt *relieved* that she wasn't eating anymore because that meant more food for us. That's the God's honest truth, I tell you, and that is something for which I can never forgive myself. So please don't tell me I have any integrity left."

After a long silence, Barous spoke again, his voice deep and steady. "Guarin, listen to me. You must not let yourself dwell on things like this; it only prolongs your suffering and makes it seem worse than it really is. It's not like you would have eaten her food if she wanted to eat. And you clearly are not willing to give your children away—if anything you were trying to do what's best for them. We all do things that we regret in such dire circumstances. You were fighting for your very survival, not to mention your children's survival. You can't expect to have rational thoughts in those moments."

"Some say it is precisely moments like those that matter most and bring out our true character." Guarin leaned his back again against the stone wall, stretched his legs out in front of him and closed his eyes, reflecting back upon his life. "What manner of men do we become when everything that we hold dear to us is ripped from our lives. One by one I've lost my trade, my wife, my dignity, my health, and now even my dear starving children. I have let down my children most of all. The conditions I have endured, the mistakes and choices I have made to end up where I am now...I tell you my very soul has been worn thin." He paused to take a deep breath, opened his eyes and looked up to the ceiling. "I was so full of vigor in my younger days, nothing could bring me down. I thought I could go anywhere, be anybody I wanted to be. But every decision I make seems to offer less possibilities going forward, constricting this vision of a man that I had hoped to become. Now here I sit, trapped in this tiny bleak cell, right where I belong."

"Don't be absurd! Of course, you don't belong here. Neither of us belong here, but you certainly less so than me. Once you get released, go find your children. Show them how much you love them. This weather will eventually clear, our crops will produce and ripen, and you, my friend, will raise your axe once again. But first, you must look past your mistakes and misfortunes, forgive them as God intended. The only thing that matters is what you choose to do going forward. That choice begins with each moment that you still breathe—this moment—it's the *only* thing that matters. What good did it do you to simply give up? Perhaps that is the crux of why your son hasn't regarded you with the admiration that he once did?"

Guarin chuckled, realizing for the first time how pathetic he had become, wallowing in self-pity these past few years. "Perhaps you are right." He turned his head toward Barous's cell and continued with a stronger voice. "I'll have you know that I did try to stand up to the intruder who came for my children. I brought out a knife to ward him away and told my kids to run. He got the better of me, but at least I kept him busy long enough for them to escape from the house." He paused, reflecting back on that fateful moment, then smiled. "I had actually forgotten until now—barely even noticed at the time—but now that I think back, I seem to remember the look of surprise—and, dare I say, a spark of admiration?—on Han's face when I confronted the man."

"Well, that's more like it! Good for you! I'm sure that will be a moment your son will never forget."

"I tried anyway, but I don't think it was enough. He knocked me out, so I don't really know what happened after that until the guards came to my home the next day and brought me here. So, I still don't know where my children are."

"I truly hope you find them again, my friend. I would have to assume this man will return to town for more work sooner or later." Barous groaned, trying to shift his position. "We need to get out of this shit hole. I've broken out of prisons stronger than this while on crusade, believe me."

"If you lead, I'll follow, and help as I'm able. I feel my strength beginning to return, but I don't think I'd be of much use in a fight just yet."

"Come to think of it, neither am I," Barous groaned again.

Chapter 20

GRETA AWOKE IN THE DARKNESS OF HER NEW ROOM. She sat up, yawned and stretched, and looked beside her where Han still slept. *Is it morning?*

She heard footsteps coming down the hall and then the door creaked open. The soft glow of candlelight illuminated The Lady's face from below as she peered into their room. The long shadow of her nose slowly stretched across the ceiling as she pushed her head further through the doorway. Greta sat up, smiled, and waved good morning.

The Lady beamed a huge grin at her, swung the door open the rest of the way, and stepped inside. "Oh, good morning, my dear!" she exclaimed, her voice ringing out with high-pitched glee.

Han yelped and almost jumped to the ceiling as she startled him awake. He sprang to his feet in his under-breeches and then lurched back again once he saw the tall figure of The Lady standing before him in the room. He pulled the sheet up to cover himself and managed to utter a feeble "good morning".

"Oh, I didn't mean to scare you, my little monkey," she giggled. "I thought you would both be awake by now. Did you sleep well?"

They both nodded their heads; Greta smiled but Han did not.

"Good, I'm glad to hear that. Come outside after you've dressed to splash some cool water on your faces before we eat. I left a bowl of water for you on the porch. And don't forget to empty your chamber pot. Han, would you be a dear and take it to the trench out back?" She smiled and twiddled her fingers under her chin in a silly gesture of waving goodbye as she stepped back out.

Greta began changing into her new clothes. "I slept like a log and feel so much better. How about you?"

Han didn't answer right away. He looked a bit uncertain as he just stood there staring at the doorway. "Greta, do you notice anything… strange about her?" he asked in a whisper.

She shot him a puzzled look, "What do you mean?"

"I had some really weird dreams last night. Actually, one of them wasn't a dream, at least I don't think it was, but it sure felt like it. I woke up in the middle of the night and heard people chanting, kind of like Sendy did when the wolves were chasing us. I went out to see what was going on…"

Greta's jaw almost dropped off of her face. "You went outside last night? Are you crazy? What if she caught you out there?"

Han tossed his hands up, "What? It's not like we're prisoners here. I was curious. Anyhow, it was pretty scary— actually insanely horrifying. They brought Roland back."

Her stunned expression lightened up, "Sendy is back then too?"

Han looked at her as though she wasn't really following him. "Yeah, she's back, but you should have seen what they were doing to Roland." He stopped short when he heard footsteps and chatter in the hallway, so he quickly began to dress himself. "I'll tell you later. We better head out for breakfast."

Greta stepped outside in the cool morning air to a blue sky with big puffy white clouds. She closed her eyes, basking in the warm sunlight that had been missing for months. Then she splashed some water on her face from a deep wooden bowl that sat on the porch bench. She couldn't even remember the last time she felt so good and refreshed. Glancing up at Han, she noticed that he wasn't faring as well.

He stepped outside and set the chamber pot down on the porch. "Why is it so bright outside? It actually hurts my eyes!" he complained, squinting and shading his swollen eyes with his hand as though he were a vampire being blasted by direct sunlight.

"Maybe it's because we haven't seen this much sun in so long. I like it, it feels good," she said with a smile, closing her eyes again, letting the sun dry her face.

"It's probably because I barely slept." He quickly splashed his face and dried it with his tunic. He held his hand up to block the sun and gave one last look toward the sky, but he shook his head back down and wiped his tearing eyes. "Or maybe it's from that stupid leaf I ate. And all this time I couldn't wait to see the sun come out again. I guess I'll go empty our piss bowl," he said, picking up the chamber pot and heading out to the yard.

After a couple minutes of enjoying the morning sunlight, Greta took a deep cleansing breath and then stepped back inside to the dining room where Sendy was helping The Lady prepare breakfast.

"You're back!" Greta blurted out as she charged across the room and threw her arms around her.

Sendy knelt down to return her embrace and kissed her cheek. "Wow, look at you! Don't you look refreshed and happy this morning!"

Greta smiled, nodding her head enthusiastically. "Oh yes, I slept really well in my new bed. And last night, The Lady made us such a delicious stew with pie for dessert and everything!"

"There now, didn't I say you would like it here? And now we can enjoy a nice breakfast together; that is, unless you're not hungry anymore after that big dinner last night," she said with a playful smirk.

Greta knew she was being teased. She widened her eyes and nodded her head excitedly again, stretching her lips into a tight grin.

She gasped. "You are? If you keep eating like this, you're going to get fat!" she giggled, tickling her belly until Greta laughed out loud. "Ok, what do you say to helping us set the table? I'll teach you just the way she taught me."

When Han entered, they all turned in his direction. "Well, I can't say your brother looks as refreshed as you do," Sendy said to Greta as she studied his face. "I wish I could say good morning to you, but you don't look like you slept a wink."

"I slept ok." He opened his mouth again to speak but then quickly closed it.

"What is it, Han?" Sendy asked.

He looked down and then back up at her face, squinting one eye with his half-scrunched face, "I was just wondering what ever happened to Roland. Did you bring him back?"

The Lady passed into the room just as he asked the question. Sendy exchanged a cautious glance with her before continuing. "Yes, we found him, but he remains gravely ill. The Lady and I cleaned and dressed his wounds. We performed some... healing spells on him last night." She looked intently at him, almost suspiciously as she said this. "We revived him for a short time, but he remains very sick. He is resting now, and we mustn't disturb him."

"I see. Well, I'm glad he didn't die or anything," he replied respectfully enough.

Sendy smiled. "That is kind of you to say so, but it looks like he will have a long, slow recovery ahead of him."

"Does that mean you will stay here a little longer, so you can help take care of him until he is better?" Greta asked.

Sendy looked over to The Lady with her eyebrows raised. "If you feel you could use my help, I would be glad to stay here until he is back on his feet at least. What say you, My Lady?"

"I think that is a most splendid idea, my dear. My back does not allow me the stamina that I used to have, and my eyes do not allow me to see very well either. Perhaps you can teach our new little visitor some of the healing arts while you're here," she said, winking at Greta.

Her face beamed with pleasure at Sendy. "Oh, please do! I will be your best student ever. I promise!"

The back door to the kitchen opened and heavy footsteps plodded towards them. "Good morning to you all," Jehan's voice boomed. "Looks like you all decided to finally wake up."

They all greeted him with bright smiles.

"Sendy has offered to stay with us a little longer to help care for our new patient. Looks like we will have a full house!" The Lady informed him.

"They're going to teach me how to be a nurse so I can help out too," Greta told him, looking up as he towered above her.

He knelt down beside her, his knees creaking and cracking as he did. "Is that right? I think that is a fantastic idea. I bet you are a fast learner too. Am I right?"

She nodded her head happily, so excited she even felt a rush of chills behind her ears.

He then looked over to Han. "And I can teach you some things about gardening and repairs, and I can show you how to use the furnace too. What you say to that, young man?"

For the first time this morning she noticed a sparkle in his eyes. A look of determination came over him that she hadn't seen since their Papa first showed him how to cut and chop wood—kind of like how a man looks when he has a job to do.

"Yes, absolutely, I would love to help you work outside. My Papa is a woodcutter. He used to show me some things with his tools, but that was years ago, before the rains started."

"Very good. Then I bet you are a fast learner too. It's hard work, but I'm sure you will enjoy it, yes?"

"Don't worry about me, I like to work hard," he said eagerly.

"Well, I have just the thing to get you two started this morning," The Lady said, removing a warm loaf of gingerbread from the oven for all to share.

Chapter 21

HAN TOILED IN THE YARD ALL DAY LONG: chopping and hauling wood to the cellar, repairing the animal shed, tilling and raking the garden soil, milking the goats, cutting the wool from the sheep, collecting the ripened fruit and vegetables into a box, and on it went. Busy days passed by, one after another, until the days turned into weeks. Rain or no rain, he always had work to do outside with Jehan, while Greta worked inside with The Lady and Sendy. They always enjoyed some kind of bread with cheese or tart jelly for breakfast, a good hearty meal in late afternoon, and sometimes a bit of soup or desert before bedtime.

The color and fullness returned to Greta's cheeks, and her hair began to grow back over the wounded patch of scalp. He felt relieved to see his sister looking healthy again instead of like a "demon child" that she resembled after getting attacked by the bat. He used to tease her about her appearance, but now as they sat on the grass eating their afternoon snack, he told her how good she looked. She rewarded him with a genuinely appreciative smile, a healthy smile no longer marred by those puffy, red gums. She smiled much more after that which made him feel even better.

Growing eager for his own compliment, he decided to show off some of the new muscles he built up over the last few weeks. He stood before her in his breeches, grunting and flexing his arms and then puffing out his chest in funny poses like a muscle man in a circus, sending her giggle pitch to almost imperceptible levels.

Given how miserable he felt every day at home, he almost wondered why he felt so apprehensive about coming here in the first place. He still missed his mother, of course, and his old friend, Amis. He thought about them almost every day. He missed his Papa too and wondered if he was even still alive. He regretted the way he'd been treating him lately, but at the same time he couldn't seem to forgive him for giving in to his stepmother's demands.

For the most part, he enjoyed working in the yard and learning from Jehan, who took his time to explain everything and never made him feel stupid. He didn't realize how much there was to know about gardening.

He felt a rush of pride by demonstrating his skill with the axe, using proper body position and arm swing. Jehan boomed with laughter and cheered him on with every deep chop. After he finally split through the thick log, Han raised his foot on top of it, thrust his fists to his waist, and puffed out his chest in a show of domination over his conquered foe.

Jehan enjoyed watching him show off, clapping his hands and doubling over with laughter, "Oh, you a big man now!"

Just to show him up, Jehan took the axe and split the next log with one mighty stroke and then mocked the same macho pose. Han tried his best to look impressed, considering how his Papa split even bigger logs than that with a single chop.

He got used to bringing the wood down to the cellar after a while too. He learned how to use the furnace for smoking larger quantities of meat to make it last longer. He also learned how it served a more important purpose: producing charcoal. By closing the solid metal door over the grating, it turned the furnace into a superheated kiln. When the wood logs are placed on the rack above the fire and burned over several days, they transformed into a much lighter fuel called charcoal, which burned much more efficiently than wood or even coal. The Lady used the charcoal to heat her oven and fireplace, and then Jehan would cart off the excess to be sold over in the next town for a decent profit.

When Jehan wasn't working or teaching Han, he usually relaxed in his big wooden chair and played the fiddle. The lively melody brightened his spirits and lifted his imagination while he toiled away with his chores.

One rainy day, he called Han over to where he played under the shelter of the barn. He taught him some basic notes and chords until he was able to put together a simple tune.

Han thanked him and then looked up at him with his half-scrunched face. "Jehan, can I ask you something personal?"

"You want to know where I come from?" Jehan surmised with a smile, taking back his fiddle.

Han nodded his head politely. "Yes, please—if you don't mind, that is."

"Why should I mind?" he asked, broadening his smile as he strummed quietly with his fingers. "I come from a land very far and very different from here, called Africa. Have you heard of it?"

"Africa?" Han sounded out the unfamiliar word and shook his head slowly. "Does everyone in Africa have dark skin like you?"

Jehan chuckled, "Yes, everyone's skin looks like this in the part of Africa I come from. But if you go further north toward the great sea, their skin is almost as light as yours."

Han stared at him with amazement. "So how did you end up way over here?"

He chuckled again and tousled his hair, "That is a long story from a long time ago, my little friend."

Han's imagination began to go wild with excitement and wonder. He gazed into the rain until he couldn't hold it in any longer. "Can you at least tell me a little bit about it? I've always wanted to learn about faraway lands. I've never been anywhere besides Riquewihr, and now here. Please, just a short story? How old were you? Did you sail in a big boat with sails? Did you come by yourself?"

"Ok, ok, ok, I tell you," he laughed deeply, holding up his hands to stop Han's barrage of questions. "I grew up in a very small village. My father was a healing man—we call them shaman." His eyes widened, his voice growing with enthusiasm, as he went on to explain. "Shamans use gifts from the earth and summon magical powers to heal the sick, protect the village and curse enemies; they pray to the sky for rain, welcome all new babies into this world, and help the dead transport safely to their eternal resting place.

"Just like here, the son always takes after his father, so he taught me to become a shaman," he said proudly with a thump on his chest. "I took over his duties after he died, and I ushered him safely to his eternal home." He closed his eyes and paused.

Han stared at him with bewilderment. "You're a shaman? You can do magic?"

He nodded.

"Did you teach Sendy some of that magic? I heard her chanting in the forest when the wolves were chasing us, and then they stopped...for a little while at least." He jumped to his feet, "Could you teach me how to be a shaman?"

Jehan focused his eyes on Han, his expression turned somber. "To learn the arts of the shaman, you must open your mind to knowledge that is forbidden to Christians. You must appreciate the importance of sacrifice, recognize the presence of our ancestral spirits and learn how to interact with them."

Han backed away without realizing, remembering the horrific ritual with the goat they performed on Roland. "Oh, I didn't know it was like that. I...better not...I'm sorry—"

Jehan reached out and placed a firm hand on his shoulder. "It's ok, Han. It is only a choice, you do not need to learn it, and I do not expect you to understand it either," he said sincerely, patting his cheek with his other hand.

Han sighed with relief. "Thank you, sir, I just don't want to get into any trouble with anybody, you know? My stepmother told me I could get burned alive for talking about any of that stuff. She calls it evil...but I can tell that you're not evil...right Jehan?"

Jehan shook his head with a puzzled expression for a moment before responding. "Evil has no meaning as my people understand it. Like you, we believe in only one almighty creator, The Lord of Light, but he is also the almighty destroyer. For every creation there must first come destruction. In order to live, one must consume something else that lives. The thing being eaten or destroyed may perceive the act as evil, but the consumer certainly does not. There is no evil in it; there is no good in it. Do you understand?"

Han nodded his head. "I think so. I never thought of it like that before." He thought for a minute in silence. "But what if I eat a piece of fruit from a tree? I'm not destroying the life of the tree. That couldn't possibly be perceived as evil, right? Unless you're Adam in the Garden of Eden, of course."

Jehan put on a big smile and chuckled. "Oh, there you go, everyone always has to ask about the damn fruit! Now, you want to talk about good and evil, or you want me to finish telling you my story of how I got here?"

"Your story, please!" Han sat back down on the ground, his legs crossed under him, his hands propped under his chin, showing his full attention.

Jehan went back to slowly, almost hypnotically, plucking his fiddle as he resumed his tale.

"One day, a group of missionaries arrived to discuss their religion of Christianity. They treated us with generosity and kindness, offering us food and gifts, to which we were most grateful. Nevertheless, I forbid them from speaking about this One God and his son, Jesus, unless they could convince me of their strange new religion first. We talked for two full days about both of our religions. In the end, I thanked them for their aid and for the interesting debate—and then I asked them to leave our village.

"Weeks later, I received word that their company of missionaries had been attacked by a local tribe. They killed most of them but kept one woman as prisoner. When I arrived at their camp, she looked barely alive and caged like an animal. I was able to negotiate her freedom for some of the valuable items that her company had left us. I healed her with medicines and the aid of the spirits, nourished her with our food. In time, we resumed our debate and eventually I convinced her to see the world as I do. At last, she allowed me to teach her to practice the ways of the shaman and our ancient religion."

He paused as his plucking transformed into a brief melody, and then faded back to a sporadic strum or single note once he continued on with his story.

"She remained as a guest in my village for more than two years until she decided to return to her homeland. She asked me to come with her to help her cultivate the land and continue her father's business of producing charcoal since he was getting too old." He paused to look up at Han with a smile, "I can tell by your expression that you know who this woman is by now?"

Han's eyes widened even further. "The Lady!"

Jehan smiled and nodded. "She is my most gifted student. In fact, you could say she even taught me things that I only *thought* I understood. I made a difficult decision to leave my family, my village, my life as I knew it. By this time, my own son had come of age. I had prepared him to take over my duties as shaman to our people. The prospect of traveling across the great sea to foreign lands intrigued and excited me—an opportunity I would never get again, and if I refused, I knew I would always regret it. So, after all these years, here I am."

Han saw Jehan in a different way now. "Thank you for sharing your story with me. I can't imagine traveling overseas to a foreign land." But then he thought of his own father and swallowed hard. "I bet you really miss your son. Have you ever returned to see him again?"

He looked down and lost his smile but continued softly strumming. "Yes, of course I miss him, but to travel back there on my own is quite expensive, not to mention dangerous for a man of my skin. Besides, after all these years, I doubt my village even survived."

Han creased his brow and remained silent for a minute before he looked back up at Jehan, "It must be hard not knowing if he is still alive, and if he still thinks about you. I still wonder if my Papa is alive. I think about him a lot, and it's only been a few weeks."

"Leaving someone you love is always hard, but we must move on and let our life path lead us where it will." He strummed another slow melody, then stood up, sighed, and stretched. "It seems the rain is letting up. What do you say we get back to work?"

A few days later, Jehan left for the nearest town to sell the charcoal, get some needed supplies, and visit some old friends. He said he would probably be gone for a couple of weeks and left the yard work in Han's now capable hands. He left several sizable logs in the stable, enough to keep him busy chopping for a good while. Han was sorry to see him go; working by himself in the yard became rather dull.

The evening that Jehan departed, Han offered his reassurance to The Lady that he would keep up with the yard work while he's gone. As he talked though, a disturbing sensation crept over him. He sensed that she wasn't really listening to him at all; instead, her face slackened, and her glazed eyes seemed fixed upon his flesh. The smile that she initially put on began to slowly transform into something strange as her expression took on a look of yearning, of hunger, of craving. A slobber of drool dribbling from the corner of her mouth finally aroused The Lady out of her daze.

"Oh, I know you will, my little dumpling," she said, giving his cheek a hard squeeze.

He remembered seeing that same kind of crazed expression only once before, at a church picnic of all places. He couldn't help but notice how one of the fat priests stared with eager anticipation at the juicy pig roast, licking his thick, moistened lips as the cook sliced it in front of him. With his flabby jowls, bulbous nose, and small round eyes that seemed too close together, he actually resembled the pig staring him in the face. Han recalled how his lascivious expression didn't change as his eyes roved around from the pig to the children seated around the table.

Over the last few weeks, he had noticed something odd about the way The Lady regarded him when they spoke: a quick dart of her eyes from his face to his arms or legs and then back again to his face, a squeeze of his arm or a pinch of his cheek as she passed by. She often called him one of her nicknames while forcing her lips into a weird grin. He remembered seeing that grin the first day he met her and noticed something peculiar about it in the back of his mind. But the more he thought about it, the more it bothered him: like she was smiling to herself about some mischievous secret, while her eyes appeared to be studying him somehow.

Thankfully, Han got to spend most of his time in the yard, and away from The Lady. One day, after carrying down another load of wood to the furnace for what felt like the hundredth time, he grew curious to explore the rest of the cellar. There wasn't much to explore really, just some old equipment and broken tools and what looked to be remnants of old kids' toys and shoes strewn around the floor. A few rats scurried about but always kept their distance.

Then he noticed some small primitive looking pictures etched in black on the walls and wooden posts. He hadn't really paid any attention to them before. Most were pictures of animals like wolves, goats, and owls, others of children and houses and trees. One that caught his attention was of a woman wearing a tall pointy hat, her arms upraised, standing beside a podium or alter of some kind and in front of a crowd of children. An indistinct shape surrounded her, a cloud perhaps, rendered in a different shade of charcoal. As he looked closer, he could barely make out a faint reddish hue underlying the cloud. He had to back up again and view it from just the right angle to realize that the cloud was actually a flame; the light from the furnace somehow lent the image a glowing red color that flickered almost like a true flame within the borders of the charcoal outline, dancing around the image of the woman with the weird pointy hat.

He saw another miniature sketch, again where the light shown brightest. This time it seemed to represent a face of some sort. He had to study it for several minutes to make it out. He slowly backed away again until the image suddenly focused into a stark and terrifying clarity--the unmistakable visage of a demon—that sadistic grin, those black eyes that seemed to pierce his soul, and two twisted horns atop his head. The flames of the furnace reflected brightly and directly off its face, bestowing a lurid and frightful appearance, pulsating with rage and fury.

A scrabbling sound from across the room startled him out of his trance, followed by the sound of rats scurrying hastily around the cellar. For the briefest of moments, he thought he saw a pair of eyes staring back at him from the darkest shadows. Merely a fleeting flicker of light flashed off the eyes before disappearing, barely enough time to register in his mind but just long enough to make him look twice. He listened closely, peering into the darkness. *Just silence and shadows.* He knew it couldn't be a rat since the eyes were too high off the floor, and they weren't little dots either—they looked distinctly human. *It's probably just my stupid imagination again*, he reassured himself.

As he followed the wall to the other side of the room, away from the light of the furnace, his hand passed over a doorway. He felt for the handle and pulled—locked tight, piquing his curiosity.

He moved back towards the light until he reached the steps. He took one last look around to be sure that he didn't see any more movement or mysterious pair of eyes before heading back up. His eyes strained to adjust to the light of day as he closed the cellar door. When he looked toward the yard, he realized he was being watched. Standing rigidly with her hands on her hips, The Lady scowled at him before swiftly turning away around the corner of the house.

Chapter 22

GUARIN HEARD THE HEAVY FOOTSTEPS of a group of men marching up the steps of the prison tower. Whenever he heard men coming toward the prison in a group, that usually meant they were coming to bring a prisoner to the interrogation room for questioning, and then he would hear the agonizing screams. Yesterday it was Barous, but he knew they were coming for him this time.

Three men emerged from the darkness and stopped in front of his cell door, Father Linhart along with two grim-faced guards. Guarin recognized one of them as the gaunt, scar-faced man—Joff was his name. Without waiting for him to rise, they yanked him from his cot, shoving him out of the prison room and down the hallway, before stopping in front of a heavy wooden door. Joff unlocked the bolt, slid the iron rod aside from the door, and then, heaving with all of his strength, pulled the great oaken door open. A crude wooden stairway led down into a dank dungeon room.

"Let's go, nice and easy," said Joff. "We wouldn't want you to fall down the steps and break your neck."

As he descended into the chamber, his legs stopped in the middle of the stairway as he felt his breath leave him, a heavy weight sinking from his chest to his abdomen. *This won't be pleasant*, he thought, staring at the grand instruments of torture arrayed before him. He almost started whimpering like a little boy who got himself into big trouble and there was nothing he could do about it. He swallowed hard, reminding himself that he was a man, and he needed to stay strong, or at least act strong.

An open window built deep into the thick stone wall provided adequate natural light to the modest sized room. Hanging menacingly above him, a massive wooden beam attached to the high ceiling supported a long, heavy chain looping through a pulley system. One end of the chain wound tightly around a horizontal drum-like winch with three long wooden spokes jutting out from it, resembling the captain's wheel of a ship. A horizontal wooden rod suspended like a trapeze from the other end of the chain.

"Don't worry, Mr. Guarin, we won't be using the strappado today," said The Cleric.

A sturdy narrow table, about six feet long, sat across the room from the winch. Against the wall, a smaller table displayed about ten different instruments, most bearing sharp blades or points for cutting, some clearly meant for bludgeoning, and others appearing so barbaric that he feared to imagine their use. A few other objects on the table caught his eye as well, such as tubing, some kind of a funnel, and several large jugs of water.

"Keep moving," the guard barked, shoving him from behind.

When he reached the bottom of the steps, they lifted him up and slammed him onto the wooden table. He didn't bother to resist as they secured his arms and legs with leather straps. They secured his head between two wooden blocks with another strap over his forehead.

The black silhouette of The Cleric moved over his vision, his features veiled in shadows beneath his cowl until he brought the candlelight closer, accentuating the deep crevices lining his face and brow.

"Are you thirsty, Mr. Guarin? We have been most kind not to have deprived you of food and water during your stay here, wouldn't you agree? While I am in charge here of Thieves' Tower, no one shall be deprived of these basic needs. You should be thankful to us for how we have treated you thus far. You would not have even survived your illness had we not brought you here." He paused to cast a glare of intimidation before continuing. "Your importance to me in this case has just risen substantially. I've received word from an eyewitness that you had a long talk with the Templar here in Riquewihr. You told me that you only met him briefly by the waterfall, did you not?"

"That is true, but Barous and I were not talking about Templars, we were talking about the witch you brought up on stage. I didn't share that with you because he didn't tell me any information that you would find useful."

"Is that so? I don't like it when you keep any information from me, Mr. Guarin. Let me decide what is useful and what is not. In any case, I will offer you one last chance before I begin to compel the truth from you. If you agree to testify in trial that you are certain he is a Templar based on your conversations, then I will let you off this table and reward you with some of our finest food and ale. If not, you get water. In fact, I will give you so much water, your stomach will nearly burst open, but I will try to stop just short of that. This is a new technique that I learned in Paris—quite effective for getting the information that I want, but most unpleasant, I'm afraid."

"You may give me all the water you want. I will not be coerced into lying for you so that you can reap your 'just' reward."

"Games, Mr. Guarin. We both know you are just playing games with me," he replied in a patronizing tone. Then he put on a sarcastic frown. "But I don't want to play anymore. After you've had your fill, I don't think you will want to play anymore either."

The Cleric held up his hand, into which the guard placed a crude wooden funnel with a hollow reed attached to the narrow end. Something resembling a piece of pig intestine, about as long as his finger, dangled from the tip of the reed. Joff proceeded to clamp a metal pincer tightly over his nose, followed by a foul-tasting wooden wedge between his teeth to hold his mouth open. Before he could even wonder why he would need help keeping his mouth open, given that was all he had left to breath with, The Cleric moved the tip of the reed over his face, the piece of intestine flopping and jiggling about like a worm. He then carefully fed it past his tongue and into his throat, his lips pursed nearly into a pucker, and his eyes focused on his task like a surgeon. He met some resistance as he tried to force it further down into his throat. Leaning in for a closer look, his neck scrotum lightly brushed across the tip of Guarin's nose.

The Cleric plucked his mouth open. "I'm going to need you to swallow now, Mr. Guarin. Don't worry, you can still breath around the tube."

This induced a fit of spasmodic gagging and retching that lasted several minutes as he felt the tube sliding past his throat. Just as he was able to calm himself enough to breathe again, he heard The Cleric try to offer him some words of encouragement. "There, now that wasn't so bad, was it?"

He nodded to Joff who proceeded to pour a large jug of water into the funnel, slowly distending his stomach. The pressure intensified until it induced an overwhelming sense of nausea and pain. Once he finally stopped pouring, Guarin sucked in breaths as best he could around the reed jammed into his throat.

"Very good, Mr. Guarin! I'm impressed that you are able to hold that down. You must have been very thirsty indeed," he chuckled, lightly patting his pregnant-looking belly. "We're going to let that settle in your stomach for a moment, we don't want it to burst open so soon. Joff, would you kindly bring another one of those water jugs for him, please?" He then turned back to Guarin, displaying a polite smile, "It will be just a moment."

Guarin knew that he would be vomiting up the water soon, with or without the other jug, but when it spilled into his stomach, he was unprepared for the degree of pain and nausea that he experienced. As his abdomen continued to distend, he felt a sickening and suffocating sense of dread. He tried to thrash and wrench his mouth away, but the straps permitted his head no movement at all. Just as he thought his stomach would truly burst, the water began spewing back out through the funnel, soaking himself and the guard, until the reed itself was forced out by the geyser erupting from his mouth. When the air hunger in his lungs forced him to inhale, he sucked in the water that had pooled in his mouth, stimulating a harsh coughing fit that fought against his burning desire to pull in a breath.

After what seemed like several long minutes of spasmodic coughing and struggling to catch his breath, he felt the slimy, wriggling worm again on his tongue, followed by the reed tube poking into his raw throat. This set off another round of gagging and retching, quickly followed by The Cleric forcing even more water into his stomach than the first time. This cycle repeated itself three more times before they finally removed the wedges from his mouth and unclamped his nose.

"Have you had enough of this nonsense, Mr. Guarin? Is there something you would like to tell me now?"

Guarin was in such a state of shock that he barely heard his words. Still trying to clear his throat, The Cleric nodded to the guard to resume another round. He finally relented as he felt the clamp tighten over his nose again. "Stop, please! I will tell you the truth of what I know! No more, I beg you!" His voice came out in a hoarse whisper that burned his throat.

The Cleric smiled under the shadows of his cowl, first to him, then to the guards. "You see how effective my techniques can be? I believe this water treatment has cured him of his desire to lie to us. You may let him up now."

Once the straps were removed, they pulled him up to a sitting position. His body felt limp, requiring support from the guards to keep from slumping back to the table.

"Now, what is it you wanted to tell me?"

The Cleric's face appeared blurry, his words muffled and distant and drawn out, as though speaking in slow motion. Guarin opened his mouth to speak, but instead regurgitated another bolus of water, spilling out of his mouth and over his chest. He tried to speak again, but his own words were like mush, and then his vision faded to black.

Chapter 25

WHILE HAN SPENT MOST OF HIS DAYS TOILING out in the yard, Greta worked mostly inside with The Lady keeping everything spotless. She followed the same routine every day: clear and wipe the table and countertops after breakfast, wash the dishes, mop the floors, and assist The Lady in preparing for dinner. After that, she had to repeat the routine and also clean the oven, which The Lady always closely inspected to be sure it was immaculately clean. Once a week, she would have to clean out the fireplace in the living room, which always left her hands and face coated with black soot and ash. When the chores were finished, she taught her how to knit and mend clothing, make dolls out of thick yarn, and even how to design and fabricate interesting styles of hats.

Despite working hard every day, Greta appreciated all that she learned from The Lady. She was a much better cook than Aunt Lutrud and her own mother ever were.

After just the few weeks since they arrived, she felt like she had grown three years older and ten pounds heavier. Her hair had grown out and felt softer to the touch, allowing Sendy to style it in different ways. She loved Sendy and thought of her almost like a big sister, but lately she has been too busy in Roland's room or sleeping in her own room. Apparently, he got really sick again with a high fever last night and they feared the worst. She could hear him moaning from her room through much of the night.

The Craving

While mending some clothes on the couch, Greta saw them both wearily leaving his room. The Lady went directly to her bed. Sendy looked about to do the same until Greta caught her eye, peering expectantly from the living room. She put on a smile and walked over to sit beside her.

"I'm sorry that I haven't had time to spend as much time with you as I had hoped," Sendy said, running her fingers through Greta's golden hair, delicately brushing it behind her ear. "I know we had promised when you arrived that we would teach you about healing and caring for the sick, but she has kept you so busy with all these other chores. The Lady has been up all of last night with Roland and she needs to rest now, so I could really use your help. Would you like to start tonight?"

Greta hesitated before agreeing. She felt her stomach flop when she thought about going into that smelly room of his but quickly decided she would rather spend as much time learning from Sendy as she could.

"I think I'm ready. Thank you, Sendy." she replied, trying to look more excited than nervous. Still, the thought of seeing Roland for the first time since the attack weighed on her. "Has he awakened yet?" she asked.

"He comes and goes. He doesn't speak yet and sleeps most of the time, but occasionally he will open his eyes and look around for a little while. He swallows when I place some food in his mouth." Sendy offered her a look of concern, as though she could sense her anxiety. "I want you to know that he doesn't look nearly the same as he did when you last saw him. He has lost a lot of weight and the color is gone from his face. His wounds haven't healed yet which is causing that odor you've probably noticed near his room. Don't be frightened, I just want you to be prepared when you see him."

"It's ok. I remember how my mother looked when she was sick…before she died…and I saw lots of people that looked like they were dying in the streets of Riquewihr. I even saw a whole cart load of rotting dead bodies being carried out. Nothing could ever smell worse than that."

"Oh my goodness, is it that bad in town? Well then, if you have seen all of that then I think you will be just fine," Sendy reassured her. "I'm going to lie down for an hour or two, and then after dinner we can get started."

Those were just about the longest two hours that she could ever remember, her thoughts consumed with apprehension. The Lady didn't even come out of her room to join them for dinner, so Han looked more relaxed and became more talkative at the table than usual. But when Sendy asked him to join them in Roland's room, he stretched and yawned and tried to make his face more tired than he looked a minute ago, saying he was exhausted and wanted to go to bed early.

Leaving Han to clean up the dishes, Sendy led her down the darkened hallway toward Roland's room, turned the handle and let the door swing open. Despite the open window, the sour stench of death that remained stagnant in the room rushed out to envelop them in a thick cloud of miasma. Greta coughed and covered her mouth, fighting back the urge to vomit.

Sendy stepped inside and walked to the bedside set against the opposing wall. Greta followed her into the room but stopped to take it all in. She felt like she had just passed through the threshold into the underworld of the dead. Two candles glowed on nightstands set to each side of the bed, casting an eerie light onto each side of Roland's bloodless face. Because of his fever, the sheets were cast aside, exposing Roland's mostly naked, corpse-like body. Large pillows behind his back propped him up, but his eyes remained closed. Deep red scars lined his face and neck, some remained open, weeping a clear fluid onto his pillow and sheets beneath him. His fingers and toes looked black and bony from frostbite.

She noticed curious symbols drawn or tattooed in black over his skin. The most prominent of them covered his bare chest: an empty circle surmounted by a horizontal crescent moon—*or was it a set of horns?* Each of his cheeks bore an image of a cross, not a Christian cross though, more like a plus sign. A diagram of a spoked wheel was etched onto his forehead. The setting looked more like an elaborate funeral display than a bed of healing, making her knees tremble.

Sendy stepped toward Greta. "Come," she beckoned, holding out her hand to join her beside his bed.

Greta shuddered, then accepted Sendy's hand, grasping it tightly.

She looked back to the doorway. "Did you change your mind, Han?" Sendy asked as he stood staring hypnotically from the hall.

He shook his head slowly and backed away to his own room. "No...that's ok. Good night."

Greta surveyed the room and saw more symbols painted in broad prominent strokes. The wall facing Roland featured a large spiral diagram, while each side wall displayed an encircled five-pointed star.

"What do these symbols mean?" Greta asked in a whisper, sounding more like a whimper. "I saw this one carved into the tree out back."

"These are called Pentagrams; they are a symbol of protection, a symbol that has been used for thousands of years. I've been told that even the early Christians wore Pentagrams as jewelry. The spiral symbol represents spirituality and the journey of life. Roland is on a most arduous journey right now. When he wakes, I try to get him to follow the spiral inward. It gives him something to focus on and calms him down if he becomes anxious."

They walked closer to the bed. His breathing seemed kind of shallow and faster than she would expect from somebody that was sleeping. His scarred face appeared much worse than she had imagined; several large gashes extended from his cheek to his scalp, crossing over his left eye.

"What are these symbols on his face and chest?" she asked, tracing a finger along his forehead. She couldn't feel an impression so assumed it was drawn rather than etched permanently into his skin.

"We can talk about the meaning of these symbols after we have finished, for now you can think about what they might mean to you."

"Yes, of course." She looked down to a tray on the nightstand containing a small pile of ground herbs. Sendy picked it up and held it close to her nose.

She raised her eyebrows with delight. "It smells really nice. What is it?"

"It is a mixture of cinnamon and sage. It doesn't take the smell away, but it does help a little bit at least. Here, this works much better," she said as she opened a drawer and removed a fuzzy narrow twig. "This is lavender incense, it burns slowly and has a calming scent." She placed it on an ornate metal tray atop the nightstand, then lit the tip by striking a flint mechanism.

Greta didn't think she would ever be able to rid her memory of this stench, but the lavender helped quite a bit.

"Now for the hard part," Sendy sighed. "I need you to help me roll him over onto his side so we can clean his wounds. Be ready, the odor is worse when we turn him," she cautioned, handing her a cloth. "Here, tie this around your face to cover your nose and mouth."

Greta couldn't imagine how it could get much worse. It smelled just like the cart of bodies, except this was inside with nowhere for the smell to go.

"I'm going to reach over and pull from his shoulder, I want you to push his hip onto its side," she said, placing Greta's hands where they needed to be. "Ready? Push!"

With a grunt, they heaved him over. Roland groaned but didn't otherwise arouse.

"There, great job!"

Greta immediately noticed the extensive open wounds covering his back just as they blasted their reek into her face, as though emanating from a decaying death pit containing a hundred bodies. She retched. Puss oozed out from some of the swollen pockets, some of them rimmed with dusky or black tissue. Tiny little worms danced around, plunging into and out of the gooey slop, seeming to move way too fast for their size. It looked like a gruesome painting with the colors of red and yellow and black and green. A wide gash across his lower back became a sinister grin, just as the open wounds over each scapula, and the large one on the center of his back transformed the whole masterpiece into a most grisly visage glaring back at her. Her vision began to fade, and her legs trembled until she felt herself collapsing to the floor.

She awoke with her back against the wall to the aroma of the pleasant spice that Sendy wafted before her nose. "Ahh, there she is, waking up now," she said, waving a fan in front of her face. Greta tried to stand back up. "Ah-ah, just stay where you are for now. Look at me. Can you see me ok?"

She crossed her legs under her, sitting up straighter against the wall. Her cheeks felt flushed and another wave of nausea struck her. She swallowed hard and shuddered. "Yes. I'm so sorry. I must have passed out. I think I'm ok now."

"That's alright, my sunshine. Just rest here a minute before you stand up again. Take some deep breaths," she said, dabbing a cool, damp cloth on her forehead.

She felt embarrassed more than anything, wanting nothing more than to impress Sendy. "I'm sorry, I guess I'm not much of a nurse."

"Oh, don't you worry about that. This can happen to anyone, especially for the first time. You're going to do just fine if you want to try again."

She crinkled her nose in disgust. "What are all those things crawling around on his back?"

"Yes, I forgot to warn you about those. They are just maggots—larvae of flies. Believe it or not, they actually help the wounds heal faster by consuming the dead tissue, so we just leave them there for now. They usually just fly out the window once they become flies. You must have seen maggots before though, haven't you?"

Greta's face showed utter revulsion. "I guess so. Only on dead animals, but even then I try not to look too close."

Sendy smiled. "Don't worry, they won't bother you since your skin is nice and healthy." She called for Han but he didn't answer. "He must be sleeping. Now don't move or try to get up. I'm going to bring you some cool water from outside to drink. I'll be right back. You're alright for now?"

Greta nodded nervously. "I'm ok, but hurry back, Sendy." After a minute alone in the dim room, she began to feel scared and anxious and wanted to get out for a minute to clear her head. She stood up and felt steady enough on her feet so moved toward the hallway, until she heard the sound of Roland's voice.

"Stop."

She turned to look back at him. His eyes were closed. She turned toward the door again, this time in haste.

"Help me," he grunted.

She didn't want to stop but she did. His eyes remained closed. She took a closer look and noticed that his eyes were moving rapidly behind his lids. *He is just dreaming.* He said something else, just a whisper now. *What was it, a name?* Again, he whispered, clearer now, perhaps a name that sounded all too familiar. *It sounded like...no, it couldn't be.* She crept closer. "Guarin." *Unmistakable this time. Why would he say Papa's name?* She searched his face for meaning.

"Go on, what about Guarin?" she coaxed him.

He mumbled something in a whisper. She leaned in closer. A sudden jerk of his hand caught her forearm in a tight clutch, his grip as cold as ice. A scream caught in her throat. The tips of his bony fingers were black and the nails were gone, leaving a tapered appearance, more like talons than fingers. She tried to jerk her arm free but his grasp held tightly. She looked up into his penetrating gaze, his left eye scarred into a milky white slate, his right eye burning fiercely like an emerald flame into her own. She screamed. This time it came out rampant and raging, a wild scream of terror and desperation that pierced the silence, a frightful scream loud enough to rouse the souls of the dead.

Greta jerked and twisted her arm until, at last, she wrenched it free. Making a dash for the door, she ran into Sendy just as she entered, spilling the pitcher of water onto her and the floor. Still lost in a panic, she tried to run past, but Sendy held onto her, spinning her out into the hallway. She kneeled down and hugged her tightly, trying to calm her down. "It's alright, you're ok. Tell me what happened. Don't be scared." Greta breathed a heavy sigh as she stroked her back for comfort. "I'm sorry, I shouldn't have left you alone."

Han opened his door just as The Lady opened hers and called out from the end of the hall, both clearly alarmed and asking what had happened.

"Yes, I think she just got scared, that's all. Please, go back to bed. She just needs a minute to calm down."

"My word!" exclaimed The Lady before turning back and slamming her bedroom door shut behind her.

Greta cried and drained her tears onto her shoulder until she could speak. "I'm sorry, Sendy. I know you told me not to get up, but I just wanted to get out of the room. I couldn't breathe and didn't want to be alone with him in there for another second."

"I understand, believe me, don't worry about that." Sendy grasped Greta's shoulders and looked into her eyes. "Tell me though, what made you so scared to scream like that?"

"He spoke to me", she blubbered. "He spoke my father's name."

Sendy cast her a look of doubt.

"He did, I swear he did. Then he whispered something else. When I leaned closer to hear him better, he suddenly grabbed my arm. He looked like he wanted to kill me! That's when I screamed."

Sendy looked over to where Roland lie motionless and asleep, then placed her hands over her cheeks. "I promise I won't leave you alone with him in that room anymore, you understand?" Greta nodded. Sendy kissed the top of her head, then bowed forward so that their foreheads were touching. "Good, now follow me outside to get some more water and fresh air, and then we'll start over again, sound good?" As she nodded, their foreheads rolled up and down together, making them giggle.

Chapter 24.

GUARIN AWOKE ON THE FLOOR OF HIS CELL in a puddle of his bloody urine and liquid feces. Rolling out of it onto his hands and knees, he retched until the taste of bitter bile lit his throat on fire, which he spewed into the putrid puddle as well. *This is happening much too often of late.* He crawled away, slumped his back against the cold stone wall, wondering how many more times he would find himself staring into his brightly colored blend of body fluids.

"Are you surviving over there, my friend?" asked the welcoming voice of Barous.

"Barely, that was much worse than I ever could have imagined," Guarin rasped.

"What did they do, hit you with the water cure?"

"Is that what they call it?" He winced from a strong hiccup that nearly sent his chest into spasm, then let out a stifled groan.

"Just be glad they didn't mess with your balls, that's about as bad as it gets."

"The man is a cleric! What would he want with my balls?"

"These kinds of men will do just about anything to get someone to talk if they want it badly enough. Listen, if you haven't already, I'm going to confess when they return. I cannot bear the pain of another suffering on my behalf. I have escaped persecution for much longer than I could have hoped for all these years. As I said before, you did nothing to deserve this."

"Neither did you, Barous. I am not a world traveler like yourself, but I have seen enough to understand what drives powerful and ambitious men, even in the best of times. Now, through these years of desperation, it is easy to see how vices like greed corrupts our very souls. From what you have told me, it corrupts even those we are supposed to hold in the highest regard, including popes and kings." He paused. "Promise me you will not admit to anything, for your word will go against what I intend to say, and my efforts will be in vain. So far, they only have Lutrud's word against my own."

"Your courage and fortitude are unrivaled, my friend. I have admired many men for less; still, I beg you to reconsider."

Guarin found himself smiling from the compliment. "I thank you for your kind words, but surely you must have witnessed the bravery of men mightier than me through your travels."

"Mightier, yes, but few willing to stand up for principle and loyalty as you are doing. I believe you are correct in what you said a moment ago: the more power one holds, the more corrupt they become, with a couple notable exceptions. I've already told you about the Grand Master, Jaques de Molay. Dante is another great man that I admire, a man who prides himself on principle over money or power."

"Dante? I am not familiar with the name," he admitted, his chest spasming from another violent hiccup.

"Dante Alighieri, a famous Italian poet and politician. He preferred exile from his beloved home in Florence to paying a fine and public penance to the city for alleged crimes that he swears he did not commit. I had the great pleasure of meeting him just last year during my travels through Verona. Quite an interesting man, possessing deep knowledge of Christianity and philosophy alike. He read me some passages from an epic poem he is writing, called Inferno. He takes the reader on a tour through Hell itself, introducing us to famous souls such as Virgil and Homer, Cleopatra and Julius Caesar, the monster Cerberus, and Satan himself."

"This Dante sounds like a fascinating man. If only I knew how, I think I would enjoy reading a book like that. If I see a word often enough, like on a storefront, I'll eventually remember what it means, and I might even recognize the word if I see it again somewhere else. I just can't fathom how you can possibly remember the meaning of all those countless words in a book, and then be able to put them all together into a story."

Barous chuckled, "It's not as difficult as all that, my friend. You can quickly learn to sound out letters into words that you already know. You don't need to memorize every word. Writing is the same thing, but sometimes more fun because you can create and write down your own story or poem."

He heard Barous laughing to himself again. Feeling embarrassed, Guarin went on to explain, "I'm sorry, it's just that nobody has ever taught me the first thing about reading. Lutrud started teaching the children…"

"Oh no, I'm not laughing at you. I was just remembering a funny poem I wrote together with some of the other knights while traveling through the Holy Land—more of a fable actually. I'm sure you've told your children some of the old Aesop's fables to get them to sleep?"

"Hmmph," he let out his own little chuckle, "Just as my own parents told to me. The stories always seem to have the same silly names of animals like The Fox and the Hare, or the Cock and the Mouse, or The Lion and the Ass."

Barous shouted back enthusiastically, "Exactly! That's why we just decided to call our story, The Cock and The Ass."

An unexpected burst of genuine laughter escaped Guarin for the first time that he could remember. "You've got to be kidding me! I can't wait to hear this!"

As Barous recited his bawdy tale, the humor tickled at places deep within him, arousing sensations that had been lost for so long, and yet felt so familiar as they bubbled up into laughter. The rising sound of amusement from the other prisoners, who had remained mostly silent until now, became infectious as the tale went on, his own laughter escalating until it finally piqued in a breathless cachinnation, inducing his cheeks and torso into a euphoric spasm of glee. "That is the craziest damn thing I've ever heard! I didn't even think it was possible to laugh that hard!" He let out another peal of laughter. "I lost all control and literally crapped the rest of that water out of me at the end there!"

Barous and the others let out another round of boisterous howls and guffaws. "I thought I heard something; thought maybe you were just providing sound effects. You alright over there?"

"My face feels numb, and I think I pulled a muscle from my ribs to my belly, but otherwise I feel great! I'm sorry, but that is just so wrong. Please, don't ever try to write a story for children. The Cleric would hang you by your balls if he heard that story!"

He laughed, "Yes, you're probably right about that. At least I know I can trust you to keep it secret from him."

"It's been so long since I laughed like that, I thought I'd forgotten how! It's like I'd been storing it up all these years inside of me until it finally came pouring out. Thank you, Barous, I really needed that."

The sound of the cellar door grated open, arresting their attention from a fleeting moment of mirth back to the dire reality of their situation. Captain Erec entered, bearing a large bucket of water and a relatively clean loincloth. He set the bucket down on the floor, then proceeded to Guarin's cell and rattled the lock open.

"Looks like you survived to see another day," he said, then looked down at his mess on the floor and let out a dry wretch. "Come with me... You're going to have to get your own ass up. I don't want to step one foot closer into your filth," said the Captain, shaking his head with disgust—*or was it pity?* "You've been sick since I picked you up at your home last week. What the hell is the matter with you anyhow?"

"Between my kidney stone and the gallons of water they forced down my throat yesterday, I'd say I'm doing pretty well actually," Guarin rasped, struggling to his feet. He tried to walk as best he could, but realizing how dizzy and wobbly he felt, he had to reach out to the wall for balance before making his way out of the cell.

"Stand right here and hold onto the cell gate so you don't fall over while I rinse you off. Drop what you're wearing on the floor." He covered his mouth like he was trying not to retch again. "Damn, you really stink," he uttered under his breath as he dumped the bucket of cold water over Guarin, spilling most over his head and torso, splashing the rest over his cock and ass.

"Good enough, dry off and put this on," said the Captain, tossing him a towel and the new garb, his mouth still set in a grimace of revulsion.

Still struggling to keep his balance, he held onto Captain Erec's arm for support as he led him out of the prison room, past the interrogation room, and into a private office room.

The Cleric sat behind an ornately carved oaken desk, thumbing through some papers, his cowl hanging loosely behind his neck, exposing sparse gray hair and prominent turd-colored spots that appeared to be stuck onto his scalp. A large bookcase occupied one of the walls, containing countless volumes of thick, dusty record books, some looked to be over a hundred years old. The Captain ushered Guarin to a chair across the desk from The Cleric, then took up his post at the doorway.

"Thank you, Captain Erec," said Father Linhart, without bothering to look up from his papers. He continued to ignore his presence for another couple of minutes while he focused on one of the papers in particular, holding it up to the light making its way through the narrow window. At last, he put the paper down with the others, folded his hands on the desk in front of him, and looked up to find Guarin glaring directly at him, waiting impatiently for him to begin.

The town administrator with the curled mustache entered the room, sporting a dark red jerkin over an even darker red linen doublet and a fancy mauve hat, sizable enough to show off his status and wealth. He offered a curt nod of his head. "Good day to you, Mr. Guarin. I trust you will be more forthcoming with information for us today?" he asked rather pretentiously, taking the cushioned chair in the corner of the room.

Guarin returned him a stiff nod but decided not to engage his question. A hard silence engulfed the room. He looked back to The Cleric who stared quietly at him for a long moment before beginning. He felt himself cringe with annoyance when he smacked his pursed lips open to speak. "Mr. Guarin, I see you have recovered from the interrogation this morning. As I'm sure you are aware by now, we have the Templar in custody. One of the night watchmen found him drunk in a whorehouse. Not what you expect from a man of the Holy Order, is it?" He paused, waiting for a response. "Do you still hold this man in such high esteem? Was he really worth risking your freedom and enduring such harsh interrogation?"

After all he had been through, Guarin found it easier to lie to him now. "You mean the merchant that I met at the waterfall? Yes, I still hold him in high esteem, very nice fellow."

The Cleric stared at him unblinkingly for another long moment, then pursed his lips in annoyance before pressing him further. "You don't want to try my patience, Mr. Guarin. I will have the confession that you promised me. If not, we can always bring you back down to fill your belly with more water. I can also inquire into any other contacts this man has made in town and extend my interrogations to them as well, beginning with those women in that whorehouse. Why don't you just make this nice and easy for all of us. All you have to do is confirm what your wife has already told us."

"She is not my fucking wife," he growled, matching his glare for a tense round of silence before speaking again. "Where is Lutrud now?"

"She is being kept under a watchful eye. You need not concern yourself with her right now."

"She has information as to who took my children and where they might have been taken. Did you make your inquiries into this matter with the town officials?"

"Indeed, I have. But all I ask is some of your cooperation in return. Does that sound fair, Mr. Guarin?"

"Yes, it does, Father." Guarin closed his eyes, bowed his head in a show of submission, and swallowed hard. "I regret that I told you a lie and concealed the truth. I beg your forgiveness, but I can make it right. If you can give me some information about my children, then I will give you tell you all I know about this case." He leaned forward, imploring him with his eyes. "Please, tell me where they were sent."

"Very well. Lord Endris, could you help Mr. Guarin with his inquiry? I believe you could answer him better than I."

"Of course, Father." He stood up, crossed his hands behind his back, and approached the table. "The man who took your children goes by the name Roland. He is not employed by the city in any official capacity, mind you, but he is a very capable man, quite efficient at what he does. We pay him for more of the…" his eyes looked up, searching for the right word, "…irregular work that needs to be done around town. You understand?"

"A bounty hunter," Guarin surmised, his gaze firm and intent.

Endris put on an expression that suggested he wanted to divulge more sensitive information but was struggling with how to say it. He sat down with one leg on the side of the desk, as though trying to appear more personable, trying to lower himself to Guarin's eye level, yet remaining a full head's length above him.

"You were deemed unfit to care for your children, you understand? Even your wife—sorry, their stepmother—admitted that she could no longer care for them—not by herself. This man, Roland, he knew of some kind of an orphanage or foster home run by a healing woman, but he did not tell us where she lives, and we did not care to ask at the time. Perhaps if your illness resolves and you provide us with your cooperation, I can obtain more information from him when he returns."

Guarin remained silent, letting it sink in before responding. "Roland." He let the word echo in his head. "Did he give a general direction, or say when he would return?"

Lord Endris shook his head solemnly. "I'm sorry, but that is all I know for now. He is a bit of a rogue, comes and goes from town to town at his own whim."

The Cleric leaned forward. "Now it's your turn. What can you tell me about our Templar?"

Guarin stared him down, his frustration mounting, a deep crease deepening between his brows. "You have declared me unfit to keep my children. Am I not unfit to give public testimony?"

He smacked his lips open again; Guarin winced at the sound. "Mr. Guarin, please understand. You looked like you would die any day. I'm sure you would agree that you were in no condition to care for your children. If you looked as you do today, this would have gone much differently."

"But you obviously couldn't know that I was going to die, could you?" he countered, more as an accusation than a question.

"I was of sound mind and able body the morning this—Roland—took my children from my home by force."

The Cleric shrugged his shoulders. "I have obtained a statement from Lutrud that says otherwise. She said you were delirious with fever and could hardly stand on your own on the day before he came to your home."

"Yes, let's talk about Lutrud. You have her on record of being investigated for witchcraft. I think it must be in some of those papers before you—is it not?"

He scowled, smacked his hand on top of the papers, and blurted out, "Enough of this nonsense!" He stabbed his finger toward Guarin's face. "That is precisely why I need your testimony, now let's have it out."

Lord Endris, looking exasperated, left the table and began pacing the room. Guarin eased himself away from his pointed finger, settling back into his chair with a wry smile. "What did she do, make some kind of a deal with you? She testifies against this so-called Templar, and you drop the charge of witchcraft?"

The Cleric abruptly rose to his feet, his voice rising to a shout, "I've had enough of this. Guard!"

Guarin raised his hands up. "Alright, alright. I promised you information about this case, and that is what I still intend to provide."

He waved off the guard. "This will be your last chance, do not try to waste another moment of my time."

"As I said earlier, I lied to you and withheld important information that would be useful to this case. I would like it on record that if I clarify my statements now, this charge will be stricken from my record, and I can leave here a free man."

He nodded, slowly lowering himself back into his chair. "You have my word on that."

Guarin waved his finger over his papers. "I would like it writing please, like a contract."

The Cleric stared him down, then put on a stiff smile. "Very well then, as you wish, a contract," he said as he began writing it out in bold strokes, then held it up to Guarin. "There you are."

Guarin looked it over, nodding his satisfaction before signing, even though he couldn't read a word of it. He was pretty sure that they were aware of this as well. "And you will notify me when Roland returns?"

"Yes, of course. I will pass the word on to the civil authorities. Now please, may we proceed with your statement?"

"Thank you, Father," Guarin said, leaning forward once again, folding his hands over the edge of the desk. He kept his eyes averted from The Priest's intense gaze, instead focusing on his hands as he began to nervously rub them together. "I hope you can understand my reasons for not divulging this to you earlier. I suppose I felt a sense of obligation or commitment to keep my word." He then looked up, matching his gaze. "You see, I believe that Lutrud is indeed a witch."

A heavy silence hung between them, their eyes locked in an unwavering stare, The Cleric's lips tightly pursed in growing frustration. When he finally smacked them open to speak, the Captain standing at the doorway flinched, as though it startled him back into the moment from his wandering thoughts.

"I don't see how this is relevant to the case against the Templar."

Guarin feigned a look of innocent surprise. "Father, don't you see? I couldn't have you going into trial, providing information obtained from a woman who engages in witchcraft. If this became public knowledge, you would be disgraced! I could not have that on my conscience. Nor could I stand to live with myself, knowing that I could have prevented the persecution of an innocent man. Barous is no Templar, at least as far as I am aware."

"You are playing games with me, Mr. Guarin. You are forgetting the evidence that I presented to you. Explain how you obtained that Templar coin."

"Ah yes, the coin," he sighed. "An insignificant thing really. He said he collects many different coins during his travels—you'll remember, he is a traveling merchant. He gave that particular coin to my son because Han is fascinated with knights. Barous said he had others like it, so thought nothing of it really."

The Cleric settled back into his chair, clasping his hands over his chest, assuming a more relaxed demeanor but never detaching his unblinking eyes from Guarin's. "I suspect you are lying to me, Mr. Guarin. You were much more believable when I first questioned you in front of her."

"As I say, I never believed she might be a witch until I thought about it afterwards. In any case, I should have been more honest with you in my cell, after my suspicions had taken root."

"I will bring her in for more questioning and a thorough examination. I am not finished with you yet, however. I still believe you know more than you say in regard to the Templar."

"Father, you promised me! We had a deal!" Guarin shouted.

"A deal? You mean this?" he smirked, holding up the written contract. "This means nothing. I asked you to provide me with a statement regarding The Templar. Instead, you lie and play games with me," he said, ripping up the paper in front of him. "Captain Erec, take him back to his cell."

Chapter 25

HAN WRAPPED HIS CLOAK TIGHTLY AROUND HIM as the evening drizzle quickly turned to a driving rain. The chill wind whipped the stinging rain into his face and flapped his hood over his ears. He looked up to see a darkening sky, laden with heavy clouds. Though most of his chores were completed for the day, he preferred to look busy and stay outside, away from The Lady for as long as he could.

He ducked under the shelter of the stable to wait out the worst of the rain, rubbing his hands together and blowing on his fingers to keep them from going numb. The longer he stood there, the harder it rained and the louder the wind howled. *Looks like it's time to join the others,* he thought, and ran across the yard to the back door of the house.

"It looks miserable outside, aren't you freezing?" Greta asked.

Han grabbed a towel, rubbing it vigorously over his face and hair. "Parts of me are. It wasn't too bad until a few minutes ago."

The savory aroma of goat and vegetable stew wafted into his nose, making his mouth water. "It smells great in here. Did you make it yourself?"

"Thank you, I made most of it, but Sendy helped me too."

"Have they been busy with Roland all day again?"

She nodded as she carried a pitcher of wine to the table. "Yes, either that or trying to catch up on their sleep. I guess he keeps them up all night moaning and yelling and trying to get out of bed. Sendy said he seems better today though."

"Yeah, I hear him too. I'm just glad we don't have to get up and go into his room when he does that."

He hoped The Lady would be too exhausted to join them for dinner again tonight, but his spirits dropped when she finally showed herself. She lumbered through the dining room with her neck and back stooped forward, her face slack, looking exhausted and older than usual. She didn't bother to address either of them as she set her wine glass on the table and then made her way into the kitchen.

"Sendy won't be joining us this evening. Why don't you both have a seat and we'll get started," she said, her voice sounding deeper than usual and her tone flat.

They all remained quiet during dinner that evening, listening to the wind and rain rattle the windows and the thunder bellow overhead. They each seemed to be lost in their own thoughts, but Han felt a growing tension that spoiled his appetite. The Lady poured the stew into Han's bowl which smelled as good as the first day they arrived. He stirred the contents, and then his stomach turned as a large eyeball, cloudy and discolored, rose to the surface with a soft, plopping sound. He sat there staring at it, and it stared back up at him as though daring him not to eat it.

The Lady noticed his hesitation and turned back to him after filling Greta's bowl. She didn't say anything, but he felt her hovering over his shoulder, watching him. He didn't look up at her, instead he took a bite of his stew, gently pushing the eyeball to the side as he stirred.

"It's really good, thank you ma'am," he said.

She moved along without acknowledging his compliment and took her seat across from him. She wore another of her hats, this one simpler and rounder in design, taking the shape of her head. It was made up of torn scraps of fabric, each of a different color.

"I like your hat. The colors are really pretty," Greta commented, breaking the silence.

"Thank you, dear," she replied with a curt smile.

He stirred his soup again. He kept trying to push the eyeball down into the soup, but it kept popping right back up. He then tried turning the eyeball side down into the soup with his spoon, but it kept spinning back around to look at him again. He took a drink of his wine. It didn't taste watered down as usual—quite strong in fact.

A thump and a skitter from the cellar below them caught their attention.

"Rats!" said The Lady, her lips curling in towards her teeth. "They can get a little noisy sometimes," she added, her left eye beginning to twitch now.

They resumed their meal in silence which amplified The Lady's slurping and gushy chewing sounds. Han quickly lost his appetite with each bite he—and she—took. Greta must have noticed as she cast him a sharp glance and then darted her eyes to his soup.

The Lady put down her spoon and folded her hands on the table, staring at him for a few moments before addressing him with her flat tone of voice. "Han, what's the matter, you don't like your stew?"

He nearly jumped when her question broke the tense silence. His eyes jerked up and down from his stew to The Lady nervously. "No—I mean—yes, I like it, but…it's just that I'm not that hungry today." His eyes finally dropped again to his stew and stayed there.

"Are you getting sick? You've been busy working in the yard all day. How could you not be hungry?" she asked, almost accusingly.

"No, I don't think I'm getting sick. Maybe I just had such a big breakfast and a lot of cheese as a snack, that's all."

"Well, that's good," her voice creaked, stretching her lips into a brief, tight smile before pressing him further. "But I want you to eat some more. I want you to finish what is in your bowl."

Han could tell by her stern expression that he would have to keep eating. He pulled out another spoonful and lifted it to his mouth but stopped short. He noticed at the last moment that somehow, as though just to spite him, the eyeball ended up on his spoon. He dropped it back into the bowl and fished around for some beans and mushrooms.

"I want you to eat that too, Han. It is good for you, and it's time that you try new things."

He hesitated and looked up at her with his mouth hanging half-open. He didn't know what to say, so he just shook his head at first. She nudged her head into a slight tilt, burrowing her eyes deeper into his, as though daring him to disobey her. "I can't....I can't eat that." His words came out like he was choking on them.

She stared intently at him a while longer without saying a word, but she set her mouth into a tighter grimace, her left eyelid now twitching more frequently. Abruptly, she rose from her chair and walked briskly over to his side of the table. He quickly spooned himself another bite, then picked up his bowl and drank a few large swallows of broth. Something soft and smooth bumped up against his nose as he drank. He set it back down and saw the eye glaring at him now from the center of the bowl.

He winced as he glanced back up at The Lady who suddenly appeared at his side, looming over him like she was ten feet tall. A crazed smile suddenly split across her cheeks, her lips pealing back over her swollen, blood-red gums. "That's a good boy! Just one more bite!" The words came out in a flurry with that unnatural high pitch, almost like a scream.

He looked back into his bowl. He felt the eyes of The Lady—and the one in bowl—boring into him. Forcing his trembling hand toward the bowl, tears rolling down his cheeks, he slid his spoon under the soggy orb and raised it to his mouth. He gagged immediately when it touched the back of his tongue. The eyeball shot out of his mouth and plopped right back into the bowl, spattering broth over the table and onto his face and clothes, as well as The Lady's.

Her smile transformed instantaneously into a fiendish scowl, and the loose flesh on her cheeks shook with rage. "EAT IT!!!" she screamed into his ear, her face so close that he could feel the hot stench of her breath on his neck, almost taste the heavy scent of alcohol emanating from her mouth.

He felt his own face contort uncontrollably like a baby and then wept out loud, "I'm sorry, I tried but I just can't eat that—it's disgusting! Can't we just have desert now?"

"I SAID EAT IT!!!" This time her voice came out in a deep roar, as though shouted by a man like Jehan instead of an old lady, her left eye now seized in a spasm of successive blinking.

Without warning, she swung her arm around and struck him across the head with her open hand, the force of the blow knocking him backwards off his chair, slamming his head onto the floorboards. His body continued to roll backward, his legs flipping violently over his head, until crashing hard into the wall behind him.

He lay stunned on the floor, looking up at the ceiling, unable to move. His ear rang louder than a church bell directly over his head, and it throbbed worse than any blow he ever took from Lutrud. Through his daze, he began to see a long shadow creeping along the ceiling toward him. Then the horrid figure of The Lady passed into his blurred vision. Her hat must have flung off when she struck him, her long gray hair spilling down past her shoulders, much of it tangled in mats, some hanging down into her face. Several bald patches exposed her scaly scalp and open sores. She looked truly wicked as she crouched over him, hands held rigidly in front of her like claws, lips drawn back and glowering with rage. Her tattered hair and feral expression reminded him of the wolves that stalked him in the forest, but she looked more like a monster from his worst nightmare.

He wanted to scream, but it caught in his throat; instead he urinated. He felt like he had to vomit, but instead he felt a warm gush spill and bubble out of him into the back of his undergarment. He faintly heard his sister crying through the ringing thrum in his ear before he even realized that she cowered at his side, screaming and pleading to leave him alone. Han repeatedly kicked his legs and pressed his feet against the floor, struggling to push himself away from this raving witch, lifting his back up against the wall, as her hands slowly drew closer to his neck.

Chapter 26

GRETA FELT AS STUNNED AS HAN LOOKED, watching him lay there in a daze. She threw herself to his side and screamed for her to stop as The Lady crouched over him, her hands reaching out for his neck. *My God, she is going to strangle him!* "Please, leave him alone! He didn't do anything! Why did you have to hit him? Can't you see he's hurt?"

She could see her words had no effect as her devilish eyes remained focused on Han. Frightened and shocked by this sudden transformation from a respectful lady to this fiend before her, she just hugged her brother tighter, buried her face in his chest, and cried until she heard an unexpected voice. She looked up to see Sendy step into the room. She appeared exhausted but spoke calmly and reassuringly.

"That should be enough for tonight, My Lady. I will deal with the children and clean up the table. It has been a long day. You need to rest now."

The Lady—*the Croon*—stood up and backed away, brushing her hair out of her face with one hand and fumbling to pick her hat off the table with the other. "I just wanted to make sure I didn't hurt the boy too badly. I…I don't know what came over me so suddenly. I guess that wasn't very lady-like of me, now was it?" Looking clearly flustered, her hands shook as she placed her hat back upon her head. "Yes, well perhaps you are right, my dear. It has been a long day indeed, so I think I will take my rest. Good night to you all." She nodded curtly and slinked away, disappearing down the dark hallway to the bedrooms.

Sendy knelt down to look over Han, her eyes showing concern and sympathy. "Where does it hurt, Han?"

He raised his hand to his forehead, then moved it to his ear and finally toward the back of his head and neck. "It all hurts, and my ear is still ringing." he moaned. He rubbed his hand over a patch of blood that matted the back of his hair.

"You're bleeding. Let me see," Sendy said, inspecting his wound. "Greta, can you please fetch me a clean cloth from the kitchen?"

Greta quickly brought back a piece of cloth and handed it to Sendy. "Thank you, sweetie." She dabbed the cloth gently to wipe most of the blood away, took a closer look, and then pressed it firmly over the wound. "It is just a small cut but looks like you will have quite a bump there soon."

"What the heck happened to me? How did I get on the floor?" he asked.

"I heard some yelling and then a loud crash through the bedroom wall. I don't imagine that you fell off your chair," she answered with some levity.

Greta's initial shock gave way to indignation. "She hit him. She hit him just because he wouldn't eat her stupid, disgusting eyeball," she snapped, wiping her tears with quick strokes of her hand.

"That will do, Greta. Thank you but keep your voice down please. We don't want to anger her any more than she is already."

"Oh yeah, that's right," Han said with a frown. He heaved a deep sigh and moved to sit up straighter against the wall, then turned to Greta. "I'm sorry, but I can't stay with her any longer."

"Don't talk so silly. Wherever would you go? You'll starve like everyone else," Sendy said, still pressing the cloth over the back of his head.

"It doesn't matter. I'll figure something out. Anywhere is better than living with her," he said softly.

"You would leave your sister here and go off alone? That doesn't sound like a very wise thing to do."

"We could all leave together—that is, if you'll allow it," proposed Han hopefully. "You said yourself that you wouldn't be staying long."

"How can I care for two young children when I don't even have a home myself? Besides, have you forgotten that I am wanted for witchcraft? I have to start a new life on my own, far away from here. I'm afraid My Lady has just exhausted herself these past couple days, and she didn't sleep much last night again either. I bet if she could take it back, she would. Why don't you stay a while longer? Once Jehan returns, you'll see things go back to the way they were. You're doing such a fantastic job in the yard, and he is depending on you. Please don't let him down."

She peeled back the dressing to reassess the bleeding. "I think it has stopped," she said, folding the blood to the inside of the cloth before pressing it back to his scalp again. "Hold it here tightly, Greta. I'm going to grab something to hold it in place."

She returned from Roland's room with a long, thin bandage and wrapped it around his head a few times over the dressing, then showed Greta how to tie it in place. "There, that should do it. What do you think?"

Greta smiled. "I think he looks kind of funny."

"How do you feel, Han? Better?"

He nodded.

"Ok then, let's see if you can stand up," she said, helping him to his feet. "No problem, right?"

"I'm ok, I guess, but my head still aches and my legs feel kind of wobbly."

She turned to look out the window. "It looks like the storm has passed over for now. Why don't you grab a fresh set of clothes from your room and go outside to clean up and change," she said, picking up his chair and replacing it under the table. "I can smell something good baking in the kitchen. I'll have it ready for you when you come back."

"Yes ma'am," he replied politely. Greta could tell he looked embarrassed for soiling himself. He started to turn away but then looked back up at her earnestly. "Thank you, Sendy. I want you to know that I really appreciate what you did for me tonight."

Sendy reached for his shoulder and gave it a light squeeze. "I'm just glad you're alright." She dismissed him with a warm smile and a soft pat on his cheek.

Greta smiled to herself as she noticed a reddish hue blotch his cheeks when he turned toward his room.

Sendy turned to Greta, "Would you mind clearing the table and washing these dishes while I start cleaning up in the kitchen."

Greta nodded happily. "Yes, of course." She picked up the empty bowls and began carrying them through the kitchen, but then noticed a look of sadness or concern on Sendy as she wiped the countertop. Greta paused and spoke in a low voice. "I'm really glad you came out when you did. She looked like she wanted to strangle him."

"I've never seen her like that before. I was frightened too," Sendy said, absently staring down at her rag. Then she turned toward Greta. "I'll talk to her tomorrow after she has had a good night's rest. I'll ask her what made her so angry."

Greta smiled, "Thank you, Sendy. I can help you again tonight if you need help with Roland."

"That would be nice. I could really use your help. After dessert then."

Greta nodded and brought the dishes outside through the back door of the kitchen to wash in the large basin filled with water and lye. Han met her carrying his fresh clothes and began cleaning his soiled clothes with a bucket of rainwater.

"How is your head feeling?" Greta asked.

He looked up at her and then went back to washing without a response until a minute later. "I really don't want to stay here," he whispered across the chill night air. "This lady is crazy—beyond crazy—she's as evil as the devil himself. If Sendy hadn't stepped in, she would have strangled me to death right there on the floor. I saw it in her eyes—hatred. Surely you can see it now, can't you?"

Greta had to think hard before she spoke. She knew they wouldn't make it on their own, and she didn't want to be left here by herself either. "Well, I agree she looked pretty crazy tonight when she hit you so hard—and she had no good reason to hit you either—but maybe Sendy is right; maybe she was just tired and angry and had no temper left to deal with us kids."

Han stared at her like she was the dumbest person he'd ever met. "So, you think she walloped me just because she was crabby?"

She giggled. "It's not like Aunt Lutrud never got mad enough to hit you before. And remember that time Papa even went off and hit you when Mum was really sick?"

Han just shook his head. "This is different. There is something about her that has been giving me the creeps; after tonight, she scares me to death! Remember what I saw her doing to Roland that first night? Well, the other day I noticed a bunch of strange drawings in the cellar. I don't even know how to explain them except that they looked…well, evil. I don't know if that woman we saw in town being accused was really a witch or not, but if ever there was one, this old lady has got to be the queen of all witches!" he said harshly, growing more animated as he spoke.

Greta stomped her foot and put her finger to her mouth. Han paused and looked around, then continued on more softly. "This time she hit me because I couldn't eat that goat's eyeball. What's it gonna be next time? Could be anything!" He wrung out his clothes and strung them up on the clothesline. "Come on, we'll talk about it later. Let's get back inside."

Chapter 27

HAN LAY ON HIS BED THAT NIGHT, his head still pounding, unable to sleep. He left the candle burning so he could at least focus his eyes on something. He couldn't take his mind off of his hatred for The Lady, which burned as hot as his hatred for Aunt Lutrud. The only difference was that he never feared Aunt Lutrud like he feared The Lady. He shuddered as he recollected what Sir Barous had told him: *Alas, I'm afraid some people are truly and irredeemably evil.*

He wanted to leave this house, but more importantly, he thought about where he would go. Eventually, he could find his way home but wasn't even sure he wanted to go back home, back to Aunt Lutrud, and back to his hapless father. If he left, would he leave Greta behind? Could he leave her behind? He didn't want to take the responsibility for her safety—for her life. She was the only person he even cared about anymore. He wouldn't be able to live with himself if she died on his account.

To take his mind off of The Lady and his predicament, he tried to shut everything out of his mind except for the small candle flame. He watched it dance and flicker, melting the wax into a tiny pool around the wick until it spilled over, dripping thick liquid down the sides of the candle before quickly cooling to a solid once again. Then he followed the wispy tendrils of smoke rising off the top, swirling upward until disappearing into the darkness.

As he steadied his mind and relaxed, his decision became clear: he would stay here with Greta, at least for the time being.

Sendy would smooth the tensions between him and The Lady, and Jehan should be coming back soon too. He had been gone for almost three weeks already, so he hoped he might return any day now. He didn't really spend much time with The Lady anyhow since he spent most of the day outside. He would just try to put this night behind him and remain respectful toward her.

After a time, he began to drift asleep until Greta came into the room and closed the door. "How did it go in there, better than last night?" he asked with a yawn and a stretch.

"Yes," she squeaked, sounding embarrassed, "He is better now. He just slept and didn't even wake up when we cleaned his wounds." Her expression turned to one of revulsion. "They are so awful! They smell even worse up close and have a bunch of disgusting maggots crawling around in them. At least I didn't pass out again."

Han started cracking up at this, "I can't believe you actually passed out on your first lesson? How embarrassing!" he teased.

"I couldn't help it," she shot back defensively, but then, realizing the absurdity of it, started laughing along with him. "You would have passed out too, I bet."

"Better you than me, that's all I'm saying. I don't know whether I'd rather be forced to eat that eyeball again or get too close to those maggot infested wounds of his," he said with a shudder.

"Well, you never know, maybe she will put some of those maggots in your stew and force you to eat them next time."

"Alright then, how about if Sendy makes you clean his butt the next time he craps the bed?"

They went on like that, each trying to come up with something more disgusting than the last, until they ran out of ideas.

As they settled back in their beds, Han decided he owed her a bit of reassurance. "I've been thinking about what I said outside tonight. I've decided to stick around here for a while longer. At least until the weather warms up, and as long as she keeps her hands off of me. I don't want you to worry about me leaving you here by yourself, ok?"

Suddenly she popped into his bed and gave him a big hug. "Thank you, Han," she replied, breathing a deep sigh of relief. "Good night. I hope you feel better in the morning." Then she kissed his cheek and lay back into her bed.

"Good night, Greta," he said with a warm smile.

He leaned over and blew out the candle. Darkness never really frightened him very much, but it did lately. Nightmares haunted his dreams. He knew they were coming when he tried to fall asleep: horrors of the furnace below him, of children burning, children that reached out to him, pleading for him to help stop the burning; ghastly visions of Ferrand staring accusations into his soul and threatening to take his revenge once they meet again in death.

Now, as his mind succumbed to that familiar buzz pulling him to sleep, his final thoughts turned to the drawings in the cellar as the figures became animated, moving like little cartoons across the wall. The black figure with the pointy hat standing with arms upraised in front of the small children, gesturing them toward the flaming cloud of smoke as, one by one, they moved forward, helplessly, to their senseless deaths.

The face of the black figure then turned toward him, it was the face of The Lady—The Witch—paralyzing him with her frightful gaze and wicked sneer. She motioned her long arms to him now, beckoning him toward her. "You too my clever little boy, my sweet little dumpling. You didn't think I would forget about *you* now, did you?" she shrieked and cackled at him in a piercing pitch. He tried to scream but couldn't. He tried to cover his ears, but his arms were frozen to his sides. He shut his eyes but could still see her face getting closer to his. Her shrieking became a deep growl of anger as her face transformed into that of a demon, pulsing and glowing red with fury, drawing in ever closer to him, until he could smell the scorching stench of death on its breath. The growl became a pitiful moaning sound as from a thousand tortured souls crying out their anguish from the depths of Hell itself. The demon reached out and grabbed hold of him, shook him, throttling him with rage.

Then he heard a familiar voice. "Han, wake up!"

The Craving

He awoke with a startle and flinched as he opened his eyes. "Greta! I'm sorry, did I wake you up? I was having another nightmare," he muttered, his words slurred from sleep.

"Shhh! Listen!" she insisted.

There was only silence. "What did you hear—"

"Shhh! There…you hear it now?" she whispered, her voice quivering with fear.

He sat up. What began as a faint moaning sound, grew louder and more disturbing as he listened. "I thought that moaning was just in my dream! What is that?"

"I don't know, but it sounds scary. I think it might be Roland. Maybe he is in pain or something," Greta suggested, her voice still squeaky and shaky.

Another loud, haunting groan emanated through the house, a sickening groan that wouldn't stop as it creeped under their door and penetrated through the walls. Han felt Greta trembling with fear beside him. He pulled his covers up over them and put his arms around her, holding her close. He realized he was shaking too.

"It doesn't sound like Roland. What in God's name is that?" Han whispered into the darkness as the groaning trailed off.

"It must be him, who else would make a sound like that? Let's see if Sendy is going to check on him."

Again, it began—a long, dreadful, wailing moan that filled his heart with feelings of torment and suffering. The kind of sound that would pull at the very souls of humanity, compelling all who hear such a cry of despair to provide some help, compassion, and mercy—except this moan did not sound human, it sounded unnatural—it sounded monstrous. It made him think of the sound Grendel might make from the stories of Beowulf that his father used to tell. He huddled with Greta and prayed for the sound to stop, but on it went, sometimes changing from an agonizing moan to a beastly growl to a shrieking roar.

Suddenly, a thunderous bang made them both jump and scream, as though something heavy had crashed onto the floor. A door opened hastily, violently banging into the wall as it swung open, followed by the sound of footsteps running down the hallway, then the frantic jerking of a door handle, another groan—louder this time—immediately followed by a loud scream.

"Sendy!" They both shouted together.

Throwing caution aside, they ran out of their room and peered down the dark hallway. He listened at Roland's door, but it was silent. Another sickening, ominous groan roared down the hall from The Lady's room—then another scream. Greta tugged at his arm toward the demonic sound. They stopped cold at the threshold of The Lady's room as they peered inside trying to make out what was happening through the darkness. A dark shadow writhed on the floor while another jabbed sharply at some kind of object in her hand. Brief flashes of light sparked from what appeared to be a piece of flint that Sendy struck with a tool from her other hand, each flash providing a glimpse of the horror before them.

The Lady lay on her back convulsing on the floor, her body arced backward like a bow, just like the sick man they witnessed seizing in Riquewihr. Then darkness again. Another spark—this time her mouth gaped open and roared that unnatural groan. A scuffling sound. Another spark—she suddenly appeared directly in front of Han, interposing herself between him and Sendy, her eyes wide and glaring at him with hysterical fury. With her hands and feet on the floor, her chest and belly arched upward, hyperextending her spine, her neck was thrown back to face him upside down. A jolt of terror surged through him. He jumped backwards and away from her as a cold chill erected every little hair on his body. He had no idea how she could have moved that fast toward him. She must have somehow scrabbled toward him in this position like an upside-down spider. Three more successive sparks flashed, briefly illuminating this creature that was The Lady. Her ripped and tattered gown was strewn around her waist, exposing her long sagging breasts that draped down and hung over each of her shoulders. Two of them were breasts at least, but he couldn't overlook a second set of nipples lower on her chest that seemed to be dripping a milky substance tainted with blood.

At last Sendy lit the candle, filling the room with a dim, flickering light. Averting his eyes from her beastly form, he perceived countless words and symbols and upside-down crosses and numbers and runes scrawled across her walls in a most bizarre and haphazard fashion. Many of the symbols were prominently displayed with a large bold script, whereas many of the sentences were written in tiny letters strung together in endless trains, some of the sentences intersecting others at varying angles, while others spiraled around each other. "What the hell—"

"Go back to your room, you shouldn't be here. I'll handle this," commanded Sendy. She lit a small stick of incense which began to effuse its sweet and calming scent throughout the room.

Han and Greta backed out into the hallway yet somehow unable to wrest their eyes from the macabre scene taking place in front of them. The Lady shrieked a cacophony of laughter at them, spraying urine across the room between her splayed legs, some of it splashing onto Sendy.

She let out a low, beastly growl that seemed to emanate from deep within her chest. Then a voice unlike anything he had ever heard burst forth from her mouth, shouting words that he had never heard and could not possibly understand, but booming loud and clear in his ears. Her satanic litany resonated with importance like some grand pronouncement or omen of some kind, mysterious incantations filled with a portent of evil and foreboding.

Suddenly and hastily her arms and legs scurried like a spider as she rotated her body around to face Sendy. This "creature" spat words at her, in Latin this time, as it moved toward her, backing her against the wall. Sendy began chanting her own incantation, holding the candle in front of her, trying in vain to ward her off. At last, the creature stopped speaking and stopped moving; she just stayed there, glaring at her in that strange, impossible position that she somehow maintained. Finally, she erupted with a deafening shout: PASCERE DAEMONIUM! PASCERE OPORTET DAEMONIUM!

Then her body became racked in a fit of violent, spastic contractions lasting a full two minutes before finally collapsing to the floor, as though her life was instantly snuffed out. Han knew some basic words in Latin: the word for "feed" was one of them, the word for "demon" was obvious. He felt his blood run

Scott Wojtowich

cold when he put the words together: "FEED THE DEMON! YOU MUST FEED THE DEMON!!"

A heavy silence permeated the room and pulsed in his ears after so much commotion, until Sendy broke it with a commanding shout. "Go to your room, NOW!"

Han didn't need to be told a third time. He grabbed Greta's wrist and turned back toward his room without hesitation. But then he did indeed hesitate. Something made him stop quite abruptly. He dared not take another step toward that which loomed ahead of them in the dark hallway. The dimmest of moonlight shining from the living room windows silhouetted a figure standing just steps away, directly in front of his bedroom door. The sour stench of death left no doubt as to who stood before them. He heard Greta try to alert Sendy, but her voice came out as only a soft, whining murmur of despair that caught in her throat.

Like a magically animated golem, the menacing figure didn't move or speak or even utter a sound. His body remained perfectly still, facing them directly, arms hanging down to each side—everything except for his long tapering, talon-like fingers that moved rhythmically in slow, wave-like motions.

Han felt like he was dreaming one of his nightmares, unable to move or speak or even breathe. He forced himself to finally exhale and call for help. "Sendy!" His voice, trapped by terror, came out as merely a shrill whisper. They slowly backed away from him, back toward The Witch's room and Sendy. But the door slammed behind them, shutting them out and sending their paralytic fear into a frantic sense of panic.

Chapter 28

THE PAIN IN GUARIN'S SHOULDERS THROBBED AND ACHED and burned like fire, worsening with every second that he hung helplessly in the strappado's grip. With his wrists bound behind his back, the horizontal wooden rod lifted his arms from under the crooks of his elbows, suspending his agonizing body five feet off the floor. Guarin pulled his knees up to his chest and forced his torso forward, trying to ease some of the strain threatening to dislocate his shoulders. Behind him, Joff tugged at the wheel like a ship's captain in a stormy sea, breathing heavily and grunting with each turn, slowly pulling him higher off the ground. He tuned out the droning words of The Cleric, ordering him to confess to his lies and admit the truth about the Templar. The excruciating torture seemed to go on endlessly, but just as he felt his muscles about to fatigue and his shoulder joints about to give way, he felt the tension of the rope suddenly release, dropping him to the ground like a shit sack.

"Get your ass off the ground!" He felt a hard kick into his ribs. "On your feet, prisoner!" Joff commanded.

As he struggled to rise, Joff grabbed hold of his upper arm, jerking him to his feet. He screamed as he felt his arm nearly tear loose from his shoulder. Joff callously removed his arms from the strappado and bound him to a nearby post instead. Guarin tried to shake off the waves of pain and spasms that spread across his shoulders. He had to tear his eyes away from the simple wooden rod swinging gently on the rope beside him. To anyone who didn't appreciate its use, it could almost be mistaken for a child's swing. To Guarin, the water torture seemed like child's play now compared to the misery he felt hanging from that monster. With his muscles fatigued, he knew his shoulders would snap out of joint the next time they hoisted him up there.

But underneath the agony that racked his shoulders, a familiar affliction began to rear its ugly head again. He felt that nauseating pain build up inside—not the throbbing ache in his lower back as before, but a heavy pressure, lower in his abdomen, and even deeper into his balls. It seemed as though the sudden jolt to his body from striking the ground awakened his stone and moved it along. He hadn't felt his kidney pain for days, and the blood more or less seemed to clear from his urine as well, so he had hoped that it finally passed unnoticed. He knew better though. He had been through this before and knew what was coming. He would know when it passed, and it most certainly had not.

The door to the chamber opened and a woman—a prostitute by the looks of her—was escorted down the steps by one of the younger guards. An expression of abject horror crossed her face as her gaze fell upon the terrifying instruments of torture. "NO! NO! NO!" She began screaming hysterically and fighting with the guard, trying in vain to claw her way along the banister to get back up the stairway.

Guarin remembered the sinking feeling of dread he felt the first time he laid his eyes into this dungeon. *Has it only been two days?* As if the water torture wasn't bad enough, they brought him back and dropped him straight down into a narrow chute under the floor called the oubliette. Without even enough room to sit, he was forced to stand between four narrow walls of stone in absolute darkness for twelve hours. Once daylight finally made its way into the chamber, he looked up to see a metal grate about ten feet above his head. Above that, the wooden rod dangled menacingly from the strappado, waiting to take him for a wild ride.

He looked over to Barous now, his arms strung over his head by chains suspended from the ceiling, his skin covered with fresh lashes from just days ago, as well as others scarred over from years past. The burly captain was working him over pretty hard, striking him from behind with a club and then pressing it deeply against his spine as Barous cried out.

The younger guard strapped the woman's arms behind her back and secured the wooden rod under her elbows. Her hysterics calmed down to what can only be described as deep despair as she stood whimpering, her body trembling with fright and utter helplessness. Her shirt had torn open from trying to escape up the stairway, exposing her large quivering breasts, glistening with beads of sweat, to all of the men in the room. Joff couldn't seem to take his leering eyes off of them.

"I'll take it from here, you can resume your post," Joff said to the younger guard.

Guarin noticed an expression of relief wash over the young man's face as he departed the chamber.

The Cleric jabbed his face in front of Guarin's, so close that he could smell the old man's sour breath as he spoke. "You are a stubborn man, Mr. Guarin. Because you would not cooperate, you forced me to involve others," he said, slowly turning his head toward the woman. Snapping his head back to Guarin once again, he offered one final chance for him to confess. "If you have nothing further to say, I will move on to question her, and then to your friend, Barous, and then back to you again—round and round we go," he threatened as his lips twisted into a confident smirk.

"I'd rather you brought Lutrud down for questioning instead of this innocent woman. I think I'd rather enjoy seeing that actually. Where is that little witch anyhow?"

"Do not concern yourself with her. She is under our close watch. As for the woman here before us, we shall see just how innocent she is. She will have her chance to cooperate, just as you did," he said, moving toward her as he spoke.

He lifted her chin to face him. "Before we begin, I would like to offer you a chance to answer some questions for me. If you tell me the truth, then I will let you go free. Does that sound fair?"

"Yes, I guess so," she answered, her mouth hanging open stupidly.

"You can start by telling me your name."

"My name is Rose."

"Are you a prostitute, young lady?"

She shook her head, her long dark hair waving across her face.

"It's ok if you are, you needn't lie. I won't punish you for that. Just tell me if you have seen that man before," he said, pointing to Barous.

She looked over to Barous and nodded. "Yes, I've seen him."

"Good! Now tell me what you two talked about."

"We didn't really do much talking."

Barous yelled across at her, "That's right, Rose, you tell him like it is!" followed by a sudden groan as the captain clubbed him in his back.

"I'm told he is quite fond of telling people that he was a Templar. Didn't he mention that at all to you, either before or after you…stopped talking?"

She stared at him blankly with her mouth hanging open for a couple seconds before responding. "What's a Templar?"

His mouth tightened in frustration. "I'm sure you know very well what a Templar is. Now just admit that he made mention of this and you can go free. Your shoulders are not as strong as this man's."

She became very apprehensive once again, "No—wait—please—I'm telling you the truth! He never mentioned anything like that to me. You can't do this, I beg you!"

The Cleric stared her down with a dour grimace. "That is not what I want to hear, you little whore. Maybe this will jog your memory." He then gave a curt nod to Joff, who jerked the wheel around, turning the winch and pulling her arms up behind her until her body lifted off the ground. She screamed in agony, instinctively trying to hunch her body forward, kicking her legs in different directions, her head writhing in circles and then shaking back and forth.

The Cleric hollered questions at her over her screams, but she clearly wasn't listening. Suddenly, she dropped as the guard lost his grip on the wheel, but then caught her again as she fell, jolting her arms further upward from behind her back. He heard a clunking sound as both of her shoulders dislocated, her body now swinging limply, her arms stretched grotesquely straight over her head in a backward fashion. Her face lost all color as her eyes rolled back, losing consciousness for a few moments before arousing again, moaning pathetically as her listless body was lowered back to the ground.

"You can't hold your grip on this little lady?" The Cleric chided Joff. "Free her wrists and see if you can't get her shoulders put back in place."

"It must be her big tits; they weigh more than you think!" Joff said with a smirk, groping and shaking one of her breasts.

"I'll have Captain Erec take over the strappado then. Lift her up onto the table; I've not finished with her yet," ordered The Cleric. He walked over to a different table on which the cruel instruments of torture were neatly laid out.

Guarin watched helplessly as the Captain removed the chains from Barous's wrists and then secured his arms over the strappado bar. He grimaced as Joff untied Rose's wrists and moved her slack arms through different random motions, first one and then the other, her moans only interrupted by bouts of momentary unconsciousness, until they finally clunked back into place.

Meanwhile, the pressure in his bladder and balls continued to build into a throbbing pain, and he had a strong urge to piss that grew worse by the minute. "I'm sorry, I know you're all very busy, but I have to take a raging piss," he grunted out.

"Oh, Christ," he heard Captain Erec mutter under his breath from behind him.

Joff shot a glance at him while carrying Rose to the table. "For shit's sake, just piss on the floor like everyone else does."

"I will if someone can just remove my garb. Captain Erec here was kind enough to bring me a fresh one, and I don't want to soil this one up with piss and blood all over again."

Erec jerked the cloth off of him, tossing it across the floor. "Good to go. Anything else we can do for you? Would you like me to shake it when you're finished?"

"That'll do, thank you," Guarin grunted and then strained to urinate. It felt like trying to force a spear through his penis but released merely a scant trickle of bloody urine for his efforts.

Joff looked over and chuckled at him. "Having a little stage-fright, are we? Hey everyone, let's all look away and give the man some privacy," he mocked.

"I feel like my bladder is about to explode, but I can't get it out," he groaned, still straining, his naked body drenched in sweat. The misery he felt began to overwhelm his senses, and he actually looked forward to passing out at any moment, but for now he could only pant and push and grunt and groan.

The Cleric returned from the table across the room, bearing one of the crude instruments in his hand. It looked like a large pair of metal tongs, like one might use to pick up chunks of ice, with two sharp claws pointing inward at each end. He could only assume its purpose was for tearing flesh, not for picking up ice, but he still couldn't have imagined just how gruesome this man was willing to get.

He looked down upon her, his stone-like visage and intense gaze peering out through his cowl, studying her face, her breasts, her body. "We don't need to go any further, young lady. Simply tell me what he told you about being a Templar, and agree to admit to this publicly, then you will be set free. Otherwise, you will be punished like a whore," he threatened, bringing the breast-ripper in front of her face so she could see its menacing claws.

She spit in his face, "I don't even know what the hell a Tumbler is! I told you, we didn't talk much, he was drunk, I was tired and hungry. I had other clients waiting, I just…" she began to whimper as he slowly moved the instrument over her breast, pulling the spring-loaded tongs apart to encompass as much of her flesh as he could.

"Allow me to assist," said Joff, lifting up her breast and squeezing it between the sharp claws. Once The Cleric let go, the two ends recoiled and pierced through her flesh, inducing a horrific, bone-chilling scream. A fresh gush of blood spilled down from her torn breast onto the table and then began dripping down to the floor. A crazed grin erupted on his face as he watched her writhe in pain.

Guarin and Barous both yelled out, pleading for him to stop and leave the woman out of this. The Cleric abruptly turned away from Rose and strode toward the men, leaving the breast-ripper in place, protruding straight up from her chest. He approached Barous first, his eyes now flaming with intensity, but his expression set in grim determination. "You end this now! Look at what you are making me do to your acquaintances. I've sent letters to Paris, and we should be expecting someone to arrive who can identify you, so no reason to delay this any longer."

"Ha! The only men who can identify me are all dead!" Barous growled defiantly. "Go ahead and string me up; let's see if it makes me say anything different. Just leave the woman alone, for God's sake."

The Cleric's scowl drew into a smirk, "We shall do just that." Turning to Guarin next, he grabbed hold of his face in a tight grip, lifting his head until he locked in on his furious gaze. Just as he plucked his mouth open to speak, something seemed to snap in Guarin at that moment. He wanted to savagely bite his nose off, gouge his eyes out, pry his jaw loose from his skull with his bare hands. He thrust his head forward like a horned ram, but The Cleric flinched back just in time to avoid the blow. As though transfixed by Guarin's sudden and unexpected change in behavior, The Cleric remained standing directly in front of him with a look of utter surprise and dismay. Shaking with rage, Guarin bellowed like a roaring lion, boring his raving eyes into his adversary's until he finally felt a release.

He closed his eyes as his roar faded to a moan and his body slackened. A smile of relief crossed his face as he felt his urine finally begin to drain from his distended bladder. He heard a boisterous, unrestrained laughter from Barous. Opening his eyes, he looked down and watched with delight as he emptied his bladder onto The Cleric, his bloody piss soaking into and dripping down his long white robes, pooling on the floor around his cloth slippers. Guarin began to laugh along with Barous. A look of disgust crossed The Cleric's face as he stepped back from the red puddle of urine and shook his feet like a wet dog. He was surprised to hear a restrained chuckle from Captain Erec standing behind him instead of his usual gagging or retching. Looking closer into the puddle, Guarin identified the tiny and insignificant looking stone that had caused him so much misery over the past week.

"Enough of this! String him up!" he barked at Captain Erec, throwing his arm up in the air. "We'll see who is still laughing."

Captain Erec grunted as he turned the wheel with all of his strength, hoisting the heavy body of Barous off of his feet. Guarin could see his impressive chest, arms, and abdominal muscles ripple and flex as he fought to ease the strain on his shoulders. He seemed to be having an easier time with it than either he or Rose had, at least for now. After a full two minutes of this, Erec suddenly slackened the rope, letting him fall momentarily just as the other guard did to the woman, but purposely this time. Amazingly, Barous had the strength to maintain the position of his body: his knees pulled up, chest thrust forward, head tucked. He looked as though he were trying to roll into a summersault, maintaining this perfect balance without even expressing any groans of pain, his face showing only intense focus.

The Captain dropped and jerked him again, but this time the bonds on his wrists broke free before his shoulders did. Instead of collapsing to the ground in a heap, he righted himself, landing squarely onto his feet like a circus acrobat, arms spread wide for balance, as though he were anticipating his sudden release.

A jolt of excitement ran through Guarin's spirit as he watched with awe-struck wonder as this powerful knight immediately went to work dispensing with the guards. With one mighty blow from his fist, he sent Captain Erec flying backward against the stone wall, his head striking it with a hollow sounding smack, rendering him immediately senseless. Joff rushed him from across the room, unsheathing his short sword and roaring as he charged. Barous waited until he was almost upon him before making his move, reaching for the chains that hung from the ceiling, deftly sidestepping to avoid his thrust, and then rapping the chain around his skinny little neck.

Joff continued to flail his weapon at Barous who caught hold of his wrist with his free hand; then, momentarily letting go of the chain with his other hand, he grabbed hold of his forearm just below his elbow, snapping it down over his knee like a thin tree branch. Joff let out a squeal of pain as his weapon dropped to the floor, his broken forearm hanging limply down from the rest of his arm, a jagged piece of bone jutting out from his skin.

Barous moved his hands back to the chain, tightening the stranglehold on his neck, watching as his ugly, cadaverous face discolored into a mottled bluish-purple, his lips visibly swelling and gulping for breath like a fish out of water.

All the while, Guarin kept a watchful eye on The Cleric, who looked to be in a state of shock, backed up against the table where Rose lay, the breast-ripper still attached to her torn, bleeding breast. Barous now turned his full attention to him as well. Finally coming to his senses, The Cleric reached for any method of protection he could find. Prying the breast-ripper free, he held it out in front of him to ward off the Templar. Bits of yellowish-tan colored tissue mixed with both fresh and coagulated blood dripped from its menacing claws.

"You will stand down, prisoner," he warned, backing away toward the stairs. For the first time, Guarin noticed a look of utter surprise and dread on his face.

Barous finally let go of the guard, leaving his corpse dangling from the chain around his neck. He picked up another long iron chain from the floor and stalked toward The Cleric with a grin. "What are you going to do with that thing, rip my tits off too?"

"You cannot escape this town. Harm me and we won't have to establish that you are a Templar to execute you."

"I'll take my chances. I've escaped prisons and cities more fortified than this," he said, holding the lower end of the chain with his left hand, swinging the other end like a lasso with his right.

The Cleric suddenly threw the bloody breast-ripper at him like a spear, then turned and ran for the stairs, yelling for help. Barous closed in on him quickly. Hurling the chain at his back, it wrapped around his torso a few times, binding him tightly. Barous yanked on the chain with all his might, twisting his hips and pulling with the full length of his arms, sending The Cleric spinning violently through the air before crashing back to the ground, his body whirling across the stone floor.

He then dragged him by his cowl toward the strappado, pulling him deliberately through Guarin's puddle of bloody piss. The Cleric choked from the cowl tugging on his throat as he frantically reached and clawed at his neck to loosen the constriction, then began pleading for his life as Barous bound his arms onto the strappado.

"Let's see how long *you* can last in this contraption now," he said, heaving back on the wheel, lifting his kicking and flailing body into the air. His pathetic pleading quickly turned to incoherent howls and shrieks of pain. "This should hold you for a good while," he said, securing the winch with the chain to a latch on the wall. Even while he continued to scream, Barous picked up the breast-ripper, opened it wide, and closed it over his face, the blood-soaked claws stabbing through his cheeks and into his gaping, screaming mouth.

Despite the morbid, grisly scene of horror all around him, Guarin felt a rush of excitement and overwhelming joy. He had seen plenty of fights but had never witnessed the unmatched skill of a true professional knight.

"Thank you, Sir Barous," Guarin said as he untied him from the post. A gleam of admiration shone from his eyes, much like his son had regarded the knight the day at the waterfall. He felt he should kneel to him out of respect, but then realized how silly that would look. "You weren't kidding when you said you could break out of here. I knew you could still fight, but that was incredible! How the hell did you do that?"

Barous beamed a big smile at him, "The pleasure was all mine, my friend. You could say I've had some practice with that contraption before," he said, gesturing to the strappado. "I must admit though, I also had a little help from this man," he said, gesturing toward Captain Erec, sprawled out against the wall and just now beginning to regain consciousness.

Rose began to arouse as well. They both walked over to release her from her bondage, helping her up to sit on the table, pulling her gown back over her chest. "You will need to have that wound tended to right away," Barous cautioned.

"The Cleric had a point. How can we make it out of this town, let alone this tower?" asked Guarin. "There are only two gates, and both are guarded."

"You are correct, but they only pay attention to who is coming *into* town, not leaving it—at least not until word of our escape gets out," Barous answered, clapping him on the shoulder.

After a few minutes, The Cleric lost consciousness. Captain Erec pushed himself up to a seated position on the floor, propping his back against the stone wall.

"Before we leave, I need to give thanks to a new friend," Barous said.

"I said you could hit me, but I didn't mean for you to knock me out," Erec grumbled, rubbing his hand over the side of his face, which was already beginning to swell and discolor.

"That was for jerking me around up there," he chided, offering his hand to help him up.

"Yeah, sorry about that. I guess I didn't loosen the knot enough around your wrists as well as I thought. I figured one more jerk ought to do it though," he replied, staggering to his feet.

Guarin stared incredulously at Captain Erec. "You guys planned this out?"

Erec shrugged his shoulders, "Not really planned, no, but when they broke the woman's shoulders, I decided I'd seen enough. I think I have a pretty good idea what's going on here, and none of you deserve what they've put you through, much less your lady friend over there."

"You are a courageous man, Captain. We appreciate the risk you have taken for us," Guarin said, shaking his hand.

"Good luck finding your son, Mr. Guarin. This is the key to the door. Take my blade as well; you will need to fight your way out of here. There are several more guards inside the tower, but most can't fight worth a shit. I would just ask you to try not to kill any of them if you can avoid it. Some are my friends and only doing their jobs."

"I don't suppose we'll be able to talk our way out of here," Guarin said, accepting his sword and strapping the scabbard around his waist. "I can't thank you enough. May fortune repay you if I cannot."

Barous lifted Joff's sword off the ground. "This will have to do for now," he said, taking a few practice swings.

Take my leather jerkin and trousers for now, they should fit well enough and offer some protection. Guarin can take his. He won't be needing them," he said, motioning his head to Joff, his dead body still suspended from the chain around his neck.

He looked down at his corpse and shook his head, "I don't think they'll fit, but I guess they will have to do."

"Thank you again, Captain, I shall do my best to repay this debt I owe you," Barous said earnestly, shaking his hand with a single hard pump. He then looked up to The Cleric, still dangling from the strappado. "I'll let you decide what you want to do with this sadistic piece of shit."

Erec looked up, appearing mortified, as though he hadn't even noticed him hanging above him like a ceiling fixture, the breast-ripper engulfing his face. Reflexively, he brought his hand up to his mouth, swallowing hard, "Seriously?!"

Chapter 29

GRETA TURNED HER BACK TO THE SILENT SHADOW in the hallway, banging her fists frantically on The Lady's chamber door, crying out, "Sendy, open the door! It's Roland—he's awakened! He is in the hallway! Help us!"

Sendy jerked the door open with alarm, but as she assessed the situation, almost immediately assumed a calm and reassuring disposition. She briefly embraced them without taking her eyes off of the dark shadow in the hallway. "Go to my room and close the door, children. Don't be alarmed by him," she said quietly, motioning them away. She moved cautiously but steadily down the hallway, not bothering to look back to see if they obeyed her, which they hadn't. They remained at the end of the hallway with their backs pressed up against the wall. Greta stole a glance into The Witch's room to see her lying unconscious on the floor. Sendy had straightened her onto her back and placed a pillow under her head.

She looked back as Sendy slowly approached Roland until their silhouettes merged, stopping about an arm's-length away. He remained motionless as a statue except for those eerie, writhing talons of his.

"Roland, is that you, my dear? How did you get out of bed? Are you feeling better?" She asked, her tone calm and soothing.

He remained silent and still, staring blankly at her.

"Did you hear the noise, is that what aroused you? It was not a pleasant sound now was it?"

She stood facing him, patiently waiting, but he still gave no response.

"Are you thirsty? Can I get you some water, Roland?"

He looked like he tried to utter a sound but then just exhaled with a soft gurgling groan.

"How about if I help you back to your bed?"

He remained silent but his fingers stopped moving. Sendy supported him with her arm and ushered him back to his room, tossing a glance over her shoulder at Greta and Han.

"I could probably use a hand. Do you mind helping me?" she asked.

After getting him back into bed, Han excused himself, looking rather peaked, but Greta offered to stay and help her until he was settled in.

She woke up late the next morning to the smell of baked bread. Stretching, she looked over to see Han sitting up with his back against the wall, staring intently at his ball. "Good morning," she yawned.

"Hey," he replied curtly, then began bouncing his ball off the floor and the wall. She noticed that he tended to do that when he got bored or frustrated.

A large bruise had swollen up on the right side of his temple overnight. "That looks pretty painful. Does it hurt?"

"Eh," he said equivocally, as though he didn't care.

"Did you sleep ok?"

"Eventually."

"That was pretty creepy last night, like she turned into a demon or something. Sendy said she has been having these spells ever since she knew her. She said it's called the falling sickness, but The Lady insists on calling it The Gift because it helps her communicate with spirits. Anyhow, they make her do weird things like that, especially when she gets really exhausted. That's what the incense was for, it helps calm her down so the seizure stops." She paused but then continued when she realized Han wasn't going to say anything. "She also said The Lady—"

He abruptly snatched his ball off the bounce and turned to face her, snapping at her in a coarse whisper. "Why don't you quit calling her The Lady. She isn't a lady, she's a goddamned witch! Can't you see that?"

Greta jerked her eyes to the door and back again, eyebrows pinched together. "Are you crazy? What if she can hear you?"

Han scooted closer to her and spoke softer this time. "Did you see her room? Did you see the bizarre writing and symbols drawn on her walls? She is crazy! You think she is communicating with gentle healing spirits when she gets like that? More like demons! Do you know what she said in Latin before she collapsed? She said: 'You must feed the demon!' What kind of a person says something like that? And what if Sendy hadn't been there last night? Now that Roland can walk, what if he creeps into our room when we're sleeping? We don't know what is going through his mind—hell, I don't even trust him when he *is* in his right mind! It's dangerous to stay here, Greta. We have to leave, and the sooner the better."

"Stop it, Han. You're trying to scare me. You don't need to worry about Roland. I was with him last night. He is too weak to harm anybody. The Lad—, she just had a bad seizure. Sendy said she would be back to herself again today. Just see this through. You'll feel better once Jehan comes back."

Han rubbed his face with his hand, then scratched his head in frustration. "I can't understand why you would want to stay here. I don't like this house, and I certainly don't like her."

"You think it's dangerous living here? How safe do you think it would be wandering on our own with all those thieves and bandits and wild animals out there? Don't you remember how hungry and miserable we were before we came here? I don't want to be hungry like that again." She regarded him with an almost pleading expression, then her face softened. She sniffed long and slow through her nose, closed her eyes, and half-smiled. "Smell."

Han cracked a smile as well. "Alright, that smells pretty good. Let's see how it goes today, and we'll talk about this later."

They walked out together to the dining room. A fat loaf of bread packed with blueberries awaited them on the center of the table. From the kitchen, she heard someone humming under the crackling sound of frying eggs.

"Good morning," Greta called into the kitchen. "Everything smells delicious. We're just going outside to wash up. Do you need any help with breakfast?"

Expecting to see Sendy answer, she was surprised when The Lady popped her head around the corner, looking much like her usual self again.

Ooohh, good morning my little baby birdies! It looks like you both got some good rest and slept late this morning. That is excellent because we have a big day today. Just go on out for your little tinkle, and then have a seat at the table after you wash up. I'll have food on your plates by the time you come back." She flashed them a big grin and a wink before pulling her head back behind the wall just as quickly as she presented it, resuming her cooking and humming.

Han and Greta stared at each other silently in a moment of disbelief before heading outside.

"She acts like nothing happened! It's like she's a different person," whispered Han when they got outside and closed the door.

"See, I told you so. She was just exhausted yesterday," she said. Then she smiled and added with a giggle, "...and crabby."

"Ha! Yeah," Han chortled. He stooped over the bucket of water but paused. Turning his face at different angles, she realized he was looking at his reflection in the water. "It looks worse than I thought," he said, gently rubbing the swollen bruise with his hand.

Greta stepped next to him, reached up and placed a reassuring arm around his shoulder. She gazed silently into the still water along with him; their reflections appeared to be framed together like a circular portrait.

After a long quiet moment, she pressed her cheek against his. "See, look at that, we're brother and sister. As long as we stick together, we'll be just fine." She turned to kiss him gently on his bruise and then splashed water at him. "Now hurry up and let's go eat that blueberry bread!"

"Hey, that's cold!" he gasped. "How do you like it," he said, splashing the water back at her.

Her playful smile and laughter quickly evaporated when she realized someone was watching them from across the yard.

A very short, stout, bearded man stood there, both hands crossed together on top of a shovel, his chin casually resting on his hands.

"Hello?" Greta called out to him.

He raised his hand and gave her a wave. They waved back awkwardly. Han and Greta turned to one another, unsure whether to engage the stranger any further.

When they returned to the dining room, The Lady smiled up at them as she dished the warm blueberry bread onto their plates. She was dressed impeccably once again, her hair neatly tucked into a fluffy black fur hat, bearing almost no resemblance to the monster in her room last night.

"I hope you're hungry, I know I am. Have a seat please." Then she looked twice at Hans's bruise and moved in for a closer look. "Oh Goodness, what happened to your head? That must be from falling out of your chair, I bet. Well, we will fix that right up, don't you worry," she said as she pinched his cheek and then gave it a little pat.

Han looked up at her with confusion but tried to remain respectful. "Thank you, ma'am," he replied sheepishly before taking his seat.

"Who is that man outside in the yard?" Greta asked.

"He is an old friend of mine, one of my best workers. He will be helping Han in the yard until Jehan returns. After you've finished, he will show you what needs to be done today. He brought a new pig with him that needs to be slaughtered for dinner tonight."

The Lady watched them eat their breakfast sitting erect in her chair, regarding them with an endearing look, as though she were proud of her young children. It made Greta feel more at ease, almost like the first day they arrived.

"Sendy told me that you helped her tend to Roland again last night, is that right?"

"Yes, My Lady. He seemed much better last night and even walked out into the hall on his own."

"Very good. I'm glad that you can be helpful to me in more ways than just cleaning the house. I have much to teach you about healing. Before you know it, you will be able to manage his care without my help, just like Melisende was doing."

The Lady continued on, but Greta's thoughts were held up by something she just said about Sendy—like she used her in the past tense.

"Where is Sendy? She will still be around to help out for a while longer, won't she?" Greta asked.

The Lady looked at her blankly for a moment before moving her lips into a stiff smile. "Actually, I asked her to leave this morning. She had been telling me that she had some things to take care of and assured me that you could capably take over her duties. She may not be back for…quite a while."

The Lady remained sitting with her hands crossed on the table, slowly nodding her head and studying their faces, but maintaining that stiff smile. Greta felt like she had just ripped her heart out from her chest. She had taken away the most important person in her life, the woman that she respected and trusted more than anyone. She snuck a glance at Han to see that his face had turned a ghostly white. She could sense that his last shred of hope had just spilled out of him. Now they were alone with her; alone except for this dwarf waiting for Han outside.

"Thank you for the breakfast, ma'am. May I be excused now?" Han asked.

"Yes, Han. You may be excused."

Greta watched him get up and walk outside, without even clearing his dirty dishes from the table. She saw that The Lady took notice of this too, so Greta quickly got up and stacked the dishes together before she could say anything.

"It's ok, My Lady, I don't mind washing his dishes for him today. It looks like he wants to get started on his chores this morning before the rain starts."

Then a most unexpected tear dropped and spattered onto a dish she held. The emotion came upon her quickly. She hoped The Lady didn't notice. She didn't want her to know that she was upset about Sendy leaving; nevertheless, her lower lip began to quiver. Quickly turning her head away, she headed for the door to the yard.

"Is something the matter, Greta?" she asked, sounding more like an accusation than a question.

Maybe it was the apprehension of hearing her voice as she reached for the door, but the abruptness of her tone rattled her, setting off alarm bells that clanged in her head, jerking her to a sudden stop. One of the cups flew off the top plate, clattering onto the floor and spilling its juice. Pangs of guilt and fear and sadness all rose up and choked at her throat.

She turned back to address The Lady, her lower lip quivering uncontrollably, her eyes puffy and streaming tears down her flushed cheeks. "I'm so sorry, I'll clean it up right away! Please forgive my clumsiness, My Lady."

Flustered, she moved to place the dishes back on the table, but then turned back to the door, and then back to The Lady again, not knowing whether to clean up the mess first or take out the dishes. At last, she bent over to pick up the cup, nearly dropping the remaining dishes in her arms. "I'll just…I'll just take these outside and set them down in the water. I'll be right back to clean it up, OK?"

The Lady gawked at her in disbelief, fists planted on her hips. "Yes, I expect you will, and then perhaps you can tell me what has gotten into you."

Greta went out and carefully placed the dishes in the wash basin. She then quickly splashed some water on her face and buried it in the towel. After having composed herself, she heaved a great sigh before returning inside. To her surprise, The Lady did not punish or scold her for making a mess; she just stood over her in silence until Greta cleaned up the spill.

"There now, that wasn't so bad was it?"

Greta looked up at The Lady, standing straight and tall above her. She started using her high-pitched, unthreatening "granny" voice once again. "You looked like a scared little mousy scurrying and jumping about. You have nothing to be afraid of, my dear. Tell me why you became so upset. Is it because I sent Melisende away?"

Greta nodded her head meekly and squeaked out a quiet "Yes." The Lady continued to smile down at her, silently urging her to elaborate. "I didn't want her to go. She was so nice and friendly, and I really liked her a lot. She reminded me of my own mother in some ways, except younger." She felt her eyes begin to burn again. "But most of all, I was just surprised. I didn't even get to say goodbye." Fresh tears streamed down her cheeks again.

The Lady knelt down and lowered her pitch to a more natural voice; it seemed to Greta this was the most genuine voice she heard from her yet. "There, there, my little darling dear. Perhaps she will come around again someday. She is very nice, isn't she? I've known her since she was just a little girl, raised her as my own daughter." She stretched her smile wider and tenderly reached down to lift Greta's face toward her own. "I can be like your mother now, just as I was with her, if you'll let me."

Greta didn't know what to say to that. *You're a croon, not a mother*, she thought. She didn't want to insult her in any way, so she forced a smile. "Thank you, My Lady."

Rising back to her feet as though the conflict were resolved, she declared enthusiastically, "I have a great many things to teach you. We shall begin today."

Greta went outside to wash the dishes in the basin, watching Han dig and rake and plant beside the dwarf. Before heading back inside, she turned to give one last look at her brother—and wondered if he would leave her today.

Chapter 30

WALKING CAUTIOUSLY UP THE STEPS, swords at the ready, Guarin followed Barous with a spine-tingling sense of excitement, knowing that the moment was at hand: freedom or death. At any other time in his life, he would have been trembling with fear. Although he always considered himself a confident man in his younger days, he never really thought of himself as a fighter and preferred to avoid dangerous confrontations. At this moment, however, he felt like a man coming out of his shell. Languishing in a dingy cell for a week, sick as a dog at death's door, separated from his children, he really had all but given up on life. He realized when talking with Barous that he had actually started to give up long before he got sick, long before Roland came to take away his children; indeed, he began to give up when the rains took his trade from him, and the famine took the only woman he ever loved.

Now fate had given him a second chance, a chance at redemption. Come what may, he would not walk passively into this new life. After the exhilaration of watching Barous escape the strappado, the immense relief from finally passing his stone, and the satisfying vengeance of witnessing The Cleric agonize on his own instrument of torture, an abrupt change had overtaken his senses. A storm has been gathering within him, a storm that now swelled into a furious typhoon of unstoppable power and unlimited potential; he wanted to unleash its full fury and let it rage at whoever tried to stand in his way. Feeling stronger than he had in years, adrenaline surging through his veins, he gripped his sword tightly as Barous unlocked the door—and felt the corners of his mouth curl into an unexpected grin.

All hell broke loose at that point. Wasting not a moment of surprise, they burst forth from the threshold toward two of the unsuspecting guards down the hall. A cathartic blast of energy hurled forth from his mouth in a thunderous roar as he charged.

The guards had barely unsheathed their swords before they crashed into them, throttling them back into the stone wall. Guarin's man raised his sword arm to strike, but he was ready for it. Clutching the guard's wrist in mid-swing with his left hand, Guarin swung his sword arm across the side of his head, pounding hard with his pummel, jarring the helmet from his head, and sending it clattering across the nearby table. Seeing the guard's stunned face, he pressed his advantage, smashing the sword pummel again at his naked head until he dropped senseless to the floor. He realized then that it was the young boy who had brought Rose down the stairs.

Quickly looking to the other guard, a more formidable opponent than his own, he saw that Barous had him wrapped up from behind, his arms locked under his shoulders, hands extending up to the back of his neck, driving the big man's head into the stone wall repeatedly until he too slumped to the ground.

Guarin heard a tromping of footsteps rushing toward them just as two more guards appeared from the hallway, their swords poised to strike as they charged headlong into the melee. Barous quickly spun around and together they stepped forward to confront the assault. One of the guards rushed at Guarin, raising his sword above his head with both hands and swinging down with all his might. Instinctively, he dropped to one knee and raised his sword horizontally above his head, supporting the flat of the blade end with his free hand to help deflect the crushing blow. It worked, but the blade cut into his left hand, and his right hand lost its grip from the stinging vibrations that radiated up his arm on impact. Just as the guard raised his sword again for the final killing stroke, Guarin thrust his shoulder up into his torso, driving him backward in a bullrush, until effectively tackling him to the ground. The guard maintained the purchase on his sword and tried to stab back at Guarin but was ineffective at such close range. Guarin used the only weapon at his disposal, smashing his bald pate repeatedly into the guard's face and head until he heard bones cracking under him.

Once he felt his resistance give way, Guarin turned to assess the situation raging around him. He could hear the clashing of metal, the shouts and groans, and the thumping of flesh, but he had to wipe the blood from his eyes to see what was happening. Realizing the fight wasn't nearly over, he lurched to his feet and snatched his sword from the floor. Barous had just dispatched three more guards and was savagely fighting off two others singlehandedly while he had been struggling on the ground with his own foe.

He couldn't bring himself to pierce his sword into another man's unsuspecting back, so instead he moved to pummel him in the back of his head. But just as he raised his arms, the guard across from him called out a warning. With a sudden jerking turn, the guard spun his elbow directly into his ribs, knocking the wind out of him. Almost immediately, he saw the guard's sword coming at him, too late for him to counter. Sensing his last moment, he tried to cower away from the impending strike, but instead witnessed the man's head lift off his neck and soar across the room as Barous's sword sliced cleanly through. The top of his headless corpse sprayed a shower of blood like some hideous fountain, surging as high as the ceiling at first, then less spectacularly with each pulse of his dying heart, his body finally careening to the ground as though in slow motion. Guarin watched with morbid fascination as Barous swung his sword back around in one fluid motion, piercing it directly into the final guard's throat, then gave one final thrust until exiting through the back of his neck.

"Holy shit, that was close! You never cease to impress the hell out of me," said Guarin as he fought to catch his breath.

Barous helped him to his feet with a broad grin. "I would have been overwhelmed without you fighting valiantly beside me. I wasn't sure you had it in you."

"You know, I think I even enjoyed it, at least until the point when I thought I was going to die. Thanks for lopping his head off, by the way."

"I should be thanking you; your attack was just the distraction I needed."

They checked down the hall but didn't hear any other sounds of approaching guards. He looked down to the slain, bloody corpses strewn across the floor. "I thought we weren't supposed to kill any of them?"

Barous just chuckled. "I tried."

"Well, I hope none of the dead ones were his friends," said Guarin, rolling the loose head under his foot so he could see his face.

"Hey, that's the asshole that pulled my fingernails out! I don't give a shit if he is his friend," said Barous.

"Yeah," agreed Guarin, still staring down upon his head, rocking it back and forth with his foot, "he was a dick. Fuck him." He kicked it away then looked toward the guard with the sword in his throat. "This guy was a *major* asshole, fuck him too."

Barous laughed at his grim humor, "You got it, my friend, that's the idea! Anyhow, let's hope that was the last of them."

They brought Rose up from the chamber where she had been waiting warily on the stairway for the fighting to cease. Captain Erec found them some civilian clothes from the storage room and then ushered them to the door outside, checking first for passing guards. When they stepped into the courtyard, all was quiet and dark.

Barous whispered to Guarin, "We shall have to separate for now, at least until we make it out of town. Take the girl and make straight for Dolder Gate. It will arouse less suspicion if you walk close together. Good luck to you my friend. God speed."

Chapter 31

HAN STEPPED OUTSIDE AND LOOKED OUT ACROSS THE YARD. A cold chill greeted him in the face, along with a spatter of drizzle, but he wasn't thinking about the weather. He felt devastated by the news this witch had just announced. *What could Greta say now to convince me to stay?* He looked over at their new visitor and trudged off to introduce himself. The dwarf looked up as he approached, his face heavily bearded, weather-worn and creased like leather. His brow looked almost as bushy as his beard and deeply furrowed, giving him a gruff appearance.

"Hello, sir. I'm Han."

The dwarf just grunted and nodded his head.

Han looked over to the small fruit trees nearby waiting to be planted. Since the dwarf didn't seem to be forthcoming with any instruction, Han walked over to pick up his shovel and began digging where he thought most appropriate. He looked up to the dwarf just as he stabbed the dirt to be sure he wasn't digging in the wrong place, to which he grunted and curtly nodded his head again. After a few minutes of silent digging, Han thought he would give one last effort at introductions. "Can you give me your name at least?"

All he heard was another guttural grunt. It sounded the same but slower this time, as though he were trying to articulate a word. Han grunted back at him, trying to repeat the sound he made. The dwarf confirmed with another quick nod and a grunt. This time Hans's face lit up as though he recognized the name. "Oh, Roul! Is that it, Roul?"

The dwarf stared at him as though struck dumb. "Yah, Roul," he finally replied, clearly exasperated and mocking Hans's pronunciation of his name. "What's the matter, you got too much wax in your ears, boy?" he added with a heavy accent that Han presumed to be Dutch.

"Forgive me, sir. I understand now. You live somewhere around here?"

"Yah, some here, some there."

"Where are you from?"

"North."

"North?"

"Yah, way up north."

Quickly realizing this conversation wasn't going anywhere, Han went about his digging. They formed a broad mound with the dirt and planted the trees deeply.

After they finished planting, Roul went just outside the gate and cut down a good-sized branch, about as wide as his waist and ten feet long. He called Han out to help him load it onto a low wheeled cart.

When he stepped through the threshold of the gate, he immediately felt the vastness of the forest pressing in on him, the dense canopy of trees above him shutting out most of the daylight. It looked as dense and dim as he remembered; tangles of thorny vines, thickly packed bushes, and endless untamed, overgrown hedges concealed the ground from view.

He could barely make out the path before him as it cut through the brush, but only for a short distance before the forest seemed to swallow it up. *I could take off right now. Roul wouldn't be able to keep up with me.* The anticipation pulled at him. In a moment he could be free. *If I left, though, I would be on my own and could never come back—not for hunger, not for warmth or shelter, not even for Greta. How long would it be before I might see her again? Would I even recognize her if I didn't see her for ten years?*

"Han!" Roul called to him, startling him away from his thoughts. He nodded to the other end of the log with a grunt. He helped him lift it onto the cart, then the two of them pulled it into the yard, before Roul locked the gate behind him once again.

The Craving

After they finished chopping the wood, he told Han in his guttural accent to carry a couple cartloads down to the cellar while he hauled the rest under the shelter. Just as he turned the corner behind the house, Han pulled himself up the wall, rock by rock, as fast as he could. He raised his head over the wall and peered out into the forest, then heaved himself on top for a better view. The vegetation looked just as dense and impassable everywhere he looked. If he jumped down, he figured the full height of his body would sink right through into the thick brush.

Discouraged, he dropped himself back down. Climbing the gate was his only chance out of here. He would offer Greta one last chance to agree to come with him—if not, he would escape just before dawn.

By late afternoon, they began slaughtering the pig for dinner. Roul held the wild beast in place while Han tried to cut its throat with the long knife. It jerked wildly just as he swiped, cutting only superficially through the thick skin. This only made the pig grow angrier and fight harder to break free. Blood oozed over its skin, making it slick and even more difficult to hold onto. It took him a few more slices to finally strike the artery which, once finally severed, sprayed a warm crimson gush across his face and chest. It squealed and shrieked and thrashed about in a hideous frenzy as Roul held on as best he could, his grunts sounding just as beastly as the pig.

Han had put a few pigs down with his father and watched many more, but never had he witnessed such a chaotic struggle as this. Finally, all at once, the pig lost its strength and flopped to the bloody ground with a meaty, wet slapping sound. Han stared wild-eyed at the pig, expecting it to start thrashing again in any moment. He marveled at how, only seconds ago, it showed such robust vigor, and now it was just a lifeless carcass, much like the men who tried to rescue him from Roland. *What a peculiar thing life is*, he realized.

He looked at Roul who was covered in as much blood as himself, bracing his hands on his knees and heaving deep breaths. Han thought he might vomit over the poor beast, but instead looked up at him at started laughing. "That was one crazy pig!" he shouted through his laughter, shaking his finger at it.

The whole situation seemed so outrageous and absurdly chaotic that Han suddenly burst out laughing along with him. "I hope he tastes as good as he fought!"

They finished quartering the pig late in the evening, cold and wet, and still slick with blood. The pungent odor emanated off of him, and he steamed perspiration into the cold night air. Exhausted, he made his way to the wash basin and splashed the soapy water onto his skin, rubbing away the dirt and blood and grime as best he could.

They brought some of the smaller cuts of meat to The Lady to be seasoned and cooked for dinner that night; the rest they carried down to the large oven in the cellar to be smoked much more slowly over a low flame to make the meat last longer.

As they made their way back up into the yard, he could already smell the pork roasting from the kitchen through the open window, along with the chatter of Greta and The Lady. As soon as he stepped inside the door to the kitchen, he saw the large hunk of pork, bathing in its own juices, sizzling and crackling before him in the oven. His mouth began to water as he stood staring at it until he heard giggles from Greta and a stern throat clearing from The Lady. "Ahem!"

He broke his transfixed gaze and looked over to their smirking faces. "Oh, hello! I'm sorry, I didn't see you there."

"Yes, we noticed," Greta giggled.

"That smells really good," he said.

The Lady sniffed, "Well it smelled better before you walked in here with those nasty clothes. Why don't you both get changed. It should be ready in a few minutes."

Han nodded and started off to his room but stopped short as he passed through the dining room. "Jesus Christ" he yelled, nearly falling backward into the kitchen. What he found so unsettling was not some immediate danger or threat of harm, but rather the strangeness and the utter surprise of seeing the man that he did not expect to be seated at the head of the table. Yet there he sat, this man who should be dead, sitting calmly before him, erect in his chair, his bony and blackened fingers stretching too far from his hands as they rested on the table in front of him. His face, placid and expressionless, stared at the wall in front of him, then slowly turned to face him, revealing the jagged scar that cut through his milky-colored eye. He saw the odd tattoos that Greta mentioned, prominently marked onto his forehead and cheeks. Making no effort to speak, he just stared at Han like a lifeless phantom. The sweet, savory aroma of the roasting pork that whetted his appetite was now overcome by the redolent stench of his rotting flesh.

He swallowed hard. "Roland," he uttered at last, "I didn't expect you to be out of bed."

He did not reply, but began to tap his fingers on the table, the same finger from each hand at a time, followed by the next pair, and so on, continuing on in an incessant tapping rhythm.

The Lady swept into the room behind him, apparently as shocked as Han was to see him sitting there. "Roland, how did you get out of bed? How did you get into this chair?"

He slowly moved his eyes to The Lady. He did not speak or show any expression, but his fingers stopped tapping. Then he lowered his eyes to Greta as she crept into the room behind The Lady.

The Lady broke the awkward silence. "Well I should say, you are much stronger than I thought possible. They told me you walked last night but I didn't believe them. We must celebrate your recovery. Greta dear, would you kindly bring our friend something cold to drink?"

"Yes, My Lady."

He looked back up at The Lady and uttered a wet, gurgling sound. After clearing his throat, he spoke briefly in a quiet, coarse, and unintelligible whisper. They all stopped and stared at him in silent anticipation. Slowly opening his mouth, he croaked a bit louder, this time Han was barely able to make it out. "The children." He darted his eyes around the room and back to The Lady. Once again, he pulled open his dry, cracked lips and spoke in that barely audible coarse whisper, "Where...are...the children?"

Han and Greta exchanged confused glances, then Greta giggled. "He doesn't recognize us."

"Yeah, we must look a lot different than we did on that journey," Han realized. "I'm actually surprised that he even cares about us."

Greta turned to him. "We're right here Roland. See, I grew my hair back. Sendy brought us here safely, then went back for you. She saved your life. Do you remember any of that?"

He continued to stare vacantly at The Lady, even as Greta spoke. After a short while, his tapping resumed, and then he shifted his gaze to stare ahead of him at nothing again. Han slowly walked past him, looking closely at his fingers as they tapped away in that writhing motion. They looked like bones that were tightly wrapped in a thin layer of dried black leather, becoming so narrow at the tips that they almost resembled the claws of a raven.

"I think I'll go get changed now," said Han as he warily backed away from him. As soon as he opened the door to his room, he heaved a deep sigh, as though he had been holding his breath. He wiped the sweat from his brow with a trembling hand. "As if things weren't strange enough over here…" he muttered to himself as he changed into his tunic.

After returning, Han took his usual seat at the table and looked around at the others: *a witch, a dwarf, and an undead creature called Roland*, he mused to himself. *What a dignified collection of misfits we have here.* They ate their meal in an awkward silence. Roland seemed to be handling himself pretty well without needing any help once his pork was cut into pieces—definitely more well-mannered than Roul over there with all his slurping and open-mouth chewing sounds and grunts of gustatory pleasure.

It seemed everyone at the table tried their best to ignore the overwhelming stench coming from Roland that came very near to ruining their delicious meal. Roul tried to spark conversation by telling everyone about the gruesome pig slaughter. Unfortunately, nobody could understand half of what he was saying, and before he got too far The Lady interjected.

"That is quite enough, Roul. Thank you for sharing, but I don't think we need to hear about the slaughter of a bloody pig while we are trying to enjoy eating that very same pig. And I think you would know by now not to talk with your mouth full when dining at my table, so I don't think I need to say it again."

Roul's chewing and talking stopped abruptly at this admonition, and his face assumed the expression of a young child who had just been shamed by his grandmother.

"I'm sorry, My Lady—"

"Ah-ah! Not with your mouth full," she said, cutting him off again with a sharp wave of her finger.

Like a wooden puppet, his mouth snapped shut while his eyes popped open with alarm and embarrassment. Han thought this was pretty funny and risked an empathetic smile in his direction. It did not go unnoticed by The Lady, who cast him a reproachful warning with her eyes. Roul moved his eyes from The Lady to Han and back again before he cautiously resumed his chewing, this time with his mouth closed. After that unsuccessful attempt at conversation, they finished the remainder of their meal in silence, which was fine by Han.

The only thing that occupied his mind that evening was escaping from this house of freaks. He hoped Greta would come with him, but he was resolved to go alone if she refused. His apprehension grew as the night progressed, so he confronted her as soon as he closed the door to their room.

"How was your day with *The Lady*?" he asked, accentuating her name in a mocking tone.

"It was ok. She seemed back to her normal self again, just like Sendy said she would."

Han could see a hint of sadness cross her face after she said her name.

"For how long though? Sendy won't be here to help us if she snaps again. Didn't you see the look she gave me at dinner?"

"That was nothing more than the look she gave Roul. She wasn't angry at you."

"Whatever. You want to know what I think?" He glanced back at the door and then continued in a whisper. "I think she sent Sendy away so she can get away with punishing me as she sees fit."

"That's crazy, she wouldn't do that. You're making it sound like everything is about you."

"Oh, *that's* crazy? What's crazy is that monster she turned into last night! What's crazy is that half-dead creep that suddenly pops out of nowhere and scares the shit out of me! Now I'm afraid he's going to be lurking around every corner I turn." He checked the door again as his voice began to rise. He could feel his frustration growing, so he took a breath to compose himself. "Look, you told me yourself that Sendy was the main reason you wanted to stay, and now she's gone. Tell me *now* why you would want to stay here with her?"

"She teaches me things, interesting things that I could never learn anywhere else. She treats me almost like I'm a grown-up, and she is usually pretty funny too. I think she will be in a better mood now that Roland is getting better, and she won't have to stay up into the night with him as much. She feeds us good food. We have a bed to lay on in our own room. Don't you see, Han? We won't survive on our own. If Papa is gone, where would we live? Where would we sleep?" Tears began to well up in her eyes as she pleaded her case. "It's cold and we won't have any food. Nobody else outside of this house has any either so don't expect anybody to take us in, not even Aunt Lutrud, and I doubt we could even find our way back home from here. Even if we survived the cold and starvation and wolves and bandits, the best we could hope for in town is getting put into an orphanage with other starving kids. Is that what you want?"

Han just shook his head. He didn't like what she was saying but knew she was probably right. There were no good options; he just knew that, for him, staying here wasn't one of them. *One last try.* "I can find our way back. I left markers to help me remember which path to take. I'll pack a bag with warm clothes and grab some of that smoked pork to bring with us. We can make it last; we're used to rationing food over these last two years."

Tears now trickled down her cheeks in long rivulets. "I don't want to live like that anymore though. I don't want to feel so hungry that I have to eat bark and bugs to stay alive. That's not living."

"That's just until we can find our way out of the forest," he said, becoming more optimistic. "We'll find a new town or village nearby. I've learned enough from Jehan to be able to work for money now. Trust me, I can support us. Come with me, Greta."

"I'm sorry," she whimpered, shaking her head. Her lower lip protruded and quivered like a baby. "I can't go. Please just say you'll stay."

He looked to the floor to avoid her pleading expression, searching for something else to say, but he had made up his mind. "I can't," he said with finality. He looked to her face again. "I'm sorry too, Greta. I'll be gone before morning."

Her expression had changed as soon as he looked back up at her. Gone was her pouty and pleading aspect of despair. She suddenly appeared more worried, anxious—no, even more than that—she looked alarmed. But she wasn't looking at him. She was looking past him and down toward the floor. He turned to look and noticed a flickering shadowing under the narrow space between the bottom of the door and the floor—a shadow of someone's feet, lurking, listening. They both stared in silent terror for a long agonizing moment, not even daring to breath. They watched as the handle slowly turned and the door opened with an ominous creak, breaking the thick silence that hung over the room. It sounded as though the door itself snickered malevolently as it opened toward them. Han imagined if a dead man were to rise from his grave, his mocking laughter would sound about as sinister as that creaking door.

The Lady stood at the doorway looking down at them. She held a candle at her breast, illuminating her face from below, accentuating the prominent features of her face, the deep crevice lining her brow, and that wicked scowl. She took a step forward, and then another, the hard soles of her boots clunking loudly on the wooden floor, echoing through their room. He recalled the sound that Roland's boots made on his own floor when he first entered their home—bad things happened after that.

She set the candle next to their own on the table and clasped her hands together just under her breast. "So, my little boy wants to run away from me, is that it?" her voice creaked as she continued to advance slowly, deliberately, toward him, one clunking step at a time, until her hideous face stopped only inches from his own.

He felt like he was five years old again, caught saying things he wasn't supposed to. He knew that he was being a bad boy and deserved the spanking he received.

He started to back away from her, cowering in fear, but then he straightened up. He wasn't going to be that five-year-old child anymore. Why should he feel guilty about wanting to leave? He stood his ground and stared back up defiantly at those mysterious, glazed eyes bearing down on him. Her eyebrows pinched downward toward her nose, and her lip tightened up into a snarl. He knew she was trying to intimidate him, she wanted him to back away like a scared little boy, but he refused to be afraid in this moment. *If she hits me again, then Greta will finally see my way of things, and I win.*

"I'm not a prisoner here! So what if I want to leave? You can't stop me, you can't watch me every day and night," he said with trembling voice, bracing for a strike.

Suddenly the features of her face spread out into a wild fit of fury, turning even more horrible and ugly. In an instant, she jerked her hand toward his face with a quick flick of her arm. He could just make out a small vial that she clutched in her hand, before his eyes were struck by a searing hot liquid. He collapsed backward onto the floor, shrieking and wailing with panic, trying desperately to rub the poison away from his burning eyes. Above his own cries, he could hear the piercing shrieks of The Witch's maniacal cackle, as well as the terrible screams from Greta, all reverberating together, transforming the sound into a supernatural, resounding, ear-splitting pitch.

Even as he screamed, he began to choke on a bolus of liquid that this fiend must have poured into his open mouth. Before he could even spit it out, she clapped her hand tightly over his lips, forcing the potion down his throat, spraying out of his nose, and inducing an uncontrollable fit of coughing and choking. Like a bloody pig, he frantically fought against her, trying to throw her off. He felt her full weight on top of him now pinning him onto his back, her hand still pressing over his mouth. He had no idea how this old woman could fight as hard as any man, somehow managing to keep him pinned to the floor. The burning in his eyes now took second place to the desperation that he felt of being suffocated. He bucked hard and nearly knocked her loose, but she quickly regained her position, tighter this time. He felt her grab a fistful of his hair and smash the back of his head to the floor with unimaginable strength, finally rendering his body and spirit limp like a beaten dog.

"Yes, we shall see how you escape from me now, my clever little boy!" she shouted her animosity into his face. "I'm afraid your time here is not yet completed. Oh, you will know it when it comes. It won't be long—you can trust me on that!" Quite abruptly, she removed her hand from his mouth, lifted herself up, and turned toward the door.

Still coughing and heaving deep, coarse breaths between his cries, he struggled to catch his breath. Pressing his fingers into his flaming eyes, he screamed back at her, "Why can't you just leave me alone!"

"You should have listened to your sister. She knows what is best for you," she said before slamming the door shut behind her.

"Greta, help me, please, it burns! I can't open my eyes. Please do something!"

She didn't come to his aid though.

"Greta?"

He sat up, his head spinning as a wave of nausea passed through him. Perceiving only darkness and silence, he had to listen closely to hear her quiet whimpering from across the room.

"Greta, please. I need some water for my eyes."

Just more whimpering.

"Are you ok, Greta?" He struggled to get the words out. The burning in his eyes subsided, but he suddenly began to feel very drowsy, like some magical force tugging his mind into a peaceful oblivion.

"Han!" He heard her cry out just as he felt himself falling back to the floor.

Chapter 32

GRETA HARDLY SLEPT THAT NIGHT. It took her about an hour just to move away from the corner into which she had cowered, frozen in fear as she watched this woman attack her brother with such terrible violence. This woman that had been so kind to her, this woman that she looked up to and sometimes admired. She hated herself for trying to convince Han that she would not hurt him anymore. *She wasn't a kind old woman who loved children. She wasn't a woman at all—she was a night hag—a true monster from those horrible stories—with the venom of a snake and the treachery of the devil.*

She lay on her side staring at Han through the candlelight, making sure his chest still rose with his breath. Once the candle burned itself out, she listened closely to his breathing in the blackness of their room. She tried to close her eyes but kept seeing visions of that croon pounding his head to the floor. She prayed that he would be alright, that he would wake up in the morning and still be able to see. She prayed for this madness to stop; she prayed for Sendy to return; she prayed to her mother and her father; she kept praying to distract her mind from these terrible visions. Every time she felt herself drifting off, she would suddenly awaken to the sound of their screams and that horrible shrieking laughter that blasted in her head.

At last, her mind finally let go of these tormenting thoughts as an intoxicating lullaby began to sing softly in her head, easing her towards sleep. It was a common tune, one that her mother used to sing to her at bedtime, one that Greta would occasionally hum to herself after she passed away. She let the sweet voice pour through to her very soul, soothing her anxiety and numbing her guilt. But whose voice was singing in her head? It sounded different from her mother's, more like a child's, clear and comforting—like the voice of an angel.

She felt like she had just fallen asleep when she awoke with a gasp. The Lady stood at the doorway, looking down at her, wearing one of her ridiculous hats. It was more formal looking than her others, two small cones rising at opposing angles from her head, covered and connected by a white shawl that draped down the sides of her cheeks and across her neck, exposing only her face like a nun. She did not appear like the scowling, crazed witch that left their room last night, but she wasn't acting like her cheerful "morning-self" either.

"It is past time that you get dressed and ready for your chores today," she said flatly.

The faint morning light struggled to reach down the hallway and into her room. She had barely slept and her head felt dizzy. She blinked and rubbed her eyes, then quickly turned to Han. He hadn't moved from the same position all night. She went to his side and touched his shoulder, "Han?"

"Oh, don't bother him. He won't be waking up for a little while yet."

She looked upon his face and jerked back in horror. "His eyes! What happened to his…" her voice trailed off as she stared into the blackened pools discoloring the skin around his eyes. Then she turned, shooting a fierce accusatory glare back at The Lady and screamed at her. "What did you do to his eyes?"

"I had to blind him," she said bluntly, without any hint of remorse or need to explain any further.

Greta stared back at her, shocked, speechless, devastated. She had to force her words. "You blinded him?" She stared at her again for a long moment, her lower lip quivering. "Why? Why would you do that?"

"I think you know why. I'm afraid I would have done the same to you had you agreed to go with him. His eyes will burn from the poison for a little while longer, so I gave him something to help him sleep through the worst of the pain. And don't worry too much about his sight, it should come back eventually, more or less."

Greta looked back down at Han as he lay in deep slumber, gently stroking his cheek, brushing strands of his hair back from his face.

"There, now please get dressed and wash up. I have something I would like to discuss with you over breakfast." She lingered at the doorway until Greta finally rose from Han's side, then strode briskly down the hallway to the kitchen.

Greta walked warily to the table and sat down, wishing Sendy was here with her. The Lady sat across from her, chewing her bread and studying her face without blinking. Greta felt the weight of her gaze upon her but kept her own eyes on the bread and jam on her plate.

"Tell me, did you pray to your God last night for help?" she asked, pouring herself a glass of wine from the pitcher.

Greta looked up at her, puzzled. "What? Yes…yes, I did," she replied hesitantly.

Slamming the pitcher back down, she shouted, "Your God won't help you here!" A thick silence followed her outburst, except for the fading din of the pitcher ringing in her ears. Leaning forward, she glared at her from across the table. "Do you think it was Jesus Christ that saved your life by bringing you to my house? Do you think it was The Holy Spirit that took your mother from you? Do you think God would cause or even allow such suffering and starvation in the world? Tell me this, why would He allow me to harm your innocent little brother?"

"I don't—"

"THERE IS NO GOD!" She shouted again, banging her fist on the table. Greta felt herself shrinking in her chair. She had never shouted at her this way before. "I have seen too much evil in my life—men butchering other men and women and children—and for no apparent reason. I barely escaped with my own life as a young girl working as a missionary in Africa. We were attacked, my entire group massacred by heathens, while I was knocked unconscious with a club and left for dead. How useless is this God of yours that He couldn't even protect His own missionaries?" she cried out, throwing up her arms, practically rising out of her chair to express her incredulity.

She then collected herself and eased back into her chair. "I survived though, rescued by a shaman who revealed the truth to me. How could I have been so blinded? There is no God, or if there is, He has no power in this world, not like Lucifer." Her scowl began to transform into a smile. "Through Lucifer, I have seen divine power, and I can assure you it is not the power of Jesus Christ. Lucifer allows me to harness true divine power. I can commune with spirits and demons and the Devil himself. They reveal themselves to me, talk to me, show me what is to come, what I need to know. They grace my garden while others wilt and rot. They grant me powers to heal the sick and raise the dead. They —" Her voice grew louder once again, her expression more enthusiastic, her hands rising up in clenched fists, before cutting herself off and settling back into her chair once again.

She took a drink of wine and then clasped her hands on the table in front of her before continuing. "I can teach my craft, but it requires certain…sacrifices. I've had many students that followed my teachings, and others who chose not to. Your brother has made his choice, but I have decided how he can still be useful to me. This comes as no surprise; females seem most willing and adept to learn the way of the witches. You seem to be learning well enough, but it is time we took the next step forward. It is time to admit that your God has done nothing for you or your family. It is time that you relinquish Jesus Christ altogether, just as I did long ago, and embrace the dark angel, Lucifer, as your guiding light."

Greta found herself in an unimaginable predicament. She couldn't even believe what she was hearing and didn't know what to say. The Lady wasn't really offering her a choice with that unspoken threat lingering under her words. She replied with what honestly scared her more than anything. "We could get burned at the stake if we get caught practicing witchcraft!"

"You just have to be smart and secretive. You could simply deny it and charge your accuser of seeking revenge upon you. Lucifer will aid and protect you in your path. He will make you more powerful than you ever thought possible." Her words came out with force and conviction, as did her unfaltering gaze upon her.

Greta tried to match her gaze without showing her fear. She wished Sendy had never left them alone with The Lady—then it dawned on her. She swallowed hard. "Sendy was your student." The Lady smiled at her. "So, she really is a witch then?"

"Yes, of course, my dear."

She felt lost. *I have nowhere to turn, no one to trust.*

"Think on what I have said. You shall decide your path soon, or I shall decide it for you. And I will not tolerate any more prayers to your God in my house. Is that clear?"

"Of course, My Lady. Thank you."

She spent the rest of her day in a haze, mindlessly going about her chores, washing clothes, making and straining the cheese, kneading the dough, cleaning the kitchen and that filthy oven that left her fingers as black as Roland's. Then she was shut inside Roland's dark, smelly room for hours, tending his wounds, bathing his body, applying ointments, exercising his limbs, emptying his disgusting chamber pot.

By dinner time, she felt so exhausted that she almost fell asleep at the table. Han was not present at dinner. She didn't bother to ask why. The Lady wouldn't even allow her into their room that day because she said he needed his rest. When she finally had permission to go to bed early, she walked warily to her room, hoping that Han was beginning to wake up. She opened the door and shined her candle inside—into the dark and empty room.

"Han?" She stepped inside, moving her candle into the dark shadows and corners of the room. He was gone. *Where could he be? Did he get up and leave like he said he would?* She noticed something small laying on his mattress. She stooped down and lowered the candle for a closer look. That creepy looking old doll—the one they had pulled out of the toy box on their first night here—stared up at her with those big round eyes. It seemed to be screaming at her with that wide-open mouth—or maybe it was laughing at her. With a sudden feeling of revulsion, she threw it into the box like it was a dead rat, then stared at the box as though she half-expected it to start crawling back out. A strong sense of anxiety and alarm welled up in her chest. She walked back to the dining table where The Lady was finishing her wine. Greta stood there in silent trepidation until she finally looked up at her.

"What happened to Han? He isn't in his room," she squeaked.

The Lady dabbed her lips with a napkin and then looked up at Greta with a sardonic grin. "He isn't in his room? Oh, I don't know, maybe he decided to run away? I haven't seen him, dear." Her reply sounded disingenuous, like she was rehearsing a line from a play.

Greta didn't know what to say. She just stood there staring at her, not realizing that her jaw had gone slack and hung half-way open like she was struck dumb. She had to know what happened to him, she wouldn't be able to sleep not knowing where he was. But if she pressed her—second-guessed her—she would get angry, so she just stood there.

At last The Lady broke the silence. "It's just the two of us now, the way it should be. Don't you think?" They stared at each other for a long moment, The Lady maintaining her mocking smile, as though daring Greta to confront her. Then she cocked her head slightly to the side and continued. "Is there something else you wanted to say? You look very sleepy; I think you should go back to your room now."

Greta's lower lip quivered until she was finally able to force her words out in a timid, squeaky whisper. "Han is gone?" Tears welled up in her eyes, still struggling to grasp the finality of the situation. She then dropped her head, made her way back to her room, and closed the door. She just stood there, motionless, her back against the door, all her thoughts consumed by worry, confusion, loneliness, and fear. *What did she do with Han? He couldn't have left on his own.* She could only come up with one other alternative, and the conclusion finally struck her like the weight of the world on her back: *My brother is dead. The poison... She must have removed his body when I was working, perhaps burned or buried him outside.*

She set the candle on the table, kneeled beside her bed, and prayed silently for a very long time. She never questioned why God would have allowed these things to happen to her and her family. She accepted what her mother told her before she died: that life was a struggle for everyone, including Jesus, and probably always would be. She prayed simply because she felt empty and broken inside, and praying to God filled her up, lifted her spirit, made her feel whole again.

Just as she began to feel her thoughts scatter and succumb to sleep, she heard that song again in her head, that sweet voice of an angel, sending her thoughts gently adrift down a soothing silver stream of tranquility.

Chapter 33

DARKNESS.

When Han finally awoke, he had no idea what had happened to him or where he was, only that he could not see a thing. He shivered from the cold, moist air around him. As he smacked his mouth open, an overwhelming sense of thirst came over him. *How long have I been asleep?* He felt around and realized that he was lying on a rough wool blanket spread over a cold, hard bed of gravel. His hand knocked into a deep wooden bowl, spilling a cold liquid over his skin. Instinctively, he lifted it to his mouth without even bothering to smell or taste it first and drained the entire bowl in large ravenous slurps and gulps, some of it spilling down his cheeks and neck. *Damn, that tasted good.* As soon as he emptied the bowl, he dropped it carelessly to the ground, sucking in panting breaths as if he had nearly drowned himself.

He swiped the back of his hand across his mouth and took another look around him once again. Figuring that his eyes should have adjusted to the darkness by now, he blinked to make sure they were open. He sat up and listened intently for any sound at all, but the silence was absolute. He called out for help but heard only his voice echoing back to him. He yelled louder this time, then as loud as he could. Something scurried across the ground nearby, probably a rat.

I must be in the cellar—but how did I get here? His mind felt muddled and numb as he tried to collect his thoughts, tried to recall the last thing he remembered.

He stood up, but with nothing to hold onto, nothing to see in the blackness, he quickly became dizzy and unsteady. Throwing his arms out in a vain attempt to balance, he felt himself begin to sway and stumble to the side until smacking against a brick wall. He took a breath and steadied himself, then made his way cautiously, step by step, feeling his way along the bricks, turning with each corner, making a perimeter along the walls, until he finally felt a door frame set into the third wall that he came to.

He realized that this must be the locked door that he saw in the cellar. *Why am I in here?* He felt around the wooden door until he grasped the handle. It didn't turn. He pushed, then pulled, then shoved his shoulder against it, then pressed his foot on the wall beside the door and tried to jerk the door back and forth, but it wouldn't budge. He banged the bottom of his fists against the wooden door, but it was so heavy and thick that he barely made a sound. Numerous scratches and gouges in the wood left splinters poking out of his hands that now trickled with blood.

He called out again, yelling Greta's name, louder and louder until his shouts became screams and his screams became desperate, pleading cries for help. At last, he turned his back to the door and slowly slid to the ground, burying his face in his hands, tears streaming down his cheeks, his chest and shoulders shuddering with his sobs, until he was emptied of all his emotions—and that was exactly how he felt inside—empty, like a hollow log that lay neglected in a remote and lonely forest.

He sat huddled on the ground for what seemed like hours, shivering, sobbing, hugging his knees against his chest, staring into the blackness around him, wondering how long he would have to sit here before she let him out, or at least check on him. *What had I done to deserve this? I should have left here when I had the chance. Wait—that's it!* He remembered talking to Greta last night after dinner about leaving with or without her. His mind flashed with images of what happened next: The Lady listening at the door—confronting him—throwing poison at his face and in his mouth—his eyes burning.

"My eyes!" He waved his hand directly in front of his face. Nothing. He placed his fingers over his eyes. "Am I blind? My

God, did she blind me? Did you blind me you fucking bitch?! Why can't you just let me go?" he screamed. "What did I do to you? What did I ever do to anybody?"

He thought hard about that last question, as though it came out of his mouth and bit him for even daring to ask such a question. A deluge of shame and guilt poured over him as he thought about all of the people he had hurt in some way or another. *Ferrand would still be alive if I hadn't put all three of those men in danger; they all died trying to help me. Hell, I would have even abandoned my own sister here and left her alone with that crazy witch. It's no wonder she didn't lift a finger to help me, didn't even come to my side when I called her name. Papa would never forgive me for something like that; Mum would roll over in her grave.*

He swallowed back an even deeper shame as he remembered the day his mother died. *Only the Lord knows that dirty little secret of mine.* He never told anybody, even tried to forget about it, pushed the memory deep down into the darkest pit of his soul. But now it came flooding back over him like it just happened yesterday. He recalled his last wish as she lay on her deathbed: he wished that she would just get it over with and die. Not because he didn't want her to suffer any longer for her own sake, but because he didn't want to see her anymore in that condition. She looked at him with those pitiful sunken eyes, motioning him over with a feeble wave of her hand. But he didn't want to kiss her or hug her anymore. Her sickly appearance disgusted and scared him. This skeleton of a woman didn't look anything like his mother, and he just wanted her to go away—and she did. In that moment, her last dying moment, he had turned his head in revulsion from her and walked out the door. When he returned, she was no longer breathing, her head turned in the same position as when he left, her dead eyes staring up at him as if to say, "Why did you leave me, my son?"

A tight knot constricted his throat as he tried to choke back his sorrow, but then he let it pour out of him in heavy tears and wailing sobs, "I'm so sorry Mum. Please forgive me." He craned his neck back and cried out to the heavens, "Can you hear me, Mum? I love you so much, and I miss your smiling face. Do you miss me? Do you still love me?" His words echoed off the walls, then ended in a lonely silence.

He hated himself more than anything for that selfish moment of weakness. *How could I ever forgive myself? Maybe I deserve to sit in this bleak prison of blackness*, he thought, *to think about my sins—as punishment for my sins.*

His conscience wouldn't leave him alone, so he tried to shift the blame. He thought about his father next, how he'd given up on his family, how he was willing to let Lutrud send his own children away, not even knowing where they would be sent. In the end he certainly had a change of heart, he gave him credit for that, but the stage was already set, the players were in motion—too late to make things right.

The moment of his father's stand against Roland had happened so quickly, so unexpectedly, that he hadn't really taken the time to reflect on it since then. He had been so devastated by what Lutrud said to him in that moment, that he had practically dismissed his courageous stand altogether. *"My dear, we talked about this. You agreed that we cannot feed them. We must let them go!"*

He remembered how weak and sick he appeared on the way home from Riquewihr, how he collapsed into bed as soon as they got home. He wondered how he even built up the strength to confront Roland the following morning. *I guess he did care about us after all.* He almost wished he could have stayed to watch them fight. *Did he get one or two good punches in before he was taken down?* He half-smiled and felt the back of his neck prickle imagining his father in a fight. *It almost worked too; we'd almost gotten free.* Then his smile slipped away. *What happened to Papa after that? Is he even alive now? Could he be searching for us?*

He thought about what his father must have been going through since he lost his own wife, his work, his health. *The more depressed he became, the more I disrespected him. Why couldn't I even bring myself to show him a little support that night when he broke down and cried in front of us? Instead, I just turned away in disgust, exactly like I did to Mum.*

The deepest despair he had ever felt came crashing down on him in that moment, like a physical weight, pushing his head down, slumping his shoulders, pressing his back forward until he could no longer bear the weight. He let himself topple over onto his side, locking himself into a tight fetal position, and whimpered. *I've let down everyone who has ever cared about me. Truly, this is where I belong.*

He awoke lying on his back again, staring into blackness. Time had no meaning for him any longer: he woke, he dozed, he thought, he stretched, he shivered. He walked around the room countless times, guiding himself along with his hand on the bricks, knowing that it measured exactly twenty paces along two of the parallel walls and sixteen paces along the other two.

He should be hearing footsteps overhead since he heard them from the cellar. He didn't though, so that could only mean that this room extended out from the cellar and under the yard rather than under the house. Which would explain why nobody could hear his screams and calls for help. His only company were the rats. He heard them around, skittering about. Sometimes he would try to chase them around just to break the monotony and boredom, but it usually didn't end well with him crashing into a wall.

At least The Lady was gracious enough to leave him a small chamber pot with a lid to cover his stench. He discovered her little game too, of hiding bowls of food and water randomly on the floor, forcing him to crawl and feel his way around on the cold hard gravel to find them, wondering which one held a little surprise eyeball waiting for him to consume, wondering if a rat had chewed on it first, or even crapped in the food. It didn't matter anymore though. He had found and eaten all of the bowls as far as he could tell, having meticulously searched the entire room, crawling from one end of the floor to the other, trying his best not to miss any areas in the open space.

He began to hear voices, usually when talking to himself. The voice was always the same—a soft, hoarse, hissing voice. He wasn't sure if they were threats or warnings or his own mind talking to him, but they seemed to come from behind the locked door.

"Get out! This is an evil place," it hissed.

"You will die here, very soon. Your time is coming."

"Beware of The Lady. She likes to eat children, especially babies, but she will eat you too."

"Don't eat the food. She is just trying to fatten you up so you will taste better."

At first this voice would scare him into silence, but after several of these warnings over however many days he'd been locked in here, he finally shouted back, "Why don't you quit trying to scare me and get me out of here then! Help me out or just shut up already!" He defiantly whipped a rock at the door and heard footsteps skitter away along with a snickering laugh.

He became more and more convinced that he must be that child whose eyes he saw in the cellar a while back. He knew he wasn't imagining that. He wondered if he could be a child that had escaped from here. He hoped so, because that meant that he could escape too.

"What is your name?" Han called out, but the voice was gone.

Hours later he heard a sound that he hadn't heard since his imprisonment: the faint but unmistakable squeak of the latch and the trap door to the cellar being opened. Footsteps thumping down the wooden stairs. The sound of a key, much louder now, scraping into his own door, grinding in the metal lock, and then the creaking of the hinges as the door swung open. The air from the cellar wafted into the room. He could smell the stale, wet earth mixed with the scent of burning wood and charcoal from the furnace. He could even smell, almost taste, remnants of the pig they smoked the night before she locked him in here.

For the first time, he could actually see a faint light, not much bigger than a spot, hovering at the doorway.

"Hello?" Han croaked.

The light moved slowly closer, swinging gently from side to side in rhythm with the soft metallic scraping of its metal hinge. Heavy steps crunched on the gravel floor, growing louder as they approached. Then a familiar voice replied, "What have you gotten yourself into, my boy?"

"Jehan! You're back!" Han exclaimed, jumping to his feet, letting his excitement get the better of him. Han had been thinking about Jehan and Sendy during his time in the blackness. Given how long they have known The Lady, he figured that they must have been aware of how cruel she could be. But he still clung to any shred of hope that he could. Hope was all that he had left.

"Yes, I've only just returned. I came down to see you as soon as I heard," his voice sounded even deeper in the enclosed room. "I brought you some food and drink," he said, placing a tray into his hands.

Han tried not to sound too emotional, but his voice quivered, almost choking on it as he spoke. "The Lady blinded me and forced some kind of potion down my throat to make me sleep, then I woke up in this cellar. I don't even know how long I've been down here."

"She told me it has been three days."

"Three days?" It seemed much longer. "Can I come back up now? I promise I won't try to run away, especially now that you're here."

"It seems The Lady has made her choice."

He swallowed hard. "Choice?"

Han blinked and rubbed his eyes, trying to refocus with the light in front of him. He could barely make out the tall figure standing before him, holding out a lantern between them.

After a long moment of silence, he heard Jehan draw in a heavy sigh, as though he were deliberating on how much he should say. "You have been chosen, Han. At first, I didn't think that she would even consider you given your age, you're almost—"

"Chosen for what?"

"I've told you already of The Lady's great powers. Much greater than my own, in fact. She has The Gift—the Gift of a High Witch."

His mind raced as Jehan's words came out painfully slowly. "Has she chosen to teach me this power of witchcraft?" Han asked. *This isn't making sense.*

"Your sister perhaps, but not you, Han," he said gravely, his deep voice echoing within the chamber. "You have another purpose, a greater purpose." He then paused, as though cutting himself off. "That is all I can say for now. Just know that you have been chosen for a great honor. All will be revealed very soon."

A wave of nausea spread throughout his body. The light turned and began to sway again as he walked toward the open door. "Jehan, wait!" he shouted. "Please, at least leave me the light. I can't bear this darkness any longer."

Without a word, he set the lantern down and left the room, locking the door behind him.

Han considered all that he told him. *A great honor. I've been chosen.* He knew this could be no *great honor.* All of his suspicions came crashing down on him at once as he realized what all of this could only mean. He began to tremble as he remembered the drawings on the cellar walls: the figure with the pointy hat next to an altar, the children burning, the demonic face. His neck prickled as he remembered the whispered warnings from the mysterious voice. What did Jehan said about her gift, her great powers? Jehan didn't have to finish what he was going to say. Han knew; a part of him had suspected since he first stepped down into that cellar. *Great powers usually require...a sacrifice.*

He felt swallowed by hopelessness in that moment, a sense of complete emptiness that he couldn't quite explain—as though even God himself had abandoned him now. He straightened his posture and drew in a sharp breath. *I won't give up. I must find a way to escape, maybe like this other kid.* He wondered if he was just a phantom, a figment of his imagination, but he had to hope.

He picked up the lantern and held it before him, peering into the murky darkness of his prison. He could only see a few feet in front of him despite the light, but it was something. He noticed a dark stain against the wall across from the door. Walking closer to inspect it further, he noted that the stain looked like old blood that had spattered against the wall and even onto the ground beneath his feet. He noticed the stain cut-off sharply at about the level of his chest, perhaps from a table of some kind that once rested against this wall.

He inspected the perimeter of the room but didn't see any more blood stains. What he did find were more of the drawings like he saw in the cellar: demonic looking faces, wild animals, burning children. The most disturbing one looked like a child being sacrificed on a table by the tall figure with the strange pointed black hat. He surveyed the door just in front of him and noticed some writing etched into the wood, along with countless scratch marks, as though someone had desperately tried to gouge their way through the door with their nails. He squinted and blinked, his eyes beginning to tear as he tried to focus on the writing. He wasn't good at reading, so he had to stare at it until it made sense to him: ABANDON ALL HOPE

Chapter 34

GRETA SLEPT WELL INTO THE MORNING. Her head felt clearer, but her sense of fear and loneliness remained. She went about her day much the same as yesterday, completing her chores with a mind-numbing routine. But in the back of her mind, she prepared herself for what she would say to The Lady the next time she asked her to swear allegiance to Lucifer. She concluded that she would have to fake her way through this over the next few days. What choice did she have? She couldn't try to run away now. She would never survive on her own and refused to give up on Han. *Maybe she kept him hidden somewhere locked up, like in the cellar?* She did say that his time here was not yet completed on the night she poisoned him. As menacing as that sounded, it at least provided her a shred of hope to cling to.

While taking a stroll around the yard, she stopped by the trap door and knocked, listening closely for any sounds. She attempted to pull it open even though she knew it was locked. She asked Roul to unlock the cellar door, but he immediately became suspicious and said he had too much work to do.

Roland became more alert today and his once gaping, puss-filled wounds were clearly beginning to heal into little puckers on his skin. The Lady gave her a stinky solution to spread over his wounds, killing off all the wriggly maggots that remained. He ate much better each day and started to get his color back, but his mind still had a long way to go. He seemed to stare off vacantly with his one green eye, the other remained as white as a pearl. He barely talked, even if she asked him a question.

Sometimes he seemed like he wanted to say something, like he was straining to get his words out, until finally uttering a single croak or grunt. She wondered how he was able to complete a full sentence just a couple nights ago. "Good days, bad days" is what The Lady and Sendy always said.

His became stronger each day. He was able to get out of bed his own so they took him for a walk outside. He even joined them again at dinner, along with Roul, who seemed quieter than the last time she dined with him. At one point, Roland seemed to be straining at his throat. At first, she thought he was choking on his food, so she jumped to his side, but then he started grunting words.

"Where…are…the…children?" He uttered as his eyes latched onto The Lady.

Greta rubbed his back and answered for her. "I'm right here. I've been helping take care of you for the past few days." She paused as her expression saddened. "Although, we're not sure where Han went."

He took another bite that she offered but didn't remove his gaze from The Lady, who sipped at her wine, her left eye beginning to twitch. When he didn't say anything further, she took her seat again and they finished their meal in silence.

Finally, The Lady spoke for the first time. "Roul, would you mind walking Roland to his room? He had a big day and needs to rest. Then you may retire for the evening. Thank you, dear."

Roul grunted and popped out of his chair like he was waiting to be excused from the awkwardly silent meal. Greta began washing and handing the clean dishes to The Lady who dried them with a clean cloth.

"Have you thought about the matter we discussed last night?" The Lady asked.

"Yes. It's just that this is all so strange, and it scares me."

"Once you get started on the path, you will understand it better. You will meet others like us, and you will no longer be scared. In fact, it can be quite fun and liberating." She closed her eyes and smiled. "Even ecstatic at times," she added, as though remembering a fond moment from her past.

"These powers…do they allow you to see where others are? Can you find out what happened to Han and my father?" She spoke the line just as she went over in her head.

The Lady cast her a sharp glance, pausing briefly before answering. "I can only commune with the dead, not the living. I'm sorry, dear, but perhaps it is best that you forget about Han, since he has abandoned you."

"I'm not sure I can. No more than I can abandon God," she replied honestly, forgetting her rehearsed lines for the moment. "How did you finally make your decision? I know you told me why, but I mean…was it difficult for you, after having devoted your life to Christianity until that point?"

"No, it was not difficult at all, in fact. When those heathens massacred my fellow missionaries, I felt like God had forsaken me. But soon after I began to even question the very existence of God." She shrugged her shoulders. "I realized that if he did exist, he certainly didn't seem to wield any power in this world. Once I accepted this, I felt free to live my life as I chose, not bound by rules made up by corrupt priests and theologians over centuries— all men, I might add. Who are they to us?" She put the towel down and focused more intently upon Greta.

"That's when my visions began. I am told it is a rare gift— a reward for my conversion. They are quite powerful, magical, insightful; bestowing upon me incredible visions of the spirit world, evoking feelings of great power flowing through my body like a font of the universe, allowing mighty and ancient spirits to speak through me!" She stopped then, just as the passion in her voice began to grow.

"What kind of spirits?" she asked in a frightened whisper.

Her glazed eyes widened with intensity, inching closer to Greta's. "We call them Demons." She reached and grabbed a firm hold of her forearm. "If you want a taste of this power, then perhaps I can show you soon. We shall have to await The Gift. I feel it will come upon me again very soon. You must be ready to come when I call."

Greta regarded her with bewilderment and swallowed hard before replying, "Yes, of course, My Lady."

She relieved her grip and softly patted her arm. "Very good, now if you wouldn't mind finishing up, I have some preparations to do."

Upon returning to her room for the night, she left the door slightly ajar so that she wouldn't miss the sound of her "call." The house seemed unusually quiet. She picked up two of the dolls that she made out of yarn and played with them like she used to at home. After tiring of this, she lay on her bed thinking about her parents and about Han, and then about how lonely she felt. She thought about Sendy too, wondering if she really was a witch like The Lady said, wondering if there was such a thing as nice witches or just evil ones.

After a couple hours of anticipation and then sheer boredom, she finally fell asleep. She had restless dreams of Han getting pummeled by The Lady while she just stood idly by and watched like an obedient pupil. Then she found herself screaming and tied to a burning cross while naked witches danced around her, and a pack of wolves howled their terror into the night. When she forced her eyes open to end the dream, she saw Han standing rigidly beside her bed, staring hauntingly down upon her with sinister black eyes, eyes just like the child in the forest.

She awoke with a start, realizing it was merely another dream.

After shaking off her fright, she lay back down and tried to relax. That is when she heard that comforting song again. Except this time the song didn't put her to sleep. She opened her eyes, sat up, and listened closely, realizing that the song was definitely not arising from inside her own head.

A gentle smile stretched her lips as she climbed out of bed. She walked over to close her door and then tracked the sound, discovering that it came through a small hole in her floor, situated near the back wall. *Is this real?* she mused as she lay down next to it, curling up onto her side and resting her cheek against her hands. Listening with wonderment, as though her own guardian angel was singing to her, she quietly joined in the last verse. When they finished, the room was left with a pleasant silence.

"Thank you." Greta squeaked into the hole.

"Who are you?" She asked after another moment of silence.

"Don't be shy, tell me your name," Greta persisted.

She let out an exasperated sigh. "My name is Greta. Won't you tell me yours?"

Finally, she heard a reply, raspy and high pitched like a little child, "Gidie."

A smile beamed across her face. "Gidie? That's a very cute name. You have a beautiful voice, Gidie. Who taught you that song?"

"My mother."

"My mother used to sing that to me too when I was a little girl, it's my favorite. Where is your mother now?"

"Dead."

Greta pinched her eyebrows up with sympathy, "I'm sorry, Gidie. My mother died too, just last year." She paused. "Are you hiding down in the cellar?"

"Yes." His reply sounded like the hiss of a snake.

"How long have you been down there?"

"I come and I go."

"Why?"

"I come back to see her new children."

"How did you find this place?"

"He brought me here, like you, like the others."

An unsettling sensation welled up inside her. *Like the others? Her new children?* She was almost too afraid to ask. "Gidie, what happened to the other children?"

"Dead."

Greta wanted to vomit. She could feel her heart beginning to race and pound in her chest, just as a cold sweat broke out on her forehead. She quickly sat up on her heels and pressed him further. "You escaped—before she could do the same to you?"

"Yes," he hissed.

"Have you seen my brother?"

"Yes."

"When?"

"I used to see him in the cellar sometimes."

"I mean, when was the last time you saw him? I…I don't know where he is. The Lady told me that he must have left."

"She lies."

"Gidie, please, have you seen him? Do you know where he is? I'm very worried about him."

"Yes." The hiss slithered through the hole, tickling her ears and prickling the hair on the back of her neck.

She shut her eyes tightly and swallowed hard as bile crept into her throat. "Where?" *Please don't say dead, please don't say dead.*

"In the cellar."

She gasped and sobbed with relief, her eyes brimming with tears. "He is alive then—down there with you?" She couldn't believe what she was hearing.

"Yes, but she locked him in the killing room."

Greta opened her eyes in shock, staring down into the black void of the hole. This tiny portal that offered such comforting sounds a moment ago suddenly began spewing such terrifying information at her. "The killing room?" Her words barely escaped her mouth in an almost silent whisper.

"Yes. It's where she keeps him before the sacrifice. She used to sacrifice the children in the killing room, but now with more people watching, she just keeps them there until the ceremony, then brings them outside for the sacrifice."

"She is going to sacrifice him at a ceremony?" she asked, grappling with the words, telling herself this sounded too horrific to be true.

"Yes, and then she is going to cook him, and then she is going to eat him. That's what she did to the other children. The Devil makes her do it."

Greta stared down at the hole, her eyes glaring with hysteria. She wanted to cry, to shout her anger to Gidie and to the heavens. Instead, she froze with terror, her mouth held agape in a silent scream.

And that was when she heard her "call."

A sudden hideous shriek erupted from outside her room, flooding her with panic and dread. Sounding like some inhuman, tortured cry, it gradually evolved into a miserable haunting groan that seemed to stretch on to no end.

"Uh oh. This is when she starts talking to her demons," Gidie rasped.

Greta jumped to her feet, quickly wiping the tears from her eyes. Her breathing was deep and rapid, her heart pounding through her chest and into her neck as she thought about what to do. Sendy never taught her how to treat her falling sickness. She didn't know which incense to burn, or how to light it.

As she forced her trembling legs to walk toward the door and into the hallway, she remembered how The Lady became helpless in a deep sleep once her seizure abated last time—which presented a unique opportunity. *Is it evil to murder a murderer?* This may be her only chance to save Han, if what the boy in the cellar says is true. W*hat if he is just a little devil telling lies, teasing me, taunting me?*

As she turned the handle and pulled the door open, the eerie groans and wailing cries grew exponentially louder, filling her room and echoing off the walls of the hallway like a demonic hoard. She had heard the ancient tales of the banshee women from Ireland, how they cry out like this to mourn the coming death of a close family member.

A sudden shriek split her ears in the form of her own name. Clapping her hands over her ears, she winced from the terrible sound that chilled her to her bones. Gathering her courage, she lifted the candle from the table and stepped into the hallway. She started to walk toward the kitchen to arm herself with a knife, but instead found herself nearly running into Roland, The Lady's animated golem, his long spindly fingers slowly writhing in the candlelight. He stared vacantly ahead, as though standing guard in the hallway, leaving her with only one direction to go.

Turning quickly away from him, she walked toward the sinister sounds emanating from The Lady's room; the groans, croaks, moans, and shrieks rising to a fever pitch, continuing to scream her name as she passed under the threshold of her domain. Several candles flickered, illuminating the strange symbols and chaotic words strewn across the walls, but casting deep shadows in the corners of the room. Using some sort of writing instrument, The Lady frantically scrawled more words on the wall, as though she were a font channeling the words of a demon. Everything stopped when Greta stepped into the room, imparting a lingering silence.

The Witch slowly turned her head to face her, her pen resting upon the wall in mid-stroke, her body otherwise motionless. Her straggly gray hair fell down over her shoulders and covered most of her face except for her long nose and chin poking through. She seemed to stare directly at Greta for several long seconds, though she couldn't even see her eyes through the curtain of hair. Finally, she jerked her hand from the wall, jabbed the pen into her arm like an ink well, and continued writing with her own blood. She also began speaking in that ancient language that sounded like Latin, but in a deep, growling, fiendish voice.

Greta looked to her left and noticed a large glass globe resting on a wooden base, centered on a pedestal between two chairs. Somehow, she could hear the words "Sit down, Greta," clearly stated with her true voice, right in the midst of her rambling Latin satanic sermon.

She obeyed. She almost tripped over a doll laying on the floor beside the chair. She picked it up and saw that it was that same sinister looking doll from the toy box in her room, its coarse black hair tickling the back of her hand. Except now several long needles protruded from each of its eyes, making it appear even more alive and frightful than ever before as it glared and screamed silently up at her. She tossed it as far from her as she could, landing against the wall across the room.

Several moments later, she heard the words "Drink."

She noticed a cup on the table beside her, picked it up and drank the liquid.

"Now close your eyes."

Her sermon became some sort of a chant that went on unceasingly, inducing her mind into a sort of trance, though she did not understand a word of it. After a while, the room became silent again. She didn't know for how long she was supposed to keep her eyes closed, so after a couple minutes of silence, she opened them. The Lady sat directly in front of her now in a forward lean, only inches away from her face, gazing over the ball at her through those mysterious, glazed eyes. Her unexpected appearance made her flinch, shooting an icy tingle up her spine. She held a drum encircled by tiny metal symbols between her knees. Her hands rested on top of the drum, rivulets of blood trickling down her skin from the numerous puncture marks in her arms.

"Would you like to talk to your mother now, Greta?"

Distracted by her bloody arms and the unsightly bald patches and sores in her scalp, her question caught her completely off guard. "My mother? Now?"

"She tells me that she would like to talk to you. Would you like to talk to your mother now, Greta?" she repeated in the same rapid, clipped, almost inhuman tone, lacking any semblance of empathy or compassion. Then she smiled crookedly, slowly cocking her head to the side as she awaited her answer. "I can make that happen. I can teach you this power too, if you will join me."

"Yes, I would like that, My Lady," she answered, but feeling more scared than eager.

A wide maniacal smile split across her face just then. "Good! Then let us begin. Close your eyes and relax, my dear."

Greta closed her eyes once again and settled into her chair. The Lady began chanting now in a different, more primitive sounding language, accompanied by the beat of the drum, quickly sending her consciousness into a mystical realm. She followed her voice as it gradually rose and then fell like waves, but each crescendo growing more fervent than the last. The drumbeat and rattle of the symbols intensified, resonating with the sound of her voice. Vivid images of spirits and animals and half-human creatures formed in her mind, at first floating evocatively before her, then spiraling around her in ghostly trails before soaring directly at her, through her, past her. Over time, the wave-like chant evolved into a commanding shout, rousing the dead to commune with the living, her supernatural voice rising with depth and power, until at last she heard a gasp, and a deafening silence.

Greta's head was spinning, her ears ringing from the clamor of the invocation, forcing her to open her eyes. The Lady was slumped forward in her chair, head dangling limply over her chest as though her neck had been severed, but her right arm remained rigid and outstretched, her palm placed firmly on top of the globe. What had only been a hollow glass ball when she sat down, now swirled with bright and vivid colors—elegant ribbons of violet, red, orange, yellow, blue, green, and every color in-between—formed of a substance that appeared both gas and liquid at the same time. Fascinated by the beautiful, graceful whirl of plasma dancing in front of her eyes, she reached forward and placed her own hand upon the magical glass ball, rubbing her palm and fingers gently over its smooth, curved surface. She became so captivated that she could not remove her eyes or her hand from the lurid display of swirling colors. The longer she pressed her hand to its surface, the warmer it became, its heat radiating through her hand, up her arm and into her chest, her body. She gazed with wonder as the colors coalesced, taking shape in the form of a shimmering face: a woman's face—her mother's face.

"Mum? I can see you Mum!" Greta softly cried out, leaning closer to the image. Her mother's expression appeared lost, afraid, searching. "Mum, I'm here, can you hear me? Can't you see me?"

Her expression softened. She gently closed her eyes, and then opened them again, this time locking her gaze with Greta's. A warm smile greeted her through the glass. "I can *feel* you Greta. I can feel your warmth and your love." Her spectral voice echoed in whispery rushes, like the resonant sound of a conch shell held to her ear.

"You look so pretty, Mum. I really miss you."

"I miss you too, sweetie. I'm so sorry I can't be there to take care of you, to see you grow up."

"Why did God have to take you away from us?" she sobbed.

A look of sorrow and sympathy washed over her face. "I'm afraid I can't answer that, sunshine. I hope Papa has been taking good care of you."

Greta pinched her eyebrows together. "So, Papa is not with you...in heaven?"

"With me in heaven?" She shook her head with concern. "No, of course not. I don't believe I am in heaven, not yet at least. Has your father passed as well? We've left you both alone?"

"He became very sick, so Aunt Lutrud sent us away. I was afraid he might have died by now, but I don't know."

"She sent you away?" she asked, looking even more confused and distraught.

"Yes, she said she couldn't take care of us any longer because we didn't have any food. We are living with a lady in the forest now; she keeps us well fed." Greta could see how anxious she looked already, so she didn't want to tell her about what happened to Han. "She can talk to spirits. She is the one who connected me with you."

A distinct look of alarm crossed her face as she listened. "...speaks with the dead? You mean like a witch? Greta, where is Han? Why isn't he with you now?"

Her face looked lost and alone again, then her image began to shimmer and dissipate back into the swirling ribbons of color, even as she heard her calling out her name. Greta jerked her hand away as she felt the heat searing through the glass.

The Lady's hand slipped off the glass ball as well and flopped flaccidly to her side. But then her head suddenly wrenched up and dropped backward—too far back it seemed—as though it were on a loose hinge, her face now staring up at the ceiling, her jaw hanging wide open, wide enough to fit her own fist inside. Her jaw started flapping as she began to chant again in that other-worldly voice, while the rest of her body remained perfectly lifeless and still.

Averting her eyes from that sickening posture, Greta looked back down at the glass ball roiling with flames from the inside. As she watched, the flames began to coalesce once again into a face, but certainly not a human one—this was a face brimming with evil, wrath, and power—unmistakably the visage of the devil.

From the corner of her eye, she saw a movement from one of the deep shadows in the corner of the room. A very tall, menacing figure emerged, advancing slowly toward her. He wore long flowing black robes and a deep black hood trimmed with crimson red, cloaking his face in darkness. She hunched over in fear, unable to bear the sight of him moving closer until she heard his footsteps stop in front of her.

She opened her eyes again and had to crane her neck back to see him looming directly above her. Between his arms, pressed against his chest, he bore a very large book—a tome—

like the ones she sees on the altar in church. He gestured for Greta to rise, beckoning her over to a taller table, onto which he set his tome, opening it to a page marked with a long red ribbon.

He turned to Greta and pulled his hood back, revealing the fearsome red mask of a devil. Truly a hideous visage but awesome to behold, it bore large empty black eyes, a beak-like nose, forked beard, and a deranged looking grin. Two curved horns erupted from his pate, bestowing upon him a darkly majestic countenance.

Gasping with fright, she backed away toward the door from his intimidating height and inhuman features, until she bumped up against someone standing behind her. Lurching forward, she whipped herself around to see The Lady's Golem standing rigidly before her, blocking the doorway and staring vacantly ahead. He gripped her shoulders tightly with his hard black talons and briskly turned her back around to face The Devil.

Greta hardly noticed that the chanting had stopped. The Witch now stood beside her, hands clasped in front of her chest.

"Greta." The Devil greeted her with a deep, booming voice. He wore a thick chain around his neck bearing a heavy upside-down cross that hung over his chest. "Do not be afraid of me. The Faerie Lady has invited me to meet with you, speak to you, help you understand our ways. If what I have to say makes sense to you, then I may ask you to join us, our sabbat, our movement, just like many before you have done." His voice seemed amplified and reverberated off the walls, loud enough to hurt her ears.

"Speaking with your mother tonight was just a taste of the power you can achieve. The Lady tells me you are already becoming quite adept in the magical arts of healing. Isn't that right, Roland?"

Roland grunted.

He turned back to Greta and knelt down to her level. "Tell me Greta, have you ever tried to speak to your mother through your prayers?" Greta nodded. "Did she ever speak back you? Did she ever show her face to you?"

She shook her head and wiped a tear, "I almost forgot what she looked like," she said quietly, almost to herself.

"Speaking to the dead is good for your soul, they possess infinite wisdom and can help you find your way in life." He paused, reached out and took her hand in his. "I understand your brother has abandoned you, left you alone here. How do you feel about that?"

"I don't know where he is. Maybe he will come back, maybe he never left."

"The Lady tells me that he wanted to leave on his own. Is that so?"

She nodded her head, avoiding his eyes.

"Your father agreed to your stepmother's demands to send you away. Is this not true as well?"

She held silent, remembering it differently, not so simple as that. She felt his finger under her chin, delicately lifting her face until she looked into his eyes.

"Listen to me, Greta. We will not abandon you if you join our family. You will recall that Sendy was rescued by our friend Roland here, just as she was on her way to trial. And she in turn rescued him. Coincidence? Divine providence?"

"You are alone now Greta, sad and abandoned by all who knew you, and whom I'm sure you thought had loved you. We can be your family now. Join us in renouncing God," he said fervently, glaring at her with conviction and enthusiasm. "Denounce Him for the suffering He has caused you and your family and to all of His so-called "Christendom" with this forsaken famine. Rise above this blinded society and join us!" he called out, rising to his feet.

He lifted the pen from the table and offered it to Greta. The pen felt sticky in her hand, still dripping with witch blood. Placing his hand on the small of her back, he guided her over to the table on which the tome lay opened. She looked down at the pages. On the left page and halfway down the right were a list of names scrawled in old, darkened blood, one after the other. He pointed to the space just below the last name. "Your name shall go here."

Chapter 35

THE NEXT SEVERAL DAYS OF HAN'S CAPTIVITY went much the
same, except that instead of crawling on the ground to find his
food, Roul brought it to him, along with pitchers of rainwater.
He never said anything; he just opened the door, silently placed
the items in the room, and then locked the door behind him. One
day, he was kind enough to leave him a small oil lamp after the
lantern had burned away.

As his sense of desperation mounted each day, Han knew
he had to devise a plan of escape. He finally built up the courage
to try to ambush Roul the next time he brought food for him. As
he heard the trap door open and his heavy footsteps down the
stairs, Han grasped the only weapon that he had at his disposal,
the empty wine pitcher, and pressed himself against the wall next
to the door. As soon as Roul stepped into the room, he swung
down hard on the top of his head. He heard a dull thud as the
impact jarred the pitcher from his hands, clattering onto the floor
beneath their feet. The dwarf looked up at him with a grunt as
though he had merely been smacked rudely on the back of his
head, and then sent him flying off his feet with a solid punch to
his face.

The next day, Han just sat on the ground and glared across
the room at him when he opened the door. Although he almost
started laughing when he saw Roul's wary expression as he
stepped into the room, his eyes bulging, his body ducking and
flinching, reflexively batting his free arm in the air like he was
trying to ward himself from another unsuspecting blow. When

Roul saw him sitting harmlessly away from him on the floor, he straightened himself up. "Ha, you learned your lesson, eh?" He grunted, wagging his finger.

"I'm sorry I whacked you on your head yesterday." Han still had a soft spot for Roul that he couldn't quite get past. He wasn't mean to him like Roland or Aunt Lutrud and figured he was just doing what The Lady told him to. *Maybe she cast some kind of spell on him.*

Roul reached up and rubbed his head. "You gave me head quite a lump. I bring you food, I give you light. Why you attack me?"

At that moment, Han saw a fleeting image of what looked like a small pale hand darting through the door, and then it was gone. Wondering if it could be the boy's hand, perhaps trying to give him something, he thought it best not to draw attention to it. "Why can't you just help me get out of here? How long does she plan on keeping me prisoner down here anyway?"

He shrugged, "Not for me to say."

"Be honest Roul. You've worked for The Lady a long time, what does she do to kids like me that she traps in this room?"

He shrugged again, "How should I know? After a while I don't see them again."

"That's because she kills them, isn't that right? Sacrifices them to her demon? Help me, Roul. Just leave the door open when you leave. That's all you have to do. I'll run away from here and you'll never see me again. Don't lock the door, that's all I'm asking."

Roul seemed to consider his request, stared at him silently for a long moment, then shook his head and let out a nervous chuckle, "Tried that once before. Nearly got *me* killed. The Lady would not be so merciful next time."

Roul turned back and brought the food tray that he had set down just outside the door, handed it to Han, and then left the room, locking the door behind him. He got up and searched the area around the door with his oil lamp to see if that little white hand dropped something for him. He reached down and picked up a ball that was lying in the corner and smiled. It was his own ball that his father made for him.

He rapped his knuckles on the door. "Hey buddy, you out there?"

"Yes," came the raspy, whispery voice.

"Where did you find my ball?"

"Your sister left it on the porch. She told me to give it to you."

"You've been talking to my sister?"

"A couple times."

"Is she doing ok?"

"Better than you."

Han almost laughed at that. "Roul just told me that he helped a child escape from here before. Was that you?"

"Yes. Many seasons ago."

"Can you help me escape?"

"How?"

"How should I know? I'm stuck in here! I was hoping you could think of something."

They were silent for a time as Han tried to think of a plan. "Wait, how do you get down here?"

"Through an opening against the side of the house, just above the furnace."

He remembered seeing a small hole next to the main vent to allow some of the excess smoke to escape from the basement. "You can actually fit through there? Well, I'll have to get back to you, but try to think of something, ok?"

"I'll try."

"Hey buddy?"

"Yes?"

"What's your name?"

"Gidie."

"Thanks for bringing my ball, Gidie."

"You're welcome."

"One more question: Did you draw all of these creepy pictures on the walls of the cellar?"

"Yes, some of them at least."

More time passed in his empty, cold, dark cell with no way to know how many days had gone by. Hopelessness eventually overcame his fear, followed by infinite boredom and restlessness and a sense of inescapable claustrophobia. He tried to come to terms with his impending death. *Why will nobody help me?* His anxiety rose to a near panic. He wanted to scream his anguish into this empty room, felt the urge to scratch his nails into the door and try to bore his way out like those before him.

Instead, he closed his eyes and forced his mind to relax. He imagined he was on a ship being tossed in a stormy sea, felt the tightening in his chest, heaving with each deep breath, felt the fast clip of his heartbeat, pulsating and surging the blood through his body. Now he focused only on slowing his breath. He couldn't control his rapidly beating heart, he couldn't control his captivity nor his fate, but he could control his breathing, and if he focused hard enough, he could control his thoughts too. As his breathing slowed, so too did the stormy waves at sea.

Han had never even been to the sea, but he could imagine it from the stories he had heard. He envisioned himself as the ship's captain, seated at the helm, in control of his direction, his destination. He stretched out his arms, inducing the waves to diminish even further, the sea now becoming placid and serene. He realized at this moment that The Witch could hold his body captive but not his mind. He also noticed that the more he practiced in this way, the better he felt.

Through this silent contemplation, he ultimately found forgiveness in himself for blaming and disrespecting his own father, for not showing enough compassion or love for him when he needed it most. As for his guilt about abandoning his sister, he just knew that if given the chance, he would never make such a selfish decision again. His sister may be the only family he has left.

He had more difficulty coming to terms with his mother's death, though—how he shunned her, turned away out of disgust in her last moments. He would never get that moment back. After obsessing over this for countless hours, he began to pray to God and to his mother, begging her forgiveness. At last, he envisioned her smiling at him, drawing him into her arms, and whispering, "My silly boy, there is nothing to forgive. Mothers understand their children better than you think."

He slept well after that, a long and satisfying sleep that he had not experienced since his captivity in this cellar. He stretched as he awoke, rubbing the sleep out of his eyes and letting out a long yawn. When he opened his eyes, he was startled to see a tall, robed figure towering above him. He held a lantern with one hand that swung slightly on its rusty hinge, casting a dim light back and forth across across the dank room, but not enough to penetrate the shadows of the cowl concealing his face.

Han quickly jumped to his feet and backed away. "Who the hell are you?"

"It is time, Han," boomed a deep, menacing voice.

Chapter 30

GUARIN SUCKED DOWN THE LAST OF HIS BEER as the few remaining locals sung their way out of the small tavern. They were getting drunk and boisterous, so he was glad to see them go. They had tried to engage Guarin into their senseless conversation and songs, but he wasn't in the mood for fun, he seldom was anymore.

He had been searching for information on his children for over two months, bouncing from the cities of Strasbourg to Colmar and all the smaller towns in between. After having met with countless healing ladies and bounty hunters, some said they had heard of Roland but nothing more than that. When he came up empty, he asked around for any odd job he could find, anything that would put food in his belly before moving on to the next town. He even tried his luck working for the town guard in Obernai. It paid well enough, and he learned a thing or two about combat, but after nearly getting himself killed twice in one week he decided it was time to move on again.

He recovered his health and much of his strength, but he'd grown tired of searching, tired of living from day to day, tired of being alone. If only he had a companion, someone to talk to, someone to laugh with. He thought of Barous, of the conversations they had with his back to the stone cell wall, the laughter they shared despite their horrendous conditions.

He heard rumors of Barous's death, struck down by the town guards in Riquewihr on the night of their escape. Apparently, he didn't go down without a fight, killing four more men and holding many more at bay until he was shot through the chest by a crossbow. *I'm sure he didn't mind dying like that.*

He never saw Lutrud again either but heard that Father Linhart had been murdered in Thieves' Tower, stabbed by a woman accused of witchcraft not long after he escaped. According to town officials, she wasn't too enthused about his plans to place her in a convent. *I never suspected she was capable of carrying out such a deed. I guess I should consider myself fortunate that she didn't do the same to me. Are we really just creatures reacting to our own circumstances, forcing us to act in ways so different from the person we thought we were?*

Guarin blamed himself partly for her actions. He only meant to damage her credibility, never thought The Cleric would take his accusation seriously. *Games, Mr. Guarin...* In any case, he understood that her own decision ultimately sealed her fate. *At least she took that sadistic cleric along with her to the grave.* He hoped her execution had been a quick one, but he knew it was probably very brutal, and very public.

As for himself, he remained a wanted murderer but figured the hunt for him had probably died down, especially since Barous and The Cleric had both been killed, along with most of the guards who could recognize him. He could trust that Captain Erec was not on his tail, but he could not say the same for Lord Endris.

When he eventually visited his home once again, it looked just as he had left it. Seeing his long-neglected axe still mounted on his bedroom wall, he pulled it down and felt its weight in his hands for the first time in three years. He blew the dust from the broad blade and rubbed his hands along its leather-wrapped oaken shaft until its true color shone through. What unspeakable joy he felt to wield it once again with his new-found strength as he whirled it around in his yard, practicing the striking and blocking motions he learned while working for the town guard. With growing enthusiasm, he brought it to his ramshackle toolshed and sharpened the blade, then dug out an old bottle of oil and polished it to a brilliant sheen. That evening, he mounted it back onto his wall and stared at it proudly from his bed until falling into a rejuvenating sleep.

He awoke early the next morning feeling optimistic. Strapping his axe onto his back, he left in search of his children once again. This time, he decided to head west, away from Riquewihr. He stopped at several of the dilapidated homes along the way; most looked abandoned, others didn't answer to his knock, until he arrived at the dwelling of an old man he used to know. Hadn't seen him in years, figured he'd died by now given his age. Old Man Marceau—Birdman, he'd called him.

It surprised him when Birdman opened the door, but especially by his appearance: tall and gaunt with a long white beard as usual—even had his loyal falcon perched on his shoulder—but his body wasted away to just skin and bones, and his face looked like dried parchment stretched over his skull. He looked like a walking cadaver as he stared wide-eyed at him through his sunken eye sockets. Apparently, the old man was just as surprised to see Guarin standing at his door.

"I thought you were dead!" said Birdman, his voice just a raspy whisper.

Guarin smiled, "I figured the same about you. How are you still getting along way out here?"

Birdman stepped out onto his modest porch. "Been doing it all my life, not so different now. As you can see, I don't eat much and ain't too picky with what I do eat."

He chuckled, then thought twice about what he said a moment ago. He dropped his smile and cocked his head, squinting one of his eyes and raising his other eyebrow just like his son. "Say, Birdman, what made you think I was dead? I mean, I know we haven't seen each other in a few years, but…"

"I saw a man leadin' your kids down this path a while back," he gestured in the direction away from his home. "I didn't say nothin'. Not much I could do really, and they were walkin' freely beside him. Next day, after the storm had passed, I made my way down to see if you or your lady were home. Nothin' there but a fresh puddle of shit, piss and blood. Looked like whoever it was had been dragged out, judgin' by the stain it left on your floor. Was that you, Mr. Guarin, or your new lady friend?"

Guarin's thoughts began to trail off after he heard his first words and didn't hear much after that, until the silence caught his attention. "Huh? Uh, yeah…yes, that was me. I was very sick. You sure those were my kids that you saw?"

"Pretty sure. My eyes ain't what they used to be in my birdin' days, but it looked like them well enough. Figured you'd arranged for them to be taken to a relative or somethin' like that."

"No, not really." Guarin felt distracted by the falcon staring back at him with those beady eyes, flitting its head around as though it wanted to view him from every possible angle. "Lutrud arranged it while I was sick. I didn't intend for them to be sent off like that. You haven't seen them come back this way since then?"

"No, I haven't. A pretty young lady came by askin' about you last week though. I told her I figured you for dead."

Guarin scratched his head and cast him a puzzled look. "I don't even know any pretty young ladies. Did she give her name?"

"No, and I didn't ask."

Then he remembered Rose. "Wait a minute, does she have dark hair and full lips?"

Birdman nodded.

Guarin cupped his hands and held them in front of his chest. "Big breasts, full figure?"

Now he opened up a near toothless grin and nodded more vigorously. "Yup, that sounds like her."

"I think I know who you mean then. I'm just not sure why she would be out here looking for me though. Anyone else?"

"Not a whole lot of traffic comes through this way. My ears ain't what they used to be neither, but it's so quiet I can usually hear when people are comin'. I usually come out to see who's passin' by, seein' how there ain't much to do out here anyways to pass the time." The falcon ruffled its feathers and shit on the back of his shoulder, adding to the solidified white paste that had already oozed down his back and dried like candle wax.

"I see," he said, turning to look down the path ahead of him. After a long silent stare, he turned back to the old man. "Well, I've got some traveling to do before nightfall, but I thank you for your information. You were very helpful."

"Good journey, my friend, and best of luck findin' your children."

He walked on for hours, the sun sinking well into its descent, before reaching a fork in the path. *More decisions.* At least he knew that he needed to search the towns west of his home and not east, according to Birdman, which eliminated most of the larger towns and cities. Uncertain which path to choose, he figured he would take a few minutes to search the area for any clues. *Maybe Han tried to mark his path?* Neither path looked very well worn; any footsteps would have been washed away by the rain. He looked for a mark on a tree, hell, even a half-broken twig probably would have convinced him to choose one path over the other.

He swiped his foot through the shallow brush, kicking at little rocks on the ground. Just to the right of the smaller path, a small chunk of wood skittered and bounced lightly off his foot in front of him. Something about it piqued his interest, so he picked it up, brushed and blew off the dirt, and examined it more closely. Despite being worn down by the weather and rain, he recognized it immediately as one of Han's carvings, this one of a bear. *Maybe Han had dropped it, maybe even on purpose. He was clever like that.*

With a renewed sense of vigor, he kissed the carving and placed it in his pocket, then strode ahead on the smaller branch to the right. At the next fork, he did the same thing, searching meticulously for another of his carvings. When he found a carving of a horse, he exclaimed and laughed out loud to the forest, "That's it, you clever son of mine! I'll find you soon enough! I'm on my way!"

By the time he reached the next fork, the day began to quickly fade into darkness, too dark to find another carving despite his best effort. Having never been to this area of the forest, he figured it would be too dangerous and foolish to push on any further. He might even miss another fork in the path, making it even more difficult to find his way back. Venturing a short distance off the path, he reached into his pack and pulled out the blanket he used for times like this.

The Craving

Awaking at the break of dawn, he trudged back to the fork. After a brief search, he found yet another of Han's carvings pointing the way. He again put it to his lips before placing it into his pack and continuing on his way. He wasn't as fortunate when he came to the next fork. Despite searching for over an hour, he came up empty. He decided to take the wider path that continued along the river, leading him to a small clearing littered with animal carcasses. The largest appeared to be the remains of a very large boar, mostly reduced to a skeleton. The rest were half decayed and half-eaten wolf carcasses, about a dozen of them. *What the hell could have done this?* He already knew the danger of traveling alone through an unfamiliar part of the forest, but seeing this slaughter only amplified his anxiety. Warily, he pushed on until he finally came across a sign pointing the way to a small village. It didn't look like much, but so far, the only civilization he'd seen west of Riquewihr.

He set down his empty beer mug and looked up at the bartender.

"Ready for another, traveler?" asked the bartender.

"No thank you. That hit the spot," he said, placing a copper coin on the bar. "Listen, I don't suppose you've heard of a fellow named Roland that might have come through here a while back? He's a bounty hunter, so he bounces around from town to town. Average height, long dark hair—kind of a dashing looking prick."

"A dashing looking prick, eh? Can't say that I have," the bartender replied with a chuckle, clearing away the empty mugs. "I hope you know how to handle yourself. Tangling with bounty hunters is a good way to get yourself killed."

"It's ok, I'm not looking to tangle with him, just need some information, that's all. Can you tell me if there's a healing lady around these parts?"

He shot him a look of concern, or apprehension maybe, he couldn't tell which. Locals tend to get nervous around sick strangers arriving to their town. "You sick or something, traveler?"

"No, just sick of being wet and hungry."

A look of relief passed over the bartender. "There is a young woman that settled in this village a couple weeks ago." He produced a rag and began wiping down the bar. "She fancies herself a healer, but most men around here expect more out of her than that, if you know what I mean. She's a pretty little thing, has that exotic look to her, you know? But don't try and get fresh with her; she's a woman that knows how to take care of herself. I've heard more than one sorry son of a bitch lament about getting an ass-whooping by her. She even threatens to tell their wives!" he laughed. "Makes for a good story after a few beers, I can tell you that."

"Good for her! She sounds like an interesting lady. I'd like to meet her," said Guarin, laughing along.

"You can usually see her around the village center in the morning. You won't miss her—long curly black hair, pretty eyes, and actually quite friendly despite the stories I hear. She flits around and talks to just about everyone like a social butterfly."

"Is that right?" Guarin said with a grin, then decided to take a stab in the dark. "I'm actually looking for a woman who takes care of orphaned children. I don't suppose you would know anyone like that around these parts?"

The bartender gave him a sidelong glance. "You sure are looking for a lot of different people. I'm beginning to think you're a detective or maybe even a bounty hunter yourself. If that's the case, perhaps you can pay me a bit more than this for my information."

"No, I'm none of those things, just a simple woodcutter— used to be anyway. This bounty hunter I asked about—he took my kids away from me while I was deathly sick a couple of months ago. I'm told he took them to live with an old healing lady that cares for orphaned children. Pretty sure she lives out here somewhere."

"Well in that case I feel for you, buddy. There's been quite a few folks in town trying to sell their children, some even trying to give them away, on account of the famine. Just not enough to feed a whole family. I never thought I'd see the day, but here we are. I myself don't know of anyone sheltering kids as you say, but you might find some leads if you ask around tomorrow. Best of luck to you, traveler."

The quaint village looked much cleaner compared to the other towns he visited. Several of the vendors were already busy setting up for the day. A cold spray of rain began falling from a heavy sky. He pulled on his hood and made his way under one of the eaves. He leaned back against the stone wall and watched as more villagers made their way into the open square. Once the worst of the rain had passed, he perused the vendors to see what they were selling: warm bread, salted beef and fish, eggs, spices. Some of the women sold crafts, weavings, clothing, shoes, hats. The prices weren't as high as in Riquewihr but still much higher than he'd ever seen before the famine.

He didn't see anyone matching the bartender's description until about an hour later when a tall young woman with the friendliest smile he'd ever seen made her way into the square. She walked with a lively bounce to her step, almost prancing, as though just the act of walking made her happy—and others too! He noticed how everyone's face seemed to brighten when she passed by, especially if she smiled at them or said a simple hello, which she usually did. She carried a large tray in front of her, fastened over her shoulders and around her back, displaying an array of herbs and flowers and small vials of medicine. She kept a separate basket strapped to her waist that bounced off the side of her hip as she walked. *The basket wasn't the only thing that bounced when she walked,* he mused. The young girls must have known what the basket contained as they ran up to her in turns, sometimes giggly and excitedly, sometimes shyly and needing to be coaxed by their mother, each to receive a lovely little daisy flower and a kiss on the cheek. He even saw a little boy about to approach, but when she smiled at him, he bolted back to his mother.

He understood what the bartender meant when he said she looked exotic, with her long lush dark hair bunched into tight curls, cascading down her back and over her shoulders, even spilling into the cleavage of her amble bosom. The tawny complexion of her skin contrasted sharply with her bright green eyes. He had never seen anyone that looked quite like her, arousing in him a sensual desire that had fizzled out after Kaetherlin died.

Unfortunately, it looked like everyone else in town felt the same way, so he had to wait patiently. Other than a couple of reproachful looks from wives who caught their husband stealing glances at her, most of the people seemed overjoyed that she brought her beauty and happiness into their humble village.

Finally, after the morning crowd had settled down, he sauntered up to her. "Good day to you, mademoiselle."

Though she never seemed to stop smiling, he felt blessed when she brightened it for him, deepening the dimple in her left cheek. It had been so long since he talked to a beautiful young woman that he felt like a nervous young boy again until he remembered his age. Her large and vibrant eyes were even more stunning up close. Not knowing how else to begin his conversation, he pulled his eyes down from her face to her tray of herbs.

"Have you got anything that might work for a kidney stone?" He immediately blushed, realizing that any far-fetched fantasy that she might find him even remotely attractive had just vanished with those words. And just as he thought about this, he wondered if she might think he was some creep just looking for an excuse to stare at her breasts, bulging prominently through her shirt just above her tray.

He forced his eyes back up to hers, expecting to see a look of awkward embarrassment or even scorn, but instead she showed genuine pity and concern, "Oh, you poor thing, I'm so sorry. I've heard they can be very painful. Apple cider mixed with lemon juice works well, but apples and lemons aren't growing well around here, as you probably know. Do you have one now—a kidney stone, I mean?" Her lip pouted when she asked, like she was talking to a young boy—*or an old man*, he thought.

"No, I'm ok, I don't have one right now. I had a very bad one a couple of months ago, so in case I get another one, I just thought…"

"Well, that's a relief," she sighed, her face softening back into a smile. "Is there anything else I can get for you?" She reached into her basket and pulled out one of the daisies. "A pretty little flower perhaps?" she offered, holding it up next to her beaming smile.

"Of course," he smiled back, accepting the daisy. He twirled it around between his fingers, admiring its bright color and simple beauty.

"Well, it was nice meeting you. Enjoy the rest of your day," she said, about to move along.

"Before you go, would you mind if I ask where you're from? I'd expect to see a pretty girl like you living in a city like Paris, but not way out here," he said, making a gesture around the town.

"Thank you. I get asked that quite a bit, but to be perfectly honest, I don't even know where I'm from exactly. I was taken from my family as a child, so I don't know much about them. But I do remember people telling me that I didn't look anything like my parents."

"I'm so sorry, I didn't mean to…"

"Oh, it's alright. Anyhow, some people tell me I look like I might be from Persia or Turkey or somewhere out there, but I don't even know what those people look like—Me, I guess," she added with a giggle.

Guarin smiled and gave her a friendly wink. "I imagine so. You've been living out here most of your life then?"

"Not too far from here. Why do you ask?" Her expression becoming somewhat suspicious.

"My two children were taken from me, much like you were, I suppose. I'm told that they were brought to live with a healing lady somewhere out in this area. I've been searching for two months, but I think I'm finally getting close. If you happen to know of any old healing ladies that fosters children, then please let me know."

She studied him intently but didn't offer a response, like she was deciding whether or not to say something.

"The man who took them is a bounty hunter, I'm told he goes by the name Roland…if that rings any bells."

Her mouth fell open in shock as she continued to stare silently at him, before her brow suddenly twisted into a sign of worry and bewilderment. He barely heard her whisper the names under a gasping breath, "Han and Greta?"

His stunned expression equaled hers in that moment as they stared at each other in disbelief. "You know them? You know where they are?"

"Your name is Guarin?"

"Yes, that's right! Han and Greta are my children. Can you take me to them?" His face showed relief but there was urgency in his voice.

She continued to stare at him with that worried expression in her eyes that did not waver. "I searched for you. They told me you were very sick. I talked to an old man who lived not more than a mile from you; he thought you were probably dead."

"That was you?" he asked incredulously. "I just talked to him two days ago, only I thought he was referring to another woman that I knew."

"I know where they are, but I fear they may be in danger. I am worried most for Han."

He grabbed her shoulders a bit too forcefully in his excitement. "What do you mean they are in danger?"

Melisende reassured one of the men passing by who looked about to smash Guarin in the face. He immediately released his grip and apologized.

"You wouldn't believe me if I told you. I am heading to a gathering at the home tonight to see what I can do, but any attempts on my own will be most difficult."

"Please, you must tell me. What kind of trouble are they in?"

She stared at him for a moment before answering then lowered her voice, "I've received word that there is to be a coven tonight. Members have been gathering since yesterday, perhaps over a dozen people. I've spoken with her caretaker, a man that I've known since I was a young girl. I urged him to look into the situation, but I don't think that will be enough. I don't even know if I can trust him either."

"A coven? You mean like a witch's ceremony?"

She looked warily around her. "We cannot talk about this in town. Come, I'll explain along the way."

"Wait a minute. Shouldn't we notify the Constable?"

"I tried that already. It only aroused ridicule and even suspicion against me, and I've recently been accused of being a witch in another village. Besides, she is a powerful woman who may hold considerable influence with some of the town administrators. I don't even know who to trust anymore. But at least I know I can trust their father, so come with me. If we leave now, we can be there by evening."

Chapter 37

MELISENDE AND GUARIN ARRIVED AT THE LADY'S GATE just as darkness fell. A few other guests arrived ahead of them, awaiting entrance to the coven. She knew that only those who arrived with a member of the coven were permitted inside. The only problem: Melisende was not a member.

Jehan presented himself at the gate and began greeting the guests. He regarded her with surprise. "My dear Sendy! To what do we owe this great honor?" he boomed, holding his arms open to offer one of his giant hugs.

She reluctantly accepted his embrace and returned a smile, though it came off as more restrained than she would have liked. "Hello Jehan. It is wonderful to see you again." She gestured toward Guarin. "I would like you to meet my friend…" she hesitated for a slight moment, "…Gawin. This is Jehan, the caretaker for The Lady that I spoke to you about."

"A pleasure to meet you, Gawin. Any friend of Sendy is a friend of mine," Jehan said, maintaining his welcoming smile and offering his hand.

Guarin regarded him warily before accepting the handshake.

Sendy quickly grabbed his attention back to her. "I trust The Lady is well since I left, Jehan?"

"Yes, and she is certainly keeping me busy with preparations for tonight," he chuckled, obviously trying to deflect the seriousness of her question.

"And the children?"

His smile faltered, casting her a look of concern. "Ah yes. This is something we will need to discuss." He turned to Guarin. "I'm sorry, but any new guests must be approved in advance. I hope you understand, this is a most private event."

Sendy pleaded his case. "If you allow me to speak to The Lady, she may allow my guest an exception."

Jehan led her inside and locked the gate behind him. "I'm sorry for the inconvenience to you, sir, but we will return shortly and explain to you what is in store for the night."

"I understand. I shall wait here for you then," said Guarin.

Jehan nodded to a robed man armed with a sword in his belt, and then turned away with Sendy. As he led her through the yard, he explained Han's dire situation. "I have inquired about Han as you asked. If you intend on joining the coven tonight, you should be aware that Han is to be sacrificed this very night."

Even though she suspected as much already, her heart dropped, but she did her best to contain her emotions. "Was there nothing you could say to convince her otherwise?"

"I tried. I really did. I never believed she would resort to this…"

Sendy felt nauseated just listening to his excuses, wanted to scream at him for lying to her all these years, but if she had any hope of convincing them that she wished to join their coven, she would have to play this just right. She stopped and looked up at him, placing her hand on his arm. "It's ok, Jehan. I'm not that silly, naive little girl anymore. You don't have to keep secrets from me. I've attended other covens, and I'm old enough now to understand the necessities of witchcraft. It's just that I've gotten to know Han, and it doesn't seem right. He is not a baby or small child who can't comprehend their fate. Perhaps I can convince The Lady otherwise, but either way I will abide by her decision."

Jehan studied her face for a long moment, then simply nodded his head and led her inside. He knocked on The Lady's bedroom door. "My Lady, Sendy is here to see you. I'll leave you alone to talk."

When she opened the door to her bedroom, The Lady was applying a powder to her face that had an odd greenish hue.

"Good day to you, My Lady."

She didn't look away from the silver plate when Sendy addressed her. "You have returned on a very busy night, my dear. I'm afraid you cannot stay here."

"Yes, I understand there is to be a coven tonight. If you could just hear me out..." she sighed. "I have given this much thought over the past two years, especially since I left here last month. You already know that religion is not an issue for me; I have never been a believer in Christ. I am a witch, and I am ready to serve and swear my allegiance to the Almighty Lucifer. As I just told Jehan, I am old enough to understand it better now. A witch needs power in order to grow, and I believe that is something that has been holding me back. You had asked me to join your coven when I was younger, and I refused. I was not prepared to undertake the requirements expected of me at the time. But if you would please give me another chance, I will not let you down. I have been attending lesser covens, but too many of them are phonies. I want to learn from the best. I want to learn from you."

"Tell me, whose coven have you attended?"

"Most recently I joined Lady Anstrude's group."

"Hmph," she scoffed, "I understand Lady Anstrude is claiming that she learned under my tutelage, though I only engaged her once in conversation. She certainly is a phony." The Lady continued to stare into her reflection on the silver plate as she wiped her fingers on a cloth. "Han is to be sacrificed tonight."

Sendy lifted the hairpin from the table and began to style her hair for her. "Yes, Jehan has already informed me. Do you not think he is too old?"

"He will be the oldest yet, but it matters not. I've already made my decision. If you want to join, then you will have to abide by my decisions. Do not question me."

"He also told me that Han initially showed some interest in becoming a shaman. Why not let Jehan try to convince him to join us? He is a very good worker and handy in the yard. I think he would be most useful—"

"He is an insolent boy! I have no use for children like that."

Sendy laughed softly, "Yes he is, isn't he? That doesn't mean his mind can't be changed. Please, offer him another chance. What harm can there be in it?"

The Lady finally turned around to face her directly, delivering a sarcastic, almost belittling look. "I haven't told you about the Hunger Demon that has attached itself to my soul." She let that sink in before continuing. "But you have seen what becomes of me when it does not receive its sacrifice. It has become a part of me. If it does not feed on my sacrifices, it feeds on me instead. I know you feel affection for these children, and that is exactly why I asked you to leave. The demon has awoken within me again and demands its meal. I can even feel its craving. Roland is in no condition to bring more children to me anytime soon. So tell me, what choice do I have?"

Sendy remained silent and willed tears into her eyes before replying. She looked down to her belly and held her hand over it. "I am carrying Roland's child. He cannot father a baby, and I have no desire to be a mother on my own. I still have several months to go yet before I deliver, if you—if it—can wait that long."

The Lady's expression softened into one of great sympathy as she rose to her feet and hugged her in a warm embrace. "Oh, my dear child, I had no idea. I never would have made you leave, had I known." She pulled her head back and held Sendy's cheeks between her hands, tears welling up in her eyes as well. The Lady gazed at her endearingly, in a way that she never had before. "Believe me, I know how you must feel. I too was faced with such a difficult decision."

"You have been pregnant before?" Sendy asked with utter surprise.

"Yes, but it seems like another lifetime ago, and I don't wish to bring those emotions up again. I just want you to know that I understand what you must be going through." The Lady dropped her hands from her cheeks and slid them down to her hands. "It means so much that you would consider sacrificing your child for me. I don't even know what to say. You know that I would never ask this of you?"

"Please My Lady, let me speak to Han. At least I can offer him a choice. That is all I ask."

"Very well, I will ask Jehan to speak to him again, but I would prefer—I would insist—that you not join him. I don't want your emotional attachment to him clouding his decision. It must be genuine and on his own accord. The coven is set to begin shortly, with or without our honored guest."

Sendy bowed her head. "I understand, My Lady, and thank you for hearing me out. I will abide by his decision either way. In fact, I would like to be at his side to provide what comfort I can as he passes out of this world and into the next."

The Lady regarded her with a look of admiration, one that she had not seen from her since she was a child. "You are a kind woman, Sendy. It makes me proud to have raised you. I would be honored if you join my coven. We have another new initiate tonight as well; our movement grows every year."

"My Lady, I brought along a friend of mine who wishes to attend tonight. May I bring him inside?"

Her expression took on a more serious tone. "I'm sorry, but I cannot have just anyone attend the ceremony. I need to know that I can trust any new guests, especially on a night such as this."

"Please, My Lady, I know him well. I have attended other covins with him and his wife before she passed. He has heard great things about you and wishes to meet with you."

She nodded her head. "I will talk to Jehan and see if he agrees. He is the Grandmaster, after all."

This took her by surprise. "The Grandmaster of your coven? He is the one who organizes all of this?"

The Lady nodded with a smile. "There is much about him—about us—that I haven't shared with you. But that is a tale for another night, perhaps tomorrow, once all of this is behind us."

"I look forward to hearing it." She started to leave but turned back. "Have you told Greta about Han?"

"I simply told her that he ran away from us."

"I understand. May I see her tonight?"

"You can visit with her tomorrow. You will be happy to know that she will be joining our community as well, just not tonight, for obvious reasons. I have put her to bed already and would appreciate it if you let her sleep. Why don't you stop by and see Roland? I think you will be pleasantly surprised by his recovery. And if you don't mind, would you be a dear and help him get dressed for tonight? I would like for him to look his best."

"Yes, of course, My Lady."

Sendy stopped to listen at Greta's door, but heard only silence so turned to Roland's room. She couldn't figure out why The Lady would want him to attend the ceremony since he barely spoke and always wore that dazed expression. Perhaps it was so that she could show him off like a trophy, a living display of her power and skills at necromancy.

Upon entering his room, she did indeed notice a dramatic improvement in his appearance since she last saw him, but unfortunately his mind still had a long way to recover. She felt an emotional tug in her throat to see him this way. Though she had seen him come and go since childhood, she really only got to know him over that two-day journey, after he so bravely rescued her from the guards. She felt indebted to him for that, and damned if she wasn't smitten by him for that heroic rescue either.

As she gazed upon his face, however, she did not see that same man anymore. Gone was the charm from his eyes and his confident smile that had sparked her passion, arousing her enough to throw caution to the wind and lie with him that very night in the forest. *The only thing missing that day was his white horse and shining armor*, she thought to herself and then smirked—*well that and a steady disposition.*

She tried to engage him with her eyes as she brushed his hair back, but he just stared blankly ahead at the diagram on the wall. "When will you come back to us, my prince?"

Chapter 38

HAN BACKED AWAY FROM THE TALL, HOODED FIGURE before him. "Jehan? Is that you?"

The figure reached up and pulled off his hood, revealing the face of a devil—similar to the face that he saw drawn on the wall of the cellar, except it had a mischievous looking grin instead of an expression of rage. Most frightening of all were two curved horns that grew out the top of his head.

Han backed away further, his body trembling. "Who are you? What do you want?"

The figure set the lantern on the ground, then reached up with both hands and lifted the elaborate mask off of his head. "It's me, Han."

"Jehan? Why are you dressed like the devil?"

"Because I *am* the devil. I am the Grand Master of The Lady's coven," he said with a grin, nearly matching the one on the mask. "I have given your situation much thought. I spoke with The Lady and persuaded her to give you a choice in your fate. Given your age and the time we have spent together, I thought this most fitting."

"What choice is that?" Han asked, his voice shaking with trepidation.

"I've spoken about this once before with you. You said you wanted to learn the ways of the shaman. Do you remember?"

Han nodded his head slowly, "Yes, I remember. You said it was forbidden to Christians."

"That is what I said. The ways of the shaman do not align with the ways of your God. This is not an easy choice to make in the lands of the Christians, but we will protect you from their laws as best we can. You must renounce Jesus Christ with all your being and accept The Lord of Light as your new savior. Give up and break free from this false illusion that you are under, and I will teach you powers that you never knew existed."

"Where is my sister? Do you have her locked up somewhere too, or has she agreed to join you?"

He opened his book to a page marked by a red ribbon and pointed to her signature. "This is the mark of her own hand."

He stared in disbelief, though he recognized her character, just as Lutrud taught her. *She wouldn't do that, would she?*

"Our movement is growing, Han. Just today, my daughter has returned. She wishes to add her name to this sacred book in our ceremony tonight. She requested that I speak to you now."

"You have a daughter?"

He smiled and nodded slowly. "Melisende."

"Sendy is your daughter?" Han asked with a look of shock and surprise. "But...she doesn't look anything like you, your color..."

"Her mother has skin like your own."

This revelation came crashing down on him like a bucket of cold water. "The Lady?"

Jehan nodded, still smiling.

It all makes sense, why didn't I put it together before? Then he thought back. "But she told us that Roland brought her here, when she was a young girl, after her parents were killed."

"It is true, what she said. The Lady was not well after Melisende was born, for too long. Her behavior became very erratic, as she tends to get at times. She demanded a sacrifice that I could not allow. I had to send the baby away to be cared for by others. As the years went by though, she regretted her intentions. We desired companionship, and we missed her terribly. That is when I hired Roland to bring her back to us." He paused and closed his eyes briefly. "But we digress. Let us come back to the matter at hand. I would like for you to join us, Han. Sendy and Greta wants you to join us."

Han thought in silent contemplation for a long moment but realized his choice was obvious. "What if I refuse?"

He regarded him with a look both solemn and sympathetic. "We cannot let you leave here Han. Refuse, and you shall soon learn your fate."

Han straightened his back and glared up at Jehan with as much conviction as he could muster, his voice clear and steady. "Oh yes, the ceremony in my honor. You don't have to tell me how I shall be *honored*. And after me, you will find other helpless children to be honored—sacrificed—fed to her demon. Why does she do it, Jehan? To keep her from having those convulsions? To give her magical powers?" He scoffed. "In my mind, I am already free from this captivity, this hell you have kept me in. I refuse to be held captive any longer by that old witch or by you, and certainly not by my own conscience. You have offered me a choice to live a life of sin. I could never stand by and watch you kill innocent children, no matter what powers I am granted. I only hope my sister understands what you are, and that you protect her just as you promised to protect me."

"Han, please, you will not get another chance," he pressed.

"You are the one who will have to live with your conscience after tonight. Just let me walk out of here with my sister and you will never see us again."

Jehan regarded him solemnly for a long moment until that mischievous grin crept across his face again. "So be it." He snapped his book shut and walked out of the room. He ushered a brief command, whereby two robed men entered and walked to each side of him. Han remained still as they secured his arms behind his back, then led him out of his prison once and for all.

The cellar was dark except for Jehan's lantern that he held at the foot of the stairs. *That's strange.* He had never seen the furnace fire out before.

"Are you ready, Han?" Jehan asked solemnly.

Han nodded, then Jehan ushered them up the stairs. When he stepped out into the night, he felt the cool, refreshing breeze blow gently against his grimy skin. He inhaled deeply, taking in the smell of the moist grass and citrus blooms, the sweet scent of eucalyptus and minty pine, a fragrance so strong he could almost taste it.

As he rounded the corner of the house into the yard, he heard the music of a fiddle and the collective murmur of voices. Though his eyes remained bleary, he saw about a dozen robed figures gathered around the large oak tree—the very same tree that held Roland upside down during his "resurrection" ceremony. Some conversed or clapped along to the music, while others danced in a wild and peculiar fashion, cackling with ecstatic and orgiastic glee. A fire burned under the great black cauldron while one of the hooded members stood beside it, stirring the steaming contents with a long wooden pole of some kind. A full moon shined intermittently through scattered clouds overhead, providing ample lighting for the evening affair.

He overheard Jehan tell Roul that the furnace went out and needed to be stoked for the ceremonial feast. His stomach lurched as a wave of fear and nausea welled up within him, a sense of panic rising just under the surface. He swallowed hard as acrid bile rose into his throat. *Am I to be their feast?*

Chapter 39

THE LADY BROUGHT SENDY TWO HOODED ROBES to be worn for the ceremony. She slipped hers on and helped Roland into his, then led him out into the yard where the festivities had already begun. Some of the guests seemed well on their way to becoming intoxicated from the herb they smoked, not to mention the alcohol or whatever beverage they drank from their cups. Through the darkness, she saw a giant figure dressed in an elaborate devil costume, along with two other men, leading Han around from the side of the house. He spoke briefly with Roul before walking over to her.

"Wow, that is an impressive costume, the most impressive I've seen on a Grandmaster," she said.

He lifted the mask from his head, his expression grave as he told her of Han's choice. "I'm sorry, my dear. I really thought he would come around and join us, but his mind is set."

She couldn't believe her ears. *What will I tell Guarin?* She had to think of a plan quickly so that he didn't act rashly.

"I am most saddened to hear this, but as I told The Lady, I will do my best to help him through to the end. Thank you for taking the time to speak with him for me."

"I think it will mean a lot for him to have you by his side." He gestured toward the gathering by the tree, "My guests are waiting for me to join in on the fiddle, and yours awaits you at the gate."

She racked her mind trying to think of a way to rescue Han, and how to tell Guarin about his situation, but when she reached the gate, he was nowhere to be found, and neither was the guard. *Why is the gate unlocked?* She opened it warily and stepped outside the yard, calling his name, but she only heard the wind rustling through the leaves.

A movement from above suddenly caught her eye. She looked up in one of the trees and saw the black-eyed child peering down at her. She gasped and clutched at her chest as a tingling chill aroused every hair on her scalp. Frozen with fear, she could only stare back in shock at this mysterious looking child. *He looks just as Greta had described.* With his pale, scantily clad skin seemingly impervious to the chill air, his diminutive frame straddling the tree branch and long wild hair stirring in the wind, he calmly looked down upon her with those sinister dark eyes like some child wraith, risen from his freshly dug grave. Then, unexpectedly, he spoke to her in a thin, raspy voice. "Can I trust you?"

Sendy continued to stare aghast at him until she finally gave her head a shake, as though she had forgotten that he asked her a question. "Yes, of course, you can trust me. Tell me who you are."

"My name is Gidie."

"Hello, Gidie. My name is Sendy."

"I know who you are, and I know you are not like The Lady. I need your help."

After their strange conversation had ended, he seemed to disappear without a trace. She peered once again in all directions for Guarin before returning into the yard and locking the gate behind her. She hadn't walked three steps before Guarin suddenly emerged from the shadows against the wall, dressed in the guard's hooded gown.

"Oh my goodness, I'm going to die of fright before the night even begins! What happened to you?"

"I got tired of waiting," he said with a scowl.

She looked down to his bloodstained hands. "And the guard?"

"Don't worry, I disposed his body where it will not be found. I started to search around the yard for my children until I heard you call my name. You must tell me what is happening.

This is all so very strange," he coaxed her, worry and anxiety written on the ripples of his forehead.

"Believe me, it just got stranger."

Chapter 40

THEY LED HAN OVER TO THE WASH BASIN and instructed him to clean himself thoroughly. A third robed woman stood watch, making certain that he did not miss any part of his body. He shivered in the cool night air, but nevertheless felt refreshed to scrub off the grime. When he dropped the cloth back into the basin, she handed him a towel and a single loincloth to wear. She then led him back to the gathering under the tree, the guards holding firmly to each of his arms.

Just in front of the tree stood an altar at the head of a long narrow table. Further down from the table, far enough away from the tree branches, blazed two large torches erected on posts that stood several feet off the ground. He could sense the excitement growing, their voices growing louder and their laughter more boisterous. But then their conversation stopped as he approached, all turning toward him at once, their faces concealed behind masks that resembled animal faces or buried under their deep cowls.

Jehan—The Devil—stepped forward, gestured toward Han, and announced in a loud voice: "Ladies and gentlemen of the coven, please greet your honored guest."

He heard some murmurs of astonishment and a few awkward "How do you do's," while others just nodded their heads solemnly. One of the ladies couldn't even contain her surprise: "Oh, he's a big one!"

The Devil took his place behind the altar and announced that the ceremony would begin. The pentagram carved into the tree behind him could be seen conspicuously just over his head. Roland stood stiffly and mindlessly off to the side, his eyes without focus, his expression empty. Han felt his legs begin to resist the efforts of his guards to escort him any closer, forcing them to drag him forward. He took a deep breath, reminding himself to keep his mind steady and calm—free from this captivity imposed upon him. He would not give them the satisfaction of provoking his fear.

The Devil gestured to join him at the altar. He then raised his arms to his sides and shouted for the members to assume their positions. Han's eyes darted from left to right as they divided into two groups and lined up on each side of the sacrificial table. They clasped hands with the member next to them and began to chant. Their heads turned in unison past the torches at the foot of the table as The High Witch approached through the darkness.

She came into view under the glow of the torchlight, wearing a tall black pointed hat with a wide brim, and dressed in a long sweeping black robe, just like the primitive drawings he saw in the cellar. Already possessing considerable stature, she almost looked like a giant as she approached, her eyes latching onto his own. Her whole appearance seemed transformed. No hint of the silly old Lady who used to tease and laugh with them, nor did she bear any resemblance to the disheveled monster that beat him or writhed on the floor under the spell of her falling sickness; she now appeared like a grand and formidable woman of eminent status and almost regal bearing—but nevertheless, a woman truly wicked to behold.

She stopped just inches from his face, her skin shimmering with an eerie greenish hue in the torchlight, her cloudy and mysterious eyes ominously fixed upon him. If she was trying to intimidate him, it was working. Her nose, which stretched out from her face, which once looked so absurd, now added a certain dominance and command to her features. He couldn't seem to break away from her penetrating gaze, instilling in him a visceral sense of fear, a sense that left him completely powerless and at her very mercy.

The Witch held out her hand to him and opened it. On her palm sat one of her colorful candy sleepy balls, as Han came to call them. "This should help calm your nerves as we get started."

He accepted it and placed it in his mouth.

"Good. Lie down on the table," The Witch commanded.

The long wooden table was fastened with several leather straps around its edges. He noticed several black smears and large blotches, probably stained from other children's dried blood. He thought of the blood stains splattered on the wall of his prison room and began to tremble. *This must be the same table that stood against that wall.* He had prepared his mind that he would die tonight, but what he hadn't prepared for was the method. *What will she do to me on this table, cut my heart out and feed it to these other devils?* Never had he felt such pangs of dread. His legs wouldn't budge; they felt stiff and heavy. He stared at the table in terror and shook his head defiantly.

"Lie down so we can begin," she said more forcefully this time.

Han looked directly at her, and then spit his colorful candy sleepy ball directly at her face. The crowd gasped, but then quickly resumed their chant. The Lady swiped a back-handed blow to his face, but he knew it was coming, dodging it just in time, causing her to lunge forward awkwardly. She would have fallen to the muddy ground had one of the members not been at her side to steady her. Nonetheless, this provided Han with immense satisfaction.

"Put him on the table!" she shouted to the guards with a scowl.

He felt his legs lift off the ground just before his back slammed onto the table, nearly knocking the wind out of him. He screamed and kicked and spat and punched, yelling obscenities to all who could hear. Despite his wild thrashing, they still managed to strap down wrists and then his ankles. They pulled three more straps across his shoulders, hips, and knees, until he was completely ensnared. He continued to jerk and fight instinctively against the restraints, rendering his wrists and ankles raw and bloody.

Once they secured the last strap, he heard Jehan's voice boom from directly behind him with some grand proclamation in his foreign tongue. The others made way as The Witch moved around the table and then took her position next to Han's right shoulder.

She joined in the chant, her voice rising above the others. In her hands, she brandished a spotless, glimmering dagger etched with sacred runes, its ebony hilt encrusted with bright rubies, emeralds, and sapphires. A sinister smile crept across her face, that creepy smile that exuded her insatiable carnal craving, as though this were the moment she had been waiting for since she first laid eyes on him. The chanting abruptly stopped once she raised the dagger to its apex high above her head, and then she shouted incantations into the night.

Seeing her dagger poised to strike down from above, his defiant thrashing erupted into a wild and unbridled panic. Words flew out of his mouth that he didn't even realize he was saying. He pleaded for his life as he watched her slowly lower the knife and begin cutting in a circular pattern around his chest, feeling a searing pain as she sliced through his skin.

Unable to budge, he looked to the nameless faces around him and screamed for help. "Please, don't let her cut me! It hurts! Why would you do this to me? Somebody, please help me!" He cried and wailed at them, searching for any empathetic face that he could at least lock onto. The only faces that weren't hidden in the shadows of their cowls or behind their masks showed expressions of excitement, arousal, rapture; their eyes wild and hungry, their mouths contorted in laughter or contemptuous smirks. His screams and pleading only seemed to stimulate their jeers and elation. They seemed intoxicated by his torment as The Witch continued to slowly cut around his chest, barely missing one of his nipples. He felt like that roasted pig being carved up in front of the fat cleric as he gazed at it lustfully, eagerly anticipating his meal.

At last, he heard a familiar voice call out for her to stop. She lowered her hood. It was Sendy.

Chapter 4·1

GUARIN WATCHED THROUGH HIS MASK as his son was stretched out and tied down before him on this sacrificial table, crying out for help to the faceless people around him, faceless people such as himself. Every fiber of his being wanted to pummel the robed members around him and lift Han into his arms. If he were Barous, there would be no hesitation—but he wasn't Barous. There remained a fine line holding him back. He needed to stick to the plan if he wanted to get his son and daughter out of here alive.

Sendy had told him that he was dealing with a most powerful witch, a Dark Witch, who derived her powers directly from the devil himself, a witch that may even have a Hunger Demon lurking deep within her soul. He looked over to the tall horned figure at the altar, who called himself the Grand Master or Devil of this coven, then to the man beside him, the man who entered his home and forcibly took his children. He was not a man anymore though, at least not according to Sendy—if he believed *any* of this shit, that is. He just stood there staring ahead of him with his one good eye and badly scarred, tattooed face. She told him that The Witch raised him from the dead, put him under her spell, and now appears to be nothing more than her acolyte, or golem by the looks of him, but treacherous to be sure.

Sendy said she knew enough about witchcraft and how to counteract it when necessary, but he also knew how precariously her plan hung in the balance. She told him one thing was for certain: she had to separate The Witch from The Devil. They were simply much too powerful to combat them together. Once she had The Lady by herself, she at least had a better chance of defeating her, especially if she wasn't even aware of her countermagic.

He looked down at the tortured desperation in Han's face as the other members teased and ridiculed him for reasons that he could not possibly fathom, except to call it evil. He put all of his faith and trust in Sendy and her plan, but there was a limit to how long he would allow this to continue without intervening. When The Witch raised her jeweled dagger above his chest, he instinctively reached for the axe hidden under his robe, but Sendy reassured him.

"Fear not, she merely invokes a prayer from the devil for safe passage," she whispered in his ear. "We must wait, we still have time."

Guarin's heart pounded through his chest and into his neck, his face drenched in sweat behind his mask. When she began to cut into his chest, he could take no more. "Enough!" he hollered, reaching again for his axe. But his voice was drowned out not only by his son's screams and loud jeering of the members around him, but by a shout from Sendy.

"Stop!" she shouted. The Lady lifted the bloody dagger from his chest and regarded her with a look of surprise, clearly taken aback by her unexpected interruption. Sendy lowered her hood. The look of shock on Han's face was not lost on her. "All of you, that will be enough! I would expect a ritual sacrifice to have more discipline than this. It is a solemn matter to take a child's life. We are creating a sacred bond between ourselves and the divine Lucifer. The child who is giving his life for this purpose deserves our utmost respect, whether he agreed to it or not. We owe him that much at least."

A collective silence followed her admonishment.

"Thank you, Sendy. That was well said, and we shall bear that in mind in our future ceremonies as well," added The Lady.

He let her speak, knowing she was trying to delay as long as she could. Nevertheless, he had no intention of allowing this witch to resume cutting a fucking pentagram into his son's chest.

She turned to him and explained the reason for carving the pentagram on his chest, as though his objection was not unusual to new initiates. "The sign is necessary to mark the boy as a gift to Lucifer from our coven, so that he will not have to suffer the pains of Hell as others do."

The Lady raised her eyebrows to her, the knife dripping with congealing blood like sticky black syrup, and asked in an almost sarcastic tone, "May I continue now?"

"Just give me a moment to calm the boy." Sendy bowed her head and then put her hand over Han's, regarding him with sincerity and pity. "I will help you get through this, Han. Trust me, it will all be over soon." A look of bewilderment passed over Han's face as he gripped her hand firmly.

At last, he heard a shout in the distance. "My Lady, I cannot light the furnace. A boy has put himself inside and refuses to come out. I think you need to see this."

"The rat," The Witch hissed.

"My Lady, I can stay with Han to calm him down until you return. He could use a respite from this."

She looked from Roul to Han, then dropped the dagger onto the table in frustration. "If you will excuse me, there is something that requires my immediate attention. Grand Master, if you wouldn't mind entertaining our guests until I return?" He nodded gracefully. She then looked back to Sendy as though she didn't quite trust her with Han while she was gone. "Sendy, you have a way with children. I may need your assistance with this strange boy in my cellar."

Chapter 4·2

GRETA SPIT OUT THE CANDY BALL that The Lady had given her to help her sleep. She knew something big was happening tonight, a party of some kind. The Lady seemed quite excited and much happier than she had been lately. Jehan had returned yesterday and worked with Roul in the yard all day setting things up, while The Lady made her work extra hard cleaning the house. She then sent her to bed early, instructing her not to leave her room because she was hosting a party and kids were not invited.

As she lay there staring at the candlelight, consumed in her prayers, she heard Gidie's voice calling her name.

She crawled over to the little hole in the floor. "What is it, Gidie?"

"Come down to the cellar with me."

A chill ran up her spine. "What? Why?"

"You must come. Your brother is to be sacrificed tonight."

"Tonight?" She shuddered as his words unleashed her worst fears upon her.

"You must come now so I can explain, I need your help. The door is not locked." His voice sounded shrill and anxious. "Someone is coming, I have to hide."

She stared and listened at the hole in the floor until she faintly heard Roul grunting something unintelligible. Gathering her courage, she stepped out of her room and through the dimly lit hallway. Out of the back window she heard music playing, and she saw about a dozen robed figures gathered together in the yard by the large oak tree.

She snuck quietly out the back door and crept through the shadows to avoid being seen. Just ahead, she saw two men escorting her brother across the yard. She crawled along the base of the house and turned the corner to the narrower side yard, then hurried toward the cellar. As she approached, Roul suddenly burst up through the trap door bearing a flaming torch, scaring both of them half to death.

He let out the strangest outburst of alarm she had ever heard, something between a grunt and a squeal, but quickly stifled it once he realized it was her. "What the…! You're not supposed to be out here—and by yourself, no less!"

She would have burst out laughing if she wasn't so scared. "I heard voices and music; I couldn't sleep."

"Actually, I could use your help." Roul peered around the corner of the house toward the Coven before shifting them back to Greta. He placed his stout arm around her shoulders, "I want you to come down to cellar with me. There is a boy I'd like you to meet. Says he wants to help your brother but won't come out of furnace. Don't be scared, just talk to him."

This took her completely off guard; she almost didn't know whether to believe him. She certainly didn't expect Roul to know Gidie was in the cellar, or that he even knew who this boy was. Could *Roul really be on our side and trying to help Han? Or is he just trying to lure me into the cellar?* For a moment, she started to wonder if Gidie was actually Roul, just masking his voice; but then she quickly realized how absurd that sounded. There was no possible way she could ever picture him singing with that angelic voice she had enjoyed all those nights in her room. In any case, she felt somewhat relieved that she didn't have to go into the cellar by herself without any light to guide her, so she agreed to follow him.

He led her down the steep, narrow cellar steps, holding out his torch in front of him to ward off the utter blackness. The only sound she heard was the creaking of the stairs beneath her and the soft crackling of the torch. She almost gagged on the smell and taste of the stale air as she descended deeper under the ground.

A sudden sense of dread began to overwhelm her senses as she realized the gravity and the uncertainty of her actions, striking her like a thump in the chest. *Why did I agree to sneak out in the middle of the night to meet up with a boy I've never seen? And now, this man who I barely know is leading me down into a dark cellar! He could do whatever he wanted to me down here and nobody would ever hear!* She stopped on the stairway, paralyzed with fear, unable to even take another breath of the foul air that reeked of smoke and corruption all around her. She wanted to run back up, but her legs felt like heavy weights that wouldn't move. To steady herself, she braced her arms against the wall on each side of her. She could only watch as Roul's torch strained to probe its light through the depths of the darkness below.

Roul turned back to face her when he reached the bottom of the stairs, reaching his hand out for hers. "Don't be afraid, just stay close to my side," he said softly. The torch light exaggerated the bold features of his face, but his eyes looked kind and reassuring enough.

She instinctively took his hand and allowed him to help her down the rest of the way. As her eyes began to adjust, she could make out some of the queer drawings along the walls and posts that Han told her about—the creepy ones that gave him nightmares. They seemed to move and dance about in the flickering light as they made their way across the cellar.

Out of the darkness, the furnace suddenly materialized before them, a large monstrous looking contraption lurking against the wall ahead of her. She felt her pulse and breathing quicken as he led her closer, half-expecting someone to jump out at her. Roul extended his arm bearing the torch through the door of the furnace, beckoning Greta forward with a reassuring smile.

When she peered inside and saw the face of the boy staring back at her, she screamed and stumbled backwards onto the rocky ground. She quickly scrambled back to her feet as the boy lurched to the opening, showing his face and staring her down with those terrible dark eyes. She gazed back in shock and terror at the face of the black-eyed child from the forest. Without taking her eyes off of him, she staggered back a few more steps, then turned and sprinted back up the stairs and out of the cellar.

She started to run back towards the door to the house and into her bedroom, but then remembered the danger that Han was in. She peered around the corner of the house and saw all of the robed figures gathered closely around the table under the tree.

She turned back as she heard Roul scrabbling back out of the trap door. "Why did you run away? Does he frighten you?"

Greta nodded, then looked back to the crowd around the table. She finally pushed the words out of her mouth. "I think my brother is on that table, and I'm afraid what they might do to him. Please help him!" she pleaded.

That was when Roul called to The Lady. Greta brought herself to her feet and wiped her eyes as The Lady walked toward her, along with another of the robed figures whose face she could not make out.

"I'm going to need you to trust me and that child in the cellar, there is no time to explain now," he whispered in her ear.

Greta felt herself shivering from cold and fear and intimidation as The Lady approached with her tall, pointed hat. Roul looked clearly distraught as he explained the situation. "I am sorry to bother you, My Lady, but this is most unusual. He is just a scared boy, but he won't come out of the furnace. I threatened to start the fire anyhow, but he just stares at me like he can't understand what I'm saying."

"I'm not surprised," she said wryly, then lowered her eyes to Greta. "Greta dear, what are you doing out here? I thought I asked you to stay in your room tonight."

"I couldn't sleep. Some noise in the cellar beneath my room woke me up, then I heard all of the music and people outside. I just wanted to see what was going on, that's all," said Greta quietly.

The Lady looked back to Roul, "Did you ask Greta to try to talk the boy out of there?"

"Bah! The girl is scared out of her wits. She ran up here as soon as she laid eyes on him."

She felt The Lady's hard stare upon her. "Why are you scared of a little boy?"

Her lips quivered. "I remember seeing his face in the trees on our journey here. He is not a boy, he's the black-eyed child, a ghost that haunts the forest."

"You must not fear such things, my dear. I want you to come back down with me and don't be frightened. You will see he is no ghost. Will you talk to him for me, so he is not so frightened to come out?"

The other woman stepped forward from out of the shadows and smiled down at her. She felt her heart leap in her chest.

"Sendy, you're back!" Greta exclaimed with relief. She wanted to jump into her arms and give her a hug but then held back, quickly remembering that she had just been standing by the table with the others. She had hoped Sendy was different from The Lady, that she would never allow Han or other children to be harmed. *I was wrong about her too.* Her brief moment of elation sunk down to her stomach like a rock. Despite her welcoming smile, despite finally reuniting with the woman that she had most wanted to see, Greta restrained her initial impulse and instead delivered her a reproachful glare.

Chapter 43

THE LADY DESCENDED CAREFULLY down the steep, narrow wooden steps into the darkness of her cellar. Roul, holding a torch out in front of him, stepped down just ahead of her, warily and repeatedly glancing back to be sure she kept her footing. Sendy followed, holding Greta's trembling hand as she whimpered behind her back. She had been down these same steps countless times, but they became more treacherous with each year that passed, now preferring to avoid them whenever possible.

The news of this young boy trapping himself inside her furnace intrigued her. She was almost certain of who it must be, and she wanted to finally lay her old eyes on him since his escape some years ago. No child had ever escaped her dungeon before him. *The Rat that got away.* She paid dearly for that loss; the demon tormented her mind relentlessly, demanding another sacrifice, denying her access to the dead and the divine, putting her through one senseless convulsion after another without receiving any benefit of The Gift to follow. But now she had him cornered, probably too scared to come out with all the people around.

Once she had safely descended the stairs, she looked ahead to the furnace. She took the torch from Roul and walked closer, trying to peer into the open door of the furnace. "Little boy, are you hiding in my oven?" She glimpsed a shadow moving across the back wall. "Gidie, my clever little boy, I know that's you in there. Why don't you come out? There is a little girl here with me who would like to meet you. Her name is Greta. Won't you come out and play with her?"

In the center of the floor, she could see the charcoal remnants sitting atop a mound of burned wood and ashes mixed with the charred bones of animals— as well as those of her victims. She removed her hat and poked her head inside. Pressed up against the brick wall, stood the wild-looking boy, staring back at her. He didn't look much taller, but his hair was much too long and his body much too skinny, his eyes as black as the day she blinded him. *He doesn't have as much meat on him as Han but making a meal of him now would taste extra sweet.* She could cook them both together in her furnace—*crispy on the outside, tender on the inside*—before cutting them up into bite sized morsels and adding to her stew that was already brewing.

"Did you find what you were looking for in there, Gidie? If you don't come out and play with your new friend, then you might end up like so many bones you see beneath your feet." She looked below the furnace and noted the kindling wood, already dripping and smelling of the flammable oil. *I could ignite these flames and have the boy burning in seconds,* she considered. She had never burned a child alive before. It almost made her drool just thinking about it, but she knew the others would not tolerate such an unspeakable act, and her demon required a ritual sacrifice, not some useless charred corpse.

Seeing as how he wouldn't budge, she stepped back from the opening and held her hand out to Greta. "Come dear, don't be afraid. He's just a frightened little boy, even more frightened than you are."

Greta just shook her head, trembling with fear.

"Come here, my scared little pussy cat," she snickered. "I'm going to need you to go inside. Just sit and talk with him; see if you can make him feel comfortable enough to come out."

She stepped toward the girl, still holding out her hand, but she back away, looking like she was about to panic and retreat from the cellar. *Useless little mouse.*

The Lady quickly began to lose her patience. Dark thoughts gathered in her mind like a storm cloud. The coven was waiting. The Hunger Demon was waiting. The furnace needed to be lit for the midnight feast. "Roul, light the furnace," she shouted. "That will bring him out of there."

He stammered and shook his head. "My Lady? I will not burn the boy alive. You ask too much."

"Roul is right, this isn't the way," Sendy agreed. "We cannot burn the boy alive without a proper sacrifice. We must find some other way to get him out. Maybe he will listen to me," she said, stepping toward the furnace door. She squatted down and smiled at the boy inside. "Gidie, is that your name? Take my hand, sweetheart. This is no place for a child."

After a few minutes, she turned back to the others. "It's no use, one of us will have to go inside and pull him out."

They looked to Roul.

"Don't look at me," he said patting his belly. "I've tried to crawl inside before. I don't fit."

The Lady turned to the girl, "Greta! I'm asking you to help me. Do you want to watch this boy burn?"

Greta shook her head, backing away again toward the steps. The Lady felt her anger boiling over, her eye beginning to twitch. *NO! Not now, I cannot lose myself to The Gift now! The moon is full, the coven is assembled, the ceremony already begun.*

Her face spasmed with anger and frustration. "You're all a bunch of worthless fools!" she screamed, thrusting the torch into Roul's hand, and briskly turning back to the furnace. She saw him clearly now, just inches from the opening, glaring back at her. She wondered if he was mocking her. "That's a good boy, come on out now." She stepped closer, slowly reaching out her hand. She noticed a look of hesitation and fear wash over his face as he backed away. "Just take my hand and I'll help you out. We'll get you washed up and feed you a proper meal," she said, creeping slowly forward, reaching her hand further through the window like she was luring a dog with a treat. He finally lifted his hand, cautiously reaching for her own. "That's it, come with me, child."

Chapter 44

GRETA WATCHED WITH TREPIDATION as The Witch reached into the giant oven. She wasn't falling for her trick to go inside and bring out the black-eyed child.

She would probably close the door on me and roast us both for good measure. Three children burned in a single night to feed her demon.

Shaking these thoughts from her head, she stepped back again, about to turn and run out of this stinking cellar.

If she is really a witch, then why can't she just use her magic powers and compel him to come out? She looked back to Sendy. Greta hadn't noticed before, but she seemed to be whispering to herself with intense concentration written upon her brow, twisting her hands and fingers in subtle but complex motions like a pagan sorceress casting some kind of spell. She looked back to The Witch who grew more frustrated every minute, stretching her arm further inside, reaching for the boy's hand.

She thought she heard Sendy's voice faintly in her head but couldn't make it out. She noticed Roul's expression becoming distraught and conflicted. *Can he hear her voice too?* He shook his head back and forth, stepping backward, muttering to himself, "No, no, no, I can't."

Sendy's voice rose in her own head, and suddenly her choice became clear. She glared at The Witch with a flame of vengeance in her eyes. She could end this right now.

Chapter 4·5

THE LADY WILLED THE BOY TOWARD HER using all of her power, and it seemed to be working. He began to reach for her hand but then hesitated, his eyes shifting quickly over her shoulder and then back again to her hand. Only inches away, she lurched forward, grasped his wrist, and tugged him toward her. She reached inside with her other hand, clasping onto his forearm for a better grip and pulled again, jerking him down on the furnace floor. He resisted, quickly kicking his legs in front of him and bracing his feet against the bricks on each side of the opening. Then he grabbed her own arm with his other hand and pulled back with surprising strength.

At the same moment, she felt a great impact from behind, shoving her forward into the opening. She grunted in pain as her belly struck the floor of the furnace entrance, her knees slamming onto the cellar floor. She felt another strong tug, pulling her further inside, while someone else lifted her legs and pushed from behind, sending her whole body into the furnace. She screamed as she hit the ashy ground, her face scraping across the sharp cinders and bones. Struggling to get up to her knees, she thrashed her arms about in the empty blackness.

"Where are you! You think you can escape from me again, you little monster? You won't escape. I'm going to boil you alive tonight! Then I'm going to chew on your eyeballs and feast on your heart!"

Squinting her eyes in the darkness, she searched for any movement. Seeing only the torchlight shining from Roul's hand, she lunged toward the opening, but it clanged shut in her face.

Chapter 48

GRETA STEPPED BACK AS GIDIE LEAPED OUT OF THE OPENING. The two of them together slammed the grate shut and pulled down the latch just as The Witch crashed against it, screaming vile threats into her face. She banged her fists against the metal, then stretched her long, bloody, gnarled fingers through the gaps, still trying desperately to scratch and claw at her.

"Get back!" Sendy commanded. "Roul, now!"

Gidie yanked her arm, pulling her away as Roul threw his torch into the charcoal and kindling below the furnace, which immediately erupted into a raging conflagration. The sweltering flames fanned around the furnace floor before flooding upwards into the furnace itself. Roul pressed down repeatedly on the bellows, stoking the flames even higher.

Through the openings in the grate, she saw The Witch begin to hop and dance queerly upon the furnace floor as tongues of flame licked and lashed at her, igniting first her robe and then her hair, before swarming all around, engulfing her whole body in a furious blaze. The Witch's defiant screams and shouts turned to shrieks of agony that exploded in her ears and resounded throughout the cellar as she sunk to her knees and resumed pounding on the metal grate. *Are those the screams of the demon inside of her?* Greta covered her ears but kept her eyes wide open and watched her burn, her body now a lurid glow of searing flesh, radiating through a cloud of dark smoke that billowed around the blazing black beast.

Pangs of guilt tore at Greta's conscience for pushing her into the furnace and causing such a horrible death. She thought about the woman in Riquewihr, condemned to burn alive that night, and how she felt about her. She didn't know if that woman truly was a witch—whether she deserved to burn or not—but she knew this witch certainly did.

At last, her body collapsed onto the heap of bones and ash, but just as Greta was about to tear her eyes away, she saw a form of bright red flames rise up in the shape of a man—no, not a man—more like a creature risen from the deepest crypts of Hell. A creature so abhorrent and so terrifying to look upon that she feared its loathsome visage was not meant for the eyes of mortals, yet she could not draw her eyes away from its sheer magnificence. She told herself it was just a trick of the flames, but she could clearly see and even feel its gaze upon her, searching for her soul.

She trembled with a fear like she had never known and felt a blackness creep into her. Within that very moment, a mischievous curiosity about the creature took hold in her mind, tempting her to understand and appreciate its nature, its thoughts, its cravings. But then she heard Sendy shout at The Demon in her strange language, arresting the grip it forced upon her. Warding Greta away with the back of her arm, she bravely confronted the malevolent beast, bearing an expression that she had never seen or expected to see upon her face: pure anger, hatred, and determination. She could even feel the immense power radiating off of her as she admonished The Demon, striving to rid its evil from this world and send it back to the hell from whence it came. The sounds that erupted from their struggle rose to a concussive force, like some epic battle in the heavens from ancient lore. Finally, the terrible cries ceased as the demonic form unraveled back into chaotic flames, leaving the cellar with a deafening silence.

She turned to Sendy, a sudden sense of overwhelming relief washing over her as she ran to her arms and felt her warm embrace. "You came back to help us?"

"Yes, my dear. I'm so sorry I left the two of you alone with her."

Greta sobbed into her shoulder as she felt Sendy squeeze her tighter and stroke her hand along her back. "I could feel it trying to get inside of me."

"I know, but it's gone now. You can trust me, it will never bother you or The Lady again, and she can rest peacefully, at last." Sendy released her embrace but held her at arm's length, a look of excitement written all over her face. "You won't believe this, but I found your father and brought him back here with me! We must hurry back outside. They may still need our help."

Chapter 47

GUARIN LOOKED DOWN UPON HIS SON who seemed to be in a state of shock, stretched out across the sacrificial table, his chest bleeding from the half circle carved into it. Once The Witch left with Sendy, he glanced toward The Devil and The Golem, then at the hooded and masked figures murmuring amongst each other, then down at the dagger that lay before him on the table. He slowly reached his hand back inside his robe and grasped his axe handle.

He felt the familiar body rush just like he did before he charged out to attack from the prison cellar. But that was simply a live or die moment. He assumed his life was about to end— *just go out fighting and damn the consequences.* But now his son's life depended on his success, and he had to fight alone, without the aid of a trained knight. He couldn't afford any hesitation, any mistakes, any bad luck.

He felt a hand grasp his arm as he reached into his robe. He turned to see it was one of the armed guards that had escorted Han across the yard to the table. Without removing his eyes from him, Guarin snatched the jeweled dagger from the table with his free hand and buried it into his chest. As he staggered and fell backwards, the other guard took his place, sword drawn and driving for his belly. But Guarin unleashed his axe in the same motion that he struck with the dagger, one arm following the other, whipping around like a windmill, to deflect his initial thrust. He added both of his hands to the axe now, spaced widely across its shaft, parrying each thrust and blow from the guard's sword.

He remembered Barous's brief word of advice as they ascended the prison steps: *Keep your eyes focused on your enemy's chest, not his eyes.* His confidence mounted with each parry until he found his opening, clear as day. With an arcing swing of his axe, his right hand sliding down the shaft to join his left, he delivered a devastating lethal blow across his neck, slicing his head cleanly off as though it were a long-dead tree branch. He followed the projectile's trajectory, its expression one of shock, as it struck a woman's chest with a wet thump, sending the whole group screaming frantically across the yard to escape through the gate.

Someone's arm came across his neck from behind and locked him in a stranglehold. He could feel him trying to pull him backward, so he added his own momentum in the same direction and toppled him onto his back. The man grunted heavily as he let his weight crash down on top of him. The grip on his neck went slack, allowing Guarin to roll onto his knee. He recognized him as one of the young men—couldn't be more than twenty—taunting his son just moments ago. While the man struggled to take in a breath, Guarin raised his axe, swinging for his neck, but he threw his arms up to deflect the blow at the last second. In that, at least, he succeeded. Guarin felt his axe snap through the man's forearms like they were two little twigs before it split across his face. He screamed hysterically and flailed his spurting arm stumps around as though trying to pull the axe out of his face without any hands.

The blade had only sunk in a few inches, but when he tried to lift it out, the man's head kept rising up along with his axe. Guarin pinned his head down with his foot, but when he wrenched back again on his axe, he felt his already shattered facial bones and skull collapse like a melon under the weight of his boot. His wild screaming and flailing arms stopped as abruptly as they began.

He quickly raised his axe, readying himself for the next attack. Another masked figure bent down to pick up the sword from the headless guard but turned and ran for the gate when Guarin charged him with his upraised axe.

Seeing that the others had already dispersed, he hurried back to release his son from the table and threw off his mask, finally revealing his identity to him. "Papa!" Han shouted, his expression one of both shock and elation.

He wanted to give him a warm smile and kiss his frightened face, but he knew that they remained in grave danger. "Yes, it's me, son," he said, swinging his axe onto the table, severing the strap from his wrist. "I'm so sorry I had to stand here while she cut you. I'm so sorry for everything but thank God at least I found you in time." He leaned in to inspect his wound. "It looks shallow. Can you walk? We need to hurry and get you off this table."

He looked up to see the tall man in the devil costume stalking briskly toward him from the stable with a great two-handed axe. It appeared to be almost the size of a polearm, easily twice the length of his own axe. He had discarded his horned mask, his expression looking as cocky as Roland's did when he entered his home.

He didn't know how he would be able to get inside the wide radius of his swing, and he didn't think he could simultaneously fight off Roland who followed just behind him. He stepped back warily to the foot of the table, trying to keep it between him and The Grandmaster, until he could at least catch his breath and relax the untrained, fatiguing muscles in his arms and shoulders. He swung again, splitting apart the leather restraints at his son's ankles. He kept checking behind and around him frequently to make sure nobody tried to sneak up in the darkness. The Grandmaster continued to stalk him around the table, but more slowly now, as Roland approached from the other direction.

"You'll have to free yourself the rest of the way and find your sister if you can," he said, offering Han another momentary glance before refocusing on the tall African man bearing the giant axe.

"Ah, the father rescues his son. A great hero returns," The Grandmaster chided. "You may have defeated my guards, but you will not escape here alive."

He stepped away from the table and toward the giant oak tree, giving himself enough space with which to wield his axe, but hopefully not enough for his opponent's much longer weapon. That was his plan anyway: try to draw him in close enough so that one of his swings might lodge into the tree.

Once the blows and parries started to fall, he began to think his plan might work. But with every strike he countered, he could feel the jarring pain shoot through his bones and joints like lightning, every swing sapping his strength and his breath. If he tried to lurch forward, his opponent would quickly back up and try to lure him away from the relative safety of the tree.

He began to stagger and falter as the fight wore on, until he could barely even hold his grip. A heavy blow at last knocked the axe from Guarin's hands, spinning to the ground several feet out of reach. As his assailant raised his axe for the killing blow, a wicked scream tore through his ears like a thousand fallen angels from Hell had just screamed their last shrill cries into the blackness of the night. The screams hung in the air, calling attention to every living being within earshot. It seemed as though everything remained fixed in time during those long and eerie moments—everything except for a hand with long thin black fingers that crept across The Grandmaster's neck.

Chapter 48

ROLAND STOOD IN A TRANCE, compelled to stand and watch the sacrificial ceremony unfold before him. Had his mind not been bereft of all emotion, all judgement, all human thought, he would have thought it despicable. Fleeting moments passed when he could feel a rudimentary sense of revulsion begin to rise into his consciousness, but then it would sink back into that deep mind-numbing haze that had become so familiar to him.

He had one recurring thought that kept trying to tickle his consciousness since his recovery—something that just didn't add up. Despite his clouded stupor, he had a sense of who and where he was and what had happened to him. But every now and then, this one question would surge into his conscious mind and search for answers: *Where are all of the children that I brought to The Lady?* He had been bringing her a child or two every few months since the famine began, but only Han and Greta remain. The question would even find a voice at times, but then that misty haze would return, quickly submerging his thoughts into oblivion once again.

Now he found himself watching the man whose children he himself had taken by force, about to be cut down right in front of him. But then he heard those unrelenting, almost supernatural screams in his head. In that moment he felt like something black and ugly and sinful was being ripped apart from his body, like he was suddenly being cleansed from an evil that had attached itself to every fiber of his being. A feeling of pure clarity ensued, his mind finally liberated from that murky prison. His thoughts had at last become his own—and his thoughts demanded action.

As everyone else seemed stunned by those horrid screams, Roland had awakened. He wrapped his arm around The Grandmaster's neck and took hold, forcing him to drop his axe as he reached up to pull his arm away. He felt him struggling to break free, wrenching his body this way and that, becoming more desperate with every second. He thrust his elbows back into Roland's ribs and abdomen, reached his hands back over his shoulders to claw at Roland's face and ears and hair with his long nails. He heard guttural choking sounds now as his body began to slacken. Then Roland forcefully took him to the ground, landing on his own back with his victim on top of him, but maintaining that choking death grip on his neck.

"Can you see clearly now, Devil?" Roland whispered into his ear. "I know you're looking. Everyone opens up their eyes to see the last of this world when they're being choked to death." He then flipped himself over onto The Grandmaster's chest, straddling his neck between his thighs. He reached down and clutched his throat with both hands now, boring his weight down upon his neck through his outstretched arms. He glared wildly at him, his fierce green eye blazing off the light of the torches. "Can you feel your life leaving you now? Can you see the darkness? Can you see the light?"

As his body slackened once again, Roland removed one of his hands from his neck and passed his black pointed talons in front of his face, wiggling them a little before his eyes—first all of them, and then just two of them—as they closed in toward his eye sockets. If he had any feeling left in his fingers, he would have felt the gooey squish as he popped through the surface of his eyeballs.

He wanted to hear him scream, so he let go of his throat. Instead of a scream, he sucked in a long, wet, gasping breath and then let out a feeble, pained moan. Just as he started to suck in a second breath, Roland reapplied the pressure back onto his throat, feeling his body spasm beneath him in his death throes. With one final thrust, Roland pummeled the back of his wrist, hammering his fingers as hard as he could toward the back of his eye sockets until he heard a crunching and snapping sound as they hit bone; then he pushed through a little further into the spongy flesh. At last, his body lay still beneath him. When Roland pulled his hand from his face and stood up, glaring down at his conquered foe's lifeless body, he noticed that his own fingers had snapped off from his hand and now protruded grotesquely from his eyes.

Chapter 49

HAN SAT UP AND WORKED TO REMOVE THE STRAP on his left wrist with his one free hand. He knew who was coming for his father, and he needed his help.

He looked over to see their two shadows fighting under the tree as he frantically struggled to untie the knot. At last, he broke free and dove to the ground, right next to the guard who gazed at him with lifeless eyes, blood oozing from his mouth. He pulled the jeweled dagger from his chest and then crept toward the oak tree. Seeing Roland standing guard behind Jehan, he realized he wouldn't be able to attack from behind, and he wouldn't be able to engage anywhere else without endangering himself from their blows and hampering his own father's ability to fight. He decided to climb the tree and extend himself over the branch so he could ambush him from above.

He felt emotionally spent, frightened for his father's life as well as his own. At the same time, he wanted to finally do something worthy of a hero, to make his father proud. As he crawled along the branch, Han could clearly see his father becoming fatigued, his movements slower and his blows weaker. He needed to time his jump just right, strike down into his neck with the dagger; but even if he just managed to knock him off balance, it might be enough for his father to finish him off.

He heard a dull clang and his father's grunt, as his axe spun away from his hands. Just as he poised himself to leap down from the branch, he heard an ear-splitting scream, paralyzing his thoughts and movement. And that was when he saw Roland step forward and begin to choke Jehan from behind.

He hadn't hardly seen him move except for those few rare occasions in the hallway or the dinner table, but now he lurched forward with the grace of a cat pouncing upon its prey. He watched as Jehan, a man whom Han looked up to and respected until just a few days ago, was being choked to death by the man he despised since the first moment he saw him. *Roland just saved my father's life,* he realized. For a fleeting moment he started to see him in a new light. But then his hatred returned, rebounding with even higher intensity. *No, this man is not a hero. He is as evil as The Witch herself. He thinks he can rescue my father and make up for his everything he's done? I am the one who is supposed to rescue him; now he has taken that from me as well!* All of his revelations, his spiritual awakening, his centeredness in which he had grounded himself, seemed to have washed away on that sacrificial table. Even his rescue by the sudden, seemingly miraculous, appearance of his father was not enough to pull him out of the seething hatred that burned through him in that moment.

He stared down at the dead body of Jehan as Roland slithered off of him, leaving those despicable black sticks—*My God, are those his fingers?* —protruding from his eye sockets. As he rose to his feet, he stared down his father like an undead predator. He thought about what Barous had told him about those who are truly evil. *He isn't rescuing anybody; he's just killing because he enjoys it!*

He heard Greta call out, "Papa!" and watched as his father caught her in an emotional embrace, turning his back to Roland.

Knowing full well how quickly Roland could deliver a lethal assault, Han dove down from the branch, the dagger grasped firmly with both hands leading the way. He jammed it into his shoulder blade before crashing on top of him. They collapsed onto the ground, jarring the dagger loose and flipping it into the grass. He heard Greta scream and caught a glimpse of Sendy rushing toward him from across the yard. Roland rose up to his knees. Han surveyed the ground and saw a glint of torchlight reflecting off the blade. Snatching it up, he put it to Roland's neck, yanking his head back with a fistful of hair.

His father appeared at his side. "It's alright, Han. It's over. You can put the knife down. I don't think he wants to harm any of us," said Guarin.

"You don't know all that he did!" Han hollered back. "This man is evil, he's a murderer. He killed Ferrand. He takes children like me from their homes and brings them here to be eaten by this insane witch!"

Sendy tried to defend him. "Han, please don't kill him. I don't think he knew about the children, about what she did to them, or to you. If you want to blame somebody, then blame me." Tears began to roll down her cheeks. "Please, take the knife from his throat and put it to my own. I deserve it if anyone does."

Han realized that Roland wasn't fighting back. He just relaxed his head and shoulders across Han's legs like he was being cradled. He then craned his neck back until he looked into his eyes. "Do it. Go ahead and cut my throat. End my miserable life and send me back to Hell. I've been there once already," rasped Roland.

Han tightened his grip, pressing the knife deeper into his throat, enough to draw blood that began to trickle down his neck. "What do you know about Hell? I've been left alone in total darkness for what seemed like an eternity, only to be finally brought out as a sacrifice to a goddamned demon, while you and Sendy and all the others just stood there watching! You would have let me die if my father hadn't come! You don't deserve to live after what you've done. Say the word, Father, and I will gladly cut his throat."

"Please, let him go, son. It sounds like each of us had a taste of Hell these last few months, even me." He leaned in closer. "It is Satan that tempts you even now. He is in your head, son. Can't you see that? Don't give into him. Only God and the courts may judge the wicked. Do not lose your innocence for this man. Those that wanted you sacrificed have been killed, including The Witch. Drop the knife, Han, and we will find justice for him."

Remembering the screams, Han looked to Sendy with surprise. "Is it true? She is dead?"

Sendy nodded, smiling, tears streaming down her cheeks, then stepped forward and cast a searching look into Roland's face. "She must have had him under her power. I can see his own face once again." Shifting her attention back to Han, she gently extended her hand and placed it on his, a look of pity showing on her face. "Please, Han, have mercy on him."

He loosened his grip, letting her take the dagger from his hand. Roland lied still for a long moment before slowing sitting up and turning to face Han. She was right, he realized, his countenance had changed, more like he appeared before the wolves attacked him.

"You really didn't know?" Han asked.

Roland shook his head. "She paid me good money to bring orphaned children to her. I didn't ask any questions. I just dropped them off at the gate. I never suspected anyone would pay to harm children, much less an old woman."

Han turned to Sendy, his expression one of utter despair. "But you knew what she did to them. You lied to us. You told us she was a kind woman, that you respected her. You must have known what she wanted to do to me. Why didn't you try to help me when I asked you?"

She closed her eyes, sighed deeply, and bowed her head, "Please just listen to what I have to say. I was a young girl when I arrived here. The Lady treated me kindly, like a daughter. Other children were brought here over the years as well. The girls would usually stay for years. The boys would work the yard for only a few weeks before she found a place for them…at least that's what she told me. Sometimes I woke up to the sound of a baby crying. She allowed me to hold them and sing to them, but the babies never stayed long either. She told me that they became sick and died, or that she found a new mother to take them. As I grew older though, I became suspicious. The children always seemed to disappear on a full moon, or shortly after one of her seizures. When I came of age, she invited me to one of her covens. She explained that a baby I had just held in my arms was to be sacrificed to The Lord of Light. I was horrified. I didn't want to believe it. So, I left that night while she slept and took the baby with me, found loving parents for her.

"Years later, I ran into Jehan again. He told me that she had become sick and delusional from her convulsions, that they made her believe things that weren't true. He assured me that he would never allow such terrible things to happen. But he said she was much better now and invited me to come back to visit. When I finally returned to see her, she really did seem herself again."

She placed her hand on Han's cheek and took a deep breath before continuing. "But when she struck you that night after dinner, I feared for your safety. I should have taken you away from her that very moment, I know that now. But I didn't want to admit it, so I made excuses for her behavior. I also couldn't take on the responsibility for you and Greta. I was wrong, so very wrong.

"When The Gift—her convulsions—returned to her that night, I couldn't sleep. I planned on leaving with you in the morning—believe me, I really did—but The Lady forced me out before you awoke. She must have sensed my unease, suspected that I would take you and Han away from her. I went in search for your father and for Jehan..." she fell silent and glanced over to where his dead body lie in the grass, a deep frown crossing her face. "He said he would return immediately to help you. I never suspected that he knew, much less that he arranged the covens and put all this in her head to begin with."

"Trust her, Han," said his father, kneeling beside him. "One of our neighbors—the old Birdman—he gave her description and said she was asking about me. He said he even saw the two of you being led away with a man he didn't know and told me the direction you were headed. Then I found one of your animal carvings on the forest path. I followed your trail, and it somehow led me to Sendy. She brought me here and planned your escape."

"I killed her, Han!" exclaimed Greta. "Along with Sendy and Roul, and Gidie most of all," she added, looking up to the tree branch upon which Gidie climbed so effortlessly. "They all helped me. We pushed her into the furnace and burned her alive, just the way a witch should die."

He couldn't believe what he was hearing. "But you signed his book? He showed me where you signed your character."

She shook her head as her eyes glossed over with tears. "He promised me that nothing would happen to you if I signed it. He lied to me!"

"Greta, I'm so sorry I doubted you. And I'm sorry I threatened to leave you here alone. I don't know what else to say." He looked around to each of them, their faces all turned toward him. He felt his throat tighten. "So, I wasn't really alone down there after all? You hadn't left me alone to die?"

Nobody answered him; they didn't need to. They just continued to regard him with unbounded sympathy and love as smiles crept on their faces. Sendy put her arm around his shoulder and kissed him on the cheek. His father pulled him into a strong embrace, pressing his bearded cheek against his own. Greta surged into them both, knocking them into a pile on the wet grass as she wept with joy. As he hugged his family, he came to the most stunning realization of all: that even God remained with him throughout his misery, spoke to him in his meditations and through the voice of his mother, helping when he needed Him most.

His face brightened as he pulled away from his father's embrace. "What happened to you Papa? You look completely different! And where did you learn to fight like that?"

Guarin chuckled. Han couldn't possibly have known how much the expression he showed his father at that moment truly meant to him, that gleam of admiration in his eyes that he yearned to see for so long. "It's a long story which I will share with you later. For now, just know that I was in a dark place for too long, but ultimately emerged as a new man. I hope to make it up to you both and promise never to let you down again."

Han smiled, thankful to see the optimism and pride back in his face. "I know you will, Papa." He gave him another emotional embrace and added the words he should have said a long time ago, "I've missed her too." He felt his father's sobs in his chest, so he held on for as long as it took before bringing up one final concern of his.

"Papa?"

"What's the matter, son?"

"I can't go back to live with step-mother again. Not after what she did."

Guarin regarded him with a solemn but reassuring expression, "Trust me; you don't have to worry about her ever again."

Chapter 50

"I'M SORRY I PUT YOU THROUGH ALL THIS," said Roland, regarding them with sincerity. "I really am sorry." He focused on Guarin, "I swear to you that I protected them with my life on our journey here, and I swear that I did not know what went on here. Had I known, I never would have brought so many children to her."

He frowned and knuckled his forehead before continuing. "During my recovery, though I remained in a deep stupor, I knew that something was wrong but couldn't express it, or even focus on it. Then tonight, when I heard those screams, it felt like something was being ripped away from me, like my mind and body had become freed from some invisible restraint, and I could finally think clearly again."

"I felt something similar when I heard those screams," said Sendy, "but instead it felt like something important was taken from me, like a great loss. I should be happy. I know she deserved to die, but for some reason...I don't know how to explain it."

"Like you lost a parent?" asked Roland.

Sendy cast him a look of both surprise and understanding. "Yes, something like that."

"It's because you have, both of them," said Roland earnestly.

Sendy nodded slowly. "Yes, it's true. They were almost like parents to me."

"They *were* your parents, Sendy," said Roland. "Jehan asked me to take you away to a new family when you were still just a baby, and I barely a man. I didn't ask any questions, I never do. Years later, they paid me a good sum of money to bring you back to them."

Sendy stared at him as though he just insulted her. "Why have you never told me of this?"

"I swore an oath to them. They did not want it known to you, or to anyone else."

A look of understanding suddenly passed over her. "So that must be what she wanted to tell me about tomorrow, that she too once had a difficult choice to make."

"It's true," said Han. "When Jehan was trying to convince me to join his coven, he told me that you were his daughter. He told me that The Lady, your own mother, wanted to offer you as a sacrifice when you were only a baby, so he sent you away to spare your life."

Her eyes filled with tears as she stared vacantly at her father's body. "I don't even know what to think. I always loved him." She wiped her eyes, then sat up straight and looked back at Roland. "At least I loved who I thought he was. But he was just a liar and the worst kind of murderer. He deserved to die for what he allowed—for what he did—to all those children, and to you, Han."

Epilogue

THEY DUG A DEEP GRAVE and placed Jehan's body inside. Then they removed the charred bones and ashes of The Witch from the furnace, interring them along with his body before filling it in with soil, leaving no stone to mark their final resting place. Sendy shed a final tear but that was all. Together, they decided it would be appropriate to hold a brief ceremony by the furnace, a funeral of sorts, for the scores of lost children that ended their lives in this desolate place.

Given that they were in fact her natural parents, Sendy took over control of the house as well as the charcoal business, allowing Roul to continue his metal working. She invited them all to stay in the home with her as long as they would like. Despite the horror show of memories they shared while living there with The Lady, they couldn't pass up the bounty of produce grown in the garden that proved so difficult to grow anywhere else. Also, living in a home this remote provided Guarin with the seclusion that he desired for now, away from any suspicious guards that may still be hunting him. Gidie stayed for only a few days, then just seemed to disappear off into the forest. Apparently, he had grown used to living in the wild and preferred to be on his own, but he still returned to visit now and then.

That summer, the cold rains finally abated, and the warm sun shined once again on a more regular basis, drying up the land and allowing for a modest but much needed fall harvest. It took European crops several more years to reach the abundance produced prior to the famine, but at least things seemed to be improving, and everyone grew more optimistic with each passing season.

Guarin reveled in the simple joy of chopping wood alongside his able son, who never let a week go by without showing off the substantial growth of his muscles and strength as he continued to bulk up throughout the year.

Greta continued to learn from Sendy in the kitchen, helping to prepare and cook delicious meals. Once the weather warmed, she walked with her in the forest, learning how to recognize edible and medicinal herbs and other natural remedies that the earth provided. She accompanied her to nearby villages where they sold their herbs for prices people could afford and offered their healing services to those in need, but mostly they enjoyed socializing with the friendly townsfolk and showing off Sendy's growing belly.

Roland seemed to grow happier the bigger it became, which he said made up for the loss of some of his fingers and toes. Over time, he regained most of the function of his remaining fingers. His mind remained as sharp as it had been before his attack, and despite all he'd been through, he never lost his smile; only now he always enjoyed it when Greta complemented him on doing a much better job of smiling with his eyes and not just his mouth.

To make up for his part in unknowingly bringing so many of the children to their deaths by The Lady, he methodically went down the list of The Devil's guest book and hunted them down, one by one, starting with the surviving members who attended the coven. To be sure that he had the right person, he remained patient, lurking in the shadows and following them in stealth until they played their hand. If he witnessed them luring an unsuspecting child from safety, or even overheard them utter such an intent, his knife would slip out in the cover of night.

In a separate town, he received word that a witch was holding a secret coven much like The Lady's, where an infant was to be sacrificed. Like a phantom shadow, he infiltrated, silently stalking and killing each of the thirteen members in turn, each successive victim becoming more and more terrified by this ghostly assassin, each becoming more and more certain that it could not possibly be human. He stabbed the head witch's own blade into her throat as he watched her die; then, after strangling her devil, he plunged two sticks into his eyes, planting them deeply into the sockets, just as he did to Jehan. He burned the bodies in a mass conflagration but left the devil's where it lay to serve as a warning to others. Lifting the babe from the table, he carried her across town and returned her into the arms of her grateful mother. At least this was one child that he saved from the treachery of the witches.

Finally, with each of the names in the book accounted for (except for Greta), he returned home to the welcoming arms of Sendy. He handed the cursed book to Greta and told her to destroy it once and for all. Besides the signatures of allegiance, the tome contained many secrets describing satanic rituals, the dark magic of necromancy, and an epic history of The Daemons including Lucifer himself. Standing before the furnace with the others beside her, she tossed it into the flames and watched it burn the pages into ashes.

Later that year, after Sendy delivered her baby, Guarin thought it best to let them live by themselves as a family should, so they departed to find their new home in a nearby village. Guarin prospered in his woodcutting trade, while Han moved to Colmar, becoming the squire for a local knight—a man who used to go by the name Barous. Greta stayed at home with her father and remained best friends with Sendy, never going more than a few days without going to see her baby girl—Greta.

The End